A Thousand Tiny Stitches

A Novel

Stephanie Claypool

A Thousand Tiny Stitches

a Novel

Stephanie Claypool

atmosphere press

For Daniel Grayson
In life and death, I love you forever

Chapter 1
Snip

Lily Wolfe hesitated at the bedroom door, watching her granddaughter, Emma, murmur to her doll. Seeing her playing after two weeks spent glued to Lily's side was a relief.

"We can go shopping today," Lily said. "Pick out a new comforter." The bed was covered in one of the first quilts Lily had ever made, but its somber pattern in indigo and garnet wasn't right for an eight-year-old. She didn't have any quilts suitable for Emma that were big enough for a queen-size bed.

Someday they could make one together, but in the meantime, Emma needed to feel the room was hers, not a guest room anymore.

Engrossed in her imaginary conversation, head bowed, a sweep of fine brown hair obscuring her face, Emma hadn't seemed to hear. It should be okay to leave her alone for a while.

Lily slipped away to the living room, hoping to find a slender crescent of how life used to be. Her cell phone had stopped its constant buzzing. No friends or neighbors were there bringing food or expressing condolences for the inconsolable. Even in the quiet, Lily knew life could never be the same, but maybe if she sat to quilt, she could forget for a while.

Settling into her favorite chair in the corner by the front window, she draped her work-in-progress over her lap and unspooled a practiced length of thread. The rhythmic rocking of her needle quieted the despondent voices in her head. Only the ticking of the wall clock marked the passing minutes. At the end of the run, she twisted a knot, fed it between the layers, and trimmed the tail. The tinny snip of her scissors made her pause. When had she last heard Emma?

Barefoot, she padded back down the carpeted hall. The bed was made. The doll lay naked on the floor, a few outfits scattered about. Everything else was in its place, except Emma.

The calm Lily had felt only moments before shattered. She forced a breath into her rigid lungs. "Emma?"

Her ears strained against the silence. Think. Emma had to be somewhere. Maybe her mother's old bedroom. Panic rising, Lily bolted to her daughter Amanda's room.

It took a few seconds to process the scene before her. Closet doors wide open, Amanda's suitcase upside down, sleeves and pant legs severed from their garments were strewn over the desk and bed. Fabric strips shorn from Amanda's dresses and blouses covered the carpet in a rainbow of colors. In the center of the floor lay Lily's ten-inch fabric shears, the blades splayed and glinting. Her eyes darted to each shred of red, expecting blood.

"Emma, please. Tell me where you are."

A muffled sob, barely audible over the rush in Lily's ears, rose from under the bed. She dropped to her knees and lifted the dust ruffle. Emma was curled in a ball against the wall, her face buried in a bunched-up piece of her mother's fuzzy bathrobe.

"Are you hurt?"

Emma shook her head.

"You scared me." Lily pressed her hand to her thudding heart, wishing she'd said something different. But what could anyone say? Lily had lost Amanda, her only child, but Emma had lost both her parents. "Can you come out?"

"No." Emma's answer came between jagged breaths as she fought not to cry.

"How about I come to you?"

"Okay."

The space under the box spring was generous for Emma's small body. Lily, although only five foot two, had to lie on her back like a car mechanic and squirm. Halfway under, her ponytail stuck on the carpet, yanking her scalp. She'd had an appointment to cut her hair shorter, but then the accident happened. She'd never gone. With her one free arm, she reached over her shoulder and pulled her hair to the front, the gray a taunting reminder that nothing stayed the same.

As she inched the width of the mattress toward Emma, the air closed around her, claustrophobic, stale, and smelling of dust. She closed her eyes until she pulled Emma into the crook of her arm and kissed her forehead.

Emma buried her face against Lily's breast and wailed, long plaintive notes punctuated only to catch her breath. What had made Lily think she could quilt for a while? She'd wanted to believe Emma was happily playing alone in her room. Something truly terrible could have happened. No quilt, no moment of peace, nothing Lily wanted or needed was more important than Emma.

After a few minutes, Emma's sobs subsided.

"Are you ready to tell me what happened?" Lily stroked Emma's cheek with the back of her fingers.

"I want to make a quilt for Mommy's shop."

"Make a quilt from her clothes? That's a lovely idea." Lily didn't have the heart to say Amanda's dream of opening a quilt shop in the dilapidated old house she'd bought had died with her. As much as Lily had looked forward to helping Amanda, she had no idea how to do it alone.

"But it's all ruined. I ruined everything." Emma shuddered, then stiffened.

"Shh." Lily pulled her as tight as she could in the confined space as if she could absorb Emma's rage and pain. "Nothing is ruined."

"But I wrecked her clothes."

"Nonsense. Quilts are made from scraps all sewn together to make something beautiful."

Her words offered little solace. A few weeks earlier, Amanda and Matt had left Pittsburgh and temporarily moved in with Lily so Emma could start the year at her new school. They'd been looking to buy a house nearby but hadn't found the right one. Now they never would.

At that thought, Lily's anger flared like a tongue of dragon fire, searing her throat, locking her jaw. Nothing in her life had prepared her to handle the rage threatening to explode inside her. Yet she had to stifle it to be strong for Emma.

"How about if we get out from under here and I find a box to save the scraps?"

Lily felt Emma nod and began the reverse squirm to freedom, grateful she kept a routine of daily exercises. Some of her friends, at sixty-five, had trouble getting up from the floor.

"I'll get the box. You come out when you're ready."

Lily raced to the basement. Somewhere, among her fabric storage boxes, she had an empty one. But the basement was stuffed with Amanda and Matt's furniture and moving boxes. Lily dumped the first plastic tub she saw. Wrapping paper tumbled out. She left it and took the steps two at a time back to Emma.

"Please come out. You can help me do this." Lily picked up an ivory silk sleeve from Amanda's favorite blouse and rubbed it against her cheek, dropping it into the box when Emma poked her head out from under the bed. Together, they had it all picked up in a few minutes. The lid snapped shut, and Lily shoved the box into the bottom of the closet. She'd deal with the mess in there another time.

"There's one thing I have to tell you." Lily held her scissors by the blades, the silver handles pointing at Emma. "Never take these scissors again or any of my cutting tools without permission, or use them without supervision. Do you understand?"

"Yes." Emma's lip trembled.

The last thing Lily wanted was to make her cry again, but this was too important. "Scraps of fabric are not a problem, but you could have seriously hurt yourself. And that is never okay." Where was the handbook on how to discipline a heartsick child? Intuition and love were all Lily had. She'd never felt so inadequate.

The next morning, Lily laid half a bagel for Emma and two cups of hot chocolate on the kitchen table to have breakfast before the first day of school.

"Would you like to float the marshmallows on the top?" Lily nudged the bag of mini marshmallows toward Emma.

"How many do you want, Gammy?"

"I think five."

Emma suspended a handful above the cup, dropping them one at a time, then counted nine into her own cup. It was good to get a glimpse of Emma the way she used to be.

"Are you excited to go to school?" Amanda had already registered Emma. After the accident, Lily briefed the school about Emma's circumstances. The principal had promised to do everything they could to ease her transition

"I guess." Emma laid her hands on her lap and pressed into the back of her chair. The innocent smile she'd worn melted into nonexistence like the marshmallows in her cup.

"You don't want to hang around here with only your grandma, do you?"

Of course she did. She still woke in the middle of the night and climbed into the empty side of Lily's bed, a comfort to both of them.

Emma pried herself, one leg at a time, from the kitchen chair. A few bagel crumbs stuck to her chin. Lily wiped them with her thumb and looked into Emma's eyes, hoping to find another spark of the girl who would've popped out of her seat in a hurry to get to school, the one who'd briefly appeared when counting marshmallows. Nothing. She needed more time to heal. Even then, a deep and ugly scar would remain.

"Let's walk to the bus stop." If Lily acted excited, kept her tone upbeat, some might rub off on Emma.

Although still August, a thin cloud cover kept the sun from warming the overnight chill. No need for a jacket, but they could make the short walk without breaking a sweat. Hand in hand, they passed identical three-bed houses like Lily's, built in the fifties, red brick, with low eaves.

At the end of the street, they met the state road. Across the way, the newly opened Village in the Hollows, a retirement community with a multi-story assisted care facility clad in white siding and green shutters, butted up to a wooded hill leading to Fellowes Run Road.

Lily couldn't see the tree that had crushed Amanda and Matt from where she stood on the sidewalk, but felt it hovering at the crest. She wanted to scramble up the hill, let the thorns on the brambles tear at her skin, to claw at the gash in its bark where Amanda had drawn her last breath until the pain from her wounds numbed the pain in her heart. She wanted to let out the grief and anger that threatened to overwhelm her and cry until she turned to dust. And she wanted the police to find the soulless driver, heedless of the double yellow line, who had run them off the road, then fled. But that wasn't likely. Paint and shards weren't enough evidence, and there were no surveillance cameras in the small town of Fellowes Hollow, nor on the back roads of Western Pennsylvania. Lily straightened her spine and pressed on.

The bus stop was on Fellowes Run Road, the main street through town, in front of a set of four old row houses next to the house Amanda had planned to convert into a quilt shop. As they approached, Emma pulled Lily to a halt and faced the would-be shop. Her eyes were unfocused and her lips curved in the hint of a wistful smile so like her mother's, looking as if she took the two steps up to the wide porch and peered through a window she'd see Amanda inside, and all would be right again.

"I want to go to Mommy's shop."

"Not today. You have to go to school."

"Why can't I stay home with you?" Normally, Emma's eyes would have been sparkling with excitement. Instead, the only thing sparkling were her tears.

"Because you belong in school. You loved your old school and you'll love this one too." Surely school would distract Emma, give her space to think of other things. "C'mon. Let's wait at the curb."

The bus rattled to a stop, and the folding door creaked on its hinges. The driver, a woman about Lily's age, smiled. "Going to Fellowes Hollow Elementary?"

"She is." Lily stooped, hugged Emma, and rotated her shoulders until she faced the bus. "It's her first day there."

"Welcome aboard."

The doors closed behind Emma. She slid into the first seat and pressed her hand against the window, staring at the shop. Were there no limits to how broken a heart could get?

Lily took a deep breath, hoping to fill the hollowness in her chest but only sucked in petroleum-scented bus exhaust. At some point, she'd have to tell Emma the sad truth. The shop would need to be sold. But that time had not yet come. It could wait, like the scraps in the box, the wrapping paper on the basement floor, her haircut, and many other things.

Chapter 2
Grilled Cheese

After Emma left, Lily had intended to go home and catch up on chores. Tackle the weeds in her flower bed, which had been growing happily in neglect, or give the bathroom a thorough scrub. Caring for her home had always been a pleasure. Over the forty-plus years she'd lived there, she'd made every inch her own. Most especially, the kitchen she and her husband Sam had custom designed shortly before he'd died. Even then, when all her friends had told her to move to a smaller place, Lily couldn't imagine anywhere she'd be happier than in her own home.

But things were different then. Amanda and Matt still lived in Pittsburgh, little more than an hour away, and frequently brought Emma for weekend visits. Lily still worked full time as a receptionist for Simon, the town's dentist. With all that and a bunch of good friends, especially her quilt circle, Lily had adjusted to living alone.

Then Amanda, Matt, and Emma had moved in. Lily would've been happy for them to stay permanently, but at least when they found their own place, it would be nearby. She retired from the dentist's office and imagined life with family around again, maybe picking up Emma from school, spending afternoons with her, cooking dinners for everyone, and plenty of time to make more quilts. There were so many patterns dancing in her head. She would have had time to try them all.

But a lot could change in five years. Or even in a single night.

As she stood at the bus stop, the thought of going home with only grief and bitterness as companions turned Lily's feet to cement. Behind her, the bell on the cafe door tinkled, jostling her out of inertia. A man exited, a paper cup in one hand, his phone in the other. Lily, a one-cup-in-the-morning coffee drinker, hadn't had the occasion to go there. But it was somewhere other than home, and she wouldn't be alone, at least for a little while.

When Lily swung open the door, the aroma of coffee mixed with cinnamon and yeast greeted her like a warm hello. Chatter from the crowd at the small, round tables dotting the floor eased her loneliness. The cafe was busier than she'd thought it would be. Becca, the owner, a young woman, stood behind the register at the counter, a large glass bakery case extended to the wall on her left.

"Good morning," she said as Lily approached.

"Good morning. A latte please." She'd normally order tea, but the hot chocolate had left Lily in the mood for something warm and creamy.

Becca turned and began the preparations, the sucking sound of steaming milk drowning out the symphony of conversations in the cafe.

"Mug or a go cup?"

"A mug. I've heard wonderful things about your coffee."

"Thank you." Becca bit her bottom lip while she brewed the espresso, then said, "Mrs. Wolfe, I want to tell you how sorry I am about Amanda."

Her words bounced off Lily like the thumping of a bass drum. Although Lily had practiced her response to condolences hundreds of times, it hadn't gotten easier. "Thank you, but call me Lily, please."

Becca's face was flushed and shiny with sweat, but past that, she was a strikingly beautiful woman. Coils of dark, shiny hair cascaded from under her gray bandana. Her full lips parted in a wide smile, lighting her hazel eyes. She filled the mug with frothy milk and placed it in front of Lily.

"Did you know Amanda?" Lily asked.

"Not really. We chatted a few times since she bought the place next door. In high school, I was a couple of years ahead of her, but everyone knew she was Coach Wolfe's daughter. We all loved him."

The mention of Sam took Lily by surprise. She blinked hard.

"I'm sorry. I didn't mean to . . ."

"Please don't be sorry. It's nice to know Sam is fondly remembered. He was a wonderful man."

"He was a great coach. Definitely upped my confidence. I'd never have been able to open this place if he hadn't been my math teacher."

Lily wanted to ask Becca how she'd done it, but someone in line behind her cleared their throat. Lily took the hint and found the only open table. Sitting sideways on the chair with her back against the wall, she let fond memories swirl in her head. Sam teaching high school math and coaching girls' soccer and volleyball. Amanda as a toddler, a big kid, a teenager, finally an adult and a mom. Lily would turn back the clock if she could. Live all those years over and over in an endless loop.

Becca passed by carrying a plate with a golden-brown grilled cheese to the man at the table next to Lily. He thanked her and leaned over, lifting half the sandwich to his mouth, gooey strings of cheese trailing. He caught Lily staring.

"Sorry," she said. "I didn't mean to disturb you. It's just that might be the prettiest grilled cheese I ever saw."

He nodded and bit the sandwich.

Lily looked away, slightly abashed. She'd been wondering if crumbs would get stuck in his scruffy beard.

While Lily nursed her latte, other customers finished their coffees and food, forks and spoons clanking against dishes, chairs scraping the floor as they stood. Some threw a few bucks on the table before leaving. Most didn't. Becca came out to pick up the dishes and wipe the tables. No wonder she had a sheen on her face. She worked hard, but her knockout smile didn't waver.

She stopped as she passed Lily. "Everything okay?"

"Yes, this is great." Lily pointed at her mug. "It's no wonder. You look like you love doing this."

"I do. Although I hate taking out the trash." With her free hand, Becca pinched her nose.

Lily laughed. "Not my favorite, either, but someone has to do it."

Becca stared at the mess in her dish tub. "That and everything else."

"You've been here about two years, right?" Lily asked. She knew Becca had been living in New York City but wondered if she'd moved back, like Amanda and Matt, to get away from city life. "What brought you back?" Was that too nosy? "I don't mean to pry."

"It's fine. Two reasons, really. The first is my marriage fell apart in about the nastiest way imaginable. Second, my parents are pushing eighty, but they haven't gotten the hang of the retirement thing yet. I thought I'd try to help them out of their routines. Give them things to do. They walk here for coffee every afternoon." She shrugged. "It's something."

If Becca was two years ahead of Amanda, she'd be about thirty-eight. When Lily was that age, she'd been married for sixteen years and a stay-at-home mom for nine-year-old Amanda. "I came here when I was twenty-four, when Sam got the job at the high school. I've never looked back."

"I don't suppose I will either. I have my cafe and great customers." Becca rested the tub on the back of an empty chair.

"I wish I could open Amanda's quilt shop, but the place is in dreadful condition. Without her, it's beyond what I can do."

"Remember what this place looked like?" Becca swooped

her arm from one side of the cafe to the other. The row houses had been abandoned for years before the first store opened. "And now, three of the four shops are filled. Speaking for myself, the foot traffic is pretty good."

"You've made the place charming." The wainscoting was painted a pale pinkish brown, and the walls were papered in a soft rose-and-vine pattern. "The smell alone pulled me in."

"Thanks. It took a lot. I'm proud of it."

Another customer came in. Becca hoisted the dish tub and greeted the woman. After preparing her order, Becca waved for Lily to join her at the counter.

"I have a bit of a lull until the lunch crowd."

"Maybe you could sit for a bit?" Lily offered.

"Doubtful, but I knew what I was getting into." Becca closed the dishwasher, tossed her rag in a bin, pulled a clean one from a drawer, then started to wipe down the equipment and surfaces.

Lily stood by the register, not quite behind the counter. "Before you opened here, had you owned a shop or worked in a cafe?"

"Nope." Becca snorted. "I married a well-connected lawyer and threw dinner parties for high-powered types. I'd still be doing it except his . . ." She paused as if searching for the right words. "His connections extended beyond business."

"Oh." Lily didn't know what to say. Did Becca mean women or organized crime?

"He was interested in most of the young females in the office. Salacious might describe it. Sa-la-cious. Sounds exactly as it should. Slimy. Anyway, I was a complete fool. Typical trusting wife and the last one to know. I guess I'd aged out of the trophy wife role." She shook her head as if to clear the image. "My only regret is that I never had children. He didn't want them. I guess pregnant wives don't look good in a display case."

As if that reminded her, Becca began reorganizing the

baked goods in her case, refilling cookie trays and cutting another pan of gooey brownies into squares. "I needed to get far away, and where better to go than home?"

"I'm sorry." Lily couldn't imagine the humiliation.

"Thanks, but don't stay that way. I'm very glad to be completely free of that bastard, and I got a great settlement. I saw this place for rent and sunk my self-pity into it. At least I didn't wallow."

"Wallowing isn't good." Neither Lily nor Emma would ever get over what had happened, but maybe they could learn to live with it.

A rat-a-tat knuckle-knock on the front window drew their attention. Philip, Lily's close friend and lawyer, pulled open the door and approached in long strides. "I saw you through the window as I was passing by. I have news."

"Good news?" Lily could hope. Philip was handling Amanda's and Matt's affairs.

"Can you come by my office at three?"

"I can't. I have to meet Emma's bus at three."

Philip pulled back the stiff cuff of his shirt and checked his watch. "I can't do it before then."

"Then come to me for dinner tonight. We can celebrate Emma's first day at school with an apple tart." A second after she said it, she realized that meant she'd have to be home to get it out of the oven before three.

"I'd love it. I can get there by six, maybe six thirty. Is that okay?" He gave Becca a quick nod as if noticing her for the first time.

"Works for me," Lily said.

He squeezed Lily's forearm. "I can't wait." He turned to leave, then spun back, addressing Becca in a whisper. "Maybe you shouldn't let that man hang out here." He rolled his eyes surreptitiously at the guy with the grilled cheese. "He might make people nervous."

"Hasn't done it yet." If Becca was annoyed, her expression didn't show it.

The man stood, no visible crumbs in his beard. He wrapped his leftover sandwich in his napkin and pocketed it, then brushed the crumbs from the table onto his plate, and brought it to Becca. "Thank you." He headed for the door, his footsteps laden in scuffed work boots, his jeans so worn they were barely blue.

After the cafe door closed behind the man, the three of them stood in silence for several seconds.

"I'll see you tonight then?" Lily said, feeling free to talk again.

"You didn't need an apple tart to tempt me." Philip left as quickly as he'd come.

Becca pulled her lips to one side, shaking her head in disbelief. "It's people like that who make me very glad I own this business and can decide for myself who to serve."

"Philip's not really so bad." Lily wished she didn't need to defend him. She knew he'd spoken out of concern for Becca's business, but wished he wouldn't be so judgmental. He could be rude but he was also generous. "I'm curious though. Who is the man with the beard? I've never seen him before."

"I don't know anything about him. He started coming in about two months ago, about the time Amanda bought the house." Becca pointed through the wall to where Amanda's would-be shop stood. "Same thing every day. Black coffee and a grilled cheese. He's always polite. You see anyone else here clean up after themselves?"

"No." Lily hadn't. "Any idea where he lives?" She couldn't imagine someone coming to the cafe every morning who didn't live within walking distance or work at one of the downtown shops. Usually, anyone living that close was well-known in town.

"No idea, but he always seems kind of sad. Lonely maybe. So, I make his sandwich with extra cheese and comp him the coffee."

"That grilled cheese looked amazing."

"Want one?"

Becca reminded Lily of those candies Emma liked, sweet and tangy. "I wish, but at my age, I can gain weight just looking at a grilled cheese."

"Nonsense. You're in better shape than most people who come in here. Speaking of people who come in here, what's that guy Philip got up his butt?"

"Nothing." If only Philip would take a few seconds to think of other people before he opened his mouth. "He's just tactless sometimes, but he's an old, old friend and my lawyer, though mostly he does me lawyerly favors. When Amanda died, he made all the arrangements, and he's handling their estate."

"Are you sure he's just a friend?" Becca arched a single brow.

"It's not like that. Philip and his wife, and Sam and I, were friends for decades. Two years after Sam died, Philip's wife, Rose, died. He's like family to me, and like family, sometimes we have to put up with . . . abrupt behavior."

"I like you, Lily Wolfe. You should stop in here more often."

"With the bus stop right in front of the cafe, you might get sick of me."

"Doubtful. Next time, your latte is on me."

"It's a date." Lily waved and left, the warmth and taste of the latte lingering on her tongue.

Chapter 3
Where's the Money?

When Lily reached the sidewalk, she froze. In her pocket, the key to the shop grew heavy. She'd put it on her key ring after the accident, carrying it like a charm containing sparks of Amanda's soul. She wasn't sure if she was ready to go into the old house. Maybe its condition wasn't as dismal as she remembered, but what if it was? Her feet, moving steadily in that direction, seemed to decide for her.

The first time Lily had seen the place, Amanda pointed out the potential street appeal, painting a vivid picture of quilts hanging in the front windows and bright flowers growing in the weedy strip of ground between the sidewalk and the porch. Although its location on Fellowes Run Road, a mere mile from the interstate, was perfect for a quilt shop, its condition was not. Somehow Amanda had seen beauty in its bones, buried deep under filth and detritus.

Lily had trouble conjuring Amanda's vision as she climbed the steps, peeled paint crunching under her shoes, nails rattling in loose planks. She turned the key in the lock and braced herself.

The morning sun had broken through the clouds, its beams highlighting rivers of floating filaments. Directly in front of her, a wide staircase with frayed, drab carpet ran up the center of the house. The floor plan, as she remembered, was simple: two rooms on either side, both upstairs and down.

As she entered the room to her left, dust bunnies quivered in corners and peeked from under two beyond-shabby recliners. Picking her way through shreds of corrugated boxes and planks of wood, she reached the door to the kitchen. A cracked leather boot propped open a dented refrigerator, a couple of cabinet doors hung crookedly, and a table with one leg snapped off lay on its side in the center of the floor. So far, nothing had changed. Not surprising. Amanda hadn't had time.

Lily scrunched her eyes shut, hearing a conversation she'd had with Amanda a couple of months before, feeling her presence as though it were both yesterday and forever ago.

"Imagine, Mom, when this is all clean. Look at that fireplace. It's huge. Wouldn't you like to snuggle next to it with a quilt? And all this beautiful crown molding, baseboards, and casings. All hardwoods." Amanda, with her eyes wide, scanned the walls of the great room. "It has amazing architectural details. We can hang quilts from the picture rails. Fill the rooms with fabrics and threads. Restore this place back to its grandeur."

Lily had felt the charge in the excitement radiating off Amanda. It was easy to understand why she'd fallen in love with the house, but no matter how beautiful her completed vision had been, there was no way Lily could accomplish what Amanda had planned. It wasn't enough that Lily knew a lot about quilting or that she'd spent hours in quilt shops. Or that her closest friends were avid quilters and would be her best customers. Lily needed knowledge about renovations and running a business. She also needed money.

Becca had said she'd gotten a great settlement. And she was young. She had many years left to earn back her investment or find another way to make a living. Lily had only her retirement money, enough to live on comfortably for many years, but she also had Emma to raise and no way to replace a substantial loss. Her only hope was if there was something unexpected in Amanda and Matt's estate.

She fingered the key in her pocket as if it might give her a hint of where to begin, how to keep this piece of Amanda alive. The answer came back the same. Impossible.

At the far wall of the kitchen, a window looked out on a wooded hillside at the back of the property. Beside it, a door led to a set of warped steps zigzagging down to a crumbled asphalt drive. A little white-and-brown, wire-haired Jack Russell terrier sprang from behind what looked like a barn. He sat on the gravel, his tail twitching.

The outdoor steps looked too risky, so Lily went back through the house to the sloping driveway at the side. When she reached the gravel, she crouched. "Hey, doggie. Are you lost?"

He turned to her, the tip of one pointy ear up, the other bent over, his tail wagging as if he wanted to say hello. He seemed to think better of it and dashed up the hill. Judging by his ease of dodging roots and ducking under tree limbs, he knew the path well. He probably lived in one of the houses at the top of the hill.

Amanda hadn't shown Lily the barn, but if she was going to sell the property, she needed to know what she had. The garage-sized door was unlocked and glided sideways on a sturdy top rail.

The inside was cleaner and more organized than the house. Parked in the center was a silver Chevy pickup with flat tires oozing black rubber under the rims. Clearly, no one was using the truck, but around the perimeter were power tools, some a little rusty, but none had cobwebs of neglect.

Hammers and wrenches hung in size order from nails in the crossbeams. A forest of lumber leaned against every open stretch of wall. Behind the truck, an earthy scent rose from hay bales, folded rags on the top, and an overturned enamel bowl on the floor next to them.

Did all this belong to her? Or to someone else. Someone

who clearly wasn't using the truck but perhaps renting the space. If so, Lily shouldn't be there. Anyway, she needed to get home to start on the apple tart.

"The napkin goes on the left with the fork on top, and the spoon and knife go on the right." Lily had watched Emma fold each napkin, then stand muted, weighing a fork in one hand and a knife in the other.

Since Lily had picked her up at the bus stop, Emma hadn't completed three full sentences. They'd gone to Giant Eagle to buy something for dinner with Philip. When Lily asked about school, the teacher, the kids, all three questions got the same one-word answer.

"Fine."

Before the accident stole her blissful ignorance of how fragile life could be, Emma would have been bubbling over with excitement, eager to share every detail of her first day at school.

"Would you like to drop the spaghetti into the pot? You're tall enough now." Emma had been begging to be allowed to do it.

Emma laid the last fork down and joined Lily at the stove without even a smile.

"Can you talk to me? Did something happen at school?" Lily wasn't sure how far to push her. It might be better to wait until she was ready to talk.

Before Emma answered, the doorbell rang. Lily, knowing it would be Philip, called out. "It's open."

Philip entered carrying a box. A thin folder on top slid precariously close to the edge before he straightened his hold. "It was on the porch. Where should I put it?"

Lily wasn't expecting any packages until the next day. "Thanks. I guess I didn't see it there." She and Emma had come in through the garage. "Just put it in the corner."

He laid the box in the dining room and brought the folder to the kitchen, leaving it by the refrigerator. Then, with a huff as though he'd reached the end of a long day, he slid into his usual chair at the table. "How was school, Emma?"

"Okay."

Okay had one more syllable than fine. A small improvement.

"How about a glass of wine?" Lily showed him the bottle. "I have an Argentinian Malbec."

"Yes, please." He rubbed his hands together. "It smells fantastic in here."

"The smell is garlic bread. The single most irresistible scent in the universe," Lily said. "It's Emma's favorite."

"Good choice. It's my favorite too."

That wasn't true. Philip never cared what was for dinner. He was happy to join Lily anytime she asked. Since losing his wife, Rose, he had little to go home for. And Lily was glad to have another person at her dinner table.

Without Emma's usual chatter, the conversation through dinner was perfunctory. The weather, the extra traffic since the addition of The Village in the Hollows, Philip's stiff knee.

Lily's mind was on the folder. There couldn't be more than a few pages inside, but they contained the news Philip had come to share.

"I'm done. Can I open your box, Gammy?"

Emma hadn't eaten much other than a large piece of apple tart, but that wasn't an argument worth having. She'd said a full sentence, and that was a good thing.

"You can. Use the little kitchen scissors, though, and be careful. Do it like I showed you."

"Okay." Emma pushed back, moving faster than she had all afternoon. When she lifted the box to bring it into the kitchen, she nearly dropped it.

"Be careful," Philip said.

Lily sprang up, but Emma wrangled it safely to the ground. The towels Lily had ordered shouldn't be heavy. She checked the label. "It's for you, Emma."

"For me?"

With a little help from Lily, Emma opened the flaps and pulled out a small, kid-friendly sewing machine and a note. "It's from Auntie Vic." A genuine smile glimmered on Emma's face.

Vicki, Amanda's best friend and coworker, had known Emma since she was born and was practically part of the family. The last time Lily and Emma had seen her was at the funeral, but she was never far from mind. Apparently, Emma wasn't far from hers either.

"Can you carry it to your room, or is it too heavy?"

"I can do it."

"Use two hands and make sure you keep all the papers and pieces together. I'll help you with it after I finish talking to Philip."

Emma nodded and headed down the hall, her shoulders rounded under the weight.

Lily returned to the table and topped up their wine glasses, twisting the bottle at the end of the pour.

"How's she doing, Lily?"

"I suppose about as well as can be expected for a child who's lost everything."

Philip grasped Lily's hand. "She didn't lose everything. She has you."

"I hope that's enough." Lily's grief fought to escape as she remembered the horror of that night. The knock on the door. The uniform. Telling Emma. How do you explain to an eight-year-old her parents are never coming home? "And lucky for me, I have her too."

"You're not alone either. I'm not going anywhere."

"Thank you, Philip. Thank you for everything. You're always here when I need you."

"We're here for each other." He tightened his grip on her hand, then let go, pointing to the open box on the floor. "And it looks like Vicki isn't going anywhere either."

"She's as good as a real aunt. Leave it to her to make Emma smile. A sewing machine is a perfect gift. Maybe more perfect than she knows." Lily explained about Emma cutting up Amanda's clothes. "I guess she can make the quilt now. It just won't be for the shop."

"Have you thought about counseling for her?"

"Of course, but it's too soon. I don't want to make her think there's something wrong with her. She's started school. I want to give her a little more time to settle into a routine, to heal. She's still in shock. We're both still in shock."

"What about counseling for you?"

"I need more time too. It hasn't even been three weeks. I still forget sometimes. Then it hits me fresh all over again." She wrapped her arms around herself, feeling the urge to rock. "No one should bury a child, and for Amanda and Matt to be taken in such a senseless, irresponsible way by a driver they'll never catch makes it worse." The fury boiling inside her threatened to burst, leaving a jagged, gaping hole in its place.

Philip's lips creased in concern. It helped to know he'd be there if she needed him.

"Maybe it's not the best time to talk about the estate." Philip turned his head to look at the folder, where he'd left it by the refrigerator.

"No. I'm okay. Tell me what you found out." She needed to know, even if only to confirm there was no large unexpected sum.

Philip brought the folder to the table, taking the seat next to Lily. "I've received the will and estate details from Matt's lawyer. I've also spoken with his parents. You have sole custody of Emma, and they do not dispute that she is better off with you. They say they trust you completely and they're available for any help you need."

Lily hadn't worried that they might fight to get Emma, but she wondered if Emma, who was as comfortable with Heather and Ben as she was with Lily, would be better off with them. She'd have two grandparents, and she'd be able to go to her old school with all her friends. Either way, no matter who had custody, they would all be a big part of Emma's life.

Philip slid his reading glasses from the inner pocket of his suit jacket, which he'd hung on the back of his chair. Even with his starched shirt open at the collar and sleeves rolled up, he looked like a lawyer, neatly trimmed salt-and-pepper hair, his black-rimmed glasses perched on the tip of his straight nose.

"There's a bank account with money, not a lot, but enough for you to cover additional expenses of caring for Emma for a few years." He held the tip of his pen to the balance for Lily to see. The next paper was from a brokerage. "There's also a college fund. If you leave this as is, you should have all you need to send Emma to college. Ben and Heather intend to continue making contributions."

At least she didn't have to worry about that.

"Now, here are the big pieces."

Lily sat forward, elbows on the table, her breath catching in anticipation.

"Matt's investment in Simon's dental practice. We're having an accountant work up what the payout from the partnership will be, something north of what he'd put into it. It's left to Emma, but you have sole discretion on how it's spent to care for her."

"I doubt Simon has any of that cash on hand," Lily said, feeling deflated. She'd still worked for Simon in his dental practice when he'd first started looking for a partner. He'd been unsuccessful for a couple of years. When Amanda and Matt decided to leave Pittsburgh, Lily connected Matt with Simon. She'd thought it was a match made in heaven, a heaven intended to be lived in Fellowes Hollow. "We bought new equipment and furniture. We upgraded the computers and moved to a larger office. I doubt there's any cash left."

Philip lowered his glasses and stared at Lily for a second. "He's obligated to pay out Matt's share. How he finds the money is up to him."

Philip would protect Lily's interests at any cost, but Lily didn't want to, couldn't, prosper at the expense of someone else, especially someone she knew well like Simon.

"The last piece is the house on Fellowes Run Road. Amanda left it to you. Looking at it from the outside, I can only imagine the condition on the inside. She'd bought it at a distressed price. You may not get much, but you should sell it."

Lily rubbed at a rough cuticle on the side of her thumb. For a moment, when Philip had said there were big pieces to the estate, she'd felt something turn inside her like a key popping open a lock. What if she had money? She mulled over what Becca had said about knowing nothing about running a cafe, that she only had determination and a great settlement. Lily was one step ahead in that she owned the property outright.

Even if she was wrong and Simon was sitting on a wad of cash, risking that money was reckless. No matter how much she and Emma wanted to open a quilt shop, even if Lily could justify spending it for Emma's sake, she couldn't risk it. Lily's heart seemed to stop pumping and grew heavy.

Amanda's dream may never come true, but until Lily sold the place, the dream still lived.

"I don't have to sell immediately, though, right? There's no mortgage."

Philip took the last swallow in his wineglass, then lowered his glasses, fixing Lily with a stare. "Correct, but why would you want to wait? You'll have expenses. There will be utility bills, possible repairs, and you'll need to pay property taxes and insurance."

"I'm sure I can float it for a few months."

"I think that's a terrible idea. Save your money."

"Do you know if the barn at the back is part of the property or if it's rented out to someone?" Maybe there was rental income.

"Barn?" Philip tilted his head.

"Yeah. I think it's a barn. Or a garage. Or a workshop."

Philip unfolded a blueprint and laid it on the table. "Here's the plot plan. Do you mean this building in the back?"

It took Lily a moment to get oriented. "Yes, that's it."

"The house, its outbuildings, and all the contents are yours. I don't know of any leases, and that shouldn't stop you from selling. Do it as soon as you can. You have no use for it."

She drummed her fingers on the table. "I know, but I don't want to make any decisions too soon."

"Like I said, save your money. In the meantime, I'll have the deed transferred to your name so you can list it. And I'll talk to Simon about the payout."

He collected the papers and kissed Lily on the cheek. "Thank you, as always, for a lovely dinner. I wish I could do more for you. Say bye to Emma for me." He let himself out.

While Lily cleared the table and stacked the dishwasher, she thought about the flat-tired truck and all the tools in the barn. Maybe there was some money she could use if she sold those things. For the moment, it didn't matter. Emma was waiting for Lily to help her with the sewing machine.

Chapter 4
The Quilt Circle

When Lily pulled her Camry into the driveway, Robin Blank slid into the passenger seat and leaned in for a one-arm hug.

"I'm glad you're coming today."

"Me too. I need something to help me feel normal again." It was quilt circle day. Lily, Robin, and two other friends had been meeting every week for twenty years with rare exceptions, including the last two weeks. Lily needed her friends, maybe Robin most of all.

"How was it getting Emma off to school today? Any better?"

"She still doesn't want to go, but it's only her second day. It'll get better. I hope. It doesn't help that the bus stop is next to the . . ." Lily wasn't sure what to call it. "That old house Amanda bought. All she wants is to go to Mommy's shop. But it's a wreck. I don't think I should take her there. Not yet, anyway." She winced on the inside. Giving Emma excuses would be hard.

"She might not notice that part as much as you, though."

"If only." Except being there, despite the condition, had made Lily feel closer to Amanda, hearing her and feeling the warmth of her presence. If that had comforted her, why was she so sure it wouldn't comfort Emma? "I'll tell you more when we get to Maggie's."

Maggie and Trish greeted Lily, enfolding her in tight hugs, pouring their love and sympathy over her, eroding the walls containing her suppressed emotions like the surf against a cliff.

Maggie pressed her palm to Lily's cheek. "I worry about you."

"I'm okay. I have to be." Lily's sinuses heated until she sniffled. "I can't believe my beautiful daughter is . . . It makes no sense."

Maggie gave her a tissue and led her to the dining room table. Lily sat with her hands in her lap, twisting her tissue. "Let's not talk about this, okay? I want to pretend things are normal for a while."

"I brought scones," Trish said, "and blackberry jelly." Of course she did. Trish lived at the western edge of Fellowes Hollow in the only development of McMansions. She had an award-winning garden and when she wasn't working in it or making flower quilts, she was in the kitchen cooking or pickling or canning the bounty of her efforts, which rarely failed to pay off.

"And I made us a pot of Earl Grey. Who wants?" Maggie filled the cups, not needing an answer. "So, what are you working on, Robin?"

"Yesterday, I basted that wall hanging I made last year. I'm going to quilt it. I just wish I had a hand stitch like Lily's."

"I've had more practice than you, that's all." Lily wasn't a fan of machine quilting. Although faster, she enjoyed the deliberate and meditative movement of working by hand.

Maggie was working on a runner for the top of the console table in her entry hall.

Trish pulled a spool of apricot-colored ribbon from her bag. "I'm going to look for an idea of what to do with this. I found it on sale at this tiny sewing store in Ohio and I couldn't resist." She specialized in silk ribbon art quilts as colorful as her garden.

"And I see you dyed your hair to match," Robin said.

All four women were within a few years of each other in

age. Robin and Maggie had let their hair go gray and cut it short years earlier. Lily's first gray hair hadn't sprouted until she was in her fifties. She fingered her ponytail, tied at her nape, glad she hadn't cut it.

After Trish's hair had turned nearly white, she used it like a clean palette. Every few weeks, she'd change the color. It could be anything from spring green to shocking pink, even jet black. "It's almost a perfect match, isn't it?" She was already skimming through embroidery books for ideas.

They snuggled into a large, velour sectional in Maggie's living room, chatting while they worked. Maggie shared a story about a dog she'd fostered for a week for Fellowes Hollow animal control. "He was so sweet. I wanted to keep him, but when we finally found his owner, he was so excited, he peed like a river. Left a trail across my floor as he ran to greet them."

"And you were sad to see him go?" Robin asked, teasing. There wasn't a dog Maggie had helped that she hadn't wanted to keep.

"Speaking of strays, do you know if there's a wiry Jack Russell who lives around here?" Maggie's house was on the street above the back of the shop. Lily explained how she'd seen him dart up the hill.

"No." Maggie shook her head. "I don't know any Jack Russells around here. And nobody's said anything about a stray, but I'll keep an eye out."

"If you find him, let me know." Lily felt an attachment she couldn't explain like he was somehow connected to Amanda.

"Are you thinking of adopting a dog, Lily?"

"Not really, although it might be nice for Emma. For me too. Some company, so I'm not alone in the house all day." Lily had a flash of Emma running in the backyard with the dog jumping and chasing her. "It's just because I saw that dog. I'm not actively looking."

"How is Emma?" Trish asked. "Is she feeling better?"

"I saw her smile for the first time last night. Vicki sent her a little sewing machine." After Philip had left, Lily stopped in the doorway to watch Emma huddling over the machine, trying to set it up. The slope of her back, the way her hair fell forward as she looked down, and the way she squinted when she concentrated were so like Amanda. "But I'm worried." Lily told the ladies how two days earlier, she'd found Emma with her mother's clothes in shreds.

"She needs more time," Robin said. "It's good she's started school."

The other two women agreed. "But she's with you, Lily," Trish added, "and that's the best place for her to be."

"I hope I can do right by her. I sometimes wonder if she'd be better off with Matt's parents."

"No way." Robin's tone left no room for disagreement. "I don't doubt they're wonderful grandparents, but you, Amanda, and Emma are all cut from the same bolt of cloth. She belongs with you."

"I wish I could do something to help her. Time passes slowly when all you can do is wait. I can't stand watching her suffer. She doesn't want to go to school, and she doesn't speak much. I miss my little chatterbox. All she wants is that quilt shop." Lily had lost track of how many times in the last two days Emma had mentioned it.

"So, you're going to do it?" Maggie asked.

Lily dropped her quilt in her lap, her needle idle. "I can't. Not if I can't afford contractors. You should see what that place looks like. The dust bunnies and shredded wallpaper alone would fill a dumpster."

"How had Amanda planned to do it?" Trish asked.

"Slowly. She was working her PR job remotely, but it was still full time. She hadn't even started on it."

Three pairs of eyes stared at Lily as if a bully had just stolen their roller skates. "Don't look at me like that. I'd love to have a quilt shop as much as any of you, but it's not a reasonable thing for me to take on."

"I bet it would do a great business. The closest quilt shops are around Pittsburgh." Maggie took her eyes from her work, her expression unfocused as though she were on a shopping trip in her imagination. "I know I'd be there all the time."

"I'd teach silk ribbon and embroidery classes for you," Trish said. "You wouldn't even need to pay me. I'd work for fabric. Imagine how big my stash would get."

Lily shook her head at Robin in a plea for support. She, like Lily, was more practical. Sensible.

"Don't look at me," Robin said, hands out like a crossing guard. "I have plenty of room for more fabric. I couldn't wait for Amanda to open it."

Maggie tapped her mouth with her finger. "Maybe we could have one of those quilt frames where we could sit around and all work on the same project. You could teach us to quilt by hand like you do."

"I thought you all were my friends. You're supposed to console me, not guilt me with your enthusiasm. I would love to have a quilt shop too. I know this sounds strange, but it would keep Amanda with me and Emma. Even if we can't see her or hear her, it's part of her." Lily paused to take a breath. "But how, exactly, do you propose I do it? Come look at the place. Then tell me what you think."

And yet, it might be the one thing that would help Emma heal. To help them both heal.

Chapter 5
One Thing at a Time

The only good thing about Lily's nightmare was that she'd had it in the slip of time between sleep and wakefulness and could force her eyes to open. She'd been trying to scale the hill behind The Village community but couldn't reach the tree. Someone was calling to her, telling her to go up by the road. It would be easier, but Lily knew she had to go the hard way. She was scratched and muddy and as long as she climbed, she got no closer.

Dawn hadn't broken yet, but she didn't dare close her eyes for fear of falling back into the dream. She rolled out of bed, wrestling free of the blanket wrapped around her legs and pulling her sweat-soaked nightgown away from her skin.

In Amanda's room, she pulled the box of scraps out from the closet, dropped to her knees, and rummaged through until she found a piece of the fuzzy bathrobe. She pressed it to her nose, much as Emma had done, craving Amanda's scent.

There was none. She grabbed another, one with the satin trim of the collar, and drew a long deep breath, pressing different parts to her face, hunting for a trace. Amanda was gone. It was only a piece of cloth. Lily bent over her knees, plugging her nose and mouth with the collar to silence her wails.

She stayed that way for a few minutes to regain her composure, then stuffed everything back into the box and shoved it into the closet. Someday, she and Emma would turn the chaos into a quilt.

While she waited for the electric kettle to boil, she spread her yoga mat on the kitchen floor and began her routine of simple exercises, enough to keep her large muscle groups strong. Even in grief, especially in grief, she was determined to stay spry. Emma didn't need a doddering substitute mother.

For the third day in a row, as Lily took Emma to the bus stop, Emma stopped to stare at the shop, begging to go in. Other than that, she was quiet. When the bus arrived, Lily's chest constricted as Emma reluctantly released her hand, climbed the steps, and sat alone, eyes downcast, in the front seat.

If only Lily could lift some of the weight Emma carried. Maybe Philip was right. Emma needed counseling, not more time. But then Lily thought of her own spirit, also badly broken, worse than after she'd braved the death of each of her parents, or her only sibling who'd died too young, and more recently her husband.

Emma had only been three when Sam died. Too young to remember, to understand. She had no road map for how to cope. Losing both her parents was unbearable, and yet it had to be endured, leaving Lily with only one mission: to help Emma recover and thrive. Nothing else mattered, not her own grief or her loneliness, both of which went with her into the cafe.

Only the table by the counter was open. Lily sat with a latte, contemplating how to spend her day. The thought of going home made her feel like her insides had been sucked out. She could look for that Jack Russell. The idea of having a dog was growing in its appeal. Or go to the local animal shelter or to a quilt shop in Pittsburgh. Find some new fabric for a distraction. Perhaps Trish would take time from her canning and jamming to join her. Or she could continue to hang out at Becca's for a while.

By nine o'clock, the crowd had thinned enough for Becca to escape the counter. She brought a plate with a muffin and the pot of coffee to the grilled cheese man at the table beside Lily.

"Muffin's on the house. Would you like more coffee?" she asked as she laid the plate in front of him.

"I can pay for the muffin."

"Except it's from yesterday, so I can't sell it. It's still good though." She topped up his cup, then came to Lily. "It's just regular coffee, but can I refill your mug?"

Lily passed but asked Becca if she wanted to sit for a bit. "It's pretty quiet here now."

"You know what?" Becca checked over her shoulder. "You're right. I could use another cup this morning. I'm dragging." She took the pot back to the burner, then returned, cradling a steaming mug in her hands. "You look deep in thought."

"Not deep. More like meandering," Lily said. "I need a routine, something to do other than spend the day alone in my house."

"What do you like to do?"

Lily thought for a moment. "I love to cook, but that's only good when there are people to feed, and I love to quilt."

"Quilting, of course. I guess it runs in the family." Becca put her hand to her mouth. "Oh, Lily, I'm sorry that was thoughtless."

"It's okay. It's not like I wasn't thinking about it already. It does run in the family. Even my granddaughter has the bug. But I was thinking about something outside the house like a job. I used to work for the dentist until I retired a few months ago. And many years before that, when we first moved here, I worked in the hardware store."

"Half my customers are from that retirement community." Becca blew a strand of hair that had escaped her bandana off her forehead. "With all these new people in town, all the shops are getting busier. Someone probably needs help. Maybe try the bakery. You could put some of your skills to work."

"And eat myself to death." Lily laughed. It felt like a foreign activity. "I need to find purpose. I mean beyond Emma, who is always my top priority. Something for me. Even if it's volunteering."

"I know what you mean. When I first moved back here, I was heartbroken and thoroughly humiliated. Worse, strange as it sounds, I still loved the bastard." She snorted, her mouth twisted in derision. "I was completely blindsided by his infidelity and the extent of it. It took awhile for the shock to wear off and for me to come to my senses."

"How did you manage to open this cafe? I know you had a settlement, but you said the place was a wreck and you had no experience. So, how did you do it?" The conversation she'd had with the quilt ladies the previous day had loitered in the back of her mind, poking her once in a while to make sure she didn't forget.

"Almost by accident. I'd come to stay with my parents while the divorce was happening. One day, I took a walk and wanted a latte and there was no cafe. No place to grab a coffee and something quick, like a muffin or a panini. I saw the 'For Rent' sign." Becca blew again at the hair on her forehead. "I didn't really think it through. I just signed the lease."

"Did you freak a little?" Lily wanted to tuck that strand back into Becca's bandana as she would've done for Amanda or Emma but thought it was too forward.

"Are you kidding me? I freaked a lot. I thought I'd gone nuts. All I knew was that I wanted to stay in Fellowes Hollow. So, I had to do something. It was this or find another rich husband. And that might be the most unappealing idea ever."

Lily laughed again. Twice in one morning. There was something open and self-deprecating about Becca. She liked her more and more.

"That's close to where I am right now except I don't have money. I'd love to open a quilt shop, but the only thing I have going is that I don't have to worry about making rent payments. That's something. But then what?" Lily leaned in like she'd asked for juicy gossip.

Becca shook her head slowly for a moment, chewing on her thoughts. "You know what, Lily? If I had tried to think it through like you are, I never would've have signed the lease. I just focused on each thing as it came up. One at a time."

"How did you know where to start?"

"I didn't. I went to other cafes and talked to the owners. People are very generous. If you ask, they'll tell you lots of stuff." Lily sat back as Becca listed out some of the things she'd learned about equipment and suppliers and the crap she'd had to sift through on the internet.

"What about the space, though?" Lily scanned the room. "You said it was a wreck, and look how beautiful it is now."

"Thank you." Becca blew on her fingernails and wiped them on her shoulder. "I chose the decor myself. But for the rest, like the counters and the plumbing and the electrical, I hired contractors."

Lily deflated. There was a small hope that Simon would come through with the payout, but that was Emma's money, even if Lily could use it as she saw fit.

"The truth is, it sounds easy when I say it, but it was hard work. Every day. And I often thought I'd gone crazy but somehow I found a way through."

"I wish I could do it. Talk about crazy."

As Lily gave Becca the list of the many obstacles she had, Becca put her hand up like a stop sign. "Slow down. If you want to do it, don't think about the end. Just tackle one thing at a time. Even a small thing. They add up." She stood. "I need to get ready for the lunch crowd. Let me know what you decide."

As Lily wandered back to her house, past The Village and the brick houses of her neighborhood, Becca's words hitchhiked on Lily's shoulder. "Don't think about the end. Just tackle one thing at a time."

There must be one thing she could do. It wouldn't hurt to make a list of what needed to be done. Who knew, maybe on a second look, it wouldn't seem so bad. Then she could scout the barn for tools to help her clean up some of the debris, and as a bonus, she might see the dog again.

After changing into old jeans and a t-shirt, Lily threw back her shoulders and marched to the shop. One thing at a time. Any small thing was a start.

The key turned in the lock, and she swung open the door with such force the knob slipped from her hand, and the door banged against the wall. Lily checked for damage, then realized there were so many scuffs and dings already, one more wouldn't matter.

As she peered into the great room on her left, everything was the same as the other day, except Lily had a mission. She pulled her phone from her back pocket and started a list. Item one: move out the old, broken furniture.

At sixty-five, Lily hardly felt different from when she was fifty-five or forty-five. Surely, she could move some of the junk. As she tested the weight of one recliner, the mechanism creaked in protest but remained firmly rooted on the floor. Carrying it by herself wouldn't work, but she could push it. To where, though? There wasn't a clear path anywhere.

If she could find a big trash can and a shop vac in the barn or somewhere on the property, she might be able to make one room, if not clean, at least bearable.

When she rounded the bottom of the driveway, her shoulders slumped. The dog wasn't there. She hadn't realized how much she'd hoped to see him, but if he was tucked safely in his home, that was a good thing. And there were plenty of other dogs needing to be adopted if she really wanted to get one.

The barn door slid open with a light touch on the handle. What she didn't expect was the dog running to her as if he'd been waiting, his pink tongue like an exclamation point in a big grin.

"Hey, little guy. How did you get in here?" She stooped to pet him, searching for a collar or tags. He had neither, but she was rewarded for her efforts with a kiss on her chin.

He trotted behind her as she examined the neatly arrayed tools. She was no expert, but they all seemed to be for woodworking, which made sense considering the yards of lumber against the walls and in the house.

As she progressed down the side, she pulled things away, looking for a gap or hole in the siding where the dog could have gotten in. At the hay bales, the bowl was full of clean water, and the rags weren't rags. They were a neatly folded pair of faded jeans and a flannel shirt. Lily pulled back the bales. A battered leather suitcase and two shoebox-sized metal boxes were against the wall.

She froze, then looked over her shoulder like someone might be there. Someone who might be living in the barn or at least keeping the dog there. A chill ran up her spine. Whoever it was could be watching her. She looked up at the rafters to be sure no one was lurking.

Her legs twitched with the impulse to run, but she still needed to find what she'd come for. "Okay, pal. Let's get this over with." The dog wasn't the least alarmed as he followed her up the other side of the barn, closing in on the open door to freedom. Still no shop vac. Lily grabbed the broom and dustpan.

At the door, the dog sat. Lily wanted to skedaddle before whoever belonged to those jeans showed up, but what about the dog? She slid the door, leaving a gap for him to get out. "You'll be okay."

The asphalt drive crunched under her feet. As she passed the bottom of the rickety steps, she noticed a town-issued garbage can beside a door, presumably to the basement. The doorknob turned, but a deadbolt held it firmly shut. At least she didn't have to worry about anyone being inside the house.

With the broom and dustpan sticking up from the trash can, Lily took them to the front room and got working. By the time she'd collected the big pieces of cardboard and shreds of wallpaper, her hands had become dry as old leather, in need of industrial-strength hand cream, but she'd cleared enough space to move the furniture and the wood near the top of the basement steps. If she pushed it down, she might be able to wrangle it out the back door.

Whether it would work remained to be seen, but it was a plan and the only one she had. Before she could move anything else, she needed to deal with all the boards propped against the walls or splayed across the floor. Given her height versus the length of the planks, she had to grab the sides of the boards at shoulder height or they tipped as she moved them. She'd taken two steps with the second one before her grip slipped and a piercing pain sliced into her right hand between her thumb and forefinger. She dropped the board, which smashed into the wall, then clattered to the floor.

A two-inch, toothpick-thick spike of wood projected from her hand, at least half an inch visible under her skin. She leaned against the wall for support as her peripheral vision faded and her skin became damp.

Carefully, with her left hand, she pulled the splinter. Pain, as though a needle was passing through her, shot up her arm, but the splinter didn't budge. A wave of nausea made her gag. This was beyond what she could handle herself. And with all the filth, she'd probably need an antibiotic and a tetanus booster. Her legs shook as she climbed to the upstairs bathroom to wash her hands.

There was no soap or towel, but it didn't matter. She'd have been afraid to touch them. Gingerly, she ran her throbbing hand under the water to get the worst of the dirt off.

She needed to get downstairs to her cell phone to call for help. At the top of the stairs, vertigo made her sit, sending a puff of dust around her. She pulled her t-shirt over her nose to breathe and closed her eyes. She'd always been squeamish. It was just a splinter, not even bleeding. Nasty, but not life-threatening.

When she thought the room wouldn't spin anymore, she opened her eyes. From where she sat, she could see into two rooms. One had a bed cracked in half, the foot- and the headboards leaning toward each other. The other had loose wires dangling from where a ceiling light should have been. There was no end to the mess in this place. One thing at a time.

Each step seemed to wobble beneath her feet. She tightened her grip on the handrail. Instead of calling Philip, she pressed the icon for Robin, who worked in the town building across the street. With luck, she'd be able to sneak away to drive Lily to the urgent care. It was only ten minutes away in Ainsleyville on the other side of the interstate. And unlike Philip, Robin wouldn't give her another lecture on why she should sell the place.

Chapter 6
No Money

"Next time, wear a pair of leather gloves." Robin sat next to Lily in the waiting room on hard plastic chairs that offered little comfort.

Lily slouched and propped her elbow on her hip, her pulsating injured hand held high, the bright lights highlighting long smears of unwashed dirt on her forearm. She could only imagine what her face and hair looked like.

"Lifting a board didn't seem like a big deal. I was trying to do what I could by myself." She told Robin about her conversation with Becca. Lily laid her head on Robin's shoulder. "I wish this could be easier."

A tiny woman in scrubs called her name.

"Remember," Robin pressed Lily's good hand between her own, "if you're not out before it's time to get Emma, I'll come back after I pick her up."

As Lily walked to the exam room, she tried to talk herself out of feeling like a failure. What did it take to move a plank of wood? Couldn't she have managed that small thing? For Emma's sake? For Amanda's sake?

"Your hand will be fine." The nurse squeezed Lily's shoulder to reassure her.

Lily didn't tell her the splinter wasn't what distressed her.

Whatever they had given Lily to numb her hand had worn off in the hours since she'd left the urgent care. The throbbing had subsided, but a lingering ache cut across her palm. The bulk of the bandage wouldn't let her make a fist, but she doubted she would've been able to anyway. She was lucky the whole splinter had been near the surface of her skin. No stitches required. A few days to heal, and that part of the ordeal would be a memory.

Since Robin had dropped them both at home, Emma had been sitting at the desk in her room, bent over her sewing machine, working on the drawstring bag project that had come in the box. Lily had been sitting at the kitchen table, listening to the intermittent clatter of the bobbin case and feed dogs, wondering what she could do about dinner with one hand virtually useless.

She lifted the receiver of her kitchen wall phone, propping it against her ear while she rummaged through her cabinet for the bottle of ibuprofen, counting the rings until Philip answered.

"How do you feel about going to that new pizza place in Ainsleyville? The reviews are awesome and they have a kid's corner with Lego tables."

"You're on." Philip's breathing was heavy. He was probably walking home from his office, expecting an evening alone. "My treat, but to what do I owe this late decision? Not that I'm complaining."

"I'll explain later." Lily replaced the receiver in its cradle and called down the hall. "Emma, we're going to go to that new Lego pizza place. Can you stop sewing and come talk to me?"

Emma came into the kitchen, her lips still pursed in concentration. "Does your hand feel better, Gammy?"

"It does, thank you."

When she'd told Emma how she got the splinter, she'd been truthful. It also gave her a believable reason why it wasn't safe for Emma to go to the shop. "Do you have any homework you need to do?"

"I did it at school."

"Wash up then. Philip will be here in a few minutes."

After a twenty-minute wait, they were seated on metal chairs between tightly packed tables full of families. The Lego stations were near the back of the restaurant, but that didn't dampen the noise and chaos of kids weaving back and forth between tables to play.

As soon as they had walked in the door, Lily knew this place wasn't Philip's style. "Thanks for taking us here." Even with the top button of his Henley t-shirt undone, he looked out of place, but good food might make up for it. Judging by the number of people in and out of the front door, they also did a brisk takeout business. A positive omen.

Lily thumbed through the menu. "Do you want plain pizza, Emma?"

"Can I have cheesy garlic bread too?"

"I'll cast a vote for cheesy garlic bread." Philip rubbed his hands together.

"That makes three of us." Lily snapped shut the menu and laid it at the edge of the table. "You can go play while we wait for the food."

Emma shook her head. "I can go later."

Lily dropped her hands in her lap, reminding her of her wound and how insignificant it was compared to what had been inflicted on Emma. Lily had hoped the Lego tables would lure Emma into having some fun. She'd been to school for three days, and while she was using sentences, Emma was far from normal.

"Did you do anything fun today?" Philip asked Emma.

"No."

"It had to be more fun than your grandma's day." He nodded toward Lily.

"Gammy lets me use straight pins as long as I don't hold them in my mouth like she does. She gave me a magnet to hold them. I can match the edges up perfectly like Mommy used to do."

Lily smiled, but a lump stuck in her throat. Maybe if Simon did have cash available, it was worth risking for Emma's sake.

While they waited for their food, the silence between Lily and Philip was unusual, but she didn't want to discuss anything about the shop in front of Emma.

The server returned with the garlic bread and placed a pizza on a wire rack on the table. Lily pried up slices for each of them, the cheese oozing and stretching. The lack of conversation no longer mattered as they pulled strings of sumptuous cheese with their fingers and wiped tangy sauce from their lips. The garlic bread was golden and crunchy, covered in salty parmesan, and sprinkled with oregano.

"I'd say it's worth the noise and the hard chairs, don't you think?" Philip laid his napkin on his plate and leaned back.

"I could do this again," Lily said. The crowd had subsided, the Lego tables deserted. "Emma, maybe you want to go play for a bit now?"

She nodded and left the table.

Lily watched her for a few seconds, then turned to Philip. "Do you think she didn't want to go when other kids were there?"

"You'd be the best judge of that." He lifted her damaged hand. "How bad is it?"

"I skewered myself but I think my ego hurts more."

"You shouldn't be doing that kind of work."

She'd expected a lecture, but he held on to her hand, running his thumb over the back. "You saw Emma. She hardly says anything unless it's about quilting or the shop. I wanted to see if I could do something."

"That brings me to Simon." Philip let go of Lily. "I spoke to him this afternoon. You were right. They'd invested all of

Matt's money in the practice."

"So, what happens now?"

Philip pulled at his watchband instead of his nonexistent cuff, a mannerism Lily associated with Philip the lawyer, not her friend. "He could find a new partner and use the money to pay you or he could sell the practice. They hadn't taken life insurance. I would have advised them to, but that ship has sailed."

For a second, the thought of finding a new partner lifted some of the weight Lily carried in her heart. She'd get a wad of cash, but she couldn't force that on Simon. There wasn't a plethora of dentists looking to move to Fellowes Hollow. "A partner is a personal thing. It can't be just any dentist."

"It's a tidy sum, Lily, and it does belong to you."

She crossed her arms and shook her head. "I'm not going to make him sell. He's always been wonderful to me." Her jaw tightened. The accident had done enough damage already. Lily wouldn't let the fallout ruin anyone else's life. Not if she had the power to stop it. Even if it meant losing the shop.

Philip shook his head and blinked slowly. "Remember, you planned your retirement around supporting only yourself. Now you have Emma you have to care for."

Lily didn't live lavishly, but she had no complaints. "I think I can manage."

Philip interlocked his fingers and pressed them to his chin. "Lily, I can't stand by and watch you get into financial straits."

He could be a little overprotective. Rose used to laugh about him for that. She'd once told Lily that Philip would offer to drive her to the store if it was raining. Never mind that Rose had never had an accident.

"I'm not going to get into financial straits." She sounded more certain than she felt. Sam had always managed their affairs. After he passed, Philip became her advisor.

"What if he made payments? Something he can afford without risking too much? I don't want his practice to go south."

Philip sighed, one side of his mouth rising, and shook his head the way he always did when Lily didn't take his advice. "I could arrange that, but you could also sell the shop."

"I know, but Emma isn't ready yet. Neither am I. Maybe I'll have to sell, but I can't make that decision now. Not until Emma turns the corner." Lily couldn't see corners anywhere in the future. Only a long, dark road.

Philip's forehead creased with concern. "Hanging on to it is costing you money for no reason."

Lily deflated, resting her elbows on the table for support. Philip was insistent, and he didn't even know about the clothes or the dog in the barn. But she wasn't willing to give up without a fight, splinter or no splinter.

She needed time to think and focus on helping Emma. Teach her to quilt and to cook. Go to movies and museums. Find other ways to ease her sadness. And get Philip off her back. Rose used to agree with him, then do what she wanted. When he hadn't wanted to redo their bathroom, she agreed it was too much money, then called in a remodeler, and handed Philip her signed contract. He got angry but he got over it. "I'll call Greta George, the agent Amanda used. See what she thinks." It couldn't hurt to get Greta's opinions and find out what the shop was worth.

Chapter 7
The Agent

With her index finger, Lily traced the pale pink line running from the outside of her first knuckle, following her life line, toward the center of her palm. She made a fist. Nothing hurt. Six days since she'd been to the shop, including three lazy days with Emma over Labor Day weekend, and the wound had closed, leaving a mark like a nasty paper cut. Her hand had made a dramatic improvement, but Emma's attitude toward school had not.

While they waited for the morning bus, the corners of Emma's mouth turned down as if she had to pull a slug off a basil leaf in the garden. She didn't ask to go to the shop. The splinter had convinced her it was too dangerous for her to go. When she took her usual seat alone at the front of the bus, Lily shuddered as if a chilly breeze had blown by.

Greta George had agreed to meet to talk about options for the shop. As Lily climbed the creaky steps to wait, she saw more decay. Split boards that probably weren't safe to step on. Balusters lying where they had fallen from the railing, rust stains where nails should be.

Once upon a time, the old house was a beauty, but the intervening years had robbed its luster and grandeur. The imposing front doors no longer welcomed guests. They had become a warning written in grime and gunk so thick it was impossible to tell what kind of wood they were. Amanda's voice reminded Lily to look closer. Underneath the crud, the ornately carved vine-and-leaf pattern remained.

"I'm so sorry for your loss."

Lily jumped, startled from her daydream to see Greta approach. They'd never met in person, but Lily recognized her layered, shoulder-length hair from the photo on the magnetic refrigerator calendar everyone in town had gotten in the mail. When The Village had begun to sell the active-senior patio homes, Greta had moved her office from Ainsleyville to Fellowes Run Road. Within a few weeks, it had become impossible not to see Greta's face on leaflets and advertisements all over town.

"Thank you for coming." Lily shook Greta's hand and opened the door, motioning for her to enter.

"Wow," Greta said, her head pivoting to take it in. "She cleaned it up a lot."

How much worse could it have been? Lily followed Greta into the front room. Then her jaw dropped. It didn't make sense. "When I was here last week, there was broken furniture and tons of wood and trash. It's gone." Lily grabbed the newel post for support. Who would have done it? Who could have done it? No one else had a key. Amanda's presence lived in Lily's mind, not as a poltergeist. "It's strange."

Greta didn't seem to listen as she circled the room. "This is such a well-built and beautiful house. I hope we can find another buyer who wants to restore it, not demolish it to build an auto body shop."

Demolish. What an awful word. It pressed on Lily like chain mail draped over her shoulders. Amanda's dream. Demolished? "I told you I'm not listing immediately. I'm looking for info and options. I'm not ready to part with it."

"Of course not." Greta patted Lily's forearm with her pearly-polished fingers. "Let's take a look around and see what your options are."

With much of the mess removed, details Lily had overlooked before became obvious. Cracked and gouged plaster, traffic patterns worn into the floorboards, but beside the scars of life, Lily saw what Greta did. What Amanda had. Oak wainscoting paneled the bottom third of the walls, and decorative cornices and molding framed the tops. Artfully turned balusters graced the stair rails, and a stone mantel framed the hearth and fireplace.

They wandered to the two rooms on the other side of the staircase. They weren't as ornate as the great room but equally lovely with oak millwork, crystal chandeliers, and stained-glass transoms over the doorways and windows. Like most of Fellowes Hollow, it was all hiding under layers of muck and neglect.

"Amanda had planned to restore it and open a quilt shop, but it needs more work than I can manage by myself." Lily held up her hand as proof. "But I want to find a way to do it."

Greta swiped the air dismissively. "A quilt shop would do wonders for this town, but this house is for flippers. They come in like a swarm and fix everything, then sell for a profit. They have tools and they have expertise."

"If I sold to them, how much would it cost to buy it back?"

"Probably a lot more than Amanda paid, but I doubt I can attract flippers to Fellowes Hollow." Greta looked over her shoulder as if reminding herself what she'd just seen. "Although if it's cleaned up a bit, who knows? We might find another person like Amanda willing to put in the time, sweat, and money."

As they walked across the back hall, Greta paused to look out the window of the door at the steps down to the yard. "That garage thing looks a lot better than it did." She moved into the kitchen. "There isn't much worth keeping in here. If you painted the cabinets and put on new hardware, a new countertop, and appliances, it would help."

Lily was only half listening. The cabinet doors had been rehung, and the broken table was gone. Maybe whoever took care of the dog in the barn had been in the house. Lily peered out the back window. Nothing looked different there, but Greta had thought the barn did. Tingles ran up Lily's spine.

"Let's look in the basement. I don't recall any problems."

Greta was halfway down the stairs before Lily's heart lodged in her throat, and she croaked, "Be careful. Someone might be there."

Greta had either not heard or ignored Lily, but neither had she screamed, and nothing had thudded, so Lily followed her.

The bare stone foundation was dry with none of the typical Western Pennsylvania mustiness. A furnace and water heater occupied one corner beside the Pittsburgh potty—a toilet, small sink, and shower in the open without walls. The rest of the space was filled with gardening tools, stacks of boxes, a ladder, sawhorses, and the shop vac she'd hoped to find in the barn. Like the barn, it was organized and cleaner than upstairs.

Lily checked the door she'd seen from the outside. There was a deadbolt, but it needed a key. She searched the floor and ran her hand over the sill of the small window nearby, finding nothing except the broken latch.

"Maybe paint the floor and walls down here. It wouldn't take much to make a proper bathroom either." Greta ran her hand over the sink. "I think you have a leak. It's wet." She pointed. "Shower drain too."

Lily had forgotten Greta was there. She was connecting the dots. And with the addition of wet drains, she didn't like the picture that was forming. What if it wasn't a leak, but someone was using the facilities? Someone who had cleaned up the barn and maybe the basement and, most recently, the main floor? "We should go upstairs."

Greta took a step and stopped. "When you're ready, I can list it as is, but if you deal with the cosmetic stuff like cleaning, painting, and refinishing the floors, you'd get more and maybe find someone interested in restoring it."

Lily nodded, but she couldn't concentrate. Her hair rose like a chorus line from her shins to her head. They needed to get out of there as fast as they could. "I'm not sure how much work I can do, but I can't let this place be demolished. Thanks for your advice."

"Anytime and don't forget to mention me to everyone you know."

Greta's fruity laugh echoed off the walls, but Lily couldn't smile until they were safely out the front door.

Chapter 8
Suspicions

"Please, Gammy. I hate school." Emma tugged on Lily's arm, trying to drag her away from the bus stop.

Week three of school wasn't starting off any better than week one or week two. If anything, Emma had grown more reluctant. "I can't help you if you don't tell me why you hate it so much."

Emma rolled her eyes and balled her hands at her side. "I don't like it there."

Why had Lily expected that asking this time would yield a better answer? "Is it because you're new there?"

"No."

"Are you making friends?"

"Yes." Emma turned her gaze to the ground.

If true, that would be good. "Which friends do you like the best?"

"Is Mommy's shop safe yet?"

The shop. As always. Lily fought the scream rising in her throat, compelling it back to the black hole that sucked in and stored all her grief and anger. Emma's problem wasn't school or being new or making friends. She had separation anxiety, clinging to Lily and the shop. And who could blame her? It had been little more than a month since her world turned upside down.

Lily's shoulders sagged at the hopelessness of it all. With

the junk cleared out, there wasn't much risk of a splinter or other accident, but the danger was worse. A stranger. Someone who could be peering out the window even as she and Emma waited at the curb.

But that someone had also been extremely helpful. For a week, Lily had vacillated between calling the cops and hoping her phantom would get more work done. She was too afraid to go back inside to check, yet she hadn't been willing to call the police either. She hadn't even mentioned her fears to anyone. Whoever it was—the dog certainly hadn't moved all the furniture—had done her a great favor. Eventually, she'd have to deal with it, but for the moment, the question was what to tell Emma.

"Emma," Lily bent to look her in the eyes. "I'm not entirely sure when. There's a lot that has to be done. Do you understand?"

Emma nodded, but a pout formed on her lips and her nostrils flared. Any second, the bus would arrive. Lily didn't want her to get on board with a sob hanging in the back of her throat. "But we'll talk about it. Okay?"

"We can go to the shop now. I'll help you."

"Now it's time for school. Go have a nice day and don't worry about it."

As Emma took her seat, Lily's heart settled somewhere beneath her stomach. She wanted to grab Emma and hold her, protect her, assuage her broken spirit. Instead, her head filled with a list of adjectives like burning embers. Defeated. Lonely. Depressed. Inadequate. She snuffed them all, sucking them down to fester with the rest of her angst. She'd pretend. For Emma.

When the bus was out of sight, Lily turned to face the porch, expecting a pair of eyes to stare back from one of the picture windows, but saw only the dingy lace curtains. If she dared, she could go in to clean as Greta had suggested. She could use the shop vac for the dust, wash the walls and floors, she could even learn to paint. Alone, she was no swarm of house flippers, but the intruder had done the heavy lifting.

It didn't make sense that whoever had been in there posed a real threat. Why would someone help if they'd intended to hurt her? And she had a growing suspicion of who it might be.

Lily headed for the cafe.

"Good morning. A latte?" Becca was always cheery, but Lily understood Becca also had a cynical core. Probably remnants of her divorce but also a quality she needed to take on the world and make her business thrive. "Not this morning. Green tea, I think. Plain."

Becca lifted the flap on the paper envelope, dangled the tea bag into a mug, and filled it with steaming water from the espresso machine.

"Do you have a minute?" Lily dunked the tea bag twice, then left it to steep. "I need to ask you something."

"Sure."

Lily checked to be sure no one could hear them and that her suspect wasn't around. "That guy who comes in for grilled cheese. Was he here already?"

"No. Lately, he's been getting here a little later." Becca's eyes focused over Lily's shoulder. The bell on the front door tinkled. "Speak of the devil."

"I'll have to tell you later, then."

Lily sat with her mug at her usual table, watching as the man ordered his food. He was taller than she'd thought. Through his threadbare t-shirt, she could see the bulges of muscles. Strong enough to have moved heavy furniture out of the house by himself? He seemed like a loner, but maybe he had friends. But if that were true, why would he bother to clean out Lily's shop, and why was there a Jack Russell in her barn?

After the man sat at the table next to Lily, Becca caught Lily's eye and tipped her head toward the back of the cafe. Lily followed.

"I think someone is living in my barn. Someone with a Jack Russell." Lily gave Becca the bullet-point version of what she'd seen. "Do you think it may be that guy?"

For a few seconds, Becca seemed only to concentrate on the grilled cheese sizzling in butter on her griddle, then cast her gaze toward the ceiling as if sorting her memories for a clue. "Could be. One day last week, when I got here in the morning, my trash can was knocked over. Huge mess. A raccoon, probably. Anyway, I came inside intending to clean it up once the muffins were in the oven, but when I did, it was already done."

"It would make sense that he'd help you since you spot him coffee every day, but why would he clean up my shop?"

Becca spread her hands and shrugged. "No idea, but that trash can is around back. It's not something my customers ever see. Someone had to have been back there for a reason. Maybe someone who lives in your barn. Remember when we were talking about the shop the other week? He was at the table right next to us."

"But you have no idea where he lives?"

"Nope. I never see him talk to anyone either."

"When he leaves," a chill ran through Lily with an idea, "I'm going to follow him. See where he goes."

For a second, Becca's eyes widened in alarm. "Just keep a safe distance, okay?"

"I will. If he walks past the shop, I don't have to go any further." Lily wasn't certain if she hoped he would go to the barn. What would she do then? On the other hand, if he didn't, then who'd been in the shop?

She returned to her tea to wait, her heart pounding as she adjusted her chair to keep the man in her peripheral vision, but not enough to tempt her to stare at him. The second hand on the wall clock ticked at half speed until he finally took his plate to the counter and thanked Becca. Lily counted to ten, then followed him out.

With his long legs, he was already halfway past the porch steps. Lily walked to the curb as if she was about to cross the street and held her breath. He turned down the driveway on the far side of the shop.

Without thinking, she fumbled for the key in her pocket, ran through the front door, straight to the window at the back. The barn door was partially ajar, and a joyous Jack Russell was eating the grilled cheese crusts the man handed to him.

Transfixed by the sentimentality of him saving some of his own meal to give to a stray dog, Lily watched until she feared he might look up and see her. There was little doubt about who had done what, but huge doubt about what to do except to get out of there.

Lily dashed into the cafe, her hand pressed to her chest as she gulped air. "He was standing right there feeding the dog. I'm freaking. What do I do?"

"Ready for a latte now?" Becca asked.

"I think caffeine would give me a heart attack. A shot of something stronger is a better idea."

"I have a bottle of scotch in the back."

Lily almost choked on her own saliva, trying not to laugh. "I didn't really mean it, but that's good information. There might come a time."

"There are plenty of times." Becca crossed her arms. The cafe door opened. "Take a seat. I'll talk to you after this customer."

A few minutes later, Becca joined Lily at the table. "Feeling better?"

"A little. Now that I've calmed down, I think it's better that it's him than a complete stranger. At least we know him a little?"

"I think if he were a bad guy, he wouldn't be so polite and respectful. If he'd wanted to steal from you or vandalize your place, it would have happened already."

"Is there anything threatening about him besides his size?"

Lily was more shocked than scared. Bad guys don't feed stray dogs and clean up other people's trash.

"On the contrary," Becca said, "he strikes me as someone who's been badly hurt. Grieving maybe."

"Like me." Lily hadn't meant to say it aloud.

Becca rubbed Lily's arm. "Yes, but you are not alone and you are not going to be alone."

"Emma keeps me going. I don't have a choice, but what if I did?"

"Then I'd make you a grilled cheese."

Lily snort-laughed. "You're good for me. Every time I come in, you make me laugh."

"I'm glad." Becca recrossed her arms. "So, what are you going to do?"

"I have no idea. What should I do?"

"I'm not sure, but if he hasn't caused any trouble yet, I doubt he will. Why would he?" Becca's eyebrows rose with her shrug.

Was that a good enough presumption to risk going back inside? "He hasn't had a reason to yet. He's had the place to himself."

Becca shook her head in disbelief. "If Doug was worried about being discovered, why would he have cleaned things up? That's a pretty big giveaway someone was there."

Doug. Becca knew his name. That was encouraging. "I think I'm afraid more because I should be afraid than because I actually am. Does that make sense?"

"He did you a huge favor."

Lily nodded. "I have a chance now to spruce the place up."

"So, you're going to give the quilt shop a whirl?"

"Someone once told me not to think about the end. Just tackle one thing at a time." Lily tapped Becca twice on the shoulder. "Right now, I'm just trying to save the place from destruction."

And at some point, she'd have to thank Doug for his help.

Chapter 9
Clean Windows

Lily pulled her jacket closed, wrapping her arm across her middle like a belt. The breeze was a sure sign of an incoming cold front and the promise of fall's arrival.

The hardware store was across the street from the hotel at the other end of downtown, as locals referred to the three-block commercial strip. Originally part of Ainsleyville, the interstate highway had slashed through the town, separating a half-moon-shaped segment of Fellowes Run Road and leaving the town behind in space and time.

Traffic had always been light, but the population had grown since the addition of Trish's McMansions neighborhood and, more recently, The Village. Lily had to wait for several cars to pass before crossing the road. No one wanted to have a red light in town, but a crosswalk seemed like a good idea. She'd suggest it to the town council even though they'd debate it for months. Then nothing would change.

The curve of the brass handle on the hardware store door felt familiar, as did the scent of old wood and solvents that wafted out when she opened it. When she and Sam had first moved to town, before they had Amanda, Lily had worked for the original owner, processing paperwork. Like the rest of the town, the store had its original features. Oak shelving, every nook stuffed with things from light bulbs and batteries to chimney caps and mortar.

Lily ran her hand over the drawers of an old apothecary chest, remembering when she would open each and take inventory, counting nuts, bolts, and washers. Little brass frames, blackened with patina, held labels ochred with age, many lettered in Lily's hand.

"Lily, it's good to see you." Ed, son of the former owner, came out from behind the counter and embraced her. "What brings you in? It's not gardening season."

He knew her habits well as he should. They'd known each other for over forty years, since he was a teen learning the trade from his father.

"I need advice on something completely different."

"I'm your guy." Ed drew his shoulders back and puffed a bit.

"I want to clean up and do cosmetic repairs on that house Amanda bought." Ed's eyes flickered with sadness. Lily tried not to let it fuel her own. "Easy things I can do myself to help it sell."

"Great. What do you need?"

"I was hoping you could tell me. I thought I'd start with painting, but I only know enough to know that I don't know what I need to know."

"That sounded confusing, but painting is not." He crooked his finger.

Lily followed him down the side aisle to an assortment of paintbrushes, roller pans, and putty knives. "Preparation of the wall is more important than the paint itself. You'll want to vacuum the walls first and then wash them."

As Lily listened to him explaining all the steps to a flawless paint job, words juggled for her attention. Rags, buckets, spackle, sandpaper. Sam used to love watching all those home repair and improvement shows. Lily had always stuck to the cooking and quilting shows. But there was YouTube. She could learn anything there.

Finally, Ed ended with a question. "Do you have a mop

with an extension handle? It'll save you climbing up and down a ladder."

Did she? What had she seen in the basement? "I don't have anything. Or I should say, I have a lot of things, but I'm not entirely sure what." Going back to the barn for anything was out of the question, and she wasn't crazy about the basement with its wet drains either. "It might be better if I start fresh."

"I'll tell you what. How about if I collect the basics for you and have the kid drive them over there. You can pay for what you keep and return what you don't."

"You don't mind?"

"Nah. Brandon loves making deliveries. He'll be thrilled." Brandon, Ed's son, hardly a kid in his late twenties, would someday take over the business, just as Ed had from his father. The passing of the torch. For Lily and Emma, it would skip a generation.

"Will you be there this morning?" Ed asked.

"All I need is time to walk back. Thank you." Lily hoped her expression was communicating how grateful she was for his help. "Oh, and one more thing. Do you have a portable radio?"

"I do. Heavy-duty contractor types. They can survive most spills and falls."

"I'll take that with me now." She'd play music, so Doug would know she was there.

"Take these too." He handed her a pair of leather work gloves. "Wear them. Especially if you're dealing with rough wood."

"Did Trish tell you I got a splinter?" Trish, with all her gardening, jarring, and canning, was probably at the hardware store at least once a week.

He ducked his head and gave a sheepish smile. "She did. I'd asked her how you were doing."

"Thank you." It mattered to her he cared.

"One thing before you go." He picked up a gallon paint can by the wire handle and swung it around so Lily could read the label. "Do you need to use a stain-blocking primer?"

"How would I know if I need one?"

"You probably do. At least where there was wallpaper. You don't want to paint and, a few months later, have stains ghosting through."

Ghosts. She could wish for Amanda's ghost to be there.

First thing when she got back to the shop, Lily turned on the radio and found a strong signal for an oldies station. Hall and Oates singing "You Make My Dreams" filled the front room. While she waited for Brandon to drop off what she expected to be half the hardware store, she left the front door open, sat on the porch steps, and tapped the YouTube icon on her phone.

When the Fellowes Hardware truck pulled up, it was Ed, not Brandon, who got out of the driver's side. "I thought I'd come see what you're up against."

"You think I'm in over my head."

"Let's just say I want to give my old friend the concierge service." He tugged at his chin. "Let's take a look."

When they went in the front door, "Daydream Believer" was playing. That's what Lily needed to do. Believe in daydreams. Like Becca said. Tackle one thing at a time. She knew nothing when she started and had found a guide.

Ed stopped in the middle of the great room and spun as he took in the walls and ceiling. "I forgot how beautiful this house once was. I envy you."

Lily practically choked on her laugh. "Seriously? This was all Amanda's dream."

"As long as you're not dealing with structural issues or electrical or plumbing, you can do most of this yourself."

Lily deflated and wondered if Ed had heard her sigh. All this? And only in the space of time while Emma was at school.

Ed studied her face. "I have an idea. Before we do anything, let's clean the front window. It will brighten the place up. Do you have a ladder?"

Lily looked at her radio as if it knew the answer. "Dream On" by Aerosmith was playing. Maybe it did know? All these songs about dreaming. If they played "Hotel California" next, she'd run out the door and not come back.

"I think there's one in the basement." In case someone was below, despite the radio, Lily stomped across the floor. Then, she opened the basement door, turned on the light, and counted to three in her head before taking the first step.

The A-frame ladder was propped against the shop vac and a wheelbarrow. Ed carried it up and opened it by the front window while Lily mixed a bucket with the vinegar and alcohol he had brought.

Each swipe he made over the glass, repeatedly rinsing the rag and wringing it, worked like an eraser, lifting the thick film of gloom. Two fresh buckets later, light streamed through the transom, revealing jewel-toned flowers and leaves with leaden stems. It was like one of Trish's quilts, except able to splay its color across the walls and floor. Amanda was right. The house was a hidden gem and absolutely perfect for a quilt shop.

A smile burgeoned from inside Lily, lifting her spirits and spreading across her face. She'd forgotten what it felt like to smile from pure joy. It made her stronger, hopeful. When she could bring Emma here, maybe she'd find joy and feel better too, even if only for a minute.

"Imagine when you have every window clean." He pointed to the transoms over the interior doorways. "And all the wood will shine once it's cleaned and polished. No one will be able to resist coming in to visit."

"Don't get too excited. It might take me years."

"A quilt shop would be great to bring visitors into town." He rubbed his chin for a moment while he looked around. "All right, let me show you some other things and then I have to leave you to it."

An hour later, Lily had sorted out the enormous pile of things Ed had left her. Brushes, roller pans, cans of sealer, drop cloths, a caulking gun, two different putty knives, sanding blocks. Things which that morning Lily hadn't known existed. She'd learned where to start. That alone felt like an accomplishment.

No doubt, the bill would be more than she'd intended to spend, but after seeing the results of cleaning one window, it seemed worth it. The idea of someone turning the old house into an auto body shop was too awful. She could hope the town would never approve such a thing, but with the influx of population from retirees moving to The Village, even Fellowes Hollow might not be able to escape the pressure of commercial progress.

Lily felt as though invisible arms were squeezing her, making it hard to breathe. She dropped onto the five-gallon bucket of stain blocker to sit. Could she do enough to make a difference? Was Philip right? She was wasting her money and making her life hard for nothing.

Lily bent forward and held her hands over her ears and closed her eyes. When she quieted her mind, she knew the shop was exactly the thing Emma needed. Lily pressed her fingers to her lips, remembering the smile she'd worn only a few hours earlier. Lily needed the shop too. Maybe the invisible arms weren't squeezing her to make it hard to breathe. Maybe they were holding her in place so she couldn't quit.

Lily turned up the volume on the radio when the beat of Abba's "Dancing Queen" began to play. It surged energy into her screaming shoulders, which begged for rest. She'd been cleaning for two full days, six and a half hours each day. She'd swiped the wand of the shop vac across every surface, using the upholstery brush to get into the nooks and crannies of the cornices. Even the doorknobs had dust. The harder part was using the microfiber mop to wash the ceiling. The extension pole helped, but not enough to prevent giving her a headache from constantly looking up. It blossomed at the back of her neck and crept like ivy up to the crown of her skull. Her arms felt as though they weighed twenty pounds each.

Only the fabulous tunes playing and the relative wake of freshness left after each pass of her mop kept her powering through the job. After she'd finished, she took a dry cloth to erase a few drips from the front window. A trio of women on the sidewalk stopped to wave wildly like a fan club waiting for Lily to deplane.

Robin, Maggie, and Trish were at the front door before Lily could put down her rag.

"We thought we'd drag you off for an afternoon tea at the cafe." Trish's hair, dyed cherry-red and curled, bounced like springs, mimicking her enthusiasm.

Lily lowered the volume on the radio. "I wish, but I need time to clean up before I turn into a coachman for Cinderella's pumpkin, aka the school bus."

Robin's gaze roamed the walls. "This isn't as bad as you'd made it sound."

"I'm not covered in dust and smell like a pickle from all the vinegar for nothing." Lily led them through the kitchen, past the door to the dilapidated outdoor stairs, and into the room on the other side of the house. "That's what it used to look like. There are these two rooms and the kitchen, then four more and a bathroom upstairs. And this is without all the trash and broken furniture. You missed the worst of it."

Like a chorus line, their faces dropped one after the other.

"Jack was the man who owned this house," Robin said, her

gaze on the floor. "I didn't know him as much as know of him. He was a furniture maker. I think he used to sell things at a store down in Little Washington."

"That explains all the planks of wood that used to be here and all the tools out in the barn." Lily rubbed her hand where the splinter had been. Only the memory hurt.

Robin watched her. "You got gloves, I take it."

"I did." Lily was about to explain how the planks had mysteriously moved with all the other trash but decided not to. Until she figured out what to do about it, the fewer people who knew about her secret helper, the better. So far, the only place she'd seen him was in the cafe when she stopped to get her morning latte.

"I knew Jack's wife a little," Trish said. It sounded like an apology. "She used to help out at the garden club from time to time. She got cancer and passed away years ago."

"I remember that," Robin said. "She was doing okay until their son died in Afghanistan. Then she went downhill."

"A broken heart can do that." Maggie slapped her hand over her mouth. "Oh, Lily, I'm sorry. That was inconsiderate."

"It's okay, Mags. I'm not the only one who knows what it's like to lose a child. I guess Jack stopped taking care of the place after that." Might Lily be doing exactly the same thing if she didn't have Emma?

"I wish I'd known," Maggie said. "I would have rallied some troops. We could have helped him."

"More like he should have remarried," Robin said. "My husband would be lost without me. I don't think men do as well as women when facing widowhood. It didn't help Jack that he lost his wits a bit." She often knew things about residents because of her work in the town's tax office.

"He may have had Alzheimer's," Trish said.

"He does. He's in the memory ward at The Village now," Robin said.

The four women stood for a moment, their gazes anywhere but on each other, saying nothing. Lily was processing what she'd learned. "Wait. How did I not know any of this?"

Robin put her arm around Lily's shoulders. "His son died about the same time as Sam."

Lily nodded. Her memories from the first few months after Sam's sudden death had huge gaps. She'd gone into a depression. Sleep, the only reprieve from loneliness, was preferable to all else. But she went to the dental office every day. She saw Amanda, Matt, and Emma regularly, and before long, she'd made a new life. With Amanda's death, she didn't have the luxury to curl into a ball and retreat to grieve, although she craved it. Maybe that's what happened to Jack after losing his son and then his wife. He had no one to live for.

"On that happy note," Trish clapped her hands together, waking them all from their thoughts, "if you can't join us for tea, we should let you get back to it, Lily."

With the ladies gone, the front room seemed bigger. Cleared of all the trash and cleaner, Lily could imagine it filled with bolts of colorful fabric. It would rival even the quaintest quilt shop.

Lily turned up the volume on the radio. "Calendar Girl" by Neil Sedaka buoyed her steps as she dumped her bucket, rinsed it, and straightened up. It would take her months at this rate to get the entire house clean. At least she'd be busy. No time for wallowing.

Chapter 10
A Cry for Help

When the alarm on her phone chimed the five-minute warning until bus time, Lily took a last look at the great room. After four days of work, the walls and ceiling were clean but yellowed and blotchy. Ed was right about the stain killer. She still needed to spackle and sand before she could lay that first fresh coat. With the next day being Friday, that wouldn't happen until next week.

Lily undid her ponytail, finger-brushed her hair the best she could, then retied it behind her neck. She bent over the chipped enamel kitchen sink and washed her face and hands with water only a few degrees above tepid. As fall settled in and the outside temperatures dropped, so would the waters of the Ohio River. By winter, they'd be close to freezing. She pulled her phone from her back pocket and added a water heater to her growing list.

When she left by the front door, she breathed deeply of the fresh air, shook her aching arms, and smiled, ready to greet Emma, happy and confident.

Emma stepped off the bus as if the effort to take the next step seemed more than she could bear. Lily pulled her into a hug.

"How was school today? Do you have homework?"

Emma looked up. Her chin quivered and her eyes pooled. "Gammy, I don't want to go to school anymore."

"I know you don't, but it's only been a few weeks. I'm sure things will get better."

Emma shook her head with enough force to rattle her brains.

Lily took her hand. "Let's go home. Then you can tell me about it." It was better to give Emma some space, wait until she was ready, than to force her to talk about it while standing in front of the cafe.

"I want to go to Mommy's shop." Emma yanked her arm away and stomped.

"I know you do, but it isn't safe yet."

"When will it be?" It wasn't like Emma to whine, but nothing about Emma was the same anymore.

"I don't know exactly. There's a lot of work. It will be a few weeks at least. We'll go when it's safe. I promise." When she no longer had to play a radio to ward off the homeless man? Lily crouched to look Emma in the eyes. Once hazel, round, and bright, they'd morphed into a lifeless brown, turned down at the corners.

"How about if I see when Vicki can come and we all go together? And you could show her how good you are with your sewing machine."

Even the mention of Vicki didn't brighten Emma's spirits. Lily clenched her hands, digging her fingernails into her palms. She wanted to hurt something, break something, anything to distract her from the ache in her chest. She wanted to rage against the senseless unfairness of poor, sweet, innocent Emma bearing the weight of tragedy.

"I know you're sad and that's okay, but can you please tell me why you hate school so much? Is it just because you'd rather be with me? Is it because you're new there and haven't made friends yet?"

Like a wave crashing, Emma burst into tears. Her breath preventing her from speaking, her mouth stretched wide, a black hole with enough gravity that even sound couldn't escape.

Lily pulled Emma close. "I'm sorry, baby." Her fingers, roughened from cleaning, caught on Emma's silky hair. Gloves couldn't completely protect her hands, and they certainly couldn't protect an orphaned child. Emma didn't need gloves. She needed Lily. "Gammy's here. I'm not leaving you."

People walking past on the sidewalk gave them a wide berth. An older couple sitting at the table by the window in the cafe kept looking and then looking away, their mouths turned down in helpless sympathy.

"Emma, please tell me what happened at school."

"This boy . . ." Emma spluttered and started over. "He sits behind me." She hugged herself, hiccupping and gasping. "He said . . ."

"Slow down. Catch your breath."

"Arthur called me weird because I have no hair." Her words spilled out quickly as she tried to complete a sentence before her next hiccup.

Kids are cruel. Why would he say such a thing? It made no sense. "You have beautiful hair."

Emma stomped in frustration. "He said I have a bald spot."

"That's not—" Lily stopped herself. The truth didn't matter. Only Emma's feelings mattered. "Let me see."

To her horror, there was a thin patch of hair on the back of Emma's head, about a half-inch in diameter, hidden by the longer hair from higher up her scalp. How had Lily not noticed?

She'd been so singularly focused on the shop, hoping that starting back at school would help Emma. She hadn't paid enough attention. What could she say that wasn't alarmist or dismissive? She briefly gripped the bus stop signpost, then got to her feet. "Let's walk home, okay?"

After Lily hung up with the pediatrician, she called Heather, wanting advice and reassurance from Emma's other grandmother. She stepped out the kitchen door and cupped her mouth and the phone, guarding her words. Even though

Emma was in the dining room working on the project that came with Vicki's sewing machine, Lily didn't want her to overhear the conversation.

"What did the pediatrician say?" Heather asked.

"She said Emma is probably pulling out her own hair. She called it trichotillomania. Say that fast—trik-o-til-o-MAY-nee-uh. Probably stress-induced."

Lily understood how Emma felt because she also wanted to feel anything other than the pain of loss. One pain to block out another, like her dream of the brambles tearing her skin or digging her fingernails into her palms. She leaned against the bricks of her house, the surface rough against her back.

"How do they know it's not medical?"

"I'm taking her in tomorrow morning. They'll take a look, but it makes sense." Lily explained about Arthur, the boy in her class. "I checked her clothes and her pillow. Not a single hair in sight. I haven't seen her doing it. She must be pulling it out when she's at school."

"Poor baby. What can you do about it?"

"I'm going to call the school and let them know. They can change her seat. Keep watch. As for her hair, if it's stress-induced, the doctor thinks it will go away as Emma feels better. If not, I have to get her into behavioral therapy. I asked about grief counseling for her, but it's only been a month since—" Sympathy for Emma's suffering sputtered through Lily's veins like a fuse of gunpowder.

"I suppose I could have waited longer before I made her go to school, but it seemed best for her to start on the first day. To get her back to a routine. Something like normal. Now I'm not so sure. I don't want to make her feel like there is something wrong with her. What do you think?"

"It isn't like Emma to hate school. Is it just that boy?" Heather's concern bled through the phone.

Lily rubbed her forehead. "All she wants is to go to Amanda's shop. I can't take her there. It's a total wreck." Heather didn't need to know the truth. Lily dropped to the concrete porch, the cold seeping through her clothes. "I'm failing her. This is my fault."

Heather was silent for a moment, then took a deep breath and cleared her throat. "No one can do a better job than you. Don't imagine that I have a magic wand and can fix her. You, Amanda, and Emma are peas from the same pod. You know that. So cut yourself some slack. You suffered a terrible loss too. We all did, but I have two other children and I have Ben." Heather choked up and didn't speak for a moment.

"When was the last time you slept well? Remember to take care of yourself. We love you. Just tell us what we can do to help."

"I thought maybe Emma could spend the weekend with you. A change of scenery might do her good." Emma was comfortable with her grandparents and she needed to separate a bit from Lily. Being with Heather and Ben would give her distance but not in a threatening way, like a new school.

Heather agreed.

Later that evening, Lily tucked Emma into her bed and turned off the lamp. The night light glowed in the corner.

"Should we read a book together?"

Emma lay back on her pillow and nodded. Every day she looked more like Amanda, her bowed lips curving into a hint of a smile, a smattering of freckles on the bridge of her nose. "Okay, but can you read it to me?"

"Of course. How about one of the Ramona books?" Lily was sure Emma knew those books had been Amanda's. As soon as she asked, she worried it was a bad idea, but Emma snuggled under the covers and closed her eyes.

As Lily read, time turned back to when she'd read that book to Amanda. If one thing in the progression of life had been different, maybe they wouldn't have been on that ill-fated trek to the Home Depot. It would be Amanda reading to Emma.

"Gammy, can we go to mommy's shop tomorrow?" Emma's voice was heavy with sleep.

"We have the afternoon off tomorrow." After her doctor's appointment, Emma wasn't going to school. "I thought we could go to a movie or play mini golf or we could go shopping. Then in the evening, we'll go to Grandma and Grandpa's. Would you like that?"

Emma didn't answer, her breathing soft and regular. Lily slipped from her room and thought about Heather asking her if she'd been sleeping okay. Maybe if she could sleep, deep and dreamless, she'd feel more capable of deciding what to do for Emma and what to do about the shop.

Chapter 11
White Tablecloths

"I finished it." Emma rounded the corner from the hallway into the kitchen, her arm held high over her head. The drawstring bag dangled in front of her.

Lily laid it on the kitchen table, smoothing the patchwork with her hand. "You sew like a pro. Your corners match perfectly, and you spread the colors evenly." It wasn't quite perfect but amazing for her age, even considering she'd started sewing with chubby needles, yarn, and cardboard when she was three. Lily gave Emma a skeptical one-eyed squint. "Are you sure you're only eight years old?"

"I am." She twisted from side to side and the biggest smile Lily had seen in weeks spread over her face. "Can I use it to go to Grandma's?"

"I don't see why not. If it doesn't fit everything, I have another small bag you can use for the rest." Lily pulled Emma close and kissed the top of her head, her tiny body molding into Lily's curves. "I'm so proud of you." Amanda would be too, and if she could see the sparks of delight flickering in Emma's eyes, Amanda would rest better.

"Gammy, can I bring my sewing machine?"

"Just make sure you check with Grandma where you set it up. I don't think she'd want you at her dining room table."

Emma had one finger in her mouth, her gaze to the ceiling. "Can I take some squares of Mommy's clothes? To make the quilt for the shop."

Lily tried to keep her expression neutral but was fairly certain her smile had faltered. When they'd been at the pediatrician that morning, the doctor hadn't found a physical reason for Emma's bald spot, confirming her suspicion of stress. Lily agreed to get Emma into counseling and also to indulge her love of quilting. But Lily had not yet told her there may never be a shop. Lily couldn't let herself think beyond what she was working on or she'd freeze up. Best to stick with Becca's one-thing-at-a-time philosophy.

"How about if I help you cut some squares? We don't have much time. Philip will be here soon to drive us to Pittsburgh."

Emma bounced on her toes, clutched the bag to her chest, then grabbed Lily's hand, pulling her down the hall.

When the bell rang, Philip let himself in.

Lily met him in the dining room. "Emma's packing the last of her things."

"Is everything okay?" Philip cocked his head. "You look beat."

"Oh, no." Lily pressed her hands to her temples. "I was thinking, that's all." She'd had an idea and wanted his opinion when they had time alone to discuss it. "Do you mind if we go out for dinner in Shadyside instead of here? I don't want to drop Emma, then run. I want to make sure she's settled first."

"Whatever you want is fine with me, but I wish you'd stop worrying. Emma will be okay."

"You're right." Lily wanted to believe it, but after the hair scare, she couldn't stop worrying.

"I know just the place too." He pulled his phone from his jacket, typing with one finger.

Usually, when Lily saw him, he was in leisure clothes or with his jacket and tie off and sleeves rolled up, but he was still in his suit, a crisp navy pinstripe. He wore his sixty-five years well, his sharp angles softened.

Emma came down the hall, one shoulder drooping under

the weight of the sewing machine, her patchwork bag over the other. Lily had laid out everything Emma needed to pack. Somehow, she'd managed to stuff it all in. Judging by the squared-off corners, she'd even squeezed in a few books.

"Are those Ramona books?" Lily asked.

Emma nodded. "I can read them by myself."

"Of course you can, but I bet you'd make Grandma happy if you asked her to read one with you. Maybe you could read it to her?"

Philip pocketed his phone. "I got us in. Are we ready?"

When they arrived at Heather and Ben's, Philip parallel parked into a tight space at the far end of the tree-lined block of stately old homes. A few prematurely fallen leaves, browned and curled at the edges, crunched under Lily's shoes as she stepped out of the car.

Inside the house, lamps glowed with warm light, illuminating the muted blues and burgundies of the silk rugs and mahogany furniture. Curios and bookshelves, evidence of Heather's passion for antique hunting, were filled with china and crystal. Lily had her own collection but nothing to rival Heather's.

"Philip." Heather brushed his cheek with a kiss. "It's good to see you. What have you got there?"

"Emma's sewing machine."

"Auntie Vic gave it to me, and look, Grandma." Emma raised the bag. "I made this."

After the appropriate oohs and aahs, Philip offered to carry the machine to Emma's bedroom. She led him upstairs.

Heather pulled Lily into a tight hug. "Come sit for a minute. Ben ran out to get olives for martinis. Would you like one? Or can I get you a glass of port?"

Lily followed her into the living room and sat on the sofa. "Port sounds lovely."

"I'll wait for one of those martinis." Philip joined them in the room.

The rustle of a plastic bag announced Ben's return. After greetings, he took his place behind the rolling bar, popping open the olive jar and mixing drinks. In a jiffy, everyone had their drinks, including Emma's mocktail, chocolate milk splashed with mint extract in a narrow tumbler with a straw and a pair of maraschino cherries.

"What do you have planned for tomorrow?" Lily asked.

"I thought we might go see the flowers at Phipps before they change to the fall show or maybe go shopping for clothes or toys." Heather paused, looking at Emma for a reaction.

She licked the milk mustache from her upper lip. So much for straws. "Can I work on my quilt too?"

Lily caught Heather's eye to say, I told you so.

Heather nodded in response. "There will be plenty of time for that too."

Ben said, "I vote for breakfast out somewhere first. What about you, Emma? Want some French toast?"

"Pancakes."

"Pamela's Diner, then."

"All this talk about food is making me hungry," Heather said. "Emma, please go wash up."

When Emma was out of earshot, she turned to Lily. "Are you sure you and Philip wouldn't like to stay? I have plenty. It's no trouble."

Like Lily, Heather loved to have family around her dinner table. Losing Matt and Amanda was terrible for her too. Many times over the years, Lily had joined them for dinner and holidays. She knew their house was beautiful, but for the first time, she was seeing something else. A vivid portrait of what the shop could look like when its walls were smooth and freshly painted, the colors warm as if lit by firelight, the wood trim and floors gleaming in brown and gold striations, the great room packed with shelves, stuffed with upright bolts of fabric in all the colors of the rainbow. Amanda's dream in full glory.

She needed to talk to Philip about her idea.

"Thank you, but I think the sooner we leave, the better for Emma." They'd planned for Emma to stay until Sunday. Heather might get some insight into the hair pulling. With luck, maybe the visit would soothe Emma enough that she'd stop doing it. "We'll be nearby for dinner, just in case, so call if you need anything. Otherwise, I'll talk to you in the morning."

Outside, Philip looped Lily's arm through his. "The restaurant is walking distance."

"Good. I could use the air." Emma hadn't seemed to mind when Lily said goodbye and left. It wasn't surprising. She loved Heather and Ben. The idea that Emma would be better off with them percolated to the front of Lily's mind. If that's what ended up being best for Emma, she'd suffer the separation gladly.

And suffer she would. The sadness of all that she'd lost, of what Emma had lost, and all they both still might lose infected Lily like a flu. She ached in every joint.

"Emma will be okay." Philip seemed to have read her thoughts.

They strode in silence for the few minutes it took to reach the restaurant. He'd chosen a dark quiet place, each table haloed in candlelight, glowing against white tablecloths with tented napkins and rose bowls. The scent was intoxicating, floral and savory, soothing and appetite stimulating.

"How about a glass of wine?" Philip perused the wine list, running one finger down the pages.

"I'm sure I could manage one." The effects of the port had worn off while they'd walked. "This place is lovely, but you didn't have to do this. I would have been happy someplace less fine."

"If I'd had to, I wouldn't have wanted to. I thought it would be nice for both of us. A widow and a widower." Philip lifted his gaze from the wine list, but his focus was far away. "We go way back, don't we? Did you ever think Sam and Rose would be gone and it would be just us? And Emma, of course."

Lily thought back to what Robin had said about Jack not managing well after his son, then his wife died. Philip would probably do well to remarry. Rose had been the heartbeat of that household. Despite Philip's controlling tendencies, Rose always said she put up with it because Philip needed to be useful. He'd give her anything she needed, even a new stovetop when she'd grown to hate the expensive one she'd bought only five years earlier.

Lily could invite him for dinner more often, make sure he ate fresh fruits and vegetables, encourage him to do more than work sixty hours a week at his law firm. After all, friends look after friends. Where would she be without Philip's friendship?

"No. This future never crossed my mind, but life has its own ideas. By the way, I've been meaning to ask, how are your sons? Any plans for a visit?" Neither of his twin sons had visited more than once since Rose had died.

"No. I'd like to see them more, but they're busy building their careers."

One of his sons had married and lived in California doing some kind of app development. The other worked at the Green Bank Observatory in the middle of West Virginia. Only a few hours drive away.

"Any babies in the future for Bryan?"

"Not yet. And I don't think Eric is even dating, but he's happy, so that counts for a lot." Philip paused, and his forehead lines softened. "I see your unhappiness, my Lily. I wish there was a way I could carry some of the pain for you. But I'm here if there's ever anything I can do to help."

The waiter appeared with a bottle of wine, which he cradled with a cloth and showed to Philip, who nodded. The server cut the foil and twisted the corkscrew, pulling out the cork in one smooth movement. After Philip sipped and nodded again, the waiter filled both their glasses.

Lily let the deep purple wine coat her mouth before swallowing. "I want your opinion on an idea I have, but you have to first promise me you won't default to telling me to sell."

"So, this is about the shop?" His expression didn't falter, but he straightened a bit.

"It is, but it's more about Emma." Lily filled Philip in on the pediatrician's assessment. "I agreed it's better to start her in counseling than to hold off."

"I can't argue with that." Philip twirled his glass, admiring the wine in the candlelight. "Although, I have to say she was more animated tonight than I've seen her."

"And that's how this gets me to the shop. She was animated because she's working on a quilt made from Amanda's clothes, which she thinks she's going to hang in the shop."

Philip didn't say anything. Lily continued.

"I managed to get some work done on it. The transformation just from a good cleaning is amazing. The problem is, by myself, it will take forever. I spent this whole week and barely made a dent."

"What advice do you want from me?" His words were flat and dry, somewhere between bored and annoyed.

"I think I should put some money into it. Hire people to do some things." The work would get done, and Lily would have more time and energy to devote to Emma. Lily lifted her glass, resisting the temptation to take a deep swig while she waited for Philip to mull over his response.

"Then what do you and Emma live on?"

"I still have Sam's pension, so I have income and I won't spend all my savings."

"You know I think this is a terrible idea. You'll have to sell eventually and there's no guarantee you'll get your money back. It's easier on you and Emma if you sell now and get it over with." He straightened his cutlery. "Stick with your original plan. Carry the cost of the shop for a few months. Emma will go to counseling and when she's ready, off-load the place."

"But what if I want to open a quilt shop? It's a piece of Amanda. I think it might help Emma." She inspected her ragged fingernails in the candlelight. "It helps me too."

Philip's eyebrows shot up. "You seriously think you can open a quilt shop?"

Sometimes he could be infuriatingly derisive, but she channeled Rose. Give a little, then ask for a lot. "No, not seriously, but I can't abandon the idea either."

Philip dabbed his mouth with his napkin, then returned it to his lap. "I long for the day when I see you happy again, but a quilt shop won't bring back Amanda. It will just make life harder for you. When was the last time you took care of yourself? Do you even go to your quilt circle anymore?"

"I went once."

"And you're not sleeping well. You look tired."

Lily fingered the velvety petals of the roses. She knew she wasn't doing well. The dreams didn't help.

"I can't imagine what you're going through." Philip took her hand from the roses and held it in his own. "I just want you to make things easier for yourself, not harder. I wish I had a better answer."

Lily hated the look in Philip's eyes. The corners turned down and his brow knitted. His sympathy made her feel like a sad sack who couldn't get what she wanted. Deep down, she knew she couldn't afford to lose a lot of money. She'd just have to let it take as long as it would take.

The waiter returned for their orders.

"We need another minute," Philip said. He put on his reading glasses and opened his menu. After a few minutes of silence while they read, he said, "We should go out like this more often."

Lily nodded. She agreed they should spend more time together, but as for dinner, their conversation had stolen her appetite. Every appetizer, every entrée, had a mouthwatering description, but all she wanted was another glass of wine and a piece of bread to sop up the acid in her stomach.

Chapter 12
Unexpected Aid

For nearly five years after Sam died, Lily was used to waking in a quiet house with her footsteps and the gurgling of the kettle as her morning companions. Then Amanda, Matt, and Emma had moved in, and for a few weeks, her house was rarely quiet. She'd loved it. But with Emma at Heather and Ben's, all Lily had for company were memories of Philip's expression and opinions from dinner the night before.

She sat at the kitchen table with her coffee and filled the silence by watching how-to videos on her iPad. The pros made spackling and caulking look easy. Surely, she wasn't as helpless as Philip had made her feel. She didn't need to be speedy. There was no deadline.

Two things were clear. She wasn't about to give up and she had two unencumbered days until Sunday evening when Emma came home. No bus schedule, no homework, no dinner to worry about. She'd see what kind of progress she could make with what she'd already bought.

On the walk to the shop, the sunlight white against a bright blue sky, the air full of birdsong, Lily stopped opposite the retirement home to look up the hill. Fall was setting in, the leaves on the trees noticeably thinner. A year or two and the tree would grow bark to cover the evidence of the accident. All things pass with time, but life continues for those left behind, even when their hearts have stopped working.

When Lily entered the shop, she froze, then swayed as the blood drained from her head. Doug, the man from the cafe, held his hands up, his putty knife pointing to the ceiling. "I'm just trying to help." His eyes were wide and focused on Lily.

He slowly lowered one arm to balance the putty knife on the edge of a stepladder, his other arm still held high. "I heard you telling Becca how much work you had to do here. I didn't think you'd be here on the weekend because of your granddaughter."

His tone was intimate like a friend. He'd probably overheard a lot of Lily's conversations with Becca, her dislike of trash coming to mind. Neither of them knew anything about Doug, but the most confusing part of this strange scene was that she didn't have the impulse to run or scream or grab the putty knife for self-defense.

She took a long look at him, trying to get a read on his age through his scruffy beard. There were shallow crow's feet at the corners of his eyes. Probably around forty, young enough to be her son. She didn't stand a chance if he wanted to hurt her. He had to be at least six-foot-three, but there was no malice in his demeanor, nothing threatening. He even felt familiar in his worn but clean clothes, his voice soft and manners polite.

Lily cleared her throat. "You cleaned up the broken furniture?"

He nodded. "I didn't throw anything out. It's all in the carriage house."

Lily had been so grateful for what he'd done to help, she'd never wondered what he'd done with the stuff. He'd also managed to spackle the walls of the great room, white patches like bandages as proof.

"You did all this since yesterday afternoon?"

He nodded.

"You live in my barn?"

"The carriage house." He pointed over his shoulder to the back of the house.

"It's a carriage house?"

"I think so. Or a garage."

"Who are you?" Lily wobbled as her shock wore off. She wished one of the nasty recliners was still there. She needed to sit.

Doug turned over one of the big empty paint buckets, motioned for her to take it, then pulled over the ladder and perched on the second step. "My name is Doug Fisher and I've been living in your carriage—barn. I figured the least I could do is pay you back by helping with the work."

Pieces of Lily's memory interlocked to complete the puzzle. "You get in through the basement window and use the bathroom down there."

He nodded. He had eyes that sparked with intelligence, but behind that was sadness. She felt for him, imagining the same thing showed in her own eyes.

"I'm a homeless vet. I needed a place to stay. No one lived here. I thought I'd be okay for a while. You can kick me out. I'll leave immediately."

"Do you have somewhere to go?"

"No." He ducked his head as if ashamed. "But I'll manage. I've been through worse."

"I might have to sell this place after the repairs are done."

"I can help you if you can let me stay until then. I won't come in the house without your permission, not even for the bathroom."

Lily didn't know what she thought. She stared at him as if answers would appear in writing on his face.

Doug stood, his weight shifting from one foot to the other, seeming to ask if he should leave. After a few seconds of silence, he said, "There's a bigger ladder in the barn. In the rafters. I can bring it up. Between us, we can get the place primed today and start cleaning the other room. If you want." His eyebrows lifted in anticipation of her declaration of his fate.

Sentence him to expulsion or bring him on as a partner.

There didn't seem to be other options. "Okay."

He held up one finger, then pointed toward the front door. "It will be easier if I bring it through there than through the basement window."

Lily shook her head. The fog clearing. "Of course."

He left. Lily didn't budge from her bucket. Had she lost her mind? Every fiber of her intuition told her she was lucky to have him. He was a helper, not a threat. The spackling was smooth, no lumps or ridges. Better than she could do it. He'd accomplished what might have taken her a couple of days in less than half the time.

Doug returned with the ladder.

"So, it's not a barn?" Lily asked.

"I don't think so, but it's much easier to say barn than carriage house, so I vote we call it a barn."

"There's hay in it."

"That's my bed."

"And your name is Doug Fisher."

He nodded.

"I'm Lily Wolfe. Thank you for your help. You can stay in the barn and you can use the bathroom too." She'd finally gone around the twist, her sanity lost, but not her compassion. This man needed it. "But I need to pay you."

"Thank you, but I can't accept money. I can work in exchange for you letting me stay." The corners of his mouth turned up in a smile, but his eyes reflected relief, gratitude, and something else. Sympathy, like her own.

"Would you like a coffee and something to eat from Becca's cafe?"

He stood from his perch on the ladder step. "No, thank you. You've been generous enough. I'm not your problem to feed."

Lily's spirit drooped. She'd had a glimmer of happiness at the thought of bringing him food or at least a cup of coffee. "The thing is, feeding people is something I do. It's a reflex, so if you're going to stay here, you're going to have to get used to it."

For a second, his face went blank, not sure what to say. "You're exceptionally kind, but I have a much bigger favor to ask you. My dog has been mostly alone in the barn. Can he come in the house with me? He's well-behaved, no fleas."

"That little Jack Russell. He's your dog?"

Doug shrugged. "I guess. When I first came here, I thought he was a stray. He lived in the barn. Got in and out through a gap in the siding. He let me join him and never left. I suppose he belonged to the man who lived here."

This piqued her curiosity. He'd made it sound as though it was no accident he'd come to this particular house. She was curious but didn't want to pry, not yet.

"Your dog is welcome, but it comes at the price of accepting a coffee and grilled cheese from me. Deal?"

"Deal."

"Okay then," she said. "I'll be right back and you can get your dog. What's his name?"

"Jack."

"You named your Jack Russell Jack?"

He shook his head, gave a sheepish sigh. "There's a story about that. I'll tell you later."

At the cafe, Lily had to wait for Becca to finish with another customer. She thought she'd burst before she had Becca's ear to herself. "That guy, Doug, he's helping me fix the shop."

Becca's eyes bulged but returned to their sockets as Lily gave her a recap of the story.

"There's something about him. A gentleness." Dishes clanked as Becca plunked the tub she was carrying in the sink. "I never worried he was a bad man or a drug addict."

"Are you sure I'm not crazy or desperate or not thinking clearly?"

"You might be all those things, but I see no harm in Doug. What would be his reason? And why would he clean up the shop other than to help you?"

Lily's stomach settled. She'd needed someone else to confirm it for her. "Well then, I promised him a coffee and a grilled cheese. Can I get them to go? And a latte for me?"

Dusk was near when Lily and Doug finished cleaning, repairing, and caulking all the walls in the great room and had made good progress on the front room on the other side of the house. Three times what Lily would have accomplished alone. With his more than an extra foot of height, Doug easily reached what Lily needed a ladder for. Her thighs were sore from the effort. He taught her techniques and ways to make things easier. By the end of the day, she'd become adept with the putty knife and decent at running a neat bead of caulk.

Lily swept a few hairs that had slipped out of her ponytail behind her ear. "Dinner is on me. I think we've earned steaks, but I'm too tired to go further than the diner." She needed a shower and clean clothes. The hair on her arms was coated in dust.

They each washed up as best they could, Lily in the upstairs bathroom, Doug in the basement, and walked to the hotel at the far end of Fellowes Run Road. The diner was accessible through the hotel lobby and by a street entrance.

They took a seat at one of the green vinyl booths by the window. The family dinner crowd had already left, and the people hungry after a night out were still hours away.

"This is on me," Lily reminded Doug. "For all the work you did today. With your help, I have a chance of getting this done."

"You don't mind being seen with me?" Doug looked around as if checking for people staring. People often stared at him in the cafe, but it seemed more out of curiosity than scorn. Lily shuddered, remembering what Philip had said. He'd meant well, for Becca's sake, but it was still rude.

"Not at all."

The server brought over two plates with huge burgers, a trough of fries, and a side salad. Lily had a hankering to tell Doug to eat his vegetables, but swallowed her instincts with a french fry drenched in ketchup.

Doug cut his burger and set one half to the side.

"You promised me a story about why you named your Jack Russell Jack."

He chewed for a moment, long enough to make Lily hesitate.

"You don't have to tell me if you don't want to."

"It's okay. I think you should know why I've been living in your barn." He took the last bite of his half burger and wiped his fingers, then sat back. "Jack, the guy who used to own the house, was the father of my buddy, Billy. We served in Afghanistan together."

Trish had said Jack's son had died and that was the beginning of the end for Jack's wife.

"I came to see him. After a day when no one was home, I thought he was on vacation. I figured I'd stick around until Jack showed up. The only one who showed up was the dog. I didn't know I was too late." He stopped talking and held Lily's gaze. "I heard through the cafe grapevine that Amanda, your daughter . . . I'm so sorry for you."

"Thank you," she said. Why did there have to be so much sadness in the world? "It's okay. Keep going."

"Anyway, I heard Jack didn't own the house anymore, but by then, the dog and I had bonded. I figured he belonged to Jack. He's a Jack Russell. Two reasons to call him Jack."

"As good a name as any, I suppose." She wasn't sure if she should admit she knew about Billy's death, but it seemed only proper to offer condolences. "I'm sorry about Billy."

Doug's face went blank, and he stared in the distance somewhere over Lily's shoulder, then clasped his hands on the table and stared at them. "Thank you."

He blew out a breath. "That's about it. I have nowhere else to go."

"No family?"

Doug bit his top lip. "None that matters."

They sat quietly for a few minutes. Lily had a thousand questions, but it wasn't her business to ask.

Doug broke the silence. "It's your turn. I see there's a story there for you too."

Lily went through the shorter version about the accident and Emma. Her eyes welled, but she didn't cry.

"For your granddaughter, it's unimaginable." His words trembled as he spoke as if he understood how it felt because he'd lived it. Or something like it.

"More than anything, I wish I could turn that wreck of a house into a quilt shop, but I can't do it alone, and I don't have enough money to hire people. Your help is greatly appreciated. I just don't want to take advantage of you."

"You don't have to worry about that."

They sat again in silence until Doug leaned back, relaxing for the first time.

"I don't know if you noticed all the tools and fine wood in the barn. Billy taught me a ton about woodworking. If you let me, there's a lot more I can do, like repair all that furniture." Doug shifted uncomfortably in his seat. "I'm not going to pretend I have anywhere else to go or anything else to do. I don't want you to think I'm only saying this so I can stay longer. All I ask is your friendship and somewhere to stay until we get this place in tip-top shape. Then you can decide what to do."

"Either I'll open a shop or I'll have to sell. Then where will you go?" How did it make sense that this kind and intelligent man was homeless? Something didn't add up. She didn't have his whole story.

"I was never planning to stay here long, anyway. I came because I wanted to see Jack. To tell him how much Billy loved him and . . ." His eyes glistened and he blinked a few times.

In a flash, Lily understood he thought Jack was dead. "Doug, Jack isn't dead. He's in the memory unit at The Village. The retirement community." She pointed in what she thought was the right direction. "I'm not sure what shape he's in, but you can visit him."

Doug pulled back his shoulders, his posture more like a soldier than a worn-down broken veteran.

She wanted to reach out and give his hand a reassuring squeeze. What was it about this man? She didn't know him. He could be telling her lies. He could be after her money. She should be wary. Instead, she had a motherly urge to soothe his pain. "I'm sorry I didn't mention it sooner, but I didn't know you thought he'd died."

Doug pressed his hand to his beard as if he was measuring it or contemplating trimming it. "Thank you."

Lily called for the check, and Doug packed the second half of his and Lily's burgers and all her remaining fries. He might be saving it for another meal, but Lily suspected Jack the dog was about to have his dinner. Tomorrow, she knew exactly what she needed to do.

Chapter 13
A New Plan

Up before dawn, Lily left her house in the dim light and drove to the shop. As she pulled up to the curb, it was still more night than morning. She glimpsed Doug through the netted curtains on the smaller front room window, already up a ladder and working, the ceiling covered in white patches of spackle like clouds in the sky.

Jack the dog greeted her at the door, flopping belly-up at her feet and receiving a rub before Lily scoped the work Doug had done. The ceiling repairs were finished. "You are amazing."

"Practice. I used to paint houses when I was a teenager. I also got a coat of primer down in the other room." He dropped the putty knife into a bucket of water.

"Do you sleep?"

"I probably get six or seven hours. Can't linger in bed in the army." He raised one eyebrow. "You're pretty early yourself."

"I gotta take advantage of the time when Emma isn't around. She'll be back this evening. Then tomorrow, I'm back on the school bus schedule."

He nodded in understanding. "I think we can get this room primed today. If you pick out your colors and get the paint, we can finish these two rooms." He flipped his finger between the rooms. "It'd be nice to see one room done at least. Inspiration to keep going."

Lily crossed the hall to the great room, still in shock at his progress. "Even with only a coat of primer, those walls are an inspiration." The walls were crisp and white, all signs of dirt and damage erased by a coat of primer. The woodwork and fireplace popped in contrast.

Doug stood behind her. "I'm going to need a few different brushes, though. Any chance you can get to the hardware store today?"

"I was already planning on it." First, she needed to snap a photo of something in the basement to show to Ed.

"Great. Get a couple of two-inch angle brushes for latex paint and a second extension rod and roller." He patted the top of the stepladder like he would Jack the dog. "It will make painting much faster."

"Aye, aye." She saluted him. "In the meantime, I think it's about the time Becca will have her first batch of muffins out of the oven for her Sunday morning crowd. Want one and a coffee?"

His mouth formed the beginning of what looked like the word no, but he hesitated and Lily interrupted. "Never mind, I'm not asking. If you don't want to eat it, I'll save it for tomorrow."

"Yes, please. A hot muffin and coffee sounds fantastic." He grinned, Lily thought a bit bashfully, but it was hard to tell under his beard. "And I'll see what she has for you," Lily said to Jack.

After placing her order for paint and showing her photo to Ed, Lily took a detour to the big drugstore in Ainsleyville. When she returned to the shop, she left one of the packages from Ed and the drugstore items in the car and stacked the four gallons of paint on the front porch. The dog watched her through the window with a smile on his face like he expected she was hiding a toy for him somewhere. He was Hollywood cute, tufts of wiry fur on his muzzle, eyebrows, and the points of his one stand-up, one flop-down ears. Would Doug take the dog with him when he left?

Lily couldn't worry about that. She could only take care of them for as long as she had work for Doug. After that, he was a grown man and not her problem.

By midafternoon, they were covered in paint and dust. Her fingers, adept from quilting, took easily to brushwork, cutting a neat line along the baseboards.

"I'm going to need to knock off soon. I have to go home and clean up before I meet everyone for dinner, but, first, I have something to give you." She handed him a shiny brass key. She'd shown Ed the photo she'd taken of the old lock in the basement. He'd talked her through the steps to replace it. "No need to climb through the window anymore."

Besides the lock, she'd tested the appliances. Judging by Doug's clean clothes, she figured the washer and dryer in the basement worked and was pleased when the refrigerator kicked on once she plugged it in. She'd bought laundry detergent, dish soap and towels, a bag of kibble for Jack the dog, and toiletries for Doug, including a small pair of scissors and a razor. He'd seemed to be worried about his appearance when she told him Jack the person was alive and at the retirement home. She hoped when he found them downstairs, he wouldn't be offended.

"Thank you." He pocketed the key and gave her his second big smile.

It didn't completely erase the dour expression he wore in the café but it softened the edges. She'd love to see his face shaven, or at least with a trimmed beard.

"Tomorrow, I can finish painting this room. Chocolate Milk, right?"

A laugh burst out of Lily. "It's called Cappuccino, but chocolate milk works. By the way, I put plates and cups and things in the kitchen if you need them." So far, he didn't seem insulted.

He sat on the bucket. "Most people would have thrown me out. I will leave for any reason if you need me to." He hesitated. "But I keep finding things I can do. Like, get that truck running. I don't think there's anything wrong with it except the tires. I can build new steps for the back if we rent scaffolding. And I can fix the porch. I can even turn balusters to match the broken ones. Then there's all that beautiful wood in the barn. I'm not a quilter, but I assume you'd need shelving. I could build them for you. Shame to let it go to waste."

She felt as if her heart had been displaced by a bagful of gratitude, but she couldn't let herself think that far ahead. When that time came, she would need shelving. "Thank you."

"Gammy, what are all those brown spots on your arms?" When Emma had arrived with Heather and Ben, she snuggled against Lily's side in the booth at the diner. Second night in a row for Lily, she was too tired and hungry to care. Although how she'd manage to get food to her mouth with Emma wrapped around her arm remained to be seen.

"Paint. I was fixing up the shop, so it wouldn't be dangerous anymore. What are you going to have, Emma? Pancakes?"

"Yes." Emma released Lily to rub her stomach.

Heather, sitting across from Emma, said, "She couldn't stop talking about the shop all weekend."

"I have to, Gammy. It's important."

Don, owner of the hotel, restaurant, and diner, ambled over with several plates laid across his outstretched forearm. "It's good to see you again, Lily."

"You too." Lily forced a smile at Don. As it spread over her face, it became genuine. It was good to see him and to sit there with the only family she had. "You're the server now, Don?"

"No choice. Business is gangbusters. I don't have enough help to handle it. I don't know what I'm going to do when I reopen the restaurant inside."

"When do you think that will be?" He'd closed it for major renovations a few months back.

He shrugged. "Everything takes longer and costs more than you think. Another few months at least."

"It doesn't seem to have hurt your food any. I was here last night and my burger was as good as ever." At the end of dinner, she'd order one to bring to Doug and Jack the next morning.

"Thanks. Enjoy." Don laid the plates, then ambled off.

Lily turned to Emma. "Did you have a good time at the zoo?"

Emma nodded emphatically, her mouth already stuffed.

"We all did," Ben added. "I haven't been there in ages. I got some good pics. There's one with Emma holding up her bag in front of the elephant house. We sent it to Vicki. I'll send them all to you."

"And, Emma," Heather said, "tell your grandma about your quilt."

The word quilt made Emma sidle closer to Lily again. "We're going to hang it in Mommy's shop."

"I'm sure we'll find a place to hang it when it's done," Lily said. She hadn't said where, but there was plenty of time before the quilt would be finished. Time she needed. Time Emma needed. She'd go back to school tomorrow. The teacher had promised to move Arthur's seat and to be vigilant about keeping an eye open. Maybe at least that nightmare for Emma was over.

With an hour before she needed to wake Emma, Lily sat with her coffee, tax returns, and bank and brokerage statements fanned in front of her on the kitchen table. She'd never been good with money. She could keep a checkbook and knew how to live within her means, but Sam had done the heavy lifting to make sure they were set for the future. Since he died, she'd relied on Philip, but asking him again about her budget for the shop would only result in him telling her to sell. "Make things easier for yourself, Lily." She'd heard that refrain at least five times since they'd had dinner in Shadyside. What would Rose say? Probably that Philip was only being stubborn because he felt certain she was making a mistake.

And maybe she was. She'd already put a bunch of money into it. She could manage a little more, at least fix the rotting front porch. Selling the truck in the barn was a good place to start. When Doug had taken her to look at it again, she saw past the flat tires. It was in pristine condition, and if Doug was right, all it needed were tires and a battery. After visiting a few websites, she had a handle on how much it would bring in. Who knew trucks were that expensive?

By the time she had Emma ready for school, Lily had the seed of a plan.

Hand in hand, they trekked to the bus stop, but when they passed the shop, instead of the usual question, Emma stopped, put one hand on her hip, and looked Lily directly in the eyes.

"Gammy, someday you're gonna have to let me go to the shop. It can't be dangerous forever."

Lily squinted, trying to look skeptical. "When did you get so grown up?" In the two weeks since the Arthur incident, Emma had stopped complaining about school. The teacher's updates were mostly positive. She'd even had a couple of visits with a therapist. Maybe it was helping.

"You're right. It's not so dangerous anymore. At least not most of it. Soon."

"Today?"

After school, she could ask Doug to take a break and let Emma inside. "Maybe later, if my day goes okay."

Emma squealed, jumping and clapping her hands.

"Don't get too excited. I only said maybe." If it made her this happy, there was no turning back.

After the bus left, Lily followed the scent of cinnamon into the cafe and was greeted by Becca's dazzling smile.

"Let me guess, two coffees and one grilled cheese."

"If I didn't know better, I'd think you were clairvoyant." Lily always resisted ordering a grilled cheese for herself, although every time Doug bit into his, she'd start salivating. "I wish you'd let me pay for Doug's extra cheese."

Becca swished her hand as if Lily were a bug. "I can do my part to help a homeless vet." She also threw in a free muffin as always, insisting it was a day old and unsalable, which Lily doubted. Becca rarely had any left after the lunch crowd. But if it pleased Becca, and it certainly pleased Doug, Lily wasn't about to argue.

While Becca prepared her order, Lily took a seat, thinking over all the projects Doug had said he could do. He'd been worried about making her think he was creating reasons for her to let him stay. As if she needed one. Grief might play a part in her feelings, but she'd grown fond of him and Jack the dog. One thing she'd learned about Doug was he needed to earn his keep. Without work, he would leave. They hadn't yet touched the upstairs, but it wasn't nearly as bad as the downstairs had been.

Becca brought the food and coffees to the table on a cardboard tray. "I hope you can keep that shop, Lily. It would be really nice having you as a business neighbor." She made air quotes on the word "business." Although young enough to be Lily's daughter, Becca had become a mentor and a cheerleader, always nudging Lily to take the next step.

"I might have a plan to get a little more work done. One thing at a time, right? But even if not, as long as they don't move the bus stop, I'll be here most mornings for the next two years until Emma goes to middle school."

"Good news for me." Becca stood and patted the back of Lily's hand. "I haven't seen Doug in a while. Tell him to stop in."

When Lily entered the shop by the front door, her mouth fell open. Over the weekend, Doug had torn out the carpet on the central stairs and cleaned the banisters and newel posts. The dark brown wood glowed in the shafts of sunlight. He'd also painted the walls up the staircase, erasing the last remains of neglect in the entry hall. Lily could almost forget the flying dust bunnies and shredded wallpaper. The place was warm and inviting. A beautiful, old, comfy house. At least downstairs.

Doug came up the hall from the back room.

Lily handed him his breakfast. "I wish I had more than a grilled cheese and coffee to thank you."

"I don't know. Grilled cheese is pretty good."

"Becca chucked in a muffin for you too. She says you should stop by to say hello."

She'd be shocked when she saw his clean-shaven face and shorter hair. "While you were doing all this amazing work, I was thinking about what we could do next. Wanna hear?"

"Sure." He crooked his finger, and she followed him to the kitchen. "Remember this?" The old broken table stood proudly on four legs, chairs placed neatly around it. The kitchen was far from modern but serviceable as long as the refrigerator, which hummed too loudly to trust, held out.

They sat across from one another. Lily imagined brightly colored whimsical curtains on the windows, the table set with proper plates, and a home-cooked, family meal on the table. Someone could buy this place for residential use. It didn't need to be commercial.

"If we get that truck on the road, I can sell it. Then we can do the porch and, with luck, the back steps." She didn't see any change in his expression.

For the last two weeks, since he'd shaved and cut his hair,

something deep in his eyes had changed. They'd sunken a bit like he was losing a battle with some inner demon. Whatever it was had been with him long before he'd ever shown up in Fellowes Hollow. She wished she understood what haunted him.

"I got the tools in the barn working," Doug said. "That's how I fixed this table. All that wood out there is hardwoods. Beautiful stuff. Oak, cherry, maple. Then there's the rest of the furniture, all those little tables that were around and about, and the bed frames and armoires I took down from upstairs."

"Wait. How did you get those armoires all the way to the barn by yourself?" How had she never considered the possibility he must have help?

"It wasn't easy." He rubbed the small of his back. "I took out all the drawers and shelves and doors and anything I could. Then I wrapped straps around the box and carried it like a backpack. It helps to be tall."

"You are truly incredible." She couldn't decide if she should nod or shake her head and sort of did both.

"Here's what's incredible. I think Jack made all that furniture. Most of it is nicer than you can tell through the dirt. If I fix what's broken and clean it up, you might be able to sell it."

Lily let out her breath in relief. He'd meant what he'd said about sticking around to do more work. "While you do that, I can finish the painting and repairs upstairs."

Doug had taught Lily a lot. She'd replaced the hardware on the kitchen cabinets, flipped a circuit breaker, and installed a new light switch and outlet. Her fingernails were worn short and her cuticles dry, but she didn't care. Amanda would be proud. Lily was proud of herself.

"I have enough fabric to make all the window treatments, thanks to my quilt circle. It'll be nice to get rid of those dingy lace ones." Those women had come through with donations, although she suspected Trish had bought some fabrics and only pretended they'd been lying around her house "forever."

The kindness of her friends sent a pang of loss through Lily. Amanda would never know the depth of their generosity. Sure, they wanted Lily to open the quilt shop, but they'd have given it all to her no matter what. She cleared her throat before she spoke.

"I was trying to figure out where I could sew them. I need a long table to lay out all that fabric." When she'd made window treatments for her house, the widest window she had was about three feet. That could fit on her dining room table. The front windows of this house were closer to eight feet.

"I could set up those sawhorses in the basement and lay some planks on top. There are some twelve-footers in the barn."

"That'd be perfect. One more thing." Lily paused to consider her words. She didn't want to offend Doug. "I kind of promised I'd bring Emma here after school. She pesters me every day. I can't keep putting her off. She's quite determined."

"I can make myself scarce."

"Thank you." He understood without taking offense. She wasn't really worried that Doug would act in any way inappropriate or harmful but she wasn't ready to introduce him to Emma.

"I'll get started on the truck. Once it's running, I can use it to pick up pressure-treated lumber for outside. It will save on delivery costs."

Lily hadn't thought about using the truck before she sold it. She'd need to get it registered and insured, but as long as she knew the money was coming in, she'd be okay. "Philip has the title. I'll see if he's in the office. By the way, this may be a stupid question. How do we get tires if we can't drive the truck to get them?"

Chapter 14
License to Knit

"I'm heading out in a bit. I can bring it to you," Philip said, his voice booming in Lily's ear. She should have called his office and not his cell.

"Don't trouble, I can come by to get it." The last thing Lily needed was to have Philip come to the shop. He wouldn't approve of her plans or Doug.

"It's no trouble. I already have my coat on. I can be there in five."

"I was heading to get a coffee at Becca's." Sometimes ideas come at just the right moment. "I'll meet you there."

Two minutes later, Lily entered the café. Becca was bent over the counter, her chin resting in her hands. "Back so soon?" The morning crowd had thinned, leaving her more relaxed than she'd been a few hours earlier.

"Only for a moment. Philip is bringing me some papers. He doesn't know about Doug, so don't say anything. He already thinks I'm nuts for not selling."

Becca zipped her lips as Philip barged in as if something was chasing him. He kissed Lily's cheek and greeted Becca with a nod.

"Can I get you anything?" Becca straightened, her eyes on Philip as if she didn't trust him.

"Can't now. I'm heading to a client." He handed Lily an envelope. "I know a guy. He'll give you a fair deal on the truck and come pick it up. Want me to call him?"

"Not yet, thanks. Give me a few days." Normally, she'd have been grateful for his advice, but at that moment, all she was grateful for was that he didn't ask why she needed the title or why she hadn't ordered a coffee. Imagine the argument if she told him she was going to register, insure, and drive a truck.

Drive it? Could she drive it? Could Doug drive it? Did he have a license? How could she put him on the insurance if he didn't have a license? Did everything always have to get complicated? She took a deep breath. One thing at a time.

Philip looked around the cafe as if finally noticing where he was. "It's quiet in here this time of morning."

"Good thing too," Becca said. "It helps me get ready for the lunch crowd." She brushed past Philip with a rag and a squirt bottle to clean the tables.

Philip watched her for a second, then turned back to Lily. "Call me later. Let's do dinner. Anywhere you'd like is fine."

Lily stood still until Philip passed through the door and turned down the sidewalk. The air seemed to have more oxygen in his absence.

"What do you see in that guy?" Becca shook her head in disbelief. "Honestly? He's rude."

"He has his good points. Manners might not be one of them. But he'd do anything for me and I've known him a long time."

"I suppose none of us are perfect." Becca dropped the rag and bottle behind the counter and grabbed her broom. "Some of us are crummier than others though." She pointed toward two of the tables. Chunks of muffin covered the floor. Lily wondered if any of it had made it into someone's mouth.

With a green tea and a second cup of coffee for Doug, Lily returned to the shop. He was seated at the table with a metal lockbox like the ones she'd seen behind the hay bales.

"I have a license. It's probably expired by now." Doug

scratched the back of his neck. "I haven't needed one for a while."

Lily longed to ask questions. How long had he been homeless? Where was home? He'd said he didn't have any family that mattered, but why was he homeless? It made no sense. He was intelligent, capable, and generous. Tons of people in Fellowes Hollow would hire him as a handyman in a second. Surely, he could work anywhere he went.

"I have to get it insured before I can register it. And since you're going to drive it, you need a valid license. Maybe we should go to the Driver License Center?"

He nodded and opened the box, rifling through its contents. Jack the dog sat at attention at his feet as if there might be a treat coming his way.

"Ha, found it."

Lily could see it was a Pennsylvania license but couldn't read the address before Doug shoved it in his pocket. He put the remaining papers back inside, closed the lid, and spun the dials.

"You're going to need to give them a current address." It was as close to asking outright as Lily dared.

"I don't have one." Doug's expression was neutral, his tone flat, revealing nothing.

"You do for the moment." She pointed to the floor. Why shouldn't he use the shop? After all, it was where he lived.

Lily took the back roads, winding through hills. The trees still had most of their leaves, but some, exhausted from the wear and tear of summer heat, were strewn across the roads.

With each turn, she envisioned someone coming from the opposite direction, lazily driving, crossing into her lane as if the double yellow line was just a suggestion. The state was installing centerline rumble strips to keep people on their side of the road. If only that life-saving innovation had made it to Fellowes Run Road. She couldn't think about that.

She looked over at Doug. His head was tipped back, his

eyes closed. He said he slept enough, but that didn't seem possible, even for him, with the amount of work he accomplished. He cracked one eye open and caught her glancing at him.

"Are you sure you don't mind me using your address?"

"Not at all." She wanted to tell him she hoped he'd stay in Fellowes Hollow but didn't want to pressure him. "Anyway, you're doing this to help me out, right? It's our deal. You've earned this."

He pressed his lips into a tight line. His mood changes were obvious, but he didn't give away much about what he was thinking. While he'd looked for his license, Lily had glimpsed the blue of a passport, and a paper with the Department of Veterans Affairs letterhead. She suspected his demons were born during his time in service. If he had access to the VA, he could go for mental health help. Although Emma had grown to hate counseling, complaining, "All he does is ask me stupid questions."

But it wasn't Lily's place to worry about Doug, even though she always worried about those she cared about. Except before, she didn't have breath-sucking sadness to go along with it.

By the time three o'clock rolled around, Doug had his new license with an amazingly good photo, and Lily had insured and registered the truck. The price of the insurance had made her jaw drop, but she'd cancel when she sold it.

Doug planned to take the wheels off the truck. Lily had no idea how, but he didn't seem to think it was a problem.

While she waited at the curb for Emma's bus, the older couple was sitting at their usual table near the cafe window. It seemed to be their afternoon habit to people watch. They'd get a different show today. Emma would find out she was going to the shop.

Emma leaped off the bottom step and ran as if she couldn't get off the bus fast enough, her face red and blotchy, her eyes riveted on Lily. She crashed into Lily's thighs as if she wanted to be absorbed.

"Hey, what's up? Bad day?"

Emma squeezed harder. She hadn't come home this upset since the Arthur incident. Quiet always but not distraught. Lily pried her away and kneeled. "I have great news. We can go to the shop."

Instead of a cheer, Emma's chin quivered, and then her tears came in rivers that splashed on the sidewalk and her shoes.

"Take a deep breath, baby. Try to tell me what happened."

"Arthur." Her chest heaved with each breath. "At recess . . . he . . . he . . . he . . ."

Lily's knees grew numb from kneeling before Emma got the story out. Although the teacher had moved Arthur's seat, recess wasn't in her control. Arthur had brought a few of his friends to show them Emma's bald spot. Some of what Emma said was hard to understand, but Lily didn't need to hear it all. It was enough to know they'd told her she "looked like an old lady" and asked if "her brain itched" and if she "pulled out her brains" with her hair.

Lily imagined this kid with spiky hair, a piggy nose, and jutting chin. The nastiest of bullies. He may be just a kid, but she wanted to smack the imagined sneer off his face.

"Let me see your hair."

Emma turned around. Longer hair from higher up her scalp still obscured the bald spot, but it had definitely grown.

Lily redirected her anger at Arthur to herself. How could she not have noticed? Twice. She should have known to check. Why hadn't she? Because Emma hadn't seemed as reluctant to go to school, Lily had let her guard down again. She'd failed Emma horribly.

"How about if we go into the cafe and see if Becca has a sweet treat for you?"

Emma sniffled and nodded.

Instead of the morning aromas of coffee and cinnamon, the air was heady with browned butter and chocolate. Becca had her back to the door and turned as Lily and Emma approached.

"We were crazy busy today. I'm almost sold out," she said, "but I have these." She lifted a baking sheet with chocolate chip cookies. "They're still warm. Want one?" Becca's smile faltered when she looked at Emma.

"Can I have a brownie instead?"

Becca tapped her lips. "I think I may have a few in the freezer. I can warm one in a jiffy if you want."

"Yes, please," Emma rubbed her tummy. "And can I have a hot chocolate too?" Sometimes she sounded like a grown-up in a tiny body. One thing was certain, she'd been forced to face things no eight-year-old should have to face.

"You most certainly can. How about you, Lily?"

"Just a cup of tea. Thanks." She and Emma took a seat while Becca went on a brownie hunt. The only other guests were the older couple by the window. The man held a paperback near his face with two hands. The woman was knitting. She looked up and saw Emma, who was watching her with interest. From where they sat, no doubt they'd seen what had happened on the sidewalk. The sympathetic pursing of her lips before she smiled at Emma told the story.

"Would you like to see the knitting?" she asked Emma but looked at Lily for approval.

"Go on," Lily said. "It's okay."

Becca caught Lily's eye and waved her over. "What's with Emma?"

"I'm a failure. That's what." Lily gave her the details. "I need to find her a new therapist. She hates that guy and he's not doing her any good." Lily's nostrils flared in her effort not to shout, her anger almost overcoming her. "I never see her pull her hair. She's doing it at school. And what the hell is wrong with the school? How could they let this happen? If she goes to live with her other grandparents, she can go back to her old school and her old friends. Maybe distance from the quilt shop will help too. She doesn't need the daily reminder that her mother isn't here."

Becca took Lily back to the table and pushed her tea cup closer to her. "Take a sip. Breathe. Should I get my scotch?"

"No." Lily squeezed shut her eyes. "I'm just so angry at myself, the school. The whole damn situation."

"Look." Becca gently lifted Lily's chin and pointed toward Emma. She and the knitting woman were side by side chatting. "My mom is a retired school counselor."

"Those are your parents?"

"They are. Ruth and Walter. This is their afternoon hangout."

Becca had mentioned her parents were one reason she'd moved back to Fellowes Hollow.

"Come. I'll introduce you."

As they approached, Ruth had Emma engaged in a conversation. "I'm a huge fan of books. If your grandma agrees, would you like to come here after school and we can read together?"

Emma nodded. "Can you teach me to knit too? I have a sewing machine. I can make quilts."

"Wow. That's amazing. And yes, I'm happy to teach you to knit."

"Gammy, can I?"

Lily looked at Becca for approval and got a tiny nod. "Yes. Can you say thank you?"

Becca introduced everyone properly, then pulled Lily aside. "You have no idea how good this is for my mom. I could see it on her face every day as she watched Emma get off the bus. She worked at the elementary school in Ainsleyville for over thirty years. Still misses the students."

"You're sure it's not an imposition? What about your dad?"

Becca shook her head dismissively. "He won't mind at all." Walter had already returned to his book, while Ruth huddled with Emma, showing her the knitting.

There was no shortage of love and admiration there. Ruth

had gotten Emma's mind off school. Her eyes were dry, her complexion clear. If Lily kept her home from school the next day, let her spend it with Heather, this whole incident might fade. Except for the school. They'd be hearing from Lily.

Becca tapped Lily's arm. "I have to finish cleaning up. Come talk to me. Let them have more time together."

Lily followed her to the kitchen in the back, watching as Becca scrubbed a cookie sheet. The running water blocked all sounds coming from the front of the café.

"Doug came in the other day. I hardly recognized him. You've worked some wonders on him."

"He does look nice with his beard gone and his hair trimmed, but it's all on him. I wouldn't tell him what to do."

"He's rather hot, honestly." Becca fanned her face. "But he seems sadder. Or does he just look sadder without a beard?"

"I thought the same thing but I think he's sadder." It occurred to Lily that he'd shaved about the same time he found out where Jack was. Could be part of the reason. She would've loved to know what Becca thought, but Doug's story wasn't hers to share.

Emma interrupted her thoughts, peering through the doorway from the front. "Gammy, can we go to the shop now?" Somehow, Emma had eaten her brownie and finished her hot chocolate without a smear on her face or hands. "Say thank you first."

On the way out, Emma stopped at the table. "Thank you, Ruth."

"Mrs. Shaffer," Lily corrected her.

"I told her to call me Ruth. We're friends now." She opened her arms for a hug, and Emma filled her embrace.

Lily had warned Doug she was bringing Emma directly from the bus. He'd have no idea where they'd been in the meantime or if they were even still coming, but he was most likely in the barn dealing with the truck. Just in case he was upstairs, Lily stomped as hard as she dared on the old porch boards and nearly shouted at Emma when she said, "Okay. Close your eyes. No peeking."

They walked across the threshold. "I'm going to count to three, then you can look. One . . . two . . ."

Emma opened her eyes, blinked, then spun in a circle. "It's beautiful." She ran into the great room. "Gammy, this is the prettiest house ever." She twirled and twirled, arms spread wide, a look of wonder befitting Disney World on her face.

For Lily, seeing Emma so happy seemed to make the colors in the room grow vibrant. "Better be careful or you'll get dizzy."

"It isn't dangerous anymore at all."

"Not so dangerous, but there are still parts where you can't go. Not the basement or out the back door in the kitchen. Those steps are not safe."

"Okay." She ran to the other side of the house and continued spinning, mouth agape.

"Mommy was right. This will be the best quilt shop in the world."

Such sweet and innocent words spoken by a so seldom happy child were like a flaming spear going straight through Lily's chest. How could she send Emma away? Lily couldn't take this away from her, but they were stuck in limbo until Lily could figure out the next step.

"It's late, and I told Philip we'd have dinner. Maybe spaghetti tonight?" There wasn't enough time for anything complicated.

She took Emma around the side of the house to her car parked at the rear. As they drove home, they passed Doug walking on the driveway into The Village, his head bent, his gaze to the ground.

Chapter 15
Curtains and Dinner

In the upstairs bathroom of the shop, Lily unscrunched her ponytail. Bits of grout that she'd scraped from between the tiles around the bathtub clinked into the white pedestal sink. Doug had shown her how to use the Dremel tool "to make easy work" of it. It wasn't easy.

She checked the remaining walls, following the staggered grout lines between the white subway tiles to see if anything still needed to be dug out. If she had another hour, she could finish, but the bus was coming and Emma wasn't visiting Ruth that afternoon. Heather and Ben were taking her for the weekend. They'd arranged a surprise visit from Vicki. Emma would be delighted.

After the Arthur incident on the playground, Lily had called Heather to discuss Emma living with them. Feeling empty and defeated, she'd made sure Emma was busy, then gone down to the garage to call from inside her car. "No one is perfect," Heather had said. "Do you think I never missed anything with Matt or his brother? And I was younger then. Stop being so hard on yourself."

In the two weeks since Arthur incident number two, Lily had nearly stopped berating herself. She continued to work on the shop but kept her after-school attention focused on Emma and her hair. It wasn't improving, but it also didn't seem worse. Although measuring change from one day to the next is deceptive, Emma's spirits clearly had improved. Her afternoon visits with Ruth helped far more than the therapist had, if Emma's talkativeness was a gauge.

Lily splashed cold water on her face, trying to lessen the red rim from her safety goggles. Not an attractive look, but Lily had become used to being covered in paint or dust or sweat. She'd have to shower to be fit to go out for dinner with Philip that night. He'd insisted on driving them into Pittsburgh to drop off Emma.

When Lily went to the barn to say goodnight to Doug, he had his head stuck in the truck, the shop vac making a racket. He turned it off, but it left a buzz in Lily's ears. Jack the dog rolled over at her feet, pleading for a tummy rub. She obliged.

"This is one nice truck," Doug said. "It doesn't even have seven thousand miles on it." Transformed, like the shop and the barn, it was clean and shiny with brand new tires and a fresh battery, ready to sell.

"I'm going out tonight, but don't forget about tomorrow."

"Forget?" Doug smiled. She hadn't seen him do that in a while. "That isn't going to happen."

After consulting with Greta about the best use of her remaining money, Lily had canceled the plans for the outside projects, choosing to order kitchen appliances. At least she'd make the inside as good as she could. Then she'd let herself think about how to keep going. The appliances were scheduled to be delivered the next morning. She'd also made plans for later that day but had only hinted to Doug what they were.

With Emma away, and the new appliances installed, Lily had the rest of Saturday to work. She was up a ladder attaching the center support of the curtain rod on the front window when the mailman climbed the steps. Instead of the rattle of the mail slot followed by the swoosh of junk mail on the floorboards, the doorbell rang.

"Give me a sec," she shouted as she climbed down the ladder.

"I have this letter, Lily." The mailman handed her a letter from the Veterans Administration. "It's addressed to here but for someone named Doug Fisher. Should I return it?"

"No. Doug is here." She had to think quickly. "He's a friend of Jack's. He came to visit, not knowing Jack had moved out. I said he could stay here for a few days to visit Jack at The Village." If the mailman gave this explanation any thought, he'd know it was ridiculous. Visitors don't get important mail. And if that didn't give her away, she was speaking too fast. "But if you don't mind, please don't mention it to anyone—"

He zipped his fingers across his lips. "I don't tell anyone about someone else's mail. Can you imagine? Did you see so-and-so had a letter from the IRS? Nope. Not from me."

"Thank you. It's sensitive with Jack in his condition and all." Time to stop babbling.

Once the mailman was out of sight, Lily started breathing again and her heart slowed to normal speed. As much as she had enjoyed spending the last two months in the shop and on the three-block stretch of downtown Fellowes Hollow, it wasn't an easy place to keep secrets. The townsfolk were kindly, concerned neighbors, many of them her friends, but they also loved gossip. There were a few people who might misconstrue why she was letting a homeless man live in the shop, even if he was staying in the barn, but she was also certain Philip would not approve and she didn't need him finding out.

Six o'clock had passed when Lily returned from shopping and was ready to cook her first meal in the house. Darkness was nearly complete as fall ebbed away. She flicked on the ceiling light in the kitchen, then closed the new curtains on the front windows. She'd hung them that afternoon. During the day, they could be drawn far to the sides to let the light stream in. When pulled closed, they guarded her privacy.

Lily went outside to check. Across the street the town

offices were closed, the white string lights hung along the eaves had already turned on. Gus's gas station sign glowed in the growing dusk. She faced the window from the sidewalk. The fabric gave the windows a homey, inviting appeal, the kitchen light barely showing.

She went back inside, rubbing her upper arms to warm them. Fall was making its presence known. It had to be cold in the barn. Doug had faced many winters before he'd met her. No doubt he knew what to do. He didn't need her advice, but she wanted to know he'd be okay once freezing temps set in.

Her phone vibrated in her back pocket. Philip. She'd just had dinner with him the night before and hadn't expected him to call. Nor did she want to talk to him at that moment. He could ruin her plans, but it would be worse if she didn't answer. He might come around to check on her.

"How about a movie tonight?" he asked.

"Sounds great, but I'm tired and I have a bit of a headache." With the curtains up, he'd have to go behind the shop to see her car parked there to know she wasn't at home.

"Can I bring you something?"

"Thanks, I'll be okay. I think I'll turn in early." He could be so sweet. She hated lying to him.

"You're listing that place soon, right? You're running yourself ragged."

With good comes bad. He'd become a pest. "Soon. Another couple of weeks maybe." What's one more lie?

Back in the kitchen, with its freshly painted walls, cabinets, and new appliances. It was serviceable and clean. She'd scrubbed every inch of the worn Formica countertops and vinyl floor.

Although she always thought of this place as the shop, it was a house, and it had become a cozy place. With the oven turned on, the kitchen warmed quickly. She'd stocked it with housewares pulled from Amanda's unpacked boxes. They'd been waiting until Amanda moved into her own house. The shop seemed like the next best place, but as Lily used them while preparing the meal, her heart grew heavy, and her grief threatened to break free of its container. She'd gotten so good at keeping it under control, she'd almost forgotten how force-fully it could demand her attention.

Doug came up from the basement, Jack the dog with him. "Wow, Lily. It smells fantastic in here. What are you making?"

She dabbed her eyes with her tea towel, then turned to face him. "Inaugural chicken. A simple meal of roasted chicken, potatoes, and vegetables."

"Sounds like a meal fit for a president."

"It's our first meal here."

"The chicken needs another twenty minutes. I have some grapes we can nosh on, and if you'd like," she said and held up a bottle of Beaujolais and a corkscrew, "we can have a glass of wine while we wait."

They picked at the grapes, still wet from washing, and sipped wine from the crystal goblets left to her by her mother, then passed to Amanda. They'd go to Emma next.

"I bet the truck will sell quickly," Doug said. "Unless you think we'll need it to pick up decking or lumber at some point."

"You know what?" She rubbed her chin and raised an eyebrow. "That truck is a lot more useful than my Camry. What if I sold my Camry instead?"

"Are you sure you want a truck? Or have you had too much wine?"

"I've learned to do an awful lot of things these few months. Thanks to you. Why can't I drive a truck?" She must be crazy. She'd hit the end of the line with projects. What did she need a truck for? Not to mention the Camry wouldn't sell for nearly as much money.

"I'm certain you could do anything you set your mind to." He raised his glass to her.

"I don't know about that." She didn't know how to run

a quilt shop, and she was pretty certain Doug couldn't teach her that.

"If you're still serious in the morning, I'll detail the Camry for you. They hold their value well."

The oven timer dinged. Lily took out the golden bird, surrounded by a mirepoix roasted in pan juices. "It needs to rest for a few minutes and then we can eat." She admired the meal she'd made. "I'm amazed at how comfortable this house has become. If I lived here, I'd dig out the broken asphalt in the back, plant some grass, grow a garden. Maybe expand the kitchen a little or add a deck with the steps."

Doug held up his hand for her to stop. "Don't torture yourself."

"You mean because eventually I have to sell?"

He nodded. "We both need to move on."

Doug would be the one to move on. He'd leave, and she'd probably never see him again. She'd still be in her own house in Fellowes Hollow, wondering how to fill her days while Emma was at school.

Nope. That wasn't her future. She'd find a way to tackle the next thing and then the next, not worrying about the end until she got there. "That reminds me. A letter came for you today. I'll get it."

She returned and handed it to him. "Did you register with the VA?"

"I hope you don't mind."

"Of course not, but can I ask you something? You can tell me to mind my business and I'll still let you eat the chicken." Jack the dog sat at her feet, begging for his portion. "You'll get yours," Lily said.

"You don't need to worry about that. Ask away."

"What makes you so sad?"

He sat back in his chair and his hands dropped into his lap, his gaze on the table but unfocused. "I went to see Jack after you told me where he was. He thought I was Billy."

"That's dementia." Lily tried to soothe him.

"I know. But he'll never see Billy. Billy can't visit."

"No, unfortunately." What else could she say?

"I came here to tell him how sorry I was. When I thought Jack had passed away, I knew I couldn't tell him, but now it's worse. He thinks I'm Billy, and I'm a fraud."

Doug covered his face with his hands. Lily suspected something about what happened to Billy was why Doug was homeless. She wished she had words to heal him, but she didn't want to pry any further. If he wanted to tell her, he would. Of one thing she was certain, whatever had driven him to homelessness eventually would make him leave.

"Maybe you'll catch him on a good day." She knew Doug had gone at least one more time because she'd seen him walking there. She also knew from Becca that he often went to the cafe in the afternoon and bought something to take away. Maybe he took it to Jack. Even with her heart stuffed full of grief, somehow a spot hollowed for Doug. She'd miss him, maybe more than she'd miss this house.

Chapter 16
Whack

In a small bucket, Lily measured out grout and water and stirred until her arm ached and the mixture was smooth. She'd watched a few YouTube videos. It didn't look hard but neither had carving out the old grout. She scooped a blob with her trowel, plopped it on the rubber float, then smeared it over the bathtub wall, making sure the joints filled. She was nearly through when her phone rang, the name of the school flashing on the screen.

She tried not to panic. Emma was fine when she came home from her grandparents the night before. She'd spent the last few weekends with them, and they always refreshed her. She hadn't complained about going to school that morning either, only a few hours earlier.

Lily peeled off one glove and answered on speaker.

"Emma punched Arthur on the nose." The principal's voice reverberated off the bathroom walls, commanding, and yet with a tinge of sympathy.

"Emma punched Arthur," Lily repeated, stupidly. It made no sense. As far as she knew, Emma had never hit anyone.

"You need to come get her. We can't allow that kind of behavior."

They couldn't tolerate Emma's behavior? Lily's inner dragon, volcanic since the accident, fired up, angry, and fierce. She was exploding with things she wanted to say and yet she needed to be cautious not to say anything she might regret. She moderated her voice as best as she could. "But you tolerate Arthur relentlessly bullying her. I thought you had him under control."

"I understand, Mrs. Wolfe, but I still need you to come for Emma."

Lily hung up without saying goodbye. Like a video on fast-forward, she wiped down the tiles to remove any grout not in the joints. Her freshly mixed container would be dry before she returned.

She ran out to the barn where Doug was half inside the Camry.

"The school. Emma punched that kid. I have to go. But the grout. I just mixed it."

Doug whacked his head on the door frame as he stood, rubbing the spot with his palm. "I'll take care of the grout. You take a deep breath. Do you think you can drive the truck? I just shampooed these seats. They're wet."

She'd driven the truck twice on Sunday, Doug insisting she do it before deciding to sell the Camry. It hadn't been any harder than driving her car, just bigger, and she'd loved being that high. "I can do it."

"You sure? I can drive you."

Wouldn't it be wonderful to sit in the passenger seat and not have to concentrate? But Emma didn't know Doug existed. "I'll be fine."

"I never doubt that."

Emma was in a chair opposite a large desk with a brass nameplate, her hands clasped in her lap, her back ramrod straight, and her chin quivering but lifted. Principal Veronica Slater had the look of a woman who never had a hair out of place or a wrinkle in her skirt. She asked Lily to take the chair next to Emma.

"Hi, Gammy."

Lily squeezed Emma's shoulder.

"Is Arthur hurt?" Lily asked.

Principal Slater shook her head. "There's no mark, but the aide saw Emma do it." She spoke calmly and didn't seem to notice Lily's anger or that she looked like a handyman in an old t-shirt decorated with splotches of grout.

"Is Arthur being suspended too?"

"We are working with his parents."

"Was anyone else involved?"

"We're not exactly sure. Emma is having trouble telling us her side of the story."

"Did you punch him?" Lily asked.

"He deserved it." Her words came out dry without a touch of fear or remorse.

Lily couldn't blame her, but she'd never seen Emma so defiant. The scene with Amanda's clothes chopped up and strewn across the bedroom flashed in Lily's mind. Emma was angry. And who could blame her? "You have to tell us what happened."

"I punched him." Emma's chin jutted, the way Lily imagined Arthur's might when he teased her.

"We know that, but why did you punch him?"

"He pulled my hair." She grabbed the hair on the top of her head and pulled straight up, her forehead going along for the ride. "He said he would help me pull it out. I told him to let go, but he pulled harder. So, I punched him." She jabbed her fist at the air, her hair tumbling over her shoulders.

Lily felt a smile turning up the corners of her mouth and made a fuss of inspecting Emma's knuckles to cover it. She wished she could tell her how proud she was of her and demand that Arthur be suspended instead, but she'd never win that argument with Principal Slater. Instead, she kissed the back of Emma's hand and said, "Then what happened?"

"He cried and told the teacher."

"It wasn't her teacher. It was the lunchroom aide." Principal Slater said. "Emma, can you wait outside while I talk to your grandmother, please?" She watched Emma leave. When the door clicked closed, she returned her attention to Lily. "We are going to need you to get her back into counseling before she can return to school."

Lily stood. She'd never minded being five foot two, but at that moment she wished she towered over Veronica Slater. "What do you think you might have done if someone constantly made fun of you and threatened to pull your hair out? I'm not sure I'd need to be counseled to know the best way to handle a bully. You certainly haven't handled it. I seriously hope you are going to suspend him and require counseling for him too. If not, I may have to pay a visit to his parents myself."

Lily walked out of the principal's office and signed a few papers at the front desk. "Let's go." Emma, who'd been waiting in a chair against the wall, took Lily's hand and they left.

When they reached the truck, Lily pulled open the passenger door and said, "Surprise!"

"A truck?" Emma's mouth hung open.

"Yep, and you get to ride in the front." Lily helped Emma climb in. "And I have another idea. How about we go home and you relax in a lavender bath? Then we'll go to the cafe for a treat when Ruth will be there?" Ruth had promised she'd bring a new chapter book to read.

"Gammy, are you sure I'm not in trouble?" Emma's eyes were dry. Punching Arthur had been good therapy.

"You're not in trouble. I'm proud you stood up for yourself, but it's never okay to punch people. Next time, call for help." As if all the help the school had promised had done any good. Emma's punch probably had resolved the problem. Arthur wouldn't bully her anymore, and since he wasn't hurt, Lily had no regrets.

While Emma was in her bath, Lily dropped onto the sofa, the weight of the morning pressing her into the cushions.

Arthur aside, Emma needed a new therapist, one she could connect to. She had a three-day suspension, after which the school would reevaluate her. Whatever that meant. Lily could homeschool her or try to find a private school she could afford. Heather and Ben might help.

Lily needed a crystal ball. She'd do whatever gave Emma the best outcome, but how could she know what was the right thing?

With the unfairness of Amanda's and Matt's deaths and Emma's problems settling into a new environment, the shop felt like the one thing she and Emma had to hold on to. And yet, it was slipping from Lily's grasp. The porch and the back steps weren't the only things that needed work. In the last few weeks, as they'd finished project after project, more issues surfaced. Like the furnace. No way would the existing one make a dent in the full chill of winter. Neither would the water heater create anything warmer than tepid. There was probably an endless list of horrors awaiting her.

She'd known from the start a quilt shop was a near-impossible dream, but she kept holding on. Doug's help had kept the dream alive. Without him, she'd never have gotten as far as she had. It was time for Lily to accept the dream was dead. It had died with Amanda, and that hurt the worst of all.

She buried her face in a throw pillow and screamed. "Amanda, my baby. I'm so sorry." Her throat tore with the hoarseness of her words. "I tried, but I can't. But I promise you I will do what's best for Emma, no matter what. Emma is first. Always Emma."

Lily let herself cry until she heard Emma shouting for her. She was supposed to call before she stepped out of the tub. Lily blew her nose, dried her eyes, and shoved her grief and anger back into the dragon's lair.

In the cafe, Ruth and Walter were already at their usual table. As soon as Lily and Emma walked in, Emma ran to Ruth.

"I knitted something for you." Ruth handed Emma a knitted rainbow-striped ski cap. "Try it on."

Lily nodded her approval and left them to enjoy each other's company while she went to find Becca in the back.

"I think I might need that scotch you've told stories about."

Becca raised one eyebrow in response. "You look like you could use a shot."

Lily filled her in on Arthur incident number three. "I suppose I need to call the principal and apologize. I wasn't very nice."

"You should think more about complaining to the school board. It's not like they didn't have a warning about Arthur's behavior."

"But they're still requiring Emma to go back to counseling. The last one didn't do much for her, but I have no choice now."

Becca tipped her chin toward the cafe. "Take a look."

Emma, with her cap pulled low on her forehead, sat next to Ruth reading the chapter book. "My mom thought a cap might help Emma from absentmindedly pulling her hair."

"Those two certainly seem to enjoy each other. Emma never says much about school, but she'll go on and on about what she did with Ruth. Are you sure it isn't an imposition for her to come here in the afternoon?"

"It's the highlight of my mom's day. Neither of my parents like retirement much. They need to feel useful." Becca put air quotes on the word "useful." "I'm trying to talk them into selling their house and moving to The Village. They have all kinds of activities there. I'll bet she'd find lots of other knitters."

"The Village is certainly making its mark on Fellowes Hollow," Lily said.

"You should see the lunch crowd I get now. I ordered

another panini grill and I'm thinking about getting one of those giant mixing machines. I'm out of muffins before noon." Becca's face lit up like making muffins was a game.

"You're loving it though, I can tell."

"No. I mean yes, I do love it, but that's not what I was thinking about. What if my mom became Emma's official counselor? It's what she did for nearly forty years. She still knows most of the people in the school district. I can't imagine she wouldn't be considered qualified."

"Would she?"

"We can ask, but I suspect she'd be thrilled. She's been watching Emma get off the bus every day since school started. I think she wanted to reach out but wouldn't stick her nose in without being asked."

"And Emma would be no wiser." Lily didn't dare get her hopes up, but she felt lighter. This sounded perfect. A professional whom Emma already knew and trusted who could counsel her without making her feel she needed to be fixed or cured.

"Hey, Mom. Can you come here?"

Ruth put up one finger, said something to Walter. He put down his book and slid next to Emma.

Becca gave Ruth a conspiratorial glance. "We have an idea," she whispered.

Chapter 17
Some Things Can't Be Fixed

In the middle of the night, Lily turned off her morning alarm. She'd been tossing in bed, unable to sleep, ruminating about Emma, the school, the shop. Sometime after seeing the red glowing numbers flick to three o'clock, she'd fallen asleep. Then, in what seemed like no time, she awoke to a sunlit day and a dull pain behind her eyes.

Coffee, nature's prescription, might help if she drank the whole pot, but she settled for her one-cup funnel. She didn't need caffeine-induced anxiety. While the water dripped through the grounds, she gazed out the kitchen window to her backyard. Fallen leaves mottled the grass. Tomato and basil plants, blackened from the cold night, drooped lifeless on the ground.

For more than forty years, she'd lived in that house. When she and Sam had first seen it, she'd fallen in love with the three-bed ranch and the backyard. Compared to apartment-living in Pittsburgh, it was her palace. She'd never wished for more. Sam had his dream job teaching high school and coaching girls' sports. Fellowes Hollow was the perfect small town to raise a family. She hadn't expected it to take five years to get pregnant with Amanda or that she'd never get pregnant again. But they were a happy family of three.

Lily had fulfilled most of her many dreams and aspirations, but she'd never imagined she'd be the only one left. If not for Emma, she would close her eyes and will her heart to stop.

The click of a door opening down the hall brought Lily back to her kitchen. After a few seconds, Emma rounded the corner, her hair tousled, eyes crusty with sleep.

"Gammy, don't make me go to school today. Please."

"You're suspended, remember?"

"Oh, thank God." Emma plopped into a chair and rested her chin in her palms. She could be so like Amanda sometimes.

"I spoke to Grandma yesterday. She wants to take you to the movies and out for dinner. How does that sound?"

Emma dropped her head to the table. "I went there last week. Why can't I stay home and quilt?"

She had been visiting her grandparents more often. Heather and Lily had colluded, hoping time away would be good for Emma. It had been a compromise after Arthur incident number two. Heather still believed Emma belonged with Lily. "She's so devoted to you and you are the closest thing to her mother."

"I know Grandma is really looking forward to seeing you. We don't want to disappoint her."

"Okay, but I don't want to stay all night. I want to come home."

"That's fine. And we can quilt tomorrow."

After Lily drove Emma to Pittsburgh—her overnight things packed just in case she changed her mind—Lily found Doug in the barn.

"You know," he said, his hand stroking a plank of oak like it was a treasure. "There's enough wood in this barn to build a lot of shelving. Nice shelving."

When he looked up at Lily, his eyebrows knitted, the awe dropping off his face, worry setting in.

"Was it bad yesterday?"

"How about we go upstairs for coffee and I'll fill you in."

As Lily entered the kitchen, she felt as though she was home. She'd put so much work into it, so many hours, it had become as familiar as her house. "Remember what this place looked like?"

"Oh yeah." Doug winced as if his memories physically hurt. "I'd been in the basement but never upstairs. After I heard you and Becca talking, I thought I'd see if I could help." He sighed, his head bowed. "I don't know how Jack lived like that. I would've come sooner."

It occurred to Lily that his help wasn't only about paying for his room and board. He might be doing it for Jack. Much like Lily was doing it for Amanda. She wished he'd share what had broken him so badly. If not with her or a friend, then a professional. There must be doctors at the VA that specialize in whatever Doug suffered from.

Lily poured coffee into two of Amanda's mugs and sat at the table. After telling Doug what had happened at school the day before, she stopped. She couldn't look at him and she didn't know how to say what she needed to say. It would make it real. "I've been working on Becca's advice, thinking only about one thing at a time, not worrying about the end, but the truth is this time, I'm out of money. We've done all we can do."

"Not even finish the porch repairs?"

Lily couldn't get words past the lump in her throat.

"I guess there's no point to me building the shelving then."

"No." She swallowed what felt like a ping-pong ball. "But I'm not selling. Not yet." She'd keep the place as long as she could.

"I understand. I'll get ready to leave." He pushed back his chair, preparing to stand.

Lily's heart squeezed. "You don't need to go. Stay. At least a few months." She wanted him to have some stability. He deserved it.

"It's not necessary." His palms pressed on his thighs. Decision made. "You don't need to worry about me. I know how to survive. The only thing I need is for someone to take care of the dog. I can't take him with me." His gaze traveled over the walls. "And this is his home, anyway."

Jack the dog. One more victim of losing a loved one. "Whether you're here or not, I'm not giving up this place. So you may as well stay. You can see Jack the person a few more times."

"There's no point in that." Every once in a while, anger flared in his eyes, betraying his unflappable exterior. This time it was like an acetylene torch, blue-white hot, but it only lasted a few seconds. Was he angry about Jack or at himself?

"He's never recognized you?"

"I'd never met him before. He only knew of me, but he still thinks I'm Billy. One of the workers there told me I'm the highlight of Jack's day." Doug's lip curled in disgust and he turned his face from Lily, staring out the window.

"Isn't that good?"

"No. It only makes me more of a fraud." He faced Lily, his expression composed and neutral again, hiding whatever he was feeling.

"Don't give up on Jack and don't leave yet. I'm grateful for your company and you've more than earned your keep with all the work you've done."

"Thank you for your acceptance and generosity." His apology sounded like the last sentence after closing a business deal.

A tear slid down Lily's cheek. She wanted to siphon it back up, not cry. If she started, a cavern would open inside her. She'd fall in and get lost forever. "I think we came together at a time when we both needed someone or something."

For a moment, he pressed his fist to his mouth, contemplating her words. "True, but some things can't be fixed."

He had to be wrong. If he wasn't, then he'd never be better. And neither would Emma. For that matter, Lily wasn't doing so great at fixing herself.

Later that afternoon, Philip called to see about getting together for dinner. Since Rose's death, they frequently had dinner together, either at Lily's or out somewhere, but lately he'd been asking more often.

Doug had gone back to the barn. Heather had texted to say Emma decided she would stay the night with them. Lily hadn't budged from her chair in the kitchen, staring at her cold cup of coffee until the last rays of the sun faded and she was alone in the dark. It didn't take much before Philip talked her into meeting him at the diner.

Don, the hotelier and diner owner, was in the middle of the grand opening week for his remodeled dining room. Unlike the diner, which had direct access from both the sidewalk and the hotel lobby, the only entrance to the dining room was in the hotel. If you could still call it a hotel. Only the top floor had guest rooms. The rest had been converted into professional offices, including Simon and Matt's dental practice. The only telltale signs it was still a hotel were a reception desk and a few couches. Lily sat on one and waited for Philip.

When he arrived, still in his suit, Lily stood to greet him, but instead of the diner, he led her into the dining room.

"I can't believe what I'm looking at," Lily said, trying not to gape. A polished wood pedestal for a maitre'd had replaced a large counter with a cash register. The tables, once laminated tops crammed together, were well-spaced, covered with white tablecloths, and adorned with flickering votives and red carnations. "When did Fellowes Hollow get fancy? You should have told me we were coming here. I would've changed my clothes."

"You look fine," Philip said. "Good thing I made a reservation." Nearly all the tables were full.

The host, sleekly dressed in all black, grabbed a couple of menus and asked them to follow her. A minute later, Don showed up at the side of their table.

"Don, this is exquisite." Lily nodded her enthusiasm.

His head swiveled, admiring his restaurant. "Thanks. So far, business is great."

Philip shook Don's hand. "Congratulations. You've created a destination restaurant for Fellowes Hollow. Maybe we'll get the Ainsleyville people coming to our side of the highway."

Dollar signs shone in Don's eyes. "I wouldn't complain if they did, but we'd need a bigger parking lot. So far, it's locals and people taking out residents at The Village."

"There's plenty of them. I think that place is about sold out." Philip loved to discuss local businesses. Perhaps he wondered if they'd need a lawyer.

"They can build two more as far as I'm concerned," Don said.

Lily laughed. "Good luck with that. Remember how hard it was to get the town to approve that one?"

"Yeah, wishful thinking." He rubbed his hands together. "How about a glass of Petite Sirah? It's on me. Lovely wine and I got a great deal."

He walked away before they could answer. A moment later, a skinny, young server returned with their glasses. "I'll be back for your order. In the meantime, can I bring you a basket of house-made rolls?" She spoke as though she'd been rehearsing the lines.

While they perused the menu, the tannins in the wine made Lily's stomach queasy. She hadn't eaten since breakfast with Emma. The moment the rolls arrived, she unfolded the napkin keeping them warm. Yeast-scented steam rose from the soft interior.

Her first bite nearly made her moan with pleasure, wafting

her out of the doldrums of the afternoon. "I think Don outdid himself here. If the food's as good as the bread, we're in for a treat. Thanks for talking me into it."

Philip put his menu at the side of the table and took a roll. "You don't seem like yourself. You're pensive."

"I thought that roll had transported me to heaven."

"Ah, but I can see what's underneath." Philip riveted his gaze as if he could x-ray her.

"Honestly, I haven't been myself since that night. I'll never be that person again." True enough, if not the whole story.

"It's that shop," Philip whispered, his eyes shifting to see if anyone nearby was listening. "You're driving yourself crazy with it. How can you spend all day and all weekend in there by yourself painting walls?"

He had no idea how much she had done or that she wasn't alone. Neither did he need to know. "I'm going to stop working on it, but I'm not selling. Not yet."

"You keep saying that, but what are you waiting for?"

"Emma. She loves that place. I didn't tell you what happened at school yesterday." Had only one day passed since she'd walked out of Principal Slater's office? She filled Philip in on most of the details. "I let her see it. Maybe I shouldn't have, but if you'd seen her face, you'd understand why I can't take that from her."

"You don't want to let go of it either."

"No. I don't. It's a piece of Amanda. It was her dream. And if I thought there was any hope of opening a quilt shop, I would do that too."

"It's not Amanda or a dream. It's a piece of real estate and it's dragging you down."

Did he have to be so dismissive?

"Emma's just a child. You have to do what's right for her. Think of how much easier and predictable your life would be without that shop hanging over you."

Lily heard the implication that she wouldn't get surprise

phone calls from the school anymore either. "She's angry, and it's perfectly understandable. I don't want her to suffer another loss. Surely you can understand that to her it isn't just an old house or a shop. To most people, there is such a thing as sentimental value."

Philip slumped a bit. Her dig had penetrated him. She didn't want to be mean, but why did he have to push her so hard?

"Have you thought that maybe what Emma needs most is you? And a family?"

As if families just materialized. "I think about it all the time." Lily sipped her wine, wishing its soothing effects would kick in. "I'll do anything I need to if it's right for her."

"Have you asked her what she wants?"

"Of course, but she's only eight. She can't articulate it. I'm not sure she even knows what it is beyond having her parents back."

"It would be nice for her to have a family. And a father figure." His tone softened, the accusation gone, only sympathy left.

"I told Heather and Ben she'd be better off with them, back at her old school, but they both think she needs to be with me."

"I'm not suggesting that." He leaned toward her, his hands clasped, forearms resting on the table. "You've been closing me off lately. We could spend more time together. I'm always happy to be around Emma. We should do things. Weekend excursions. Zoo trips. Movies. Whatever. We'd be able to if you weren't spending every weekend in the shop."

And there he went, back to the shop theme. If he wasn't so insistent, she could include him more in what she was up to. "I only go on the weekends she's with her grandparents."

His face went blank, his eyes downcast. "I'm alone too, Lily."

Lily felt those words like pins in her chest. Rose had only

been gone two years. Had Lily adjusted to life without Sam in only two years? Yes, but she'd had social connections and she'd had Amanda, Matt, and Emma. Philip went to work and went home alone every night. "I'm sorry. I know you are." No wonder he was so adamant about her giving up the shop. It had taken her attention away from him. "I'll have more time now. There's nothing more I can do at the shop."

"Let's have another glass of wine." Philip looked like he needed it more than she did. "We're both on foot. We can walk back to my house after we eat and then I can drive you home."

He didn't know she was driving the truck or that it was parked behind the shop. No matter. She'd walk there to retrieve it in the morning.

When Philip pulled into her driveway, he took her hand. "Things will get better. Have hope."

"I will. You too. Thanks for a lovely meal."

"Don't wait too long to say yes again, okay?"

She smiled at him. She'd known him too long to stay angry. He meant well. As he backed out, his headlights swept the landscape like a searchlight.

Would things get better? What did she hope for? Certainly, she hoped for Emma to be happy again, make a few friends, have a childhood. She hoped Doug would escape from whatever demons chased him. He deserved someone special. As capable as he was of taking care of himself, no one was truly whole when their heart wasn't full. Poor Philip too. For herself, Lily didn't want another husband. No one could replace Sam, but she did want a family again. She wanted to make one with Emma. And if she was honest, wasn't that why she was hoping Doug would stay? He'd become like a son to her, even if she had no business letting herself feel that way.

Maybe some things couldn't be fixed, but it didn't mean she shouldn't try.

Chapter 18
Patchworks and Rotten Things

The next morning, Lily leaned against the kitchen counter, waiting for the kettle to boil. Even though all would be the same if Emma were home asleep in her bed, the quiet of the morning seemed louder for her absence. Or perhaps it was the residue of Lily's nightmare. Instead of the usual clawing up the hill, she'd dreamed the school bus driver had refused to take Emma, even though her suspension was over. When Lily turned around, the shop had been reduced to smoldering rubble as if a meteor had hit it. The shock had woken her.

The sun had not yet risen above the horizon, the corner of the kitchen was shrouded in shadow. Lily visualized Sam and a young Amanda at the pantry door with Barkley, their black Lab, waiting expectantly for his treat. If only she could replace her nightmares with dreams about moments of time when her world was at peace.

She didn't have those powers, but she did have control over the day in front of her. Emma would be home in a few hours. Lily had promised to teach her to make a quilt. Someday, these would be the times she'd wish to live over. No point letting the present pass her by for want of the past.

When a car horn tooted, Lily opened the front door. Ben waved from the car, then pulled away. Emma bounded up the porch steps and into Lily's embrace.

"Can we start the quilt now?"

"Good morning, Emma. How was your time with Grandma and Grandpa?"

"Good." She pushed past Lily and ran to her bedroom.

"Are you hungry?" Lily shouted down the hall.

"No, we had pancakes." She came out of her room, lugging the sewing machine with her.

"I guess I don't get a choice here." Lily helped Emma raise it onto the dining room table.

"You promised." Emma climbed onto a chair, sitting on her knees.

"Okay, I surrender. Let me get my stuff and we'll get started."

A few hours later, Lily had taught Emma to trace a template on the back of the fabric and cut on the line. While she'd been sewing her drawstring bag, Emma had finger-pressed her seams open. For a quilt, she needed to learn to iron them flat.

"I'm going to show you how to use this mini-iron, but you must be very careful not to touch this part." Lily pointed to the small heart-shaped metal piece at the end of the handle. "You'll get a nasty burn. And don't let it touch the table or rest on the ironing pad. Put it on the stand, carefully."

"I'll be very careful. I promise."

"Okay, then. Time to sew. Make sure you line your seams up exactly and pin them before you sew. One piece at a time and you have to be patient."

Lily watched as Emma followed all the rules, still on her knees, her tongue poking between her teeth, her tiny hands surprisingly adept. Emma worked for hours, doggedly determined to master her new skills, not letting mistakes fluster or frustrate her, just trying again. Other than having her striped cap pulled over her hair, Emma seemed like her old self.

Amanda had been the same once she set her mind to something. And so was Lily. She'd come a long way from the day she got the splinter, re-grouting tiles, flipping circuit breakers, and replacing light switches, outlets, and doorknobs. She'd caulked and painted, wielded a putty knife with precision, and used electric drills to hang curtain hardware. She could probably fix a leaky sink on her own.

Wasn't she pulling together the shop exactly how quilts are made? One small piece of fabric, each insignificant on its own, connected together one at a time to make larger units until the last pieces reveal the beauty of the patchwork.

Lily's current obstacle was money. Once she figured that part out, the rest would follow. Yes, she'd be taking an enormous risk, not only for her comfortable retirement but for Emma too. Yet, if things went south, the risk was too big to contemplate.

Her heart palpitated, sending a flush up her neck. She feared the unknown. More powerful than fear of the thing itself. But if she didn't try, if she quit, she stood to lose things more valuable than money. Her pride. Amanda's dream. Emma's happiness.

There had to be a way forward. She would find it.

"Gammy, I can't go to school. We're not allowed to wear hats." Emma jutted her hip and rested her fist on it. "That's the rule."

Lily had to keep herself from laughing. "You're becoming very wise." Ruth had contacted the school and arranged for Emma to return after three days of suspension with her promise that if someone bullied her again, she would tell, not punch. "That's why Ruth made special arrangements so you could wear your hat. Don't you believe me?"

Emma deflated, her shoulders rounding.

"You thought you'd get out of it, huh? You'll be fine. They've dealt with Arthur. I don't think he's going to bother you again. But if he does—"

"I know. I'm not allowed to hit him."

"Exactly, so let's go."

Doug had been spending most of his time in the barn since there wasn't much left he could do in the house. He'd set his sights on repairing and refinishing the furniture Jack had made. His latest endeavor was re-silvering the mirrors in the armoires.

Lily took advantage of the downtime by inviting the quilt ladies to a luncheon in the shop. She'd laid out fresh fruit, cut the crusts off sandwiches, and arranged a platter with fancy pastries she'd bought at the bakery across the street. A big pot of Earl Grey rested on a warmer.

All three of the ladies' mouths dropped open when they walked through the front door. Lily showed them around, especially the curtains she'd made with the help of their generous fabric donations. "You ladies are part of this place now. Forever adorning the windows."

"Until someone buys it," Robin said.

"That's if I decide to sell it. Emphasis on 'if.' And I have news on that front, but let's go eat."

Trish's jaw was still hanging when they took their seats around the kitchen table.

Robin pointed at Trish. "You can close your mouth now."

"I just can't get over it. It's like night and day. This place looked awful. How on earth did you manage to do all this?"

Maggie said, "Lily, this place is positively beautiful. Who knew?"

"Did you hire a contractor?" Robin asked.

"No. I'd like to take credit and pretend I'm superwoman. I didn't hire anyone, but I had help. I never could have done this on my own."

"Not Philip." Maggie's nose wrinkled, nostrils flaring like she'd sniffed something unpleasant.

Maggie and Philip were opposites that did not attract. She

was a free-spirit, devoted animal lover who protected stray dogs. Philip would have them rounded up and sent to the pound, believing it was for their safety.

"Are you going to tell us, or is it a mystery?" Lily detected the hurt in Robin's voice. She usually knew everything going on in Lily's life. Robin would take Lily's secrets to her grave, just as Lily would do for her and for all these women. The knowledge that a homeless man lived in her barn would be as safe with them as it was with Becca and, she hoped, the mailman.

"In the beginning," Lily started, "the mess in here was overwhelming." They nodded as Lily shared the details of Doug coming to visit Jack and why she let him stay. It wasn't the whole story, but there was no lie in it. "He's incredibly handy. So we made a deal."

"He's done an amazing job," Trish said. "Have you spoken to Greta?"

"Not yet. I can pay the upkeep for a while longer." And an idea had been percolating for how to get money.

Robin had been sitting quietly across from Lily, one eye squinting skeptically at her. "So, is this guy still here?" All the ladies turned toward the door as if they expected him to walk into the room.

She nodded. "He's fixing the furniture Jack left. Come see."

She led them into the great room where a small lamp table with an inlaid birdseye maple top graced the side of the fireplace. "This table looked like a broken piece of junk. He saw what was hiding under an ugly dark finish, caked with years of grime. Imagine, sitting in a comfy chair with your tea and sewing box on that."

"Is he a handyman? Does he want to work while he's here? I've got a few jobs he could do." Trish nodded emphatically.

"Probably half the town would hire him," Robin said, her fingers tapping the table. "Where is this guy?"

"In the barn, I expect, working on something. Or he could

be at The Village, visiting Jack. He knew you were coming, so he made himself scarce," Lily said. "But I think it's best if we don't spread the word he's staying here. I don't need Philip finding out." Lily held up the sandwich plate. "Let's eat."

"It's really quite comfortable in here," Maggie said while they munched.

"Thanks. I like being here. It feels homey." Whether she'd ever again have a family to sit around a table in this house, her house, or any other house, was a question it hurt to think about. "If I was going to live here, I'd push the kitchen out a few feet, enough to accommodate a dishwasher and a larger table. I'd refinish the floors, fix the front porch, and put a safe set of stairs out back."

"Can you imagine a quilt shop in this beautiful old house? It's perfect," Trish said. "I'd plant some flowers in the front. The place would look like it belonged on a postcard."

Lily was dying to share her idea. Get another opinion, especially one that wasn't Philip's. "Okay. I had an idea. Tell me if you think I'm nuts." She paused to read their faces. Their eyes were wide, encouraging. They would tell her the truth. "What if I get a mortgage and use the money to finish the repairs? I could hire a contractor for the roof, get a new furnace."

"It's easy to get a mortgage. Check with Greta. See how much she thinks you could borrow." Robin was always so methodical. Maybe that's why she worked in the town's tax office.

Maggie lit up. "You have the bedrooms upstairs for classrooms. I could teach a few and Trish could certainly do one on silk ribbon embroidery. There's tons of wall space to showcase completed quilts. I'd come here every day and spend way too much money. People would come from all around Western PA. Think about it. If we knew of a quilt shop like this, wouldn't we make day trips there instead of Pittsburgh?"

Lily knew she would. "I can't focus on that right now. I

first have to deal with the renovations." She was going to call the bank and Greta George. She'd known that before she'd even asked. The smoldering pile of rubble had only been a nightmare born of fear. She was done with that. And it seemed her friends didn't think she'd gone around the twist.

When bus time came, Lily asked Emma about her day, hoping the first day post-suspension hadn't been a disaster.

"It was okay," Emma said.

"How about we go home and work on that quilt of yours? If you have any homework, you can do that first."

"I finished it at school." Hardly a rousing answer, but it was a step in the right direction.

One piece at a time. Maybe things were turning in the right direction.

On a recommendation from Maggie, Lily had called a contractor. A week later, he showed up on time. Lily greeted him at the door with Doug at her side.

The guy was older than she'd expected, mid-fifties maybe. He handed her his card. "These old houses are built well, not like the new ones, but they're totally lacking insulation. You might want to weatherproof those big windows." He carried a pencil and clipboard, taking copious notes, measuring, and photographing everything as they went through the house, outside and in.

"You say you want this to be a quilt shop? Not just a house?"

"I'm not sure if it will be residential or commercial, so I guess can we plan for both?"

He nodded thoughtfully. "Either way, you're going to need to install air conditioning and a lot more outlets."

"I think the electrical panel needs to be upgraded," Doug said. "I can't use two power tools at once."

Lily silently repeated, "One thing at a time." She'd get the estimate, then go to the bank. She couldn't worry about anything beyond that. Not yet.

When they went to the attic, the contractor scratched his head and knitted his eyebrows until there was only one. Lily's stomach dropped to the floor.

"This roof has been leaking. No surprise considering its age, but, unfortunately, you have dry rot."

"And that's bad, right?" As if she'd had to ask. The name said everything.

"Won't know how bad until we can get a better look, but you can't ignore it. We'll have to deal with it before the roof, siding, soffits, and facia."

Siding? Soffits? Facia? These hadn't even crossed her radar. "Do I have to do all of it?"

"The dry rot and roof for sure, and I highly recommend the rest."

He scribbled something on his pad. Lily wished she could read it. "How much is all this going to cost?"

"I'm not sure yet. I'll have to do some calculations, but it won't be cheap."

"How soon can you have your estimate ready?"

"A few days, but as I said, I can't guarantee the extent of the dry rot until I can get a better look."

She'd expected to face problems, but not a huge one right out the gate. There was no point worrying until she knew how bad it was. But pointless or not, she would worry. If she couldn't get enough money from the bank, she'd have to find things to cut out of her plans. Whatever it was, she'd have to figure it out.

Chapter 19
Don't Bank on It

As Lily walked from the bank back to the shop, nothing on the three blocks of Fellowes Run Road had changed except the weather. A chill breeze buffeted her past the shops, familiar as always, but somehow the gray skies drained the signs of color and deepened the cracks in the sidewalk. Did everything in this town need to be fixed or cleaned or replaced? None of it was likely to happen. Not for the town and not for the quilt shop.

She'd waited a week for the contractor's estimate, certain she'd get the loan, but the bank wouldn't lend a penny until she fixed the dry rot. Yet, to do that, she needed the money. Greta had said she could try to sell it "as is," but she'd only get a fraction of what it was worth. Chances were, the only buyer she'd find was a developer who would raze the building for a modern structure.

It seemed Lily's smoldering-ashes dream had been a premonition. She could burn the shop down and collect the insurance, but even if she wasn't worried about spending her retirement in prison, the place was too beautiful and she'd poured too much of herself into it to give up.

Emma was with Heather for the day. Lily had spent the morning at the parent-teacher conference where she'd received her first batch of bad news. Emma wasn't finishing her homework at school each day. She wasn't doing it at all. The teacher said Emma was distracted, unfocused, and kept to herself.

Since the Arthur incident, both she and Ruth repeatedly asked Emma about school, but she hadn't complained about bullying or anything else. When Emma had said her homework was done, there'd been no reason to doubt her.

Each footfall on the sidewalk felt as though the full weight of the day's disappointments had settled like dumbbells tied to her ankles. Every time Lily thought she was treading on a smooth piece of pavement, she hit a pothole.

There was one good thing to look forward to. Vicki was driving Emma back from Pittsburgh and staying for dinner. It was supposed to be a celebration of Lily's new financing and Emma's apparent progress. The celebrating wouldn't happen, but she'd definitely have a glass or two of the Bordeaux she'd bought for the occasion.

As she rounded the back of the shop, the barn door slid open a foot. Jack the dog bounded out to greet her. Doug was visible through the gap but didn't seem to notice her approach. He was sitting on an overturned bucket, his face in his hands.

Lily backed up a few steps and said in a louder-than-normal voice, "Hi, Jack." She hoped she'd spared Doug any embarrassment.

He looked up and pushed his hair off his face, possibly swiping a tear or two. She wanted to put an arm around his shoulder, but he wasn't one to tolerate pity, despite whatever haunted him.

What a sad bunch of broken people they were. Doug, Emma, herself. There had to be a way for all of them to move forward with their lives. The first step might be to stop hiding things.

"I'm making dinner for Vicki and Emma. I would love if you joined us."

"Are you sure?" He straightened and squinted skeptically with one eye. "Emma will be there."

"So will Vicki, but I think it's time to stop keeping secrets.

Unless you still want to."

"You're sure?" The corners of his mouth rose enough to suggest the invite made him happy.

"Very sure." At least something was going right.

"First, look at this." He took her to the armoire he'd been working on. The mirror was back in the door, their reflections clear as could be. "I'm pretty sure Jack the human made all this furniture." The armoire was one of three. There were bed frames, dressers, chairs, and occasional tables. "The more time I spend on this stuff, the more I admire his skill."

Doug had organized everything into a woodworking studio. Tools to one side, lumber stacked in neat piles on the other, leaving enough space in the middle for the truck. Maybe this was how it had looked before Jack lost his son and wife. Clean and dry but not very warm.

"I'd still like to make something out of this wood. Maybe bookcases? What do you think?"

"I think anything you make would be great." She'd break the news about the bank later. "I'm going up to get started on dinner. Join me when you're ready."

As Lily crossed the backyard, she imagined safe steps to take her directly up to the kitchen or a deck, if she added one. Instead of crunching over broken bits of asphalt, there'd be a patio and a garden designed by Trish with flowers, vegetables, and a patch of grass.

Who was she kidding? There was a mound of obstacles to overcome for that ever to happen, but it didn't need to be a shop. It would make a cozy home.

And with that thought, a solution to the dry rot popped into her head.

Lily had the wine poured before Doug joined her. She wiped her hands on her dish towel and sat with him at the table, letting her first sips of wine soften her edges before she broke the news from the bank.

"Lily, I can leave anytime. Don't let me hold you back from doing what you need to do."

"No." She shook her head so fiercely her brain wobbled. "I decided I was going to tackle this one thing at a time. So far, I've managed. Thanks to you. And I had an idea how to hurdle this obstacle. I can't get a mortgage on this house, but I might be able to get one on mine."

"You would do that?"

"I think so. Either way, I'd have to make payments. It's not a bigger risk." Was it, though? It felt like it was. "But would you stay to help me?"

"You've already given me more than I deserve."

"Au contraire. I'd be nowhere without you."

"No. I'm the one who'd be nowhere. You'd be home with Emma."

Maybe someday she'd understand why Doug deprived himself of so much. He certainly didn't need to be homeless. Was he punishing himself? His sadness seemed to have gotten worse since he'd started visiting Jack. There had to be a connection.

"You can believe your side and I'll stick with mine." Lily lifted her glass and tipped it toward Doug. "I can only say you are very welcome here. It's good you'll meet Emma and Vicki tonight."

Doug clinked rims with Lily's glass. "I see Emma with Ruth sometimes in the afternoon when I stop at Becca's. I know it's her because of her cap."

"Ruth is good for her. It's a good thing too. I found out today that Emma has been lying to me about doing her homework."

"I'm sorry to hear that." He clasped his hands, his thumbs flicking each other. "Are you sure she should meet me?"

"I am." Lily lifted her gaze from his hands to his face. "She loves to be here and you are a part of here."

In answer, there was a rapid, hard double knock on the front door. Lily looked out of the kitchen. Dusk had descended while they'd been talking. She hadn't closed the curtains. "That has to be Philip. Wait here."

"I saw the lights on." Philip surveyed as much of the inside of the house as he could while Lily stood in the doorway. "I thought maybe we could have dinner. Emma too." Although Lily hadn't stepped to the side, he sidled past her. "It's like night and day in here. You did all this by yourself?"

"I had help."

As Philip took another step into the great room, Lily felt her blood pressure rise, each heartbeat thumping in her head. Doug was trapped with no way to escape without being seen. Lily had wanted him to come out of hiding but hadn't planned to start his introductions with Philip, perhaps the last person Doug would want to meet.

"You could sell this place easily now. Call Greta George."

"I already have, but there's dry rot in the attic. It's expensive to fix and I can't get a mortgage until it is."

"Did she tell you what you can get if you sell as is?" He nodded slowly, eyes bright as he inspected the rest of the room.

Was he pleased with how the place looked or that the dry rot would force her to sell?

"What's the rest of this place look like?"

Before Lily could find a reason to stop him, he crossed into the kitchen. Doug was pretending to tighten a screw on a cabinet, Lily's salad vegetables lay out on the counter, and the intoxicating aroma of chicken pot pie permeated the room. Standing like flares were the two wine goblets on the table.

"Is this your help?"

"He has been a wonderful help." She emphasized the word he. "Philip, meet Doug, a good friend of mine. And this is his dog, Jack."

"Nice to meet you," Doug said and turned to Lily. "I'm done for the day. Enjoy your dinner. Thanks for the wine."

Lily wished she could think of something to say, but he scooped up Jack and left through the front door before her brain reconnected with her mouth.

Philip stood still for a moment. "Isn't that the guy from Becca's shop?"

"Yes, and he's done a lot for me."

"He brings his dog?"

"Jack is very well-mannered. Any other objections?" He didn't need to be so judgmental.

"I hope you don't let Emma near him. Where does that guy even live?"

If only he knew the answer to both questions. "I'm not sure where he lives." Not exactly a lie. Technically, he was only staying with her. He didn't live anywhere, not in the true meaning of it. "He's a kind man." She didn't add, unlike you. Philip didn't mean to be unkind. He was protecting her and Emma as always.

"What do you know about him?"

"I know he's competent and that without his help, this place would still be a wreck." Lily took three steadying breaths. "Thanks for the dinner invite, but Vicki's bringing Emma home and—"

"Here?" His eyebrows rose close to his receding hairline.

"It's a treat for Emma. I've told you, she loves to be here. I got some unpleasant news from her teacher. I thought I'd soften the blow." Lily explained about the homework. "I'd ask you to stay, but I think it's better for her if I speak to her alone." Lucky she had a ready and believable excuse not to invite him. "How about tomorrow instead? We can go to that Lego pizza place?"

What more could go wrong in a single day? Lily let Philip out the front door. Once his back was out of sight, she closed the curtains, sucked down the rest of her wine, and went to the barn to beg Doug to return.

Chapter 20
Lap Desk and iPad

Doug was pacing in the barn, mumbling, and red from his neck to his ears. He looked as if he might snort steam.

"Please don't let Philip spoil our night." Lily pressed her hands together in supplication.

"You're nuts." He stared at her, one hand up to stop her from arguing. "I'm a homeless guy. A freeloader. You shouldn't let me anywhere near Emma."

Before she could cover her shock, Lily stepped back, pushed by the force of his words. She'd thought it was Philip's rudeness that had touched a nerve. She never thought Doug would agree with him.

"You are not a freeloader, and you know it." Her own anger was rising, and if she wasn't careful, all of it, everything she'd been swallowing for the past four months, would spew from her like lava. She let her arms fall to her sides and slowed her speech. "Yes, you're homeless, but not because you have to be. I don't know what made you think you don't deserve better, but you do. Emma and Vicki are important people in my life, and so are you." She paused, hoping to see a sign of him cooling off, but he remained ruddy and stiff.

"You live here and you help me. You visit Jack the human and you take care of Jack the dog. So far, I don't see a problem. There's no reason you shouldn't meet Emma."

The bucket handle rattled as he sat with his head hanging.

"Will you please come back upstairs? Let's have a lovely night."

"Give me some time. I'll be up."

He didn't look at her, but she knew if he'd said he'd come, he would. "Thank you."

Outside, the air had grown chilly. The furnace didn't have the oomph to keep the house warm, but the oven would warm the kitchen. They'd be comfortable there, but it would be a cold night in the barn for Doug and Jack.

Half an hour later, Lily opened the front door. Emma flew to her, hugging her tightly around the hips, her face tucked against Lily's belly. After two seconds, she let go and dragged Vicki into the great room. "Come see Mommy's shop. It's beautiful." She twirled, arms wide.

"It's even better than you described it." Vicki put her bag down by the stairs and properly greeted Lily with a hug and a kiss on the cheek. At close to six feet tall, she had to bend to whisper into Lily's ear. "The shop was all we talked about in the car."

"I want to show you everything." Emma tried pulling Vicki along.

"Give me a sec to say hi to your gammy, please." Vicki rolled her eyes, but she was smiling.

"How did you manage this, Lily? When I saw this place with Amanda, it was—"

"Filthy? Dilapidated? Full of trash?" Lily finished Vicki's sentence. "Emma, go make sure everything is ready for Vicki to see."

After Emma skipped out of the room, Vicki wore a bitter-sweet smile. "Amanda saw past all that. I thought she'd gone off the deep end, but she was right. What I want to know is, how did you manage this transformation?"

"Slow down. Before we talk about this place. We have to talk about you. You look awesome." Her nose had always held her back. Whether it should have or shouldn't have could be debated and was completely irrelevant. Vicki never could see past that it was far too long for her face and had a beyond prominent bump. Lily always thought it was the reason Vicki seldom had dated, throwing her energy into her career.

"After Amanda died, I started thinking. I'd been afraid of surgery, but what was I waiting for? My life wasn't going to change unless I changed it."

The two women were both quiet for a moment. Lily swallowed hard and she could see Vicki do the same. They would both gladly return all the gifts to have Amanda back.

"I'm very happy for you."

"Thanks. I feel better too. It's a huge confidence boost."

Emma ran back into the room, grabbing the newel post to stop her forward motion. "C'mon Auntie Vic."

"Go with her," Lily said. "I have to check on things in the kitchen."

When they'd finished, Lily poured Vicki a glass of wine and filled a matching goblet with sparkling water for Emma. Doug's glass was still on the table. Lily glanced out the window one more time to see if lights were on in the barn. "Let me tell you both about my secret helper. He'll be here soon."

Vicki pointed at Doug's half-empty glass. "This is his, then? Not Philip's?"

"I didn't invite Philip. He's got me a bit peeved. But that's another story. Let me tell you about Doug." She gave them the brief version, leaving out the parts that weren't for Emma's ears.

When Jack the dog's toenails clicked up the basement steps, Lily added, "And he has a dog."

The basement door opened, Jack entering before Doug.

"Doggie!" Emma made a beeline for Jack, who slathered her, his pink tongue flapping furiously on her cheek.

"Vicki, this is my friend Doug. The man who has done most of the work around here."

Vicki's gaze fixed on Doug and didn't waver. Lily wasn't

certain if she'd seen a spark pass between them. Perhaps Vicki's confidence boost? A long shot maybe, but it would be nice for something wonderful to come from all the grief and anguish.

"And this is Emma." Lily asked Emma to look up from Jack for a moment.

"Is this your dog?" she asked.

"He belonged to the man who lived here before, but I guess he's my dog now."

"I like him," Emma said.

"Looks like he likes you even more." Doug's face softened, tender. A look Lily had seen when he spoke about Jack the human before the shadows descended.

"No surprise there," Lily said. Jack the dog was getting all the attention he could ask for. "Who wants to eat? Sit wherever you like."

While Lily spooned out chicken pot pie, Vicki said, "If it's okay with you, Lily, I can spend the night. I thought it might be fun to tour the town tomorrow. Amanda always said the town and the quilt shop had postcard qualities, but I never had enough time to look around."

"That sounds fantastic. Emma?" Emma's arm was under the table, slipping tidbits to Jack the dog. "Would you like to do that tomorrow?"

"Can we get pancakes too? And can Jack come?"

"Pancakes, yes, but Jack can't go into the diner."

With nothing but crumbs left on their plates, their glasses empty, Lily listened to Vicki and Doug chatting. He was different around her. Not so dour. When she asked him questions, he opened up, although he left out a lot of details. Judging by his quick glances at Emma, he wanted to say more but held back. Although he needn't have worried. Emma's attention was absorbed by the dog. She'd probably fed him more than she'd eaten.

The day may have been full of bad news, but this evening was making up for all of it. The homework problem could wait.

As Lily stood to clear the table, Doug offered to help her wash dishes.

"If you don't mind," Vicki said, "I've been hiding a present for Emma. Can I give it to her now?"

"Yes, please." Emma said. "What is it?"

"Go grab my bag from the other room but no peeking."

It took a second for Emma to return with the bag strung over her shoulder.

Vicki pulled out an iPad in a blue cover and a lap desk.

"These belonged to your mother. They were in her office. It took me a while to find where she wrote the password." She handed them to Emma. "I left her photographs on there and turned on the parental controls. We can set it up for you."

"Can we put games on it?" Emma asked.

"Only if your Gammy says it's okay."

"It's fine, but only what Vicki or I approve."

"Can we do it now?" Emma pleaded, knowing she should help to clear the table.

Four eyes, Emma's and Vicki's wearing matching expressions that could have melted a jury made of ice, fizzled Lily's resolve. "Go see if you can figure out how to be comfortable in the other room."

After washing the dishes, Lily and Doug joined them in the great room. Vicki and Emma sat atop a stack of folded drop cloths, head-to-head, leaning against the wall beside the fireplace with the iPad between them and Jack cemented against Emma.

"Your dog is in love," Lily whispered to Doug.

"Seems so. It's good to know that he'll be happy when I'm gone."

"Don't talk about that. This is the happiest night I've had in a long time, and after the start of the day, I deserve it."

"Sorry. I'll be right back." He returned with a couple of chairs from the kitchen.

Vicki looked up from the iPad. "You know, Lily, I could

see myself living in a house like this sometime." She turned to Doug. "I live in an apartment, but when I get a house, can I hire you to fix it up?"

"I'm only staying until Lily doesn't need me anymore."

Emma looked up, one eye squinting. "Why do you call him Jack?"

"Because he's a Jack Russell terrier," Doug said. "And the man he belonged to before me was named Jack."

"That's too many Jacks." Emma patted the dog on the head. "I think we should call him Russell."

"She's got a point." Lily spread her hands in surrender. "It would certainly be easier than calling him Jack the dog all the time."

"Russell, what do you think?" Emma lifted his head, and he licked her nose.

"I guess that's settled, then." Vicki nodded and pressed herself up from the drop cloths. "Have fun watching your show with Russell."

Back around the kitchen table, Vicki kept her voice low. "I hope you find a way to keep this place, Lily. It'd be a shame to lose it."

"I just need money. I'm thinking about mortgaging my house. After I talk to the bank, I'll decide if I can afford it."

"Where will you go, Doug?" Vicki asked.

"I don't know, but I'd be leaving anyway." The creases between his eyebrows deepened. "I came here to see Jack, but he thinks I'm Billy. I can't do it for much longer."

"Don't give up." Vicki's eyes glistened. "My grandmother had Alzheimer's. Most of the time, she didn't know who we were, but she'd also have lucid moments. We all learned to go with whatever she said if it made her happy."

"I haven't given up yet." His grimace lifted. Vicki seemed to have reached something in him that Lily never had, but he stood. "Thanks for dinner, Lily. It was nice to meet you, Vicki."

He called Russell, but the dog didn't come. "Guess he

doesn't know his new name."

Emma pulled Russell into her arms.

"He needs to go home with me now," Doug said, "but you can visit him."

She squeezed tighter and kissed Russell.

"He's a lucky dog," Lily said, "but we're leaving too, so he has to go home."

After Doug and Russell left, Lily shut down the shop, and they drove back to Lily's house. Once Emma was in bed, Lily and Vicki sat side by side on the chenille sofa. The warmth and comfort of her home was a sharp contrast with the cold, empty great room.

"How are you really doing?" Vicki asked.

"You want the truth?"

Vicki squeezed Lily's hand. "I do."

Lily closed her eyes, preparing for what she wanted to say. "There is a gaping black hole inside me that wants to consume me. I don't think I'll ever be whole again. I want to give Emma her mommy's shop, but I'll be lucky if I can fix the dry rot. And if I get through this disaster, who knows what's next?"

Vicki shifted to face Lily, her eyes sparkled with wetness. The sympathy made Lily's throat tighten. "Emma's struggling. She seemed happy tonight, but she wears that hat, so she can't pull her hair out. She's not doing her homework or making any friends. Everything is wrong. Everything is hard and I'm so damn tired."

"Don't forget me. I'm here." Vicki opened her arms, beckoning Lily to fall into a hug.

"Don't hug me. I'll cry and may never stop."

"Okay, but hugs or not. I'm all in on Amanda's dream. I told you I've been thinking about changing things. A town like this is where I'd like to be someday."

"I'm surprised you don't move to Florida." Vicki's sister and her parents were near Tampa.

"I could, but I'm too attached to Emma. And I really like

the small-town idea. I guess I caught the bug from Amanda. And . . ." She nibbled the tip of her finger. "Doug's kind of special, don't you think?"

A relationship would be good for both of them, but what were the chances? Lily might not know his whole story, but if he couldn't let himself settle anywhere, it seemed unlikely he'd let himself love. "You two seemed to have gotten on well, but he's broken too." She owed it to Vicki to advise caution.

"I could tell. Life sucks sometimes. Let's make some good things happen."

"One good thing is seeing you so much more confident." Lily couldn't remember the last time she'd seen or heard about Vicki on a date. Beauty may only be skin deep, but the lack of it can hide the beauty underneath.

"I should have done this," she waved her hand past her face, "when I was eighteen. But no more regrets." She stood, her hands on her hips. "Time for bed. We have breakfast and a tour of the town tomorrow."

Chapter 21
Charming Notes

"I'll park behind the shop," Lily said. Vicki was in the passenger seat, Emma in the back. "Then we can stroll down the sidewalk to the diner and take the other side on the way back."

"No objections from me," Vicki said. "I'll walk anywhere on a sunny day."

No sooner than Lily had stopped the truck on the gravel, Emma leaped from the cab. Russell slid open the barn door with his muzzle and made a beeline for her.

"Family reunion?" Vicki asked.

"It seems so." Doug came out, wiping his hands with a rag. "Off to breakfast?"

"We are," Vicki said. "Join us. We're taking our time, sightseeing on the way."

"I can't. I'm in the middle of sanding the first coat of sealer on that armoire." He brushed sawdust from his forearm. "I need to get the next coat on."

"Can I see it?" Vicki's eyes were wide. "That birdseye maple table in the great room is beautiful. I'm curious what else Jack made."

Lily stood quietly at a distance, amazed at how talkative Doug became around Vicki. She admired the armoire as Doug explained how he'd stained it a lighter color to showcase the carvings along the top and down the side of the doors. With its new shelves and re-silvered mirror, it was a work of art.

"It's gorgeous." Vicki ran her finger down the side of the door.

He pointed to other pieces and described his plans for them. "I'm good at fixing, and I can build simple things. Billy taught me a lot, but I could never create anything like these. Check out this bed." A headboard and footboard with what looked like braided wood posts rested against the barn wall. "It's oak. When I'm done with it, you'll see the grain in the wood. It will come alive."

Lily was reluctant to break them up, but Vicki had limited time before she had to leave. "Okay, I don't know about anyone else, but I'm hungry. Emma, can you leave Russell for a bit to get some pancakes?"

Emma kissed him on the nose, promising she'd return with leftovers.

"That's if you don't gobble them all yourself," Lily said.

"I won't." She shook her head three times.

"She's very insistent when she knows what she wants," Vicki whispered to Lily. "Just like Amanda."

"You should see her when she's concentrating on something, like her sewing machine. I can almost imagine that time has gone backwards."

"It must be so hard for the both of you. I'm going to make time to visit more often."

"We'd love that. I haven't seen her this happy since the night . . ." Lily looped her arm through Vicki's. "Let's go see the town."

As they strolled along Fellowes Run Road, Lily said, "These four row houses were abandoned for years. Now three of them have been converted to shops. My friend Becca opened the cafe. I hope we get something fun, like a yarn shop, in the last one."

"That'd be good to have next to your quilt shop."

"If there is a quilt shop. Big if."

They passed a few more buildings, including the one with

Philip's office. "Most of my favorites are on the other side."

When they reached the diner, there was a twenty-minute wait for seating. The tables were full of older couples, rounded over their coffee cups and plates. "I shouldn't be surprised about the wait anymore," Lily said. "That retirement community has definitely made a difference in business around here. All the shop owners are happy."

"You would have an immediate customer base for your quilt shop too. Plus, there'll be all the people visiting relatives at The Village. That place might be the best thing that happened to this town. It didn't destroy the postcard appeal, but it did add vitality."

Vicki's upbeat attitude made Lily feel anything was possible. Maybe Doug was responding to the same thing. They both needed a dose of possible.

When the server came to clear their plates, Emma asked for a box for all the bits of toast, bacon, eggs, and pancakes on their plates. "It's for my dog."

Lily didn't want to burst her bubble to tell her it wasn't her dog, but Vicki changed the subject. "Let's go wash you up, Emma. You're icky-sticky."

Emma held up her hands. Lint-like pieces of napkin stuck on a few of her fingers.

After they left, they had to let traffic clear before they crossed the street. "It's The Village again. I never used to wait for more than maybe one car."

"That's progress, right?" Vicki shrugged. "Like most things, good and bad."

Lily pulled the familiar brass handle on the hardware store door, and let Vicki and Emma pass inside. Ed was behind the register.

"Your store is like a time capsule. I can smell the old wood," Vicki said. She ran her fingers along the patina on the edge of the counter.

"Some people don't like it, so I have the potpourri over

there." He pointed at a mini crock pot on the counter. "Seasonal fragrances. This time of year, it's pine and cinnamon."

"I think it smells great."

"Lily." Ed pointed to the garden center at the side of the store. "Mums are on sale. I thought you might be interested. And I think Trish is still back there hunting around."

"Let's go look," Vicki said. Emma grabbed her hand as they wound their way through the tumble of boxes, baskets, and Christmas tree stands and lights.

"Trish, one of my quilting friends, is an expert gardener. Even her quilts look like gardens."

Trish's hair was a rainbow, starting with purple near the roots, passing through blue to pink at the ends. "You are so lucky you get to park at your shop, Lily. I had to wait ten minutes for a spot to open."

"Park there whenever you want," Lily said.

"Traffic aside," Vicki said. "Your town is amazing. Look at this place. It's charming."

"Have you been to the General Store yet? Or the post office?" Trish asked.

"Not yet," Lily answered. "We're on our way."

"Wait till you see them, Vicki," Trish said. "They're even more retro. Rows of tiny brass boxes with windows in them. These stores were old when I was a kid and nothing has changed."

"This town would make an awesome tourist attraction," Vicki said.

Trish's face lifted. "We keep telling Lily she should open the quilt shop. It would fit in perfectly."

"Better add some parking lots though," Lily said.

"You got that right," Trish said. "But good luck trying to convince the council. I can't even get them to approve a park in the empty lot next to the town building." She pointed through the chain-link fence surrounding Ed's garden center to another undeveloped lot. "Speaking of which, a parking lot would look better there than the weeds."

"I'm not surprised they won't budge," Lily said. "They only approved The Village because it wasn't directly on Fellowes Run Road."

Vicki laughed. "So it isn't only the buildings here that are old-fashioned."

"Nope." Trish shook her head.

"We'd better keep moving if you want to see the other shops," Lily said.

After goodbyes, they continued down the street. Vicki mentioning things she thought the town could do. New light poles with pictures of Fellowes Hollow's fallen heroes, seasonal decorations, and light strings.

Lily could picture everything Vicki said, including her quilt shop. She and Robin would happily drive for miles to visit a quaint small town, shop, stroll, and eat lunch. "It would be lovely, but there isn't enough money to do all that."

"You never know, there might be with the increase in tax revenue from all the newcomers."

"Check out a town meeting sometime. Trish wasn't kidding."

"Amanda always thought the quilt shop would be a draw for the town and vice versa. Look at the wait at the diner. You'd have an influx of visitors. I could get you a magazine write-up, a few restaurant reviews, maybe a story on one of the Pittsburgh channels." Vicki had the expertise to make it happen. "Wouldn't it be wonderful?"

It would be wonderful. If mortgaging her house didn't work, she'd have to figure out something else. There had to be a way.

"Auntie Vic thinks the town is a postcard."

After Vicki left, Philip had picked up Lily and Emma for

dinner at Angelina's Pizzeria, dubbed The Lego Place. Emma, uninterested in the Lego tables, couldn't stop talking about Vicki's visit or the shop. It was good she was talkative. Not so good if she mentioned Doug to Philip.

"She says all the people will come to the quilt shop. That's what Mommy thought too."

Was that a slight wince that crossed Philip's face?

"Sounds like she enjoyed her tour of the town," he said, no annoyance in his voice.

"She was sad she had to go home, but she said she wants to move here."

Philip glanced at Lily for confirmation. "She said she'd love to live in a town like this, but she didn't say she was going to move here. So don't get too excited."

Emma crossed her arms over her chest and pushed back. "She might though."

"Yes, she might." Lily stressed the word "might" and wanted to change the conversation. The last thing she needed was for Emma to mention meeting Doug. "What are you going to put on your pizza?"

"Extra cheese."

"No surprise there." Philip smiled indulgently. Despite his feelings about the quilt shop, he was always glad to be with them. "I'm going to have pepperoni."

"I think I'll go with extra cheese, too." Lily looked at Emma. "We can share."

With their frequent visits, the place had become familiar. This time, they had a table toward the back, closer to the Legos. Philip laid his napkin on his lap, then sipped his water. "Since we know what you want, Emma, why don't you go play? We'll call you when the pizza comes."

Lily's uh-oh meter clicked up a notch. He had something to say he didn't want Emma to hear. Philip watched her tootle toward the tables, both with several kids at them. Lily almost wished Emma would come back, but she joined the other children.

"She still doesn't know you're selling?" Philip's eyebrows rose and then dropped just as quickly as if he was trying to hide his incredulity. "Don't you think she'll only be more disappointed when she finds out?"

"She doesn't need any more disappointment now. Anyway, I can't sell right now." She wouldn't know anything more until she could speak to the bank the next day, but there was no point in keeping it secret from Philip. Lying or deflecting wouldn't change the outcome. "The bank won't lend if there's dry rot, but I can't fix the dry rot if I don't have money. It's a conundrum."

"Then sell it as is."

"I'd get a pittance for it, and probably only a developer who planned to raze it would buy it."

"That isn't your real reason, is it?" Philip folded his arms. "You can't tell Emma because it's you who can't let go."

Her shoulders tensed. She forced them down, away from her ears. This didn't need to be a battle. "I haven't wanted to sell this place from the start. You know that. I really wish you wouldn't pressure me."

"Instead, all you have is work and worry."

He didn't understand. Focusing on work for the hours she spent with Doug kept her from curling into a ball and going back to bed when she was alone. She told Philip about the parent-teacher conference. "While Vicki was here, Emma was her old self, and look how she's at the Lego tables with other kids there."

Vicki's visit had helped too. Of course, Vicki had been talking about the shop. There was also the magical effect of Russell, but to mention him would lead to Doug. She didn't need to add that to her battles with Philip. "I don't need to hand her a disappointment now. I need to figure out how to get enough money to fix the dry rot. Then I'll decide what to do next."

Philip reached for one of Lily's hands, prying open her fist and stroking her palm. "Calm down. I'm sorry if I'm pressuring you. It's only because I see what you're putting yourself through. You are in deep grief, even if you try to hide it from Emma. It's always there."

"You're right, okay, but talking about it only makes it harder." She pulled her hand from his and dabbed her eyes with her napkin. "Let's order. I'd like a glass of Chianti. We can share a carafe if you'd like."

Philip raised a finger to attract the server and placed the order, then faced Lily again, his jaw seeming to chew on words he didn't want to say. "What are you doing for Emma?"

"She's been seeing Ruth after school almost every day. It's her expertise."

"It was her expertise. She's been retired how long now?"

Lily rubbed her temples. "Is anything I do good enough for you?"

"I didn't mean it that way. I just want the best for Emma."

"I had her seeing a professional. You know, the kind you approve of, in an office, with a desk, and degrees hanging on the wall. Emma hated him and clammed up. Ruth is the best for her. You should see them together. Give me some credit. I'm not helpless."

But was it really hard to believe he thought she was helpless? For years, she'd relied on Sam, then Philip. It was her own fault he believed she was helpless. She'd believed it too, but the last few months she'd proven differently. She'd stretched her limits, and she'd succeeded. Until the dry rot.

"Also, I discuss everything with Heather. She is in complete agreement with me." Why was she justifying herself? About Emma or about the shop. Yet she couldn't stand the sympathy in Philip's eyes, so she continued. "Everything Emma said about Vicki's trip is true. She believes in Amanda's vision for the town and a quilt shop. And she is a public relations expert. If anything, I want to do it more now than before. But I can only deal with one problem at a time. And my problem right now is fixing dry rot. If I can't mortgage the shop, I'm going to mortgage my house."

Philip's eyes bulged. "That's a terrible idea."

"I knew you'd say that." She shook her head. This record was getting old. But maybe he was right. She could hear him out. "Tell me why it's a terrible idea."

"For one thing, you're risking your home. You need it for yourself and for Emma. And you love your house."

"I know, but if I'm willing to take that chance, then I have to be willing to face the consequences. I'm going back to the bank on Monday. Let's see what they have to say."

"I've been thinking," he said, pinching his lips between his thumb and forefinger. "I can lend you the money. You can pay it back when you sell. No payments. The place looks great with what you already did, and with the influx of people into town, I expect you'll get a good price for it."

This was why she was friends with Philip. He had his hard edges, but he was also generous. And he looked after her, even if he was sometimes misguided. "Thank you. That is extremely generous and I appreciate your offer, but it's not a good idea to borrow from friends." It would be easy though.

"How long have we been friends? And now we're both widowed. We're family, Lily. I can do this for you. It will save you closing costs and interest. And you won't put your home in jeopardy."

And what if she didn't sell? "I could only do it if we have a note. I can't take your money on word alone. It wouldn't be right." A note would protect both of them. "And I don't want to be forced to sell. So, I have to make payments."

"I can do that. No force."

"And you don't need that money?"

"I can spare it or I wouldn't have offered. I want to do this for you. You'll be able to hire a proper contractor. You won't need to have strangers living there."

"Doug is not a stranger, and he doesn't live in the house."

Not technically. She didn't want to argue with Philip anymore. He'd listened to her, and he'd backed off, then offered a life-line. If she took it, she'd clear the hurdle.

When the pizza arrived, they called Emma back. Lily took another sip of her wine, letting the warmth slide down her throat and diffuse through her. One thing at a time. She could do this.

Chapter 22
Overrun Failing

Greta, with her extensive network and influence, had convinced the contractor to start work despite the impending holidays and deep cold of winter, but before they could begin, the electrical panel needed to be upgraded. The other problem was access to the attic. A narrow staircase in a bedroom closet was the only way up, and more importantly, the only way down. They tore down the outside staircase, a happy side effect, then poked a hole in the gable, and ran a trash shoot down the scaffolding.

It was mid-January before work began. Perfect timing for the proverbial other shoe to drop, more like an anvil. As they tore out old insulation, the extent of the dry rot grew, while Lily's hopes that Philip's money would cover the project shrank.

When she thought about the furnace and rebuilding the back steps, her ribs refused to expand enough to breathe, her shoulders ached, her heart raced. The last time she'd felt that way, she was waiting in the emergency room, wondering if Sam was going to live or die.

If Lily died, she'd rest in peace knowing Heather and Ben would care for and love Emma. They'd do the same if Lily became destitute, a thought that made her queasy. Even though she'd often thought Emma would be better off with them, the truth was Lily needed Emma. If she lost too much money and had to move into some crappy apartment, she'd lose Emma too.

She had no cushion left if the unexpected happened again. How much more could there be? What if she hit an insurmountable obstacle? Going back to work for Simon wasn't possible. He'd already replaced her.

These thoughts kept her awake at night, but luckily, during the day, thinking was impossible with the brigade of young, skinny men in tool belts climbing up and down the stairs while the trash shoot clanged a melody, accompanied by buzzing saws and concussive nail guns. Most days, Lily escaped to the barn, bundled against the cold, sitting on the hay bales, watching Doug work. She'd bought a warm coat for Russell, a space heater, and given Doug all her spare blankets. It was enough to keep them from freezing to death.

The late February day when the contractors finished and presented Lily with the final bill, she breathed freely for the first time in weeks. Doug came into the great room and stood beside her in front of the fireplace. He looked over her shoulder at the bill. "How bad is it?"

"There's good news. I'll only need to add a few thousand dollars to pay it, but we've hit the end of the line unless the bank can lend now. If Greta is right, they should appraise it for enough to repay Philip and do the rest of the work."

"Is that what you want to do?"

She could feel him looking at her but couldn't meet his gaze. Maybe she could bear to give up hope of opening a quilt shop. There was a whole other list of obstacles to running a business, but if she sold, she'd miss the place. She'd also lose Doug. She had no claim on him, no right to ask anything of him, but she didn't want him to leave.

"No, but I think I need to not think for a bit. I've survived this hurdle. I need space to decompress."

Her cell phone buzzed in her pocket. She hoped it was Robin. A visit with her friend, sharing an afternoon glass of wine, and the weekend off, would be better than a spa vacation. The caller ID nixed that idea.

After she hung up, Lily dropped to the floor, her face in her hands. Doug brought a bucket and sat next to her. "Is it Emma?"

"They need me to come in for a conference after school. I don't understand it. Ruth and I have both been making sure she does her homework. Her hair is growing back. And she's seemed so much happier lately. Don't you think?"

"I can't really answer that. She's always seemed happy to me."

Of course. Every time he saw Emma, they were in the shop and with Russell. Her happiest times. He'd never seen her forlorn. Lily closed her eyes. They ached as if she hadn't slept in a week.

"Can I help? Drive you there?"

"No, it's okay." She opened her eyes. "You go see Jack. I'll ask Ruth to hang on to Emma until I get back."

After Lily met Emma at the bus stop, they went to the cafe as usual. She handed a few bills to Emma. "Why don't you go order from Becca yourself? You're big enough now."

Lily approached the table by the window. "Walter, are you sure you're okay with this?"

When she'd called Ruth earlier, Ruth asked to go to the conference with Lily, leaving Walter to care for Emma, Ruth assuring Lily that he'd be delighted. "He's a fixer. He needs to feel useful."

Walter shut the book and patted it. "I'd love to."

Emma returned, balancing a brownie and a hot chocolate.

"Ruth and I have to run an errand. You can stay here with Walter."

She nodded, looking at Walter. "Can we play a card game?"

"After you do your homework?" Walter rubbed his hands together gleefully. "Do you have any math? It's my favorite."

Emma wrinkled her nose.

"She'll be fine," Ruth said. "Let's go."

"Mrs. Wolfe." The teacher stood at the small table in the school conference room. "I asked Principal Slater to join us."

As if Lily hadn't noticed her sitting there when she walked in. Perhaps they were expecting Lily to overreact. "And I've brought Ruth Shaffer here. She's Emma's counselor."

Principal Slater stood and shook Ruth's hand. "It's nice to see you again, Ruth."

"You too, Veronica."

They moved to a conference table. The teacher laid a folder in front of her, then folded her hands on top as if she was protecting classified info. "I asked you to come in today because Emma is struggling with her grades."

"I thought she was doing better," Lily said. Emma never had trouble with grades before.

"I think the problem is that she's fallen so far behind in some subjects, she can't assimilate new material." The teacher was young but, unlike Veronica Slater, looked sympathetic. "She can't learn division if she hasn't mastered multiplication. She's fine with reading but doesn't retain anything other than a story."

"We were thinking," Principal Slater interjected, "perhaps we should move her back a grade. This is a terribly hard time for her. Of course, it's understandable in the circumstances, but it might be better for her in the long run."

"What about tutoring?" Lily asked. "I don't want Emma to feel she's failed."

"Emma's problem is social and emotional. We think she'd be happier in the long run, being in a different class. She hasn't made friends. Tutoring would require her to be pulled out of the classroom. We don't want to make her stand out."

"And moving her down a grade wouldn't make her stand out? Worse, it could open her up to more bullying." Lily tried to hide her scorn, but it leaked into her tone.

"I have a suggestion," Ruth said, her hand on Lily's arm to calm her. "My husband, Walter, has an excellent relationship with Emma." She turned to Principal Slater, "As you know, he was a teacher in Ainsleyville. I think he'd enjoy tutoring Emma after school."

"He wouldn't mind?" Lily asked. It would be a wonderful solution.

"We'll have to ask him, but I think he'd love it." Ruth again squeezed Lily's arm, a warning to let her handle the matter. "If not, we can look into sending Emma to a learning center after school. I don't think putting her back a grade is a good idea and I don't think it will be necessary."

The teacher agreed it might be a good plan, and Veronica Slater had no objections.

Once in the car, Ruth spoke freely. "This solution is best for Emma, and it will be good for Walter. Did you see him light up about helping Emma with homework? She is the highlight of our day, Lily. We love her."

Lily choked on her words. "I don't have words to express my gratitude. I don't know how I'll ever repay you."

"It's not necessary. We don't need money, but retirement doesn't suit us. We need jobs and you've given us the best kind, a child back in our lives. We'll all work together to help her find her way. You're not alone, Lily."

Those were the most comforting words Lily had heard in a long time.

Chapter 23
Time to Let Go

"What do you mean there's a lien on the property?" Lily didn't hide her shock. There had to be a mistake.

The loan officer, a plump middle-aged woman impeccably dressed in a navy-blue suit, had a kind face. She pursed her lips in appreciation for Lily's predicament. "You have a loan from Philip Mayberry. He filed it a few months ago. I'm sorry, Mrs. Wolfe, but we can't loan until the lien is satisfied."

Lily's hope drained from her as if pressed out by a giant squeegee, leaving her dry and flat. The new appraisal had come in high enough for her to repay Philip and, if no other horrors developed, finish the work. "Satisfied? You mean paid off?"

"Yes, usually, but he could lift the lien if he wanted to."

Why would Philip put a lien on the shop? He hadn't even wanted a note. She'd been the one to insist. Was he worried she'd borrow more than she could handle? Or was he trying to prevent her from borrowing more, making sure she'd have to sell?

"Can you do me a favor? Can we calculate what the payments would be if you could loan? There's not much point in me wrestling with this if I can't afford it, anyway."

"How much were you hoping to borrow?"

Lily added what she owed Philip to the amount she thought she needed for the final repairs and, in case she tried, to open a shop. As the loan officer typed numbers into her computer,

Lily wanted to peek at the screen but resisted. Finally, the printer clicked and spit out the piece of paper with her fate written on it.

"Wow, why is it so much?"

"It's a function of the amount borrowed, the interest rate, and the length of the loan." She reviewed the numbers with Lily.

"Why is the rate higher than the sign?" Lily faced the poster on the wall advertising low-rate mortgages.

"Because it's not your primary residence. It's an investment property."

"So I could do better if I lived there?"

"If you lived there as your primary residence."

"There's no longer term to bring it down a little?"

"Afraid not."

Lily chewed on her thumbnail. This couldn't be the end. There had to be a way. "Can you recalculate the amount assuming it is a primary residence?" Maybe she could get a mortgage on her house instead of the shop.

The number came out better but still substantially more than what she got from Simon each month. And close to double what she was paying Philip. Lily hadn't fully accounted for the interest, which Philip had refused to charge her.

"I have to be honest. You might not get approved to borrow this much while you still have the other note."

That, Lily didn't need to be told. She'd be strapped if she took it on and end up needing the loan to make the payments.

If only something, one thing could work out. She'd expected to encounter more obstacles but not for everything. What next? Would she find out her foundation was crumbling? The thought made her shiver.

"Thank you for your help." She took the papers off the desk. "Can I take these with me?"

"Be my guest. Come back if I can help with anything else."

It wasn't the bank she needed help from. It was Philip.

Why would he do such a thing? Even if she couldn't get the loan for other reasons, she'd never imagined he would tie her hands.

She'd planned to go home, calm down, and think things through. Instead, she ended up in the chair opposite Philip's desk.

"It's standard form when you make a loan like that," he said.

"But this wasn't a standard loan. You didn't even want the note."

"If the bank thinks you shouldn't borrow more, don't you think it's a bad idea to do it? You don't want to end up in foreclosure."

"I'm not going to end up in foreclosure." Even though she'd already known she couldn't do it, she didn't want to give Philip the satisfaction of being right. "Both the appraisal and Greta's estimate were higher than the amount I need. Worse comes to worst, I sell the place and everyone gets their money back."

"They think it will sell for that much, but there is no guarantee, and you don't know how long it might take to find a buyer." Philip let out an exasperated sigh.

Lily wanted to smack him. She didn't know as much about finance as he did, but she'd learned a lot and she was neither stupid nor a child.

"Don't be condescending."

"I'm sorry, I just can't stand to see you stressing out like this." The corners of his eyes turned down in sympathy. Something she always used to appreciate because he looked after her. It had become infuriating.

"Sell now. The dry rot is fixed. You can get out of this and get on with life." He reached for her hand.

She pulled it away and leaned as far back in her chair as possible. He was becoming a broken record, but then again, so was she. "I still need A/C and a furnace and—"

"No, you don't. You can sell without those. Why do you even want to keep doing this? I thought we'd agreed you were going to sell."

"You want me to sell. I've never wanted to sell. Emma's struggling enough already. She's happy when she's there, but she can't be there if I don't have a furnace."

"This isn't only about Emma, is it? It's about Amanda."

"Yes. Finally, you're listening to me. I don't want to let go. It's like losing her all over again. Surely you can understand that." She also loved being there with Doug, working, cooking dinners. It had been a long time since they'd been able to do anything, between the cold and the workmen.

"And perhaps that man living in your barn has something to do with this."

His words hit her as if he'd thrown something at her. She steadied herself, strangling the arms of the chair with her clenched fists.

"I don't understand your question."

"I thought he'd move on when the cold weather hit. It has to be freezing in that barn."

She had no answer.

He waited a few seconds, then continued. "I might consider lending you more. I don't have the bank's requirements, but I can't if you insist on frittering away your money on a man you're effectively trying to adopt."

"Don't presume to know what I feel." How did he know these things? Her feelings for Doug were private. And why did she let Philip make her feel ashamed of them? She stared at her lap.

"He's a homeless adult. Not a child needing a mother. He clearly has issues. He isn't good for you and especially not for Emma. Say goodbye to him."

"I'm glad I know what you think. You may get your way." He would if Lily couldn't find a solution. She stood and left without another word, not bothering to put on her coat or worry about what Rose would have done. Philip thought she should sell, and he was trying to prevent her from making what he thought was a catastrophic mistake. Maybe he'd be proven right, but selling wasn't the right answer either. Not even close.

The air outside was a biting twenty-three degrees, under typical cloudy Western Pennsylvania skies. Lily felt the cold but was too distracted to care.

She'd expected Philip to tell her to sell. Nothing new there. But she hadn't expected him to be devoid of sympathy or to know her pathetic secret. The cafe door was beside her and she couldn't remember walking down the block. She peered through the glass. Becca had a line five people deep at the counter. Her business had more than doubled in the last few months. Lily wouldn't be able to get a word with her until after lunch.

By the time Lily reached her house, her nose, fingers, and toes had gone numb. She put up water for tea and stared out the kitchen window. She'd lived there for forty-one years, loving every moment, most of them with Sam and Amanda. Most of them full of joy and contentment. They'd both left her too soon, but their love and commitment to each other extended beyond life. Their ghosts still lurked in shadowy memories in every corner of the house, keeping her company.

More than anything, Lily wanted to have her family again. Doug and the shop filled the emptiness inside her. Like Emma, the shop and Becca's cafe were the only places where she felt whole. They gave her somewhere to go and people to be with rather than waiting in an empty house every day, talking to ghosts until Emma came home from school.

Tears dripped like her tea bag as she pulled it from the cup. She sat, warming her hands on the mug, and let her floodgates open. Pain filled her lungs like hot water bottles, drowning her. She didn't stifle her screams, letting herself wail like the wounded animal she was. An hour passed, maybe more, before she ran dry. She laid her head on her crossed arms, counting the minutes until she needed to meet Emma at the bus stop.

Before she left, Lily held ice to her swollen face. When she rounded the corner at the end of the block, she saw Doug on The Village driveway, his head bent as it often was when he was particularly down. "Wait up," Lily called out as she drew near.

He turned. "I was wondering where you were today."

"I went to the bank. Bad news." She filled him in.

He shrugged. Nothing more. "I'll be heading out soon, anyway. Jack is worse. He doesn't even think I'm Billy anymore. I'm a stranger to him."

"I'm so sorry. I know how much you'd hoped—"

"It doesn't matter." He shoved his ungloved hands deeper into his pockets.

"Where will you go?"

He shook his head, his unblinking gaze on the sidewalk in front of him. "I don't know."

She had no read on him. Was he leaving because he felt he had to or because he wanted to?

"We're both broken, I think," Lily said.

His face fell like a withered blossom, aging him by a decade. "I told you, some things can't be fixed."

He wasn't her responsibility, but she didn't have to stand idly by and not try to help him. Neither of them had to give up, not yet. It wasn't time to stop fighting. Not for the shop. Not for him. Not for Emma. And not for herself.

"Don't be hasty. Give me time. I still need your help." She checked her watch. She'd be late for the bus if she didn't hurry. "I have to go. We'll talk later."

As Lily finished the walk to the bus stop, she knew what she needed to do. The answer had been blinking in plain sight since the night of the Inaugural Chicken, but she had to think it through. Be certain it wasn't foolish. Or something she'd deeply regret.

Emma jumped the last step from the bus, hugged Lily, then flew into the cafe. By the time Lily walked through the door, Emma was in the chair between Ruth and Walter, watching him pull a book from his messenger bag. They were only three weeks into the tutoring, and Emma was nearly caught up in all her subjects. It wasn't surprising. She'd always loved school.

Within a few minutes, the warmth of the cafe defrosted Lily's nose. She grabbed a napkin and dabbed at it, then found Becca wiping down the inside of her baked goods case.

She blew the recalcitrant strand of hair that always escaped her bandana off her face, her eyes locked on her parents and Emma. "I watch her sometimes and marvel at how she's blossoming. And my parents are growing new shoots too. All my dad talks about is what lesson he's planning for her."

Lily's emotions warmed her faster than the heat from Becca's kitchen. "I can't express what their help means to me, to Emma."

Becca swished her hand. "Love goes both ways, Lily. And you exude it."

"Me?" Lily hadn't thought she did. What had she done for Becca? Or Ruth or Walter?

"You don't see it? Your friendship has made me feel like I belong in this community, like I belong in this cafe. I can't tell you how many customers told me they came in because you told them how good my muffins are."

"That's because it's true. But it's a small thing."

"You want a bigger one? Look what you do for Doug."

"Again, I've gotten so much more back from him."

"I don't see him much anymore. How is he managing through the winter? I'm surprised he doesn't freeze to death." Becca fake shivered in sympathy.

"I gave him a space heater. He says he knows how to keep warm. I think he might be part polar bear."

Even with her hair pulled back and her face ruddy from working, Becca's smile glittered. "With a very attractive exterior, I might add."

"Are you getting ready to hit the dating scene?" Maybe she was ready to move on. "You can't let Mr. Wrong keep you from finding Mr. Right." Although Lily had thought there might be something between Doug and Vicki, neither one had mentioned the other since that night. Could he heal enough to let himself love?

"Maybe." Becca batted her thick eyelashes. "I've been tempted lately. It would be nice to do something besides work."

"Just because the first one broke your heart doesn't mean the next one will. You deserve to be with someone who will make your life better."

"I think my pride hurt more than my heart, but never mind me. What did the bank say?"

"They won't loan me money because Philip put a lien on the property. But it doesn't matter because I can't afford to borrow as much as I need."

Becca raised one eyebrow. "Wait. Back up. Why on earth did he put a lien on the shop?"

"He says it's standard. But I think it's because he wants to force me to sell the place. He thinks I'm better off without it."

"You need to stop listening to him."

"It's only because he worries about me, but it is getting annoying."

"Getting annoying?" Becca's eyebrows lodged under her bandana.

"Okay." Lily conceded. "It's annoying. Very annoying. Satisfied?"

"Yes, thank you." Her eyebrows returned to their proper positions.

"I have an idea that I don't need him for. Or the bank. I want you to tell me if I've lost my mind. It's a life changer."

Becca pulled chairs out from one of the tables.

Lily whispered, "We have to keep our voices down. Emma can't hear this until I've made up my mind, but what if I sold my house and moved into the shop?"

Becca shifted her gaze toward Emma and back. "You would do that?"

"It's cheaper than affording two places like I am now. I'd get a windfall of cash and I don't need the bank's or Philip's approval to do it. All I need is a furnace. Emma and I are definitely not polar bears."

"It's a big deal and irreversible. Are you sure?"

"No, I'm not sure I'm even sane anymore. All my memories are in my house, but on the other hand, Emma and I are happy when we're in the shop. Maybe it's good to leave the ghosts behind, start fresh."

"That's a big chunk of your nest egg you're sacrificing."

"It's the only solution that I can think of."

"And if you were sorry? Then what?"

"You think this is a bad idea?" Lily could no longer tell a rational decision from one based on dreams.

"It's not the end of the world giving up your house." Becca folded her arms on the table, one grasping the other. "My parents decided to sell their house. Greta listed it. They're moving to The Village. They have activities for them. And they added a shuttle bus that runs up and down Fellowes Run Road every half hour. They won't have to worry about getting here if there is ice or snow."

"If I sell, it's irreversible. If it's a mistake, I'd have to live with regret. I'm more worried about Emma. What if it's a bad decision for her?"

"Emma will recover. Time heals all wounds."

"Does it though?" She heard Doug's voice plainly. Some things can't be fixed.

Becca tilted her head, her eyes searching Lily's. "I'm no shrink and you can tell me to mind my own business, but I wonder if you would care so much about the shop if you weren't worried about Doug leaving."

Lily flushed. Was she that transparent? "I don't want him to leave. I know I have no right to feel this way, but I care about him."

Becca huffed. "You care about everybody. But I agree there is something about Doug. Underneath his sullenness, there is a warm and caring man."

"So you don't think I've lost my mind."

"No, I don't, and neither do other people in town. Everyone is rooting for you."

"What does anyone know?"

"They remember you came out of the bank looking dejected and yet somehow managed to fix the dry rot. They see what you've been going through and how hard you've worked."

"Are people talking about me?"

"Relax. It's not people. Just Ed, Guy at the gas station." Becca touched the tips of her fingers to her lips while she thought about who else had said anything. "Elaine at the library and the mailman. I think that's it."

Lily heard Emma's footsteps running. Before she could turn to look, Emma wound her arms around Lily's shoulders, nearly knocking her off the chair. "What's the matter, Gammy?"

Time for the truth. Emma was going to have to face reality soon enough. "I'm thinking about whether we can keep the shop."

"Why can't we?" Emma's eyebrows knitted in concern, and she pursed her lips.

Becca stood to let Emma sit. "I'll leave you two alone."

Lily ducked her head, bringing her eyes to Emma's level. "It takes a lot of money to have the shop, but I have an idea. I want you to think very hard about it. It's a big deal and once we do it, we can't undo it."

"Okay."

"I could sell our house and we would move into the shop."

"You mean with Russell and Doug?" Emma clapped and jumped out of her chair, glowing like the old, innocent Emma.

"Definitely Russell, but I'm not sure about Doug. But he will be around for a while, at least. Think about it. Are you sure you won't miss the house?"

She rolled her eyes to the ceiling, thinking. "I will miss the house, and the grass in the back, but I think I would miss the shop more."

"Once I do it, we can't go back. So think about it for a few days, okay?"

Her little face became serious. "Okay."

"Can you go back to Walter and ask Ruth to come talk to me and Becca?"

"Okay."

A minute later, Becca pulled up an extra chair for Ruth. The three women sat in a small circle around the table, Ruth looking back and forth between Lily and Becca. "You two look awfully serious. I'm afraid to ask."

"First, let me congratulate you on your move. Becca told me you're going to The Village," Lily said. "Do you have a date?"

"Our unit will be ready mid to late April. Greta thinks our house will sell fast. So it should be soon." Ruth sighed as if she'd relaxed after a long day on her feet.

"I'm kinda thinking about something similar." Lily filled Ruth in on the details. "Emma says she wants to go, but I want your opinion. Is it too much change? She won't have her mother's old bedroom anymore or the house she's known since she was little."

"No one has a crystal ball, but if she thinks about it and decides she wants to go, I don't see why it's not okay. That shop is so important to her. It's as much about Amanda to her as anything in your house. The change might help. Both of you."

Lily took both of Ruth's hands in hers. "You are so good for her."

"I do my best." Ruth blushed and gazed lovingly at Emma and Walter.

It was comforting that Emma had more than just Lily

looking after her. Ruth and Walter were like another set of grandparents. And for them, Emma was the grandchild they'd never had. Maybe if Becca started dating again, they'd soon have one of their own.

Chapter 24
The Deed is Done

"Russell." Emma squealed, ran to the barn door, joining in a Snoopy-like happy dance.

Doug came out. He hadn't shaved, and his hair was sticking out as if he'd stuck his finger in a socket.

"Can I do it now, Gammy?"

Since they'd left the cafe, Emma had asked Lily three times if she could tell Doug they were moving into the shop. No amount of explaining that nothing was certain until they worked out the details could dampen her enthusiasm. Lily still wanted to discuss it with Doug and with Vicki before she did anything.

"Why don't we wait until dinner?" The evening still bore the afternoon's promise of spring, but the temperature was dropping rapidly. She needed to turn on the oven to warm the kitchen enough to enjoy a meal. "Can you join us, Doug?"

He looked over his shoulder into the barn as if deciding whether he could stop what he'd been doing.

"We're making spaghetti," Emma sing-songed to tempt him. "And garlic bread."

Doug laughed. "If you got to pick it, I'm not surprised. And sure, I'll come. I need to hear your secret." He brushed his pant legs with his hands. It made no difference. "But I need to shower and change first."

"Okay, but go fast," Emma said.

It had been at least a month since Lily last had cooked in the shop. If they moved in, it would become normal. Tiny appliances, no dishwasher, few cabinets. Nothing to rival her beautiful custom-designed kitchen. If she could make it bigger, she could fit a large table, enough for gathering family and friends. That's if she ever had a family beyond Emma, and maybe Philip if she could forgive him.

Whether she moved or stayed put wouldn't affect the size of her family, but there was something comforting about being back in the shop, making dinner, sharing it with Doug. If everything went according to plan, he'd have a reason to stay for a while longer.

Doug entered the room, wet hair slicked back, and a freshly shaven face.

"Can I tell him now?" Emma asked.

"Let him sit down first, okay?" Lily said, her smile so big she could see the tops of her cheeks in her peripheral vision. Despite her trepidation, seeing Emma so happy had to mean she was doing the right thing.

"I'm all ears." Doug pulled back a chair and dropped into it. Lily handed him a glass of wine.

"Gammy is going to sell her house and we're going to move in here."

Doug flinched and turned to Lily. "Seriously?"

Lily had thought he'd be glad. "Emma, take Russell to the drop cloths and watch something on your iPad, so I can talk to Doug."

Lily waited until she could hear the show playing and Emma talking to the dog.

She cupped her wine glass, keeping her voice low. "I am serious. I'll be spending less than I do now, keeping two places."

"If this is what you want, you should do it." Lines formed across his forehead. "Russell will be happy if Emma is around."

"I don't have any other ideas. Ruth and I both think the change might be good for Emma and me." Lily peered into the corner. There were no ghosts. Moving would give her a lot to look forward to and a lot she'd leave behind. "I'll miss my memories, but they go with me." She tapped her head. "When I'm here, I'm happy. When I'm there, I'm lonely. I want to be here even if I never open the quilt shop."

"Congratulations, then." His words were mirthless.

So far, nothing had made her doubt her decision, and yet anxiety buzzed in her ears. "I have to admit, I'm scared shitless."

"I've been scared shitless many times." His hands curled into fists. "I don't mean in battle. There've been nights when I was afraid to go to sleep. All my papers and money are in those metal boxes. I'm bigger than most people but not bulletproof. I could have lost everything. It's not much, but it's all I have."

"And now you don't have to leave." Maybe he thought if she and Emma moved into the shop, she'd make him leave.

"Most people aren't as kind as you. That day when you found me here, I thought I'd be on the road again. But it was one thing staying here while you lived elsewhere. If people found out a homeless man was living in your barn while your granddaughter lived in the house, they'd have me arrested."

It was no one's business, and Doug was no threat to Emma.

"I won't let that happen."

His eyes darkened. The same brooding expression that always dropped like a curtain at the slightest hint he might find a place to call home. "Even you can't stop some things."

"True, but I think I can rent," she said and put air quotes around the word "rent," "my barn to anyone I choose."

Both Lily and Doug were pensive over dinner, but Emma couldn't stop chatting. Which room would be her bedroom? What color should she paint it? Where would Russell sleep?

Wispy visions of how their life would be after the move floated in Lily's imagination. How could moving be a mistake when this house and Russell brought out the real Emma?

But she'd never considered that, if she moved in, Doug would leave.

Lily waited until the weekend when Vicki wouldn't be working to call her. She took the phone to the basement of her house, used a plastic storage box full of books for a seat, and kept her voice low. Emma was sewing at the dining room table. "Do you remember all the wonderful ideas you had about this town?"

"Uhhh . . ." Vicki said.

"It's not a trick question. Do you still think a quilt shop would be a good idea in this town?"

"Yes, definitely. Are you going to do it?" Vicki's voice went up an octave.

"I had an idea. The only way I can get the money to complete the repairs and open the shop is to sell my house and move in."

"You're actually going to live in the shop?"

"It is a house too." A brick seemed to drop from nowhere and land in Lily's stomach. "You think this is a bad idea?"

"Are you kidding? I think it's fantastic. Can I come move in with you? I'll help you all I can with PR for the shop. Heck, I'll help the whole town with PR. Can I ask you one thing, though?"

"Sure."

"Where is Doug going to go?"

Maybe Doug wasn't wrong. "Do you think he needs to leave if we move in?"

"No, but I think he'll think that, and if he does, he will leave."

Vicki understood him better than she did. Maybe the connection between them hadn't faded.

"You're right. He thinks that, but I don't and I don't want

him to." Lily rubbed her temple. "His living in the barn is no threat to Emma."

"I know that and you know that. But you better make sure he knows you need him. He won't stay if he thinks you pity him."

"Of course, I need him. There are still renovations we need to do, and he promised to build shelves for me." She hadn't wanted to impose on him, but Vicki was right. Doug wouldn't accept charity or pity.

Two weeks later, with the new furnace and water heater installed, the shop was cozy and ready to live in. As a kind of insurance policy, in case Emma was sorry, Lily decided to move before she listed her house.

It was midweek before she found the right moment to talk to Doug about staying. She'd practiced speeches over and over, trying to find the most convincing arguments, then decided to speak from the heart. The sincere truth was the best. He'd either stay or go. There was nothing more she could do.

Lily stood in the doorway of what would become Emma's room, watching him assemble the oak bed frame with its graceful curved head- and footboards. The pieces of Jack's furniture he had repaired were more beautiful than anything she owned at her old house. If she and Emma were to have a fresh start, why not include the furniture?

Doug rested the headboard against the wall and tucked his screwdriver into his back pocket. "What's up?"

"I've been skirting around the truth." Lily let her arms drop to her sides. "I was afraid to make you feel obligated to stay or make you think I only want you to stay because I need your help."

He held still, his face slack, his eyes wide, asking her to continue.

"But I need your help." She'd said it, not as eloquently as she'd hoped but with sincerity. What would be, would be. "Without you, I don't stand a chance of finishing this." With a deep breath and a slow exhale, she softened the rest of her body. "But I want you to stay even if I don't need you. And I don't care what anyone thinks."

He hadn't blinked, hands still clutching the headboard. The silence stretched from seconds into minutes. Was he wondering if she meant what she'd said? Or was he stuck in his own thoughts, not knowing what he wanted to do? The longer he took, the more hopeful she became. He wouldn't have to think if he'd firmly decided.

"I can't accept charity." He spoke as if he was negotiating a business transaction. He'd always said he would leave, eventually.

"You don't need charity. You might be the most capable person I've ever known."

He leaned the headboard against the wall. "I can only stay as long as I earn my keep."

"That's fine. So, you'll stay?"

"I'll stay as long as you need me."

"It's a deal." A smile that began in her heart forced tears of joy into the corners of her eyes. She wished she knew what haunted him, what made him a loner. But for the moment, she'd have to be satisfied that he'd agreed to stay for a while longer. "Do you want to hear my plans?"

"Sure. Give me a minute to finish this and I'll come downstairs."

The coffee maker was gurgling on the kitchen counter when Doug appeared. As they sat at the table, Lily felt at home. "I love being here."

"It's a long way from what it used to look like. The barn and the basement were even worse. I'd already cleaned them up before I knew . . ." His cheeks turned deep red. "That this wasn't Jack's place."

"Lucky for me." Lily poured the coffee and returned to the table. "This is what I'm thinking. After we get settled here, I want to freshen up some things in my soon-to-be old house. A few walls need a coat of paint and we can power wash the outside. While we're doing that, I'll find a contractor for the kitchen expansion here. Then if you agree, you can do the porch and the back steps and deck."

His head tilted, one eyebrow arched.

"What?" She stiffened.

"Nothing. I'm just thinking how very different you sound from the woman I first met."

For a second, his words swirled meaninglessly between her ears, but as they settled, she understood. She was different. She'd learned to take control, and she was far more capable than she'd ever imagined. "I guess I am, in a way. And I owe it to you."

He grinned. "I can take credit for some of it, but, Lily, you are a life force. No matter what happened, you kept pushing through."

She rolled the tension from her shoulders. "Thank you for everything." If only she could help him too.

Three weeks later, Greta listed the old house and a mere week after that, she called Lily with the good news. The house had sold to a cash buyer for a few thousand over the asking price. So far, so good. She and Emma were perfectly comfortable in their new home. Other than a few pangs of nostalgia, there'd been no surprises, no obstacles until she needed the deed to close the sale of her house, which Philip kept in his office.

In the nearly two months since she'd learned about the lien, she had slowly forgiven him. He was misguided but not intentionally mean. It also helped that his interference had done her a favor. If she'd gotten the loan, she wouldn't have moved. Financially and emotionally, she was far better off.

As she walked down the block to his office, the April sunshine on her face, she was about to find out how would he react.

"Good timing." He rose from his desk and motioned toward the sofa against the far wall. "I just finished with a client. Come sit."

The sitting area looked like a living room with upholstered furniture grouped around a coffee table on a silk rug. "I can't stay long. I just need the deed to my house. I believe you have it in the safe." The law office had destruction-proof document storage where Philip had kept Sam's and her documents for years.

He shook his head as if he hadn't heard right. "You mean the deed to the shop?"

"No. To my house, the one I live in." Or used to, but she didn't need to rub salt in the wound.

"Can I ask why you need the deed?" His eyes narrowed to slits.

He knew something was up. Not much point in procrastinating. He'd know soon enough. "I'm selling the house. Greta found me a cash buyer."

He seemed to shrink behind his desk and shook his head slowly. "Why didn't you tell me? Have you signed a contract yet?"

"Not yet, but there's not much to it. We both want to close as soon as possible. Greta knows what to do."

"I'm confused. Why are you selling your house?" As the truth dawned on him, he straightened. "Tell me you're not moving into the shop. It's not too late to back out if you haven't signed yet."

"I don't want to back out. Emma and I want to live there. We like it there."

He walked back to his desk, patting the papers strewn over the top as if he were looking for something. "Ever since the accident, you haven't thought straight. Don't do anything you can't undo."

"I'm not an addled old fool. Don't treat me like one." He could be beyond exasperating, but she'd been so worried about what he'd say to her she hadn't thought how keeping a secret this size would hurt him. "I know you mean well. But I want to do this. I enjoy being in town. And if you saw how happy Emma is, you'd understand."

Philip's nostrils flared. His bottom lip pushed out as if he didn't want to say the words lying on his tongue. "I'm shocked you would do this. What are you thinking?"

This conversation was going nowhere. Nothing she could do would make him understand, and nothing he could say would change her mind.

"Can I have the deed, please? If you want to review any papers for me, I'd be grateful." She didn't need him to but she didn't mind if it made him feel better.

He opened a safe the size of a closet on the opposite side of his office, rummaged through a file, and extracted the deed. "I hope you won't be sorry."

Lily softened. He really thought she'd regret it. If she thought he was making a major mistake, wouldn't she try to stop him? "I didn't mean to hurt your feelings. But I really want this and I don't want to argue about it."

"Is this why I haven't seen Emma in a while?"

"She's so excited. I didn't want her talking about it until it was done. There was no way she could have kept it secret."

He nodded as if to accept defeat.

Lily left, relieved it was over, but somehow sad too. She'd gotten what she'd wanted but she'd lost a few things on the way. Her relationship with Philip was one.

Chapter 25
Tea and a Basement

For the first few months after Sam died, Lily would wake expecting him to be beside her. When her fingers brushed against cold sheets instead of his warm body, her heart seized at the reminder she'd never touch him again.

Only a few weeks had passed since the last time she'd awakened in that bed in her home of forty years, but when she opened her eyes to the tall ceilings and cornices in her new bedroom, she wasn't unsettled. She didn't miss her old house as much as she thought she would, but no matter where she was, she'd never stop missing Sam.

Later that morning, Lily was in her kitchen, prepping for her guests when the doorbell rang. She wiped her hands on a kitchen towel, her heels echoing as she walked across the empty great room to answer the door. "Welcome, ladies, to my new home."

Trish and Maggie had come together. Robin would be along as soon as she finished at work.

"I'm always awed at how beautiful this place turned out," Trish said. "You have to let me plant flowers in front for you. Consider it my housewarming gift."

Only Trish could look at the three-foot-deep swath of rocks and weeds between the porch and the sidewalk and see possibilities. No doubt whatever she did would be stunning.

Russell's toenails tapped on the polished wood staircase as

he ran down, legs splaying when he hit the floor.

"Is this the stray you'd asked me about way back?" Maggie asked, bending over to greet the cheerful dog dancing at her feet.

"Yep."

"You never told me you took him in."

"He sort of joined us when we moved in. He and Emma are inseparable. He's been upstairs on her bed and would've stayed there until she came home if he didn't love company so much."

"What's his name?" Maggie stooped to pet him as he wriggled around her legs.

"Russell."

"Because he's a Jack Russell?"

"Not exactly. Suffice it to say, Emma named him, but I'll save that story for another time. How about a tour?"

Except for the empty great room, furniture made the shop look like a proper house. She'd put some of the pieces from her old living room into the small room at the back and the dining set into the front room on the other side of the staircase. Upstairs, Doug had completed three of the bedrooms with bedframes, armoires, dressers, and nightstands, all showcasing Jack's intricate woodworking skills.

"Jack made all of this stuff. Doug's been restoring it."

"The guy who helped you turn this place into a gem?" Trish stood in front of the full-length mirror on the armoire, fluffing her leaf-green hair. "Is he still around? Does he need extra work?"

"I doubt it. He's planning to leave once he's finished helping me, but I can ask him." Lily thought Doug would have no problem making a living as a handyman. If he had job offers, maybe he'd make a life in Fellowes Hollow. "Anyway, Robin should be here soon. Let's go downstairs."

In the hall, Maggie stopped at the only closed door. "What's in here?"

"The fourth bedroom." Lily opened the door. The room was full of unpacked boxes. "It's a storage room, I guess. Because I need space for a quilt shop, I have nowhere to put all my crystal and china or excess kitchen things. And there's most of Amanda's things." She pulled the door shut.

When Robin arrived, Lily poured tea and laid a platter with scones, jam, and pastries from the bakery in the center of the table. "So, here's the general plan."

Robin, Trish, and Maggie all slid to the edges of their seats.

"I'm saving the great room for the quilt shop. The bolts of fabric will go there. On the other side, where my dining set is, will be the cutting table, threads, notions, and books. The kitchen and small room at the back are our private spaces." Lily motioned down the hall behind the staircase that led to the back room. "I'm going to push the kitchen out a few feet, add a deck, and replace the steps to the backyard."

Trish looked out the window. "It's mostly asphalt."

"I have to keep some of it for parking, but I can tear out enough for a small garden and some grass. Emma and I need outdoor space. So does Russell."

"I have an idea," Trish said, her gaze riveted out the window. "We've been looking for a project we can document and show to Rez to get him to approve our plans for that park." Rez, the town manager, had his default answer stuck in the "no" position. "I'll talk to the garden club. This would be a perfect project to show him what we can do."

"That would be amazing." Lily had the best friends in the world. When they were around, she believed she could do anything.

"We all want to help you, Lily." Robin patted Lily's forearm.

"I'm counting on you ladies for moral support. Honestly, it's scary. I hope my big problems are over, but starting a business can't be easy, and I might fail."

"We won't let that happen." Maggie was always the defender of the downtrodden.

"No, we won't." Robin said, her voice firm, in her no-nonsense, authoritarian way. "We can work here, teach classes, and be your best customers. It's purely selfish, of course."

"I'll definitely do a silk ribbon class for you," Trish said.

Robin spread her hands, palms up to say, I told you so. "And I have a ton of fabric I'll never use that we can cut into fat quarters."

Maggie looked like she might start clapping with delight. "We can do appliqué classes and patchwork classes, but you have to do the hand-quilting class, Lily. No one has a stitch as fine as yours."

They were ready to dig in and help her get off the ground. Lily's eyes prickled with tears she couldn't let escape. Even happy tears could release the tidal wave she held inside.

When tea was over and Lily was alone, the helium seeped from her bubble of belief. It grew soft, hovering an inch from the floor. There were still so many things she didn't know, like how much each project was going to cost. She needed to have enough cash left to stock the store but she didn't even know what to buy or where to buy it.

Then there was the business side. Were there permits she needed? Taxes to pay? Her questions were endless, and when she thought about it, the oxygen seemed to leave the room. She had to not think ahead. One thing at a time. Her first priority was to make sure she and Emma were comfortable in their new home while leaving enough money to open the shop.

Later that night, after Emma was settled in bed, Lily went to the barn. Doug was chasing around sawdust with the hose of the shop vac. She waved her arms to catch his attention. Her ears rang in the silence after he turned it off.

Lily waited for him to pull out his earplugs. "I'm trying to figure out what everything will cost."

Doug offered her one of the restored chairs and pulled another one up for himself, then overturned a bucket, placing a yellow notepad and pencil on top. He'd already made a list.

"Since I can't use the bedrooms for classrooms anymore, I need to use the basement. I actually think it's better anyway. There's direct access from the parking in the back, but we'll need to turn the Pittsburgh potty into a proper bathroom, at least the toilet and the sink."

Doug made a note on his pad. "It's also easier to install all the electrical outlets you'll need. No walls need to be ripped up and repaired. But you need a licensed electrician. I'm not qualified for that."

He moved his pencil down a line. "Once that's done, I can clean and paint the walls and the floor. The new furnace keeps it reasonably warm, so you don't have to worry about that." The next item had several lines underneath it, written in Doug's neat but tiny handwriting. "The big thing is the bathroom. You'll need walls and a door and probably a new sink and faucet. That old one leaks no matter what I do. Then maybe hide the shower with a curtain and extend the wall to hide the laundry." He made a quick sketch of the room.

"Add a rug to that list or people's feet will freeze on the concrete floor." Lily had learned that after only a few minutes of folding clothes. "And I can hang quilts to cover the walls. Can you do the work?"

"Probably, since we don't need to move any plumbing, but one of Ed's guys also works for a kitchen remodeler. Maybe you can pay him to help me."

It took a second for Lily to process what he'd said. She was stuck on the idea that Doug had made a contact in town. That had to be a good thing.

"Lily?"

"Good idea." She refocused on Doug's pencil. "Do you have any idea what all this will cost? Maybe when I have the contractor here for the kitchen, they can do the electrical. And it might be easier to have them do the deck and steps too. Although, if I have to hold off on expanding the kitchen, I'd also wait to do the steps."

"But a bigger kitchen would make you happy." Doug lifted his gaze from the pad and smiled like he was looking at a Thanksgiving meal.

"It would." She was already daydreaming of a big table and people around it to enjoy that meal. "But not if it means I can't do the shop. If I end up not doing it, I can still expand the kitchen and add the steps as a consolation prize."

"Okay. I'll come up with some numbers for you." Doug gave her two thumbs up. "You're almost there. You can do this."

"We can do this." Lily swung her finger back and forth between them.

"I'm with you until it's done."

Chapter 26
The Whole Story

At the end of the last day of school, Emma and Lily joined Ruth and Walter in the cafe for a celebration. Two hours and as many brownies later, they walked back to the shop. Russell was waiting at the front door, trampling the mail that had come through the brass slot. While Emma was busy appeasing Russell, Lily picked it up.

One envelope seemed to pulsate, probably from the rise in her blood pressure as she read the return address. The Town of Fellowes Hollow. Her building permit had already been approved. The contractors' proposal was reasonable. The crews would be starting in a couple of days.

About a month had passed without issue. Maybe she'd jinxed herself by thinking all her troubles were behind her.

"Emma, why don't you take Russell out back? I think his leash is in the kitchen."

Russell understood every word and trotted off expectantly. Lily watched out the window until she saw them in the backyard, then tore open the letter.

She read the opening line twice before understanding dawned on her. It was a notice of illegal occupancy. What was illegal? Surely, she and Emma had every right to live there. Jack had.

She dropped into a chair and read further. The barn was not a dwelling, and the premises needed to be vacated. Someone had ratted out Doug. Could they make her kick him out? He didn't permanently live there. He didn't pay rent. If she chose to sleep in her barn, it was nobody's business. Certainly not the town's.

Lily resisted the urge to call Philip. She'd been doing fine without his help and didn't need or want his interference. Robin, though, might know something about it.

"Read it to me. Every word." Robin's voice was sharp with anger.

When Lily finished, Robin said, "It violates the zoning."

"But how would they know? Who would have said something?"

"I have no idea." Robin exhaled. "I promise you it wasn't me."

"No, of course not, and not Trish or Maggie, either. But only a handful of people know Doug's staying there, and none of them would tell the town."

"I can ask around, but it might be better not to draw attention to it."

Lily was about to ask what she should do when she heard Doug's tread on the basement steps. "I have to go," she whispered. "Thanks for your help." She ended the call and shoved the notice under the stack of junk mail.

"What's up?" Doug asked, a quizzical tilt to his head, paint splotches on his shirt.

"Nothing."

He crossed his arms. "It's not nothing. I only have to look at you to know that."

"Apparently, you aren't allowed to live in the barn." She handed him the letter. "The thing I want to know is who told the town."

Doug read the notice quickly, then handed it back to Lily. As usual, he wore an unreadable mask. "Don't worry about it. I'll move out. Russell doesn't need me and Jack doesn't know who I am, anyway."

"Please sit down. We've gotten through worse." She sounded

more confident than she felt. There was an easy fix, if he'd agree.

He sat opposite her, his knees apart, arms still crossed.

"What if you move into the basement?"

His face grew dark. The same expression he had when Lily first told him she was going to move into the shop. "Look, I agreed to stay in the barn. It's something completely different if I live in this house with Emma."

She had zero concerns about him being near Emma, but she knew he worried that some people in the town might not see it that way. "The basement. Not upstairs."

He closed his eyes as if praying for patience. "It doesn't matter. You can't control what people will think, and some will think the worst." His mouth curled as if he smelled something rotten. "A homeless guy living in a house with an eight-year-old?"

"You aren't homeless. You've been with me for nine months, working side by side the whole time. It's nobody's business."

"They'll make it their business." He unwound his arm and gripped the edge of the table, the tendons on the back of his hands protruding with the effort.

"Why? Did something like that happen to you before? No one I know would think that." Except Philip, but she kept that to herself. Lily was feeling as angry as he was. At the town and at him. Why did he have to be so hard on himself?

"No. Of course not."

"No one needs to know you're here. I'll tell the town you moved out. End of story."

"And if they ask where I went?"

"I'll tell them I didn't ask you. Because I'm not asking you. I'm telling you. Move into the basement. I'll put a deadbolt on the door if it makes you happy. Anyway, Emma will be staying with Heather and Ben a lot of the time. They're sending her to day camp for three weeks."

"And then she'll be back. And it's a good idea to install a

deadbolt, anyway." He released the table, his hands dropping into his lap. Softening perhaps? "And what are you going to do about the classroom if I'm down there?"

"One thing at a time, remember?"

He let out a long sigh, shaking his head. She hadn't convinced him. Maybe she could find him another place to stay.

"I'll talk to Becca. She hears lots of gossip. Maybe she heard something about this." Lily checked her watch and grabbed the notice. "She's probably still at the cafe cleaning up. Can you wait here with Emma?"

He looked like he was about to say no, but Lily cut him off. "I trust you completely."

Before Doug could argue, Emma and Russell came inside. He couldn't refuse with her standing there. Lily made her escape.

Becca looked up from the inside of the glass display case. Her mouth dropped open when Lily told her about the notice. "That sucks. Why does the town even care?"

Lily handed her the paper. "Someone must've complained. I guess they think it's unsafe. It probably has something to do with it not having plumbing or something." With each minute, Lily grew angrier. She'd hoped she was done with this kind of trouble, especially something so completely ridiculous and unnecessary. "What I want to know is who told them and why?"

Becca pursed her lips. "Who knew he was there?"

"You, your parents, my quilt friends, Philip . . ." As she listed the people, a lightbulb went on in her head. "The mailman. He could've mentioned something to Rez in passing. And you know Rez, Mr. Rule Follower. He probably told the Building Department to issue the order."

"Are you sure it wasn't Philip?" Becca ran her tongue over

her teeth as if his name tasted bad.

"Philip wouldn't do that. Besides, he's had plenty of opportunity. Why would he do it now?"

"No idea." Becca resumed wiping the glass. "What are you going to do?"

"Go home and try harder to convince Doug to move into the basement. If anyone asks, we just tell them he moved out. No need to explain where he went." Lily pinched the bridge of her nose. Her shock and anger waning, leaving her tired.

"You know what? I'm sick of him thinking he isn't good enough." Lily was yelling and toned it down. "There's nothing wrong with him. I should be able to let him stay in my house without him worrying about someone in the town sticking their nose in where it doesn't belong."

"It's disturbing to think someone complained. Maybe you're right and it came out in passing?"

"No matter who, I'd feel a lot better if I knew there was no malice in it." She'd feel better too if Doug agreed to move in.

With Emma away at camp most of the time and the kitchen under construction, Lily spent her days visiting quilt shops as far to the east as Pennsylvania Amish country and to the west into central Ohio. Most of the owners were women who had a love of quilting and started without having much more business experience than Lily had. They were extremely generous with helpful hints and essential information, giving Lily the names of their suppliers, and what kind of inventory and equipment to buy. Many had purchased existing businesses, but a few had started from scratch. They were encouraging and loved what they did. Lily was beginning to believe she, too, could be successful. So why was she lying sleepless in bed, her thoughts jumbled like scraps of fabric?

She threw off the covers for the third time, alternating

between being chilled by the recently installed air-conditioning and bouts of sweating. Her anxiety made no sense. The work was almost done. No unforeseen issues had arisen.

She got up and walked over the satiny floorboards to her bedroom window. Below her, Fellowes Run Road was deserted and dark except for the street lamps. How many of the shop owners were tucked up in bed, only to be lying awake worrying about their businesses or the uncertainty of the future?

As she headed downstairs, she pushed aside the habitual impulse to check on Emma. She wouldn't be home until the weekend.

In the kitchen, Lily flicked on the light under her new white cabinets, delighting that the room was functional again. She trod lightly on the cold ceramic tile floor as she put the kettle on. Doug's room was directly below her.

While he'd been working on the basement, he'd stalwartly refused to move into it. Still, Lily had him extend the wall hiding the laundry to create a storage room, knowing it had a small window and could also serve as a bedroom but left plenty of space for her classroom.

It had taken her the better part of two weeks for him to succumb to her cajoling. The air-conditioning helped to tempt him when the temperatures had risen into the nineties on the Fourth of July.

The kettle rumbled while the water heated. The kitchen didn't rival her old one, but the expansion had made it big enough to fit a dishwasher and her old dining room table. Good if she ever again had people to share in a large gathering. As she stared at the table, she imagined it full of people chatting, platters and bowls of food, and glasses clinking. It made her wonder, if she had her old life back with family and cooking, spending time with friends, and quilting, would she still want to run a business?

On the other hand, Trish's garden club had transformed the front with raised beds full of shrubs and annuals. Purple and pink petunias, bright spots of marigolds, and fluffy flower heads on chives. The front of the house couldn't be more inviting to quilters.

One thing at a time, she'd learned how to get a tax ID number and what permits and licenses she needed. All without advice from Philip. Since the deed incident, she'd mostly avoided him. Despite how far she'd come, accomplishing what she'd once thought impossible, he'd still tell her to not open a business.

Before the kettle could beep, she turned it off. In the silence, muffled sobs seeped from under the basement door. She'd caught Doug crying once before, but this was different. Heart-wrenching and tortured, like what came from her own misery when it escaped.

If it had been Sam or Amanda or Matt, she'd have run to comfort them, but she didn't have that kind of intimacy with Doug. The last thing she wanted was to embarrass him.

In her haste to take her tea upstairs, she accidentally knocked the cup against the kettle. Boiling water sloshed over her hand. The cup dropped, smashed against the edge of the countertop, and crashed on the floor, scalding her bare feet. She stifled her cry with her fist, hoping against all probability that she hadn't aroused Doug.

Two seconds later, he banged on the basement door. "Lily, are you okay?"

"I'm okay. I just dropped my tea cup. I didn't mean to wake you."

"Unlock the door."

Carefully, stepping over puddles and shards, Lily slid the bolt. Doug emerged wearing shorts, a t-shirt, and flip-flops. His eyes scanned her, frantically roaming from head to toe, looking for injuries.

"Your feet. You're not wearing shoes." Doug was back in control. No stress. No emotion. A matter-of-fact assessment. "Step away. Let me clean this."

"I was having trouble sleeping," she said, backing into a chair and lifting her feet off the floor. "I made a cup of tea." She needed to explain, excuse her presence in what felt like an invasion of his privacy. "And then dropped it."

He wrapped ice cubes in a kitchen towel. "Hold this on the burn."

Only when the ice soothed the pain did she realize her foot hurt. "I'm sorry I woke you up."

"You didn't." Doug grabbed the broom from between the refrigerator and the wall, his posture softening, the soldier leaving, the man returning.

She'd always known he hardly slept. That's how he got so much done. He needed to be busy. She assumed to ward off the visions or voices in his head or whatever the deep-hidden thing was that made him separate from the rest of the world.

"I was having chamomile. Can I make you a cup too? I promise not to drop it."

"You stay there. I'll make it."

A few minutes later, two steaming mugs were safely ensconced on the table. He looked haggard and sad bent over his tea. He'd been getting more melancholy over the last few weeks. The work would be done soon. She'd run out of ideas to keep him around.

There was nothing to lose by asking him about his life. If she could understand, maybe she could help. "Can I ask you something? You don't have to answer."

"Sure." He sounded like he meant it, even if he didn't lift his head.

"What's wrong? I heard you . . ." What word should she use? Crying? "I heard you before you came upstairs."

"I have nightmares."

"From your time in the army?"

"Yes, partly." He covered his face with his hands. "They were better but got worse after those firecrackers."

A few days before the Fourth of July, there had been a

few rounds of rapid firecracker explosions, probably set off by overly enthusiastic teenagers. Maybe Doug had agreed to move inside hoping he'd bear the holiday better in a proper house in a proper bed.

"Do you want to talk about it?" If only he opened up, shared his burden, he might siphon off some of his pain.

"I can't."

They sat in silence for a few minutes. Lily thought she should go back to bed. Leave him be. When she lowered her feet to the floor, he spoke.

"You'd hate me if you knew."

Hate him? That wasn't possible. "War is horrible." How could Doug, so good, generous, kind, have something so awful he'd think she'd hate him? "Maybe you could talk to someone, a professional. They must have people who specialize in these things at the VA."

His hands trembled. It wasn't her place to hug him and tell him everything would be okay. Words like that are hollow, anyway. She had no idea if it would be okay. "I doubt there is anything you could tell me that would make me hate you. I don't know what it's like to be in war, but I know horrific things happen."

He didn't meet her eyes, but he spoke. "I came here to tell Jack what happened, but I can't. He thinks I'm Billy. It should be Billy here with him. Not me. It should have been me who died." His chin quivered, his lips pressed so tightly together they disappeared.

She looked away as if she'd walked in on him undressing. Her eyes welled, but she stayed silent, waiting to let him continue or not.

"It's my fault Billy died." Doug's chest heaved as if the nightmare inside him would tear him open. "We were on patrol. Something dropped from the building. I froze. I remember Billy's arms." Doug crossed his arms, squeezing his biceps, his knuckles whitening, his eyes unfocused, staring at the wall. "He threw me down. Then the explosion. He landed on me. I felt nothing. Everything went silent. I think I shouted, but Billy didn't answer me. I pushed him off, and the world turned red. Bright red. I couldn't do anything for him." Doug shuddered and his face contorted in pain. "His eyes. I remember his eyes. He was gone."

Lily realized her shock was showing on her face and relaxed her expression. "I'm sorry." Her words were lame in light of what he'd revealed and how much it so obviously had cost him.

"You don't know the worst." He pressed the heels of his hands to his eyes, rocking in his chair.

How could it get worse? What this man had been through was unthinkable.

"For a second . . ." He clawed at his face. "I felt happy, lucky I wasn't dead. Billy had saved me and I was glad I wasn't dead."

She had no words for him. How could anyone? But she didn't want him to think she condemned him. "I don't dare tell you anything. I have no experience that can compare. My heart breaks for you."

"Don't feel sorry for me," he snapped, his words like spears. "I don't deserve it."

Lily drew back. She'd seen him angry, but never venomous. She did feel sorry for him. She'd have to be encased in a glacier not to but what could she say that would help? Thinking back to Emma after the accident, Lily felt helpless, inadequate. All she had then were her love and intuition, and that still was all she had. Maybe she would drive him away, but she spoke the only truth she knew.

"I don't know how to comfort you. Even if I did, I doubt you'd let me. But you can't frighten me away. Use my truck. Go to the VA and get help. You can't keep punishing yourself. You are too good. You can belong somewhere. And if you ask me, you belong here." She'd said it. He needed to know as much as he condemned himself, she didn't condemn him at all.

"I know you didn't get to tell Jack the truth, but from what I hear, you made an old and addled man very happy with your visits, despite the pain it caused you. In my book, that is a far better apology than any words you could have spoken."

"Stop." He reared, his chair skittering behind him. "I don't deserve this. I don't deserve anything."

Lily's dragon lit, its dormant flames tickling her lungs. She fired back at him.

"Sit down, Doug Fisher. Not everything is about you. I deserve you. Emma deserves you. We've been together, working side by side for the better part of a year. You're family now. I hope you never leave." It took every muscle in her body to keep her in her chair. She wasn't sure if she wanted to put a reassuring hand on his shoulder or smack some sense into him.

His eyes appeared to focus as if he left his memories and returned to the room. He looked straight at her. "You know I stayed because you needed me, not because I needed a place to stay."

"I know that. And I love you for it." The words were out there, and if they weren't enough, if he chose to spend his life punishing himself, she had no way to stop him. She closed her eyes in a silent prayer for him.

When she opened them, he was still there.

Chapter 27
Peace Offering

"That's it," Doug said. He stepped away from the last grouping of shelves, admiring his work.

On the back wall of the great room, he'd installed fabric-bolt-sized bookcases, matching the color and the trim to the rest of the room so they looked as if they'd always been there. In the center of the floor were several moveable cases, so Lily could create displays and groupings. All made from Jack's stash of oak and maple, their golden finishes gleaming.

"They're beautiful." They'd be even more so when stacked with colorful calicoes and batiks. Her heart swelled with gratitude, but she resisted the urge to hug him. Since the night he'd confessed the story of Billy's death, a closeness had grown between them like they shared a secret or a mission. But not quite close enough for physical affection.

He'd taken her advice and attended a group therapy session at the VA in Pittsburgh. He also had an upcoming appointment with a therapist. It looked like it was helping him. On his last few visits to Jack, he hadn't returned hunched over with defeat dripping off his face.

"I have enough cherry left to build a cutting table, but first you need to make sure you're happy with the dimensions."

Russell ran down the stairs and skidded to a halt at the front door. "I guess Emma's home." Lily peeked out the window at an afternoon of summer sunshine, watching as Emma climbed out of Ben's sedan. Camp was over and Emma was back home full time.

Ruth and Walter were waiting on the sidewalk as promised. Emma fell into their hugs. Walter smiled down at her, his lips moving. Emma nodded furiously, grabbed his hand, and led him into the cafe.

Lily's turn would have to wait, but she didn't mind. Emma was about to get a brownie and her not-to-be-missed chess lesson with Walter.

"She'll be having fun for a while," Doug said.

"No doubt there's a mutual love society going on there. Becca says Emma is the grandchild she never gave them."

"Sounds like Becca." Doug tipped his head toward the backyard. "I'll be in the barn. Enjoy your quilting friends." He always stayed out of sight whenever anyone came to visit.

Lily checked her watch. They'd be arriving any minute.

"C'mon, Russell." Lily tried to coax him to follow her into the kitchen, but he wouldn't budge. "If you don't come with me, there'll be no cheese snacks for you."

He sat quivering, his gaze locked on the door. A second later, it flew open, banging against the door stopper.

"Gammy, I'm home." Emma made enough noise that Lily could've been in the basement with the washer running and no announcement would've been necessary.

"I can see that." While Lily waited for Emma to satisfy Russell, Walter and Ruth came up the porch steps, each carrying a box.

"Becca's getting that afternoon tea crowd again, so we thought we shouldn't take up one of her tables," Walter said. "Emma thought we could use your back room." He pulled the box out from under his arm. "She doesn't want to miss her chess lesson."

Emma squinted one eye at Walter. "It's a good idea, and Russell is happy because he can be with us."

"That part I can't argue with," Lily said. Russell was always happy when Emma was nearby. Likewise, Emma was happy when Ruth and Walter were around. She still had moments, especially if she was tired, when her face grew long, her eyes unfocused, and she seemed to lack the ability to find pleasure in anything. A complete healing might never happen, but at least she found joy sometimes.

Wasn't it the same for Lily? Anytime she wasn't planning or working, her pain and anger seeped out of their hiding place, pervading every cell in her body until she felt she couldn't stand it any longer. Especially at night. In this respect, she, Doug, and Emma were alike.

"You're always welcome to be here, but are you sure you want to?" Lily looked from Walter to Ruth. "You've done so much already."

"We're very sure." Ruth put her hand on Lily's forearm. "This is our time, right, Emma?"

Emma nodded.

"Becca didn't send us empty-handed though." Ruth handed Lily the other box. "Brownies."

"Walter, can you have one today?" Emma asked.

Ruth had taken firm control over his diet, trying to get him to drop a few pounds. He rubbed his paunch. "It's not as much as it used to be, but we have to ask the boss."

"It's a special occasion," Ruth said. "We have our Emma back. But not more than one."

Lily grabbed the leash from the hook by the door. "Emma, take Russell for a walk while I get everything ready."

Ruth followed Lily to the kitchen. Walter left with Emma.

"It's night and day how she's changed, Lily."

"You and Walter get the credit for that." Their love was Emma's best medicine.

"It's not only us. You're steadfast for her. She never has to worry that she's alone in the world. And the move to the shop and getting that dog. I think he makes her happier than anything."

"I wish she was confident enough to stop wearing a hat." For summer, Ruth had crocheted a few with an open stitch. Not that Emma needed them anymore. Her bald spot had filled in, the shorter hairs blending with the longer ones. "And I'd hoped she'd make friends at camp. Her birthday is coming up. I can't exactly make her a party if she doesn't have friends to invite."

Lily retrieved a platter from a lower cabinet and handed it to Ruth.

"Then just do family." Ruth didn't sound concerned as she stacked brownies.

"I guess I'll have to. By the way, my quilting friends should be here any moment. You and Walter are welcome to join us."

"I wouldn't want to intrude. I have my knitting. I'll be happy back there with the chess players."

"Nonsense. And we certainly have enough brownies. You probably already know Trish, the one with hair that's never the same color."

"The gardener? She did some work for our old neighbor. Very creative."

"She's as colorful as her flowers," Lily said. "You'll like her."

Lily laid everything on her dining table. It fit perfectly in her kitchen with plenty of room for all eight of them. If she invited everyone for Emma's birthday, she'd even be able to squeeze in Doug, Vicki, and Becca.

Things were definitely looking up, but there were still a few unsettled pieces. She wouldn't order anything for the shop until after the birthday party. Time to think. Time to be sure.

Trish, Maggie, and Robin had driven together and parked in the back, taking the newly completed steps up to the deck.

Trish burst into the kitchen first. "It's a good thing we could park in the back because there is nowhere on the street. Someone has got to get through to Rez that this town needs more parking. If The Village didn't run that shuttle bus, it would be completely impossible."

The other two filed in and Lily introduced them to Ruth.

"Walter and I used to be the only ones in our daughter's cafe in the afternoon. Now we had to come here because she needs all her tables."

"Progress," Robin said. "It's good for the town's tax revenues. There's money for a parking lot."

"It was good for this kitchen too," Maggie said. "It turned out great. And what a view you have out the window."

"Never mind that now." Robin hung her purse on the back of a chair. "Show me the shelves." She led them single file into the great room.

Trish ran her hand over the polished top of one of the moveable cases. "Every time I come here, this place gets better and better. Did Doug make these? They're gorgeous."

"He did. He's also making me a cutting table from cherry wood."

"Nice friend," Trish said. "I want a built-in entertainment center and I keep procrastinating because I hated going through the work when I did my kitchen."

"It's been a mess with the construction, but the inside is done now. I can finally sit without having to clean a layer of dust first."

"I'd love to hire your guy for my entertainment center. Do you have a number for him?"

One of Robin's eyebrows shot up. Since Lily had received the notice, she'd been avoiding people, mostly because she was busy with the construction and quilt shop visits, but also because, in deference to Doug's concerns, she didn't want to advertise that he was living in the basement. Robin and Becca were the only two people who knew.

Lily could have lied, but she was tired of keeping secrets from her friends. "He lives in the basement now."

Ruth perked up. "I know who you're talking about." She grinned like she knew the answer to the final *Jeopardy* question. "He's a tall guy, maybe forty, with dark hair, right? He sometimes stops at Becca's in the afternoon, then he visits Jack at The Village. My knitting students all talk about him. How he's such a dutiful son, and when they're not thinking about that, they're trying to figure out who they can fix him up with."

"When are we having brownies?" Emma joined them, rubbing her tummy. "I'm starving."

"Okay, go get Walter. Everyone back to the kitchen."

Once everyone was served, Maggie, who could be shy around people she didn't know, had no trouble gushing about the shop in front of Ruth and Walter. "I can't wait until it's open. I'll have to come here just to hang out and ogle the fabrics."

Walter, who'd sat next to Emma and hadn't said a thing, piped up. "The knitting ladies all wish there was a yarn shop in town too."

"Maybe I should do a few starter quilting lessons there." Lily hadn't considered it before, but Ruth had gathered fifteen knitters in no time. All ages, both residents and workers at The Village. "Assuming I actually get the thing going."

"Of course, you will," Maggie said. "We could do beginner classes for handwork, like appliqué or quilting."

"But anything large or that needs a sewing machine or a rotary cutter and mat, we'd have to do here," Lily said.

"Lily?" Robin shifted in her chair. "If he lives in your basement, how are you going to hold classes there?"

"There's a bathroom and a little bedroom."

"Are you sure it's okay to have him here?" Maggie's lips pursed with worry.

"I trust him completely."

"Doug would never hurt me." Emma's eyebrows scrunched together, nearly touching each other.

They all seemed to have forgotten she was there. She wiped brownie crumbs and a milk mustache with her napkin. "He gave me Russell." The dog barked at the sound of his name.

"Out of the mouths of babes," Lily said. She had no doubt, not even a wisp, that Doug would protect her, Emma, and Russell with his life. Not that it would ever come to that.

"Walter," Lily said, "I think Russell needs to go out again. Can you go with Emma?"

The dog was more than compliant, but Emma dragged her feet. Once they were gone, Lily continued.

"That's not what worries me. He moved in because someone told the town he was illegally occupying my barn. What do you think people would say if they found out he lived inside the house? He thinks the pitchfork brigade would come for him."

"How will anyone know? We're your best friends," Robin said and waved around the table, "and we didn't know."

Trish had a suspicious glint in her eye. "Who knew he was in your barn?"

"Becca and Vicki. The mailman. You ladies and Philip. I suspect the mailman might've said something in passing."

"It was Philip," Maggie said, her tongue clicking with distaste.

Nods went around the table like a chorus line.

"He wouldn't." She hated having to defend Philip all the time. "I know he has rough edges and he can be impolite, but he wouldn't hurt me."

"He also doesn't want you to have the shop," Robin said.

"As he tells me that every chance he gets." She'd stopped giving him many chances. But was she really certain it wasn't him? "Why would he turn in Doug?"

"I'm sorry to say, but you are blind where Philip is concerned." Trish tapped her lips with two fingers. "He wants to marry you."

"Doug isn't competition." A wholly disgusting thought. "I'm old enough to be his mother."

"Not like that, silly. He wants your attention. He doesn't want to share you with the shop or with Doug, and if Doug makes the shop possible, that's a double reason to get rid of him." Trish pushed her plate forward. Her point made.

"He only doesn't want me to have the shop because he thinks I'm making my life harder. And let's face it, he's not wrong."

"He's a widower. He wants a wife." Robin stood and gathered plates. "We need men to fix things. They need women to live. There are exceptions, of course."

"You're all crazy. Philip isn't interested in me that way." So she said, but she really wasn't sure.

"Philip aside," Robin said, "if you trust Doug, then I trust him."

"I agree," Trish said.

Lily looked at Ruth. "Do you think there's a problem with Doug living in the basement?" She shook her head. "No. Emma's very fond of him," Ruth said.

"It's only for a little while longer, anyway. Once the work is done, he'll leave."

"I hope he'll stick around to do my entertainment center."

"I can think of several people who might want him to do a job for them," Robin said. "We can find him work if he needs it."

"We can ask him. He's in the barn. I'll see if he wants to come in."

Doug was at his workbench with paper and pencil, drawing plans for the cutting table when Lily asked him to come upstairs. "Are you sure?"

"I'm very sure. This hiding stuff is stupid. These people are my friends. So are you. It's time. And one of them wants to hire you if you're interested."

Doug seemed larger with the kitchen crowded with people, but he pulled up a chair, his hands folded on the table. Maggie pushed the brownies toward him.

After introductions, Doug said to Ruth, "I know you. You're Becca's mom."

"She speaks very highly of you. You take her trash out. She hates that job."

He laughed, his posture relaxing. "It's nice to know I'm good for something."

"The young women at The Village think so too. The staff in particular."

A blush spread across Doug's cheeks, making a lump form in Lily's throat. He was a tender man. No wonder he couldn't recover from what had happened to Billy.

The quilt ladies took turns raving about the transformation of the shop. Trish explained what she was looking for in an entertainment center.

Doug agreed to think about it. "When can I come by to take a look?"

The doorbell rang. Lily and Doug exchanged glances.

"I guess I'd better get that." As Lily walked toward the front door, she heard Doug saying goodbye before Russell started barking.

"Philip?" Lily was surprised to see him. He usually called or texted. She picked up Russell to quiet him. "The quilt ladies are here."

"I stopped by because you dodge my calls."

"It's been crazy here with all the work. Come in. My friends are here. I can make you a fresh cup of coffee."

Ruth and Walter had taken Emma to the back room. When Lily put Russell down, he went straight there.

"I think you all know Philip."

"We were just talking about how much the town has changed since The Village opened. Are you getting more clients too? It's a windfall for the town." Robin was doing a great job of changing to a safe subject. "We're planning what we want to tell Rez he should do with the money. So far, we have parking and a park. What do you think?"

"I think we need to add a few restaurants. Every time I go to the diner, I have to wait."

"It'll certainly be good for Lily's quilt shop," Maggie added. For a shy, soft-hearted animal rescuer, she could throw a good barb.

"Well, ladies." Trish stood. "I need to get home and start on dinner."

When they were gone, Lily found Philip standing by the back room, watching Walter and Emma play chess.

"They've really helped her. Do you think she's recovered?"

He'd whispered, but Lily took him to the kitchen to answer. "She's much better. Thank you."

"What about you? We hardly talk anymore." He was looking at his hands, not her.

What did he expect? He'd made his opinions clear. "Like I said, I've been busy."

"I see you're comfortable here." He glanced around the kitchen and the leftovers on the table. "And I guess with all that shelving, you're going forward with the shop."

"I need something to do. I don't care if it's hard." He didn't need to know she was procrastinating.

"I understand." He took Lily's hand. "You don't have to shut me out. I miss you. I was hoping we could have dinner tonight."

The two sides of Philip. She hadn't meant to hurt him, but maybe after seeing how far she'd come, he'd have a change of heart. "Emma's back. Is Lego pizza okay?"

"Sure. By the way, when did you get a dog?"

"He was a stray. He and Emma are inseparable."

There was a lot she'd kept from him. It took mental energy to avoid him. What harm could come from trying to repair the relationship?

<h1 style="text-align:center">Chapter 28</h1>
<h1 style="text-align:center">Birthday Party</h1>

With Emma home all day, Lily needed Ruth and Walter to keep her for a while, so she could plan and prepare for the birthday party. But afternoons in the cafe had become popular. Shuttle loads of people, mostly older women, were dropped off regularly. Only in the late morning were tables available.

Emma dragged Lily to the cafe door in a hurry to get to Walter who had promised to read a book to her. When they entered, greeted by the familiar sweet smells, Lily handed her a ten-dollar bill and told her to order the usual. Becca knew to keep Emma engaged for a while, so Lily could discuss plans with Ruth.

"I have to make a pancake dinner because that's what the birthday girl wants. I'll have a few other things, so Walter can have something different." Of course, Walter would want pancakes. The question was really whether Ruth would approve.

"Special occasion for our girl turning nine, right, Walter?" He was entranced in his book and didn't respond to his name.

"What's he reading?" It was wrapped in brown paper, reminding Lily of the old days in grade school.

Ruth's smile betrayed her amusement. "Harry Potter. He wants to make sure it's a good choice for Emma."

"Looks like it's a good choice for him," Lily said. "But why the cover?"

"He's worried what people will think."

"He needn't be. We're all kids at heart. Speaking of which, let me tell you about the party. Vicki's coming but wants to surprise Emma, so let's not mention it. Then there are the two of you and Becca. Doug and Russell, and I'm going to ask Philip." Lily paused, expecting a sour face from Ruth, but only saw a slight curl to her lip. "We had a little tête-à-tête. He says he understands why the shop is important to me. He's going to have to accept Doug too."

"So, Doug is planning to stick around?"

"I wouldn't say that, but he agreed to do Trish's job, and he's going to help me set up the shop after I order everything. He'll be around for at least a little longer."

"I've noticed his step appears a little lighter when he comes in here." Ruth was in counselor mode, her voice modulating with a slight staccato, enunciating each letter of her words.

It wasn't Lily's place to discuss Doug's affairs, but she thought she'd be safe sharing a few things. "I think so too. Ever since you told him what the people at The Village think. Especially the women. Wouldn't it be nice if he could find someone special?"

"There's no shortage of women with big hearts working there," Ruth said. "They're a special breed to do the work they do. Some of it is exceptionally sad."

"You'd need to have a big heart." Doug had a big heart if he could let himself use it. He was making progress, though. Lily looked toward the table where he'd sat the first time she'd seen him, eating his grilled cheese, silent and brooding. He'd seldom smiled then. Lately, he smiled and even laughed, regularly. "Back to Emma though. Do you think she'll be okay having a party with just us? No friends?"

"Relax. I know it's worrisome she didn't make any friends at school or at camp. But she's stopped pulling her hair. She can concentrate on schoolwork. And she isn't glum all the time."

Lily squeezed Ruth's hand. "And she will be with her favorite people on earth. Mine too."

"Never forget, it's a two-way street."

"Walter." Emma's voice got his attention. "Becca said she's making a fresh pot of coffee for you." Emma was gripping a small tray with two hands, then slid it onto the table. Ruth and Lily grabbed their cups. "And I got milk and a pumpkin brownie. Becca said they're nutritions."

"Nutritious," Walter corrected. "So, I guess that means it's okay for me to have one." He looked hopefully at Ruth.

"I can share with you, Walter." Emma smiled, revealing a gap where she'd lost another tooth.

Lily felt a pang of melancholy. Amanda and Matt would miss so much of Emma growing up. Soon it would be a whole precious year.

On the day of the party, Ruth took Emma to the library and Vicki arrived early to help Lily set up. Russell gave up moping on Emma's bed in her absence and came down the stairs to say hello.

"One second, boy. My hands are full." Vicki placed a large rectangular box on the kitchen table, then scratched Russell behind his ears, making his back leg kick. "Silly dog."

"I texted Doug to come take him," Lily said, "so he won't be underfoot."

"Doug has a phone? He's turning back into a real person."

Lily held up crossed fingers on both her hands.

"Check this out." Vicki opened the box. Inside was a half-sheet cake, bordered with yellow roses and green leaves. On one side was an edible photo of Emma and Russell. On the other side, it read: Happy Birthday Emma and Russell. Emma had decided they could share a birthday and that he was turning six years old. The vet agreed it was a good guess.

"It's gorgeous. Thank you for bringing it."

"My pleasure. Anything for my little niece." She closed the box, rubbed her hands together, taking in the room around her. "Amanda would be proud of what you've done here." As soon as the words left her mouth, her eyes widened with remorse. "I'm sorry. We shouldn't think of anything sad today."

"Don't be sorry. She's always on my mind. She's in every nook and cranny of this house. I hope I've made her proud." Lily's eyes burned with tears. "But let's not say more about it unless Emma brings it up."

Vicki nodded. "It's okay to be sad, Lily."

"I know, but tonight, I have all the living people I love most around me to celebrate my darling granddaughter turning nine. For one night, I want to focus on what I have, not what's missing. And maybe Emma can do that too."

The clumping of footsteps coming from the basement meant one thing, Doug had arrived. "Hey, Vicki."

"I have to tell you, those shelves look like they've been here since the house was built. Someday when I leave my apartment and get a house, can I hire you?"

"Stand in line." Doug grinned. "Trish knows two other people who may want to hire me."

"That's fantastic," Lily said. Happy for him and happy he was making a life. "We also have to plan how to set up the classroom downstairs, so I can order folding tables and chairs."

"Why don't we go take a look?" Vicki said.

"I can't. I have to get a start on dinner, but Doug can show you."

He swiped his hand to usher Vicki toward the steps.

Lily had the table set, the fruit cut up, pancake batter ready to go, and a quiche keeping warm in the oven, but Vicki and Doug were still in the basement. Becca would be closing up soon. It was nearly party time.

When she opened the door to call them upstairs, she heard them talking, not loud enough to make out what they were saying, but they didn't sound as though they were talking about the basement. She made a cup of tea and sat to give them a few last minutes together before calling them upstairs.

"Oh, sorry," Vicki said. "We got carried away. I should've helped."

"It's fine. There wasn't much to do." It was more than fine if they became friends.

"After we're done here, I'm going to help Doug move all the boxes that are upstairs in that spare room to the basement."

"This is a surprise." Lily looked from one to the other wondering how this had come up.

"You can't be lugging everything from a storage room upstairs every time you want to have a class. And let's face it, with only a tiny window, it's not a great bedroom."

"Vicki convinced me it's okay to move upstairs," Doug said. And for a second time, Lily saw a pinkish glow on his cheeks, while her own cheeks rose with a smile.

Lily had been bugging him to do it. Despite needing the basement for classes, and the charley-horses in her thighs from carrying things up and down, she wanted him to feel like a member of the family. "I'm very glad to hear it. You belong upstairs and the storage room belongs downstairs." This day was turning into one of the best days she'd had in a very long time.

"I want to pay rent though. I have some income now."

"Not yet. You still have work to do here. And that was our deal."

"Was our deal. Now, I use your truck, your tools, your electricity, and water. It's only fair."

"I agree, and when you have regular work, you can pay rent."

Doug crossed the room in three steps and pulled Lily into a hug. His chin brushed the top of her head.

"You're making me cry." She swiped under her eyes with

her thumbs. "Happy tears. I promise." But any tears had the potential to crack her dam. She certainly couldn't let Emma see her crying on her birthday. She had to be feeling her loss heavily too.

Philip was the last to show up. He drew back in surprise when he saw Doug but quickly recovered his composure. If he accepted Doug, the day, already wonderful, would push the barriers of belief.

At Emma's insistence, she opened the gifts while they ate, declaring each gift the best thing she ever got. Vicki had bought her a fabric marker and stencil set, so she could color her own quilt patches or t-shirts. Ruth and Walter gave her knitting needles, yarn, and a boxed set of Harry Potter books. Doug bought her a compass and a whistle, so she'd never get lost, and was the only one to remember Russell with a reflective collar and leash. Even Philip had chosen something she loved, a desk lamp that doubled as a night-light and projected stars onto the ceiling.

"Here's my present to you." Lily handed her a small box. "It's something for you to cherish forever."

Emma carefully unwrapped the tiny box, flipped it open, and gasped. She took out the heart-shaped ruby ring and slid it on her finger.

"We can get it sized if we need to. Rubies are for July birthdays."

Emma held her hand out for everyone to admire the lively red stone on a gold band.

"This is the most special thing I ever had." She clasped her ringed hand and held it to her heart.

"I love you, Emma."

"I love you, Gammy." She climbed into Lily's lap, resting her head against Lily's shoulder.

Everyone had to be thinking about Amanda and Matt. Vicki's eyes were glistening. Doug had his head down, even Philip was affected.

"I'm very glad we live here now. And I'm glad Doug and Russell are here too." Emma climbed down and hugged Vicki. "And soon you'll move here too."

"I wish, Emma. Maybe someday."

"You know what else I want?"

"What?" Vicki asked.

Lily was glad Vicki spoke because she couldn't get words past the lump in her throat.

"I want to get my hair cut short like yours, Auntie Vic."

"If your grandma agrees, I'll take you tomorrow."

"I agree. I think you'll look great in short hair." And maybe she'd give up the hats.

"What about you, Lily?" Vicki asked. "You were thinking of cutting your hair last year. Want to make it a girls' day out?"

"You know what?" Lily fingered her ponytail. She hadn't had a trim in a while and it was halfway down her back. "Not everything has to change. My ponytail is like an old friend. I'm keeping it."

Later that evening, after Emma dropped into a peaceful sleep, Doug went to putter in the barn. Lily and Vicki sipped cups of chamomile, side by side on the sofa, their feet propped on the coffee table.

"That was a very successful party," Vicki said.

"I felt like I had a family again. I should go to sleep now so nothing can spoil this day."

"Hey, if Philip didn't spoil it, nothing's going to happen."

"He seems to have accepted that I'm going to have the shop and that Doug is staying. Although he might sing a different tune when he finds out Doug is living in the house."

"Easy answer to that one. Don't tell him."

"Speaking of telling people things. What did you say to

get Doug to move upstairs? He kept telling me he wouldn't."

"We talked about a lot of things. He told me about Billy and that he's been going for help at the VA. He said he's feeling better." She crossed one of her long legs over the other. "I told him he should stay here, that Fellowes Hollow is a great town."

"None of those arguments worked for me. You have a magical effect on him."

"Not really. He changed his mind when I told him it would make you happy."

He'd done it for her. And he'd hugged her earlier. Lily didn't want to get her hopes up, but maybe Doug was forming an attachment.

Vicki had a faraway look. "He's a gentle soul. I think your kindness saved his life. You believed in him when he had given up on himself, and no one in the world cared."

"We needed each other, but I'm not sure he thinks he deserves to be loved."

"He deserves it. We all do. Me too. I'm thirty-nine." She took her legs off the table and faced Lily. "I keep waiting until I find a partner to settle down with. I can't wait forever. I want a house. I want children. I want to live in a community like this. I'm thinking I might do what Amanda did and work from home. It's easy enough to go to Pittsburgh when I need to."

"You can stay in my guest room and give it a test run."

"I couldn't prevail on you."

"Now you sound like Doug. It's not prevailing on me. It's helping me. I have a huge hole I need to fill." Lily patted her chest. "I have four bedrooms and I'd be delighted to have your company. So would Emma. But if it makes you feel better, remember you promised to help with promotion when I open the shop, so it's not a one-way street."

Could it be that everything she wanted was happening? Emma recovering. Vicki coming. Doug sticking around. And she was about to complete Amanda's dream. She'd open the quilt shop.

Chapter 29
Taxes

Lily tipped back on one of the swiveling sling chairs around the table on her deck. She'd found them at a garage sale, added an umbrella, and was enjoying Robin's company as her first outdoor guest.

"I'm nearly there." With the contractors gone, the work was complete. All Lily had left to do was start a business. The idea set her nerve ends buzzing, making her squirm with a mixture of fear and excitement.

She'd planned a celebratory lunch with the quilt ladies. While she'd been working on the preparations, she'd been fine. Her anxiety rose when Robin came early to review the paperwork for licenses and permits, making sure Lily had everything she needed for her next step, placing her order for inventory and equipment. "I suppose I could wait to do this. It doesn't have to be now."

"You worry too much. Like most things, it seems scary when you don't know what or how, but once you learn, it isn't really that complicated."

"I just want to be sure I'm not forgetting anything important." She also intended to help Doug with his business if he kept accepting handyman jobs. "I'm hiring Becca's accountant and lawyer. She likes them both and thinks they're reasonable."

"Not Philip?"

"No. He's making amends, though. He hasn't mentioned Doug and he's being very attentive to Emma."

"He's buttering you up, you know."

Lily was beginning to think everyone was right about Philip's intentions, but they hadn't seen what her relationship with him had been like before the accident. He hadn't changed much. He'd always looked after her.

When Trish and Maggie arrived, Lily showed them the photos she'd taken of the backyard before the work, with the decrepit steps and broken asphalt. "Amazing how things have changed, right?" At the bottom of the driveway, there was a small, freshly paved parking area. The rest was cleared of debris, ready for Trish and her gang to begin their project. "I'll email these to you. You can document the rest yourself."

"I can show you the plans," Trish said.

"I'd love to see them but I trust you completely. Anyway, you're doing this for free, so the least I can do is let you create what you think is best to win your park contract."

"It's so lovely back here." Maggie inhaled deeply. "The barn makes it quaint, like a quilt shop belongs here."

Lily drew back her shoulders, her confidence returning. It really had changed. She and Doug had cleaned up the undergrowth at the bottom of the hill, dragging out the dead wood and cutting back the vines. She was proud of what they'd accomplished. "The three of you were my best encouragement."

"That was easy. You were determined from the beginning and never gave up," Maggie said. "I'm impressed."

"A few times, I came close, but I can't relax yet. I have just enough money left to get started as long as nothing unforeseen happens." She crossed her fingers and folded her hands over her heart. "I think I'll be able to open in the fall."

"Perfect time of the year. We all seem to start new projects in the fall," Trish said. "I guess that's because quilts are warm and cozy."

Robin turned a funny shade of green.

"Are you sick?" Lily stood. "Can I get you water?"

"No. I just remembered something."

Lily wasn't sure what color her own face was, but her insides had definitely churned with acid.

"When I was reviewing the tax collections at the end of the deadline period, I saw you'd missed it. I'd made a note to mention it to you and forgot. I'm sorry. It will cost you a few hundred more now."

Lily's ears plugged, muting the sounds of the world. The property taxes. How had she forgotten? She'd never missed them at her old house, but then she'd always gotten a bill in the mail. When Lily had sold her old house, they'd apportioned them at the closing. Same would have happened for Amanda when she bought the shop a year before, but there should have been a current bill. "I never got a bill."

Robin cocked her head. "They went out as usual."

"Could it have been sent to my old address?"

"I doubt it, and even if it did, the mailman would have known to bring it to you here. Let me run across the street to get a copy."

While Robin was gone, Trish and Maggie helped Lily bring out the melamine plates and the food. Lily kept her breath steady. She even managed to answer questions while her ears buzzed and her heart palpitated.

She'd forgotten the taxes. Never mind the late fee. She'd forgotten the whole bill. She'd been so proud of all her calculations, carefully made to be certain she had the resources she needed for the shop but forgot the one annual inevitable expense. The one she'd known all along she would have to pay.

She laid the platter of roasted vegetables on the table. Her mouth had watered while she'd made it. All she could taste now was the tang of bile.

A few minutes later, Robin returned, her lips pressed grimly together. She handed the paper to Lily. The bill was addressed to Philip's office.

He'd never given it to her. This was no accident. If he'd given it to his assistant, she would have known to forward it to Lily. Despite all his apologies, he was still attempting to sabotage her.

He'd succeeded.

Even if she had met the discount deadline, the amount due was a big chunk of what she'd reserved for the shop. And one inevitable fact remained. The real blame for this lay squarely on her own shoulders. This had been within her control.

"Lily?" Robin sounded as if she was in another room.

"Lily, are you okay?" Maggie waved her hand in front of Lily's face, but she couldn't speak.

"I'll get a glass of water." Trish stood.

Lily heard water running, and then a glass appeared before her. Trish tipped it, forcing her to sip. The swallow brought her back to the room. "I knew. I knew I had to pay taxes. I'd thought of it dozens of times. I'm so close, and now because of my own stupidity . . ." She banged her head with the heel of her hand.

"Stop it." Robin gripped her shoulders.

"I can't believe I didn't plan for this. I could've skipped the deck and steps." She resumed beating her forehead. "Stupid. Stupid. Stupid."

Robin's cool hands closed around Lily's wrists. "You'll find a way to manage. You always do."

Lily tried to bring her hands to her face, but Robin held on tightly. "I'm going to throw up."

"No, you're not."

"Then I'm going to kill Philip. He should have given this bill to me weeks ago. I could have made adjustments."

Maggie leaned close and forced Lily's face up with a finger under her chin. "You aren't going to fail. We're all here and we won't let that happen."

"All isn't lost," Trish said. "You have this beautiful house to live in. Soon you'll have a beautiful garden. So maybe you have to put off opening the shop for a while. That's not the end."

Lily loved these women, but that wasn't the point. "It's not about delaying it, it's about competence. What else am I getting wrong?" She didn't know how to run a business. She'd never paid attention to those kinds of things. Sam had always handled finances. Then she let Philip do it.

Philip. Her shame when he found out she'd made such a stupid mistake would be unbearable. He'd feign sympathy, but he'd be gloating.

"What if I forget something I can't recover from? I have to take care of Emma. I can't put anything more into this." A throbbing headache started behind her eye. "I'm not sorry we moved here, but living here wasn't Amanda's dream. She wanted a quilt shop."

"Let the shock settle," Robin said. "It won't seem so bad once it wears off. And if it makes you feel better, we'll make a voodoo doll of Philip and stick pins in it. Everyone else in town wants you to succeed."

"Let's eat," Maggie said. "Can I get you a glass of wine, Lily? In fact, if you have a bottle, I think a glass of wine might be good for all of us. I'm not working today."

"Me neither," Trish said.

"I have to go back to the tax office, but I can manage half a glass."

"Thank you. I can't begin to tell you—"

"Enough, Lily," Trish said. "We're here and we're not leaving. But we are going to eat this fabulous lunch you made."

After the ladies left, Lily lay on the couch in the air-conditioned comfort of the back room. Russell snuggled next to her while she played with his soft ears.

Doug's familiar thumping up the steps made her sit up. "I'm back here."

He stepped through the doorway, a dark expression on his face. He looked older, more like the brooding man she'd first met. This couldn't be good. Something had happened. If bad things came in threes, she shuddered to think what calamity was next.

"Hey," he said. "Don't get up. I'm going upstairs." Russell abandoned Lily and followed Doug, leaving a cold spot in his absence.

She got up and made a pot of tea, letting it steep for a while to give Doug some time alone. When she thought it had been long enough, she carried a tray with the teapot, sugar, milk, and two cups upstairs. "Can I come in? I brought you a cup of tea."

Doug was sitting on the edge of his bed, tears streaming down his cheeks. She put the tray on top of the dresser, another Jack masterpiece, and sat next to him. "What happened?"

"Jack died. He's gone." Doug's chest heaved, his face twisted in agony.

"I'm so sorry," Lily said. Her own grief, so carefully boxed and hidden poked at the back of her eyes. What had she been worrying about? Taxes? A quilt shop? They were nothing compared to real tragedies, especially if it made Doug backslide. He'd come so far.

"At first, I hated he thought I was Billy, but the people there made me see how happy it made him. Now they're both gone."

He buried his face in the crook of his arm and broke into sobs again. Without thinking, Lily pulled him into a hug, wishing she could siphon off some of his loss. He relaxed after a moment, leaning into her embrace.

"You gave Jack the best possible ending. Better than any apology. You gave him back Billy."

"I also took Billy from him."

"Please, Doug, it's time. Forgive yourself. Billy would, and so would Jack."

He sat up straight, his eyes red-rimmed but dry. "I'm done here. Jack is gone and you don't need me anymore. It's time for me to move on."

And there was number three.

She couldn't bear the thought of him hiding in some alley or doorway, protecting his metal boxes, alone, cold. Something inside her snapped. She wasn't going to let him go without a fight.

"Move on to what?" She stood, palms up, fingers splayed as if showing him the nothingness that awaited him. "Where will you go?"

"I don't know, but I can't keep taking from you."

"You give me more than you take and you know it. You have jobs lined up. You have the support group at the VA. You belong here with me and Emma. You make us happy." She wanted to add Vicki, but that was presumptuous.

There was no light in his eyes. They'd gone dull. He was relapsing.

What more could she say? She couldn't fix him. She couldn't fix Emma. She couldn't fix herself. He'd be alone again. Amanda was still gone. There'd be no quilt shop. But she had Emma. Emma, who was spending a few days with her grandparents for a second birthday celebration.

Chapter 30
Proposal, Therapy, and a Rat

Early morning light flooded Lily's bedroom, setting off a headache and memories of the previous night. After she'd spoken to Doug, he'd gone out to the barn. She'd shifted around unpacked boxes in the basement storage room until she found her liquor stash. Most of it hadn't been touched since Sam died. To Lily, liquor tasted like solvent, but there was a half-full bottle of Grey Goose, which was tolerable. Sam used to make gimlets for Rose when she and Philip visited. The thought of a gimlet and the old days when everyone was still alive had only made her feel worse. She'd drunk from the bottle, wincing with each swallow until her mouth and throat numbed.

With one eye squinted, she looked at the empty bottle on the dresser. If she'd had sense, she would have drunk a quart of water before she'd fallen asleep. As it was, her mouth was foul, her face greasy, and she was still in her clothes.

The last time she'd had liquor was the last time she drank heavily. That was after Sam died. Jack had died yesterday. So had Amanda's dream. And Doug was a lost soul.

She undressed and wrapped herself in her bathrobe, then slipped from her bedroom quietly. Doug's door was open, the room tidy as always. He was probably sleepless again and outside working on something. Russell jumped off Emma's bed and followed Lily downstairs.

After she took him out, she sat in the great room with coffee and water, trying to count the good things in life while her brain rehydrated. Without the shop, she'd have the whole beautiful house for living space. Both she and Emma loved being in town. Maybe Emma wouldn't take the news badly. No shop. No more Doug. Such a sad end to nearly a year of hard work and perseverance, sprinkled with desperation.

With water and caffeine in her system, Lily felt better, physically. She laid a bowl of kibble on the floor for Russell and called Vicki, leaving a message about the tax bill, Doug, and asking her to come for a visit.

After a shower, she made the harder phone call.

"I need to talk to you."

"What is it?" There was a note of panic in Philip's voice. He deserved it.

"Why didn't you give me the tax bill?"

Silence. He hadn't expected to get caught. Or he hadn't thought it would amount to anything. Why would he? Even Lily couldn't believe she hadn't planned for the taxes.

"It was mailed to your office. Robin checked."

"I assumed I got a duplicate."

"Did it say it was a duplicate?" She was too angry to let him off easily.

"Honestly, I didn't think that much about it. If you'll remember, you'd pretty much cut me out."

"That's not an excuse, Philip." She wouldn't let him blame her. He should have given her the bill.

"The discount isn't much. My advice is to pay it and forget about it."

If only it was as inconsequential as missing a discount, but he didn't need to know that. The last thing she wanted was to let him gloat over her failure or bask in happiness that she could no longer make life harder for herself.

"Thanks. Great advice." She hung up.

Two seconds later, the phone rang again. She'd expected

Philip, but it was Robin.

"I have a bit of good news. If you bring me a check at the town building, I can still give you the discount."

"You won't get in trouble?"

"I'm here on Saturday to catch up on processing the checks from last week. No one will know unless you say something. I won't."

A bit of the chill inside Lily warmed at Robin's kindness. Another thing she could add to her list of things that were good. Not everything was wrong. The payout she received from Simon each month covered her monthly payment to Philip. Only her pride and confidence were injured. Although Philip could be a rat, he was right about one thing. Her life would be easier without the shop. In truth, the only catastrophic thing that had happened was that Jack died.

After Lily wrote out her check and took it across the street to Robin, she saw Ruth alone at her usual table by the cafe window. Her company, a latte, and a grilled cheese would help clear the dull vestiges of Lily's hangover. She ordered, then joined Ruth.

"Where's Walter?"

"He drove to Wheeling to go to Bass Pro Shops." Ruth rolled her eyes. "He wants to take Emma fishing."

Lily nearly choked, catching the spray of latte in her napkin. "That's so sweet, but you know Emma. She'll be horrified to hurt a fish. Or she'll want to adopt it."

"She's an acorn off her grandmother's tree, then." Ruth beamed an affectionate smile. "I tried to tell that to Walter, but actually I'm glad he's found an interest in something other than reading books. And I love the way he is with Emma. We're hoping Becca finds her way back to dating. We'd love another grandchild."

"Another?" As far as Lily knew, Becca was an only child.

"Emma, of course. You're not planning to take her away from us, are you?"

"Absolutely not." Lily brushed a tear from her eye. "I hope you get many grandchildren to dote on."

"That will depend on Becca. I hate to see her alone. I know she'd love to have a baby."

"She might be close to ready to open her heart again," Lily said. Becca had seemed to have her eye on Doug for a while, but that hadn't lasted. "She just needs to find someone."

Ruth sighed from the bottom of her lungs. "All these broken hearts. You and Emma too. Sometimes life sucks."

It could suck big time. But not always.

"As long as there is still love in the world, I guess we have to put up with the suck." Lily's words came out braver than she felt. "But at the moment, I feel the suck like a whirlpool pulling me under. Can I talk to you? I need advice."

Ruth patted the back of Lily's hand. "Of course. I knew from your face when you walked in that something was wrong, but let's go to your place." Ruth stood. "It's getting crowded in here. Becca needs the table." Ruth signaled to Becca. She nodded in answer.

Once inside, Ruth sat at the edge of Lily's quilting chair, her back straight, hands in her lap. Counselor mode.

Lily told her everything. About the taxes. About Philip's betrayal. About Doug leaving. "I've tried so hard to be strong. I'm tired."

"Can I speak freely?" Ruth asked in a tone that made Lily feel she was about to hear something important, but maybe not what she wanted.

Lily nodded.

"I may be wrong and you don't have to listen to me, but you've been trying too hard to be strong for Emma. You've never let yourself grieve properly. You lost a child, Lily, your only child, probably the worst thing that can happen to a parent. You're keeping it bottled up. It's a wonder you don't crack."

What choice did she have? "I don't want to add to Emma's

burden. She has enough grief of her own."

"She does. And she will never be the girl she was before she lost her parents but she's a nine-year-old trying to be strong like you. She loves you and looks up to you. You're the person who loves her most in the world. But she needs to grieve too. You can avoid it for a while, but there is no shortcut. You have to go through it or it will consume you both. Emma needs to see you sad and hurting and know it's okay for her too."

Other than the Arthur incidents, Lily couldn't remember seeing Emma cry since she'd cut up the clothes. She'd clung to Lily's side, crawled into her bed at night, but not cried. "I push it down because, if I didn't, it would overwhelm me. I can't die. I have to be here for Emma."

"Yes, and one of the ways you can be there for her is to let her be sad with you. Let her see you vulnerable and hurt. Let her feel her pain."

It would feel good to let go, to give into despair. She was tired of trying to live as if she wasn't broken.

"But what do I tell Emma about the shop? She wants it so badly."

"That's okay too. Shop or no shop, what Emma needs most is you. Go through it together. Teach her it's okay to make mistakes, but you still get up the next day and keep trying to do your best."

"Ruth, you are so good to me. To Emma. And so wise."

"I'm no wiser than you. I just see it more objectively. You might be the strongest person I know. How you've held yourself together and all you've done here. Not many people could have done it. But that doesn't mean you won't make mistakes, even fail. So you won't have the shop? You are whole and good and Emma needs you and you need her. Nothing else matters."

For a few minutes, they sat in silence. Then Ruth said, "I'm going to leave you now, but you know where to find me. Don't hesitate to call."

While Lily let Ruth's words sink in, her cell had buzzed.

Vicki had left a message. She couldn't come that evening, but she'd be there the next morning.

After sending a text to ask Vicki to bring Emma with her and save Ben the trip, Lily pulled the quilt from the back of the sofa, snuggled under it. She had nothing to do. Nowhere to go. No jobs on her list. A nap might be what she needed most.

When the doorbell rang, she ignored it. She couldn't have been sleeping long, wasn't expecting anyone, and she was warm and comfortable without a trace of the morning's hangover. She'd just dropped back to sleep when her cell buzzed. After slapping her hand over the end table to find her phone, it lit with Philip's name. He'd be persistent, she was certain of that. Seconds later, a text appeared on her lock screen.

I'm at your door. Are you home?

She should tell him to go away, that she was too angry to see him, but after talking to Ruth, it seemed the better course was to vent. The idea of firing her wrath at him had some appeal. She texted back.

I was napping. Give me a minute.

She took time to pee and splash water on her face, then brushed her hair and pulled it into a ponytail.

A wad of pink greeted her at the door. Philip held a bouquet, nearly as wide as his chest, of roses nestled between lilies and purple waxflowers.

He pushed it toward her. When she didn't take it, he stepped inside and laid it on top of a bookcase.

"I'm sorry. I never meant to hurt you. I wouldn't have held the bill if I'd thought you needed it."

It would take more than roses and profuse apologies before she'd even consider forgiving him. "It's not just the tax bill." She waved her hand at the empty shelving. "You never wanted me to do any of this."

"I was worried about you. It was such a shock and trauma when Amanda . . . can we sit somewhere?"

He followed her to the kitchen. By habit, she reached for

the kettle to fill it but stopped. She didn't need to serve him anything.

"I didn't want you to make your life harder. You've suffered enough." The creases in the corners of his eyes deepened as if he felt her pain. The only time she'd ever seen him lose his composure was when Rose was sick. "You're putting your retirement and Emma at risk."

"And that is my decision to make. If I want to go into the poorhouse, I'm entitled to. But that won't happen. I have a beautiful home and I love living in it. No thanks to you."

"Maybe I've tried to talk you out of it, but I never stopped you. I lent you money, didn't I?"

"Yes, but only because you'd thought I'd sell after I fixed the dry rot. I didn't want to then, and I don't want to now. You say you care, but you don't care that what I want is this house, this shop."

He rubbed his temples, then pointedly held her gaze. "You're right, but it's different now. I want to help you. The whole thing. Come live with me. Marry me. We can raise Emma, and I'll support you in the shop, I promise. But what you're doing now is making you suffer."

She might have been shocked at his proposal except it's what her friends had been telling her. Only she couldn't see it. "I don't love you that way."

"Marriage isn't only about love. It's about companionship and commitment. Think about it. We're good together. We've known each other for decades through many hardships. You could have it all. A family. A stable home for Emma. And the shop. Of course, the shop."

Despite everything she thought she believed, she was seeing sense in what he was saying. Life would be better for Emma. How many times had she'd thought Emma might be better off with Heather and Ben, with two parents?

She loved Philip, or she had before he'd started all this nonsense, but she didn't love him as a wife should. And she didn't trust he wouldn't still get in her way.

Doug came through the basement door. Russell bounded down from upstairs to greet him. Lily hadn't even noticed the sound of his boots, but she didn't need to force a smile to greet him. Her relief was great. She had a diversion from the conversation with Philip.

"Hey, good afternoon." She checked the clock. It was just past noon. How long could one day last? "I was wondering where you were."

"Sorry, I should have left a note." Amusement shone in his eyes. "A teenager had a party and someone cracked the toilet bowl." His spirits had improved since the night before, even if hers had gone downhill, but then he probably hadn't drunk half a bottle of vodka. "Anyway, I had to drive to get a new toilet. That's why it took so long."

He seemed to have just noticed Philip. "Hi."

For once, Philip's animosity didn't show, but there was no warmth either.

"I need a shower, so I'll leave you two to it." Doug went upstairs.

Lily and Philip sat in silence until Doug's footsteps faded. Philip's mouth barely opened wide enough for words to come out. "Why is that guy using the upstairs bathroom?"

"That guy is Doug. He lives here." How dare Philip.

"You can't let him upstairs with Emma in the house. He shouldn't be in the house at all. A grown man living with a nine-year-old girl. What are you thinking? Do you realize someone might call child protective services?" Philip leaned forward with his arms crossed.

It wasn't an impossible thought. "Someone already reported him living in the barn, which is why he had to come into the house in the first place."

Philip flinched, a tiny ducking of his head. In a flash, Lily knew.

"It was you. I thought it was the mailman because I didn't

think you would do such a thing." He probably hadn't thought he'd get caught. "You knew Doug was here. When you lent me the money, you told me to hire a contractor and get rid of Doug. But I didn't, so you tried to do it for me."

"He doesn't belong here. You know it and he knows it."

"He has helped me more than anyone. He's earned his right to be part of my family." She knew calling Doug family would get under Philip's skin and she hoped it stung.

"And he's going to leave you, Lily. But I will still be here. I've always been here. Why not open your shop from a position of security for you and for Emma?"

"You need to leave. I don't think I know who you are anymore. And if someone contacts the authorities, this time I will know who did it." Her knees quaked as she walked to the front door. "Please, go."

She closed the door behind him and sat on the bottom step, completely confused. Which way was up? Which way was down? Everything seemed backward. And despite it all, one shameful thought kept tickling her. With Philip, she could have the shop and security.

Chapter 31
A Thousand Tiny Stitches

The next morning, as Lily went downstairs, her sore butt reminded her of the hour, or maybe hours, she'd sat on the steps after Philip left. She'd hoped after a good night's sleep, things wouldn't feel so dismal. It would also help that Vicki and Emma would be there in a few hours.

Lily took her coffee and a notebook to the deck, determined to add to her list of good things in her life. With Russell at her feet, she took a few slow breaths of fresh air and put pen to paper.

Top of the list: she didn't need Philip. Her face scrunched with disgust that she'd actually entertained the idea of marrying him, no matter how fleeting the thought. It would take a while, but she'd repay his loan and never have to speak to him again.

Without the shop, there'd be space in the great room for her china cabinet, her beloved plates and crystal on display instead of bubble-wrapped inside boxes. She'd move Doug's bookcases to the basement and unpack all the boxes. The shelves would give her plenty of storage space, everything easily retrievable.

She'd have time to quilt again. Teach Emma. The back room could be their sewing room with a quilt design wall and tables for their sewing machines.

Trish could amend her plans for the backyard to create a space for vegetables, and Lily could grow tomatoes and herbs in containers on the deck. She and Emma would have a garden again.

If she sat for longer, she'd surely think of other things, but doing something, anything to get started would make her feel better.

In the storage room, her boxes were stacked against the back wall, three high and two deep. There was no order to the mayhem. In her rush to move, she hadn't bothered to organize or label anything. Time was no longer a problem. She'd have plenty. Another thing to add to her list.

The first box held the liquor stash. A twinge of queasiness rose as she thought of the empty vodka bottle. She wrote liquor on it in black Sharpie and lugged it near the steps where she'd put all the boxes that would go upstairs. The second box was full of seldom-used kitchen gadgets. A citrus squeezer, a pasta rolling machine, a waffle maker. She took out the waffle maker, figuring Emma would love it, then put the rest by the back door. It would make it easy to load them into the truck to take to the donation center.

Inside the next box was the plastic storage bin labeled wrapping paper. Her heart stopped and restarted, beating hard enough to feel it in her fingertips as she ran them over a light layer of dust. She could set it aside and try to pretend she hadn't seen it, but Ruth had told her she needed to grieve, to set loose the dragon inside her, let its fire burn and then go out. "I miss you so much," she whispered as if in the quiet she'd hear Amanda's response. "I'm trying my best to do right by Emma. She misses you too."

Lily dropped to her knees, lifted the lid, and grabbed a piece of Amanda's fuzzy bathrobe. When the crescendo came, she jammed it against her mouth to muffle the sound that welled up, a deep primal howl like a wounded animal. She rocked, feeling the pain of the cold concrete floor against her knees and the full weight of her loss and her anger. Amanda and Matt had been robbed of so much life, of the pleasure of watching Emma grow up.

Slowly, the tears came, hot and heavy, dropping like pearls, dampening her thighs. She heard rustling from the top of the steps, followed by Russell's familiar tapping. He climbed on her lap and licked her cheeks. She needed a hug. She needed sympathy.

With a great effort, she forced out a word, "Doug?"

He was at her side, gently raising her from the floor, his large hands under her elbows. "I didn't mean to bother you."

"You don't bother me."

He took two boxes down, offering one to Lily. They sat in silence as Lily dabbed her eyes with the bit of bathrobe.

"Before I met you, Emma cut up her mother's clothes, wanting to make a quilt for the shop. She thought she'd ruined everything. I told her a quilt was nothing more than something beautiful made from scraps."

Russell perked his ears, then ran out of the room.

"Vicki must be here with Emma. Would you mind meeting them and sending Emma to me? I have to talk to her."

He nodded. "I'm on it."

A few minutes later, a little hand grabbed Lily's shoulder. She pulled Emma onto her lap. "I found the scraps."

"Is that why you're crying, Gammy?" Emma traced the line of Lily's tears on her cheek.

"Yes. I miss your mommy. My daughter. I've made a mistake, Emma. I tried to be strong for you but I think I taught you to hold in your sadness."

Emma's chin quivered. "I don't want you to be sad."

"And I didn't want you to be sad, but it's okay. We should both be sad. Sometimes, it hurts so much it makes it hard for me to breathe. Does that ever happen to you?"

"Sometimes. And sometimes I want to run but I don't know where to go."

"We'll get through this together. I'm sorry if I made you think you had to hold it in." Emma's face crumpled, and she laid her head against Lily's chest, her shoulders heaving. Lily embraced her, rocking them both.

When Emma's tears slowed, Lily said, "I have some bad news." May as well get it over with. "I made a big mistake and now I don't have enough money to open the shop."

"Do we have to leave the house?" There was a tremor in her voice.

It hadn't occurred to Lily that Emma would think she was losing her home. "No. No, baby. This is our home. We're safe here. And because it's a lot bigger than my old house, we can have a sewing room. Would you like to start working on this quilt?" Lily pointed at the scraps.

"I didn't ruin them?" Emma's voice still trembled.

"Nothing is ruined. All we have to do is find our machines somewhere in all these boxes."

"I can help you." Emma nodded, then frowned. "Gammy, you didn't ruin anything either."

"Thank you for saying that, but I made a mistake." Indeed, she had, but Emma was right, she hadn't ruined things. They still had each other. "You know what? We all make mistakes, but it's okay. We learn from them and we pick ourselves back up and we move on. Right? We're okay. You and me." With a finger, she tapped Emma's heart, then her own.

"And Russell?" Emma pointed.

He was sitting at the storage room door, quivering, waiting for Emma. At the sound of his name, he dashed in, jumping on top of Emma, still in Lily's lap.

"Okay," Lily laughed. "I'm afraid the top of this box might give out."

Emma climbed off, Russell dancing around them.

With her short haircut like Vicki's, all evidence of her bald spot was gone. Vicki was another thing to be grateful for. Her friendship and love for Emma remained strong, even in Amanda's absence.

Emma sniffled, her eyes dry. "I think we should go upstairs. Auntie Vic is here."

Lily's smile rose from her heart to her eyes. "When did you grow up so much? Your mommy and daddy would be so proud."

"Were you proud of Mommy?"

"More than you can imagine except I'm even more proud of you."

"I'm proud of you too." Emma encircled Lily's hips, holding tight.

"We both lost a lot, didn't we? But we have each other and we gained some things too, right?"

"We got Doug," Emma said. "And Russell."

Vicki was waiting in the kitchen with brownies. Doug must have told her about what was happening. Nothing like a brownie to change Emma's mood.

"Where's Doug?" Lily asked. She wanted him to know she and Emma were okay.

"He went to the barn. Where else?" Vicki said.

"If you don't mind, I'll leave you two with your brownies. I need to talk to him."

As Lily slid the barn door open, Doug turned toward her. "Hey." He wiped his hands on a rag. "Are you and Emma okay?"

"We are. Ruth told me I needed to let Emma see me sad and to be honest about the shop. It feels good to let it out. I'm sure we'll cry a lot more, but in the meantime, I have ideas for the house." As they sat on two restored chairs, the overturned bucket between them, Lily explained her plans. "We don't need to move anything right away, but if you wouldn't mind helping me with the heavy things, I'd appreciate it."

"No problem. Let me know when you're ready."

Lily fidgeted, not quite sure how to say what she meant. "After that, I won't have any more work for you. I understand why you want to leave, but before you go, I want you to know how grateful Emma and I are that we had you in our lives.

We'll miss you and not just because you helped us."

"It's not over, Lily." He leaned toward her, his elbows on his knees. "Maybe you can't open the shop now, but that doesn't mean you never will."

She rubbed the spot on her palm where the splinter had skewered her. "I think it's probably beyond what I can do alone."

"I don't believe that. You don't give up easily. I only taught you how to do things you could've learned anywhere." He stood and paced between the door and his workbench as if he wanted to leave but then returned. "That day, when you first walked in and caught me fixing the walls, I was sure you'd call the cops. That's why I took everything, even obvious trash to the barn. I didn't want to get arrested for stealing. I just wanted to help you."

"We did good together, didn't we?" Why did it have to end?

"We did."

It was funny how differently they could see the same thing. He'd helped her and he only saw how she'd helped him. "How are you doing? Are you feeling better?"

He shrugged. "Therapy helps. Keeping busy helps."

"I don't want you to leave. Even if I have no work for you to do. You can take more handyman jobs. Use the barn for your shop. You are respected in town, never mind Philip." She stood. "Fuck Philip."

He stifled a laugh. "Did you really just say that?"

"I did. Fuck Philip. He's an arrogant ass who can't see past himself. He was the one who reported you living in the barn." She hadn't intended to mention this to Doug because she didn't want to give him another reason to leave, but her wrath exploded out of her. "He has tried to stop me at every turn. He says he loves me. He wants to marry me, make my life easier." She snorted. "He promised I could open the shop, have no financial worries." She covered her face with her hands, ashamed of what she'd thought. "I'd actually considered it for a moment but I don't even think I know him anymore. And I'm certain he only cares about what he wants." It seemed a good day to vent everything. Get it all out. She'd breathe easier.

"You don't need him. You don't need anyone's help. All you need is to have those you love near you. And there are plenty of people in this town who love you."

Did he? Enough to stay? "I know. I have friends. Good friends. And I have Emma. And I hope I have you."

He didn't answer, his expression closed, as usual, revealing nothing.

She pushed on. "We think it's the patchwork that makes a quilt, but it isn't. A patchwork alone is nothing but cloth. A quilt is when you layer it with batting and a backing and bind them together with a thousand tiny stitches."

"I knew you wouldn't give up."

Had she said that? She hadn't, but he was right. "No. I can't. I've come this far and I've figured it out before." And an idea was forming for how to figure it out again.

"Then I'll stay for as long as you need me. I owe you my life, Lily Wolfe. I wouldn't be on this earth anymore if not for your kindness."

"I need you more than you know. It's time to gather the troops."

Chapter 32
A Night on the Town

"I think most of you know why we're here, but a few maybe don't, and it bears repeating." Lily stood at the front of the private dining room in the hotel restaurant, sweat tickling her back. Don had removed the tablecloths, leaving plain, brown round tops, their pedestals exposed. They looked like mushrooms popping up from the floor, which was pretty much how this gathering had happened.

Only a week had passed since Lily's idea had sprouted. She'd asked Vicki to stay, working remotely by day and spending evenings helping Lily plan and spread the word. They'd canvassed the street to see what the townsfolk thought. Vicki, in her magical way with words, had brought their vision to life, just as she had for Lily all those months ago.

The short notice didn't seem to have dampened anyone's desire to talk about the future of the town. With four or five people per table, five tables full and one left for latecomers, at least half of the Fellowes Hollow shop owners had assembled. Ed from the hardware store, Gus from the gas station, Mel from the General Store, and, of course, Becca had been the first to sign on. Philip wasn't there. Lily didn't know if he was aware of the meeting or steering clear of Lily's wrath. Doug, Vicki, and Emma were sitting on chairs near Lily.

Lily continued, "With the influx of residents from The Village, you've all seen a dramatic increase in foot traffic downtown." A cheer went up, followed by a smattering of applause.

"You all are my inspiration, but it wouldn't be fair if I didn't give full credit to Vicki. She is the one who dreamed this up and she has agreed to use her prowess in public relations to help us make this a success. I wanted for us to get together to discuss details. When we present our plans to Rez and the town council, they won't be able to refuse."

"Don't be so sure." A woman from Trish's garden club stood, her head swiveling to take in all the people sitting at the tables. "Ask Trish. She can't even get approval to turn that weed pit into a park."

Everyone knew it was easier to turn a battleship than to move Rez and the council.

"Trish couldn't be here tonight, but we've included her plan for a park in our proposal. We are going to ask the town for the approval and for a few street improvements, lampposts, parking at either end of downtown, and a couple of crosswalks, so we don't have to wait forever to cross the street." Lily's armpits had grown damp, and she had a persistent tremor running through her body. The smell of grilling meat stuck unpleasantly in her throat. Despite how she felt, she sounded authoritative, professional. It was hard to believe she was the one speaking.

"But most of the improvements are going to fall on each of us to take care of our own businesses. We can spruce up our signage and our exteriors. If we team up, we can help each other. And, Doug," Lily turned to him, and he looked down at his feet, "has agreed to discount his hourly rate for any work on town improvement. I believe some of you are familiar with his skills. And all of you know that without his help, Jack's house would still be a dilapidated eyesore."

Candace, who owned the candy shop two doors from the cafe, turned to face the people seated behind her. "Doug is helping me pick up and install the antique display case I found in Ohio. It's perfect for my shop and with all the indulgent grandparents at The Village, the kids need to be able to see everything."

Doug already had two new jobs lined up. Lily hoped, once all this was done, he'd find it impossible to leave. And if having work wasn't enough, maybe Vicki's presence would be. The way she'd looked at him, full of pride when Lily mentioned his generosity, had to mean something. They'd certainly spent a lot of time together the past week, but whether the bond extended beyond friendship, Lily wasn't sure.

"What about your shop, Lily?" Ed called out. "We're rooting for you." The room murmured its assent.

"Unfortunately, my shop is on hold until I can find more capital, but I haven't given up."

"I've already ordered new signs for the diner and hotel," Don said, "and I'm going to add seating in the lobby. The wait time for weekend breakfast is getting ridiculous. I might need to take back the second floor for more guest rooms. We haven't had this many bookings since my dad ran the place."

"Don't touch my dental office," Simon said. "I have new patients coming here from the outskirts and even Ainsleyville. Does anyone know a dentist who wants to move to Fellowes Hollow?" He shot a look of apology at Lily.

She nodded to him to let him know it was okay. Matt may be gone, but Simon still needed a partner.

"It's great to hear everyone's plans, but we also need to listen to objections." Lily had promised herself she wouldn't steamroll anyone. "Please don't be shy. We don't want to force anything on anyone. Let us know what's on your mind."

When no one responded, Lily handed the meeting over to Vicki who listed out a lot of demographic information, then unveiled the rendition of the finished town that one of her friends had drawn for her. One of the storefront signs read Quilt Shop. When she finished, she said, "Fellowes Hollow could be a tourist town."

"You still have to get it past Rez," Mel said. "I'm not sure even a united front will get him on board." Of all the shop owners, he stood to gain the most, especially in toy sales. "Remember what Gus went through to get his tall sign for the highway? No one even knew there was a gas station at the exit before that. Didn't stop Rez from taking a year to approve it."

"But it did get approved and so did The Village, so it's not impossible. I have some ideas that might persuade him," Vicki said. "It's all in the presentation."

A mop of blue curls came through the door. "Sorry I'm late," Trish said, breathing hard, her face red.

"We were just talking about how we can get Rez on board," Lily said.

"Sheesh. Who knows with him? While I was drawing up the park plans, I thought we should make it a veterans' memorial park. Billy isn't Fellowes Hollow's only loss. Then I realized I might be able to get a grant or two or maybe find a benefactor for the memorial. Maybe we won't need him to do anything."

Lily snuck a sideways glance to see Doug's expression after the mention of Billy. Vicki had her hand on his knee.

"It might work," Ed said. "It's the town budget he's always grumbling about."

"Don't forget what's good for the goose is good for the gander." Robin stood, then her face went white. Rez had walked into the room. "Good evening, Rez," she said. "I was about to tell everyone how with all the extra people and business in town, the tax receipts are way up. We should have enough money to make street improvements."

Lily wanted to run over and kiss Robin. She'd taken a huge risk. Rez was her boss, and she had just nullified one of his favorite reasons for saying no.

"Thank you, Robin, for pointing that out," Vicki said. "All these ideas will be in the final presentation to you, Rez, and to the town council."

As they walked down Fellowes Run Road back to the shop, Emma held Lily's hand tightly, yanking her arm as she skipped. "Gammy, you were amazing. You were like a real person." She emphasized the words "amazing" and "real," drawing out the syllables.

Lily almost choked on her laugh. "I'm always a real person. Even when I'm your Gammy."

Vicki chimed in. "Very true, but you were amazing. The way you brought everyone on board. Rez would be crazy to refuse."

"And you, Vicki, with your renderings, bringing your vision to life. I've never felt as much electricity pulsing through a town meeting before. But I have to say, I think the blue ribbon goes to Robin. Can you imagine Rez walking in at that exact moment? And she was so cool."

"Everyone is awesome, Gammy."

"You're right, Emma. We're all awesome." Lily had a bounce in her step too. Even though she would have to wait to open her own shop, the thought that she'd mobilized the town to take advantage of its potential made her feel powerful and influential for the first time in her life. She liked it.

"Everyone's caught the bug, and it's all because of you, Lily." Vicki one-arm hugged Lily. "Because they watched what you did and how you never gave up."

"Thank you, but without Doug, I would've given up a long time ago." She tipped her head forward to see him walking on the other side of Vicki.

"We did it together," Doug said. Nothing he might have said could have made Lily happier. If he felt part of a team, then maybe there was hope he'd find a place to belong. "And you, Vicki, had the vision."

"It's not the vision they bought into," Vicki said. "It was seeing the two of you working day in and day out. They saw you, Lily, walking home from the bank dejected, and yet you found a way to fix the dry rot. They've been rooting for you all along."

"Like I said," Emma said and crossed her arms, "everyone is awesome."

They'd reached the front door of the shop. The porch, rebuilt by Doug, was sturdy. With the gunk scraped off the doors, the ornate carvings were exposed. Inside, the front hall and Russell welcomed her. She couldn't speak for Doug but she felt as much at home as she ever had.

With Emma tucked up in bed, Vicki, Doug, and Lily kicked back with a bottle of Tempranillo.

"You have no idea how admired you are in this town." Vicki clinked her glass against Lily's. "I think it's amazing that you and Emma have come so far. She's doing better, isn't she? I mean, she seems like she is."

"I think she's better. We've spent some time together, talking about Amanda and Matt and crying a lot. I wish I'd realized she needed me to be sad with her. Sometimes I think I don't deserve her."

Vicki scooted across the couch next to Lily. "That is something you and Doug have in common." She looked toward Doug, in Lily's quilting chair. "Neither of you thinks you deserve exactly what you do. No one is free from making mistakes and no one is free from having selfish thoughts."

"I know," he said, staring out the window at the black night.

He'd said only two words. Two very telling words.

"Wouldn't it be nice if the quilt shop could be part of this revival?" This had been Lily's last thought before falling asleep every night that week. "You know, if Simon found a partner who buys out Matt's interest, I could get the rest of the money. It's really Emma's although I can use it however I see fit, but I thought if I put this house in a trust or something in her name, then it would still be hers."

"Why can't Simon find someone?" Vicki asked, tilting her head to the side, thoughts swirling in her eyes.

"I guess there aren't a lot of dentists who want to come

to Fellowes Hollow." She shrugged. "He'd been looking for a few years before I'd mentioned it to Matt." It had seemed a fortuitous match. How could she have known the outcome? "I'll go talk to him. Maybe he can give me more now that his business is up."

"I might be able to help," Vicki said. "Maybe we can find a better way to attract someone."

Doug yawned and stretched. "I'm going to say goodnight. I'm drop-dead tired."

No surprise there. He'd probably been up since three or four in the morning.

All week, Lily had resisted asking Vicki about Doug. With only the two of them in the room, she couldn't stand not knowing anymore. "Is something going on between you and Doug?"

"I'm not sure." Vicki nibbled at the side of her thumb. "He's a hard read. I like him a lot and we get along. There's a lot to admire about him, but I don't think he's emotionally available."

"No, maybe not yet, but you have an effect on him."

"We'll see. He has a lot to process." She stretched her long legs out in front of her. "Time will tell."

"So now that you've spent the week here working remotely, do you think you might move here?"

"I don't know. Being remote was okay. It was for Amanda too, so I wasn't worried about that, but I always thought I'd wait until I settled down."

"Settled down as in find someone?" Vicki had only been in a few long-term relationships in the years since Lily had known her. Yet, at thirty-nine, she was still single through no fault or desire of her own. The nose job might change things for her though.

"The problem is that I'm getting older. It's harder to meet single men my age. At some point, I have to stop waiting. I'm not sure I'm there yet. It's one thing to live out here and start a family. It's something different to come here by myself." Vicki stood and walked to the window as if the answer might be out there.

"You'd always have us, but I know that's not the same as a family of your own." She knew it too well, having lost everyone but Emma.

"No, but it's close. You're very good to me, Lily. And Emma may not be my niece by blood, but she is all the same." Vicki had known her since she was in the womb.

"And nothing would make her happier than frequent visits from you." Having Vicki around would plug one hole in Lily's and Emma's lives. Lily grew warm with the thought.

Early the next morning, Lily went to Simon's office, hoping to catch him before he fell behind schedule with his patients. The receptionist who had replaced her slid open the glass divider. "I'm sorry, Lily. I know you were trying to see him before we got busy, but we had an emergency patient call in. You can wait if you want."

"I can come back later if you think that's better."

"It shouldn't be too long." She tapped her lip with the cap of her pen. "I should hate you, you know."

"Heavens why?" What could she have done to this woman she'd met only a handful of times?

"Because Simon misses you. It took me weeks to live up to your reputation."

Lily exhaled. "Nonsense. You must be far more tech savvy than me."

"I doubt it." The woman had to be at least twenty years younger than Lily.

"Give it time. I worked for him for years. Loved them all. I hope you'll be just as happy here."

"I'd love it a little more if we weren't doing sixty-hour

weeks. I checked. We have at least half as many more patients than last year. We're even here all day on Saturday. Simon is ragged. I hope he finds a partner soon."

So did Lily. She took a seat and picked up an old copy of *Good Housekeeping* from the side table, mindlessly flipping pages until Simon came to get her.

"It's good to see you." Simon took both her hands in his and kissed her cheek. "I think of you all the time. I know I should reach out more, but we're crazy here."

"I'm aware of that. It's part of the reason I'm here."

"Come to my office."

She knew the way well.

He closed the office door behind them and led her to a pair of chairs in the corner.

The crow's feet at the corners of his eyes had deepened since she'd last seen him up close. At fifty-one, he simultaneously had the qualities of a much older and much younger man. Even tired, he oozed energy but had a stooped back from leaning over patients for so many years. "Tell me how you're doing. Those are some great plans you have for the town."

"I'm okay." She hadn't said a word yet about why she'd come but already felt bad asking. She decided to start with Vicki's offer. "Vicki, my friend at the town meeting, thinks she might be able to help you find a partner. Can I tell her to call you?"

"Of course." He looked at her expectantly. He knew she wasn't done.

Best to just say it. "Simon, we've known each other a long time, so I want you to feel free to say no, but I came to ask if there is any way you could give me more money. I want to get the quilt shop going, but if it's going to put you in a bind, I can wait." Would he say no if he couldn't afford it? She didn't want him to sacrifice for her.

Simon looked like he'd swallowed a solvent, the way he always did when he found something particularly nasty in a patient's mouth.

The taste transferred to Lily. She ran her tongue over her teeth. "Why are you looking at me like that? I promise, I can wait."

"That's not it. Why didn't you tell me sooner? I always could have given you more. I don't have the cash to pay out Matt's whole share, but I could give you a good chunk of it or make bigger monthly payments, or both."

She should have been happy to hear the news. She'd gotten the answer she'd hoped for and believed Simon was truthful when he'd said he could handle it. Yet, a chill ran through her and she was certain her cheeks had gone white. "I told Philip I didn't want to force you to sell and to ask you for a comfortable payment amount. He said you gave me what you could."

"I offered twice what I've been paying you. He told me you didn't want that much." Simon shook his head rapidly to express how wrong Philip was.

The solvent taste solidified into iron filings that pricked her throat as a list of things Philip had done or said ran through her mind. He'd put a lien on her house. Ratted out Doug from the barn. Threatened to report her for child abuse. Hidden the tax bill. She would've still needed to borrow money from Philip to fix the dry rot, but she would have been able to afford the payments if she'd mortgaged her house. She wouldn't have had to sell it.

"How much do you need?"

Simon's voice brought her back into the office. She told him the amount she'd paid in taxes. "That's enough for me to stock up and buy some equipment I need."

"I can handle that right now." He returned to his desk, pulled a large checkbook from the drawer, and wrote. He handed it to her. It was for far more than she'd asked.

"Are you sure?"

"I'm very sure. I can increase the monthly payments too. As soon as I find a partner, I'll be able to give you the rest." He leaned back in his chair. "Which had better be soon, or I'll also need a new receptionist. She can't keep up this pace for long. Neither can I."

Lily folded the check and slipped it into her purse. Some of the blood returned to her head and she could think again. Philip. The sooner she was done with him, the better. "One more thing, Simon. When you find your new partner, don't hire Philip to do the contract."

Instead of taking her check to the bank, Lily headed for home. She needed to process what she'd learned, her mind ping-ponging between relief that Simon had the money and explosive anger at Philip. She didn't dare confront him for fear of what she'd say or do. Throw a paperweight at his head. Kick him in the shins or worse.

She almost walked into a truck parked half on the sidewalk as she passed the cafe. Becca's new sign was going up.

Lily patted her purse and the check inside. Maybe, despite Philip, she wouldn't be left out of the town revival.

Chapter 33
Doug and Vicki

"It's Friday night. How about we call in for pizza?"

Lily was sitting in her favorite chair, hand quilting a runner for the top of her dresser. Doug and Vicki were on the sofa, and Emma had sunken deep into a bean bag Vicki had bought for her. With the extra seating, they fit comfortably in the back room, gathered like a family around the TV to watch *Taylor Swift's Eras Tour* for Emma's second time.

After the town meeting, Vicki had gone back to Pittsburgh for the week. She'd sent Lily a professionally prepared proposal for the town, which Lily submitted. Once Friday came, Vicki drove back to Fellowes Hollow. So, it wasn't town business that brought her back. Maybe it was Doug. Lily could hope.

"Did you hear me, Emma?" Lily found the remote on the coffee table and clicked pause. "Should we call in for pizza?"

"Yes. Can you put the show back on?" Her gaze stayed riveted on the motionless screen.

"Only if you can tell me what you're going to be like by the time you're thirteen."

"I'm only nine, Gammy. That's a long time."

"Emma, look at me," Vicki said. When Emma turned, Vicki put on a schoolteacher's face, and continued, "You could be more polite. You are not yet an angsty teenager, so you're not allowed to act like it."

Emma wriggled out of the bean bag and approached Lily. "Yes, please, Gammy, I would like pizza. And can I please put the show back on?" She held out her hand for the remote.

"Since you asked so nicely." Lily handed it to her. "What about you two?"

"I'm up for pizza," Vicki said. "I'll make a salad too. You look tired."

Lily wasn't tired. Not physically. Since her meeting with Simon, she hadn't had the stomach to let Philip know she knew the full depth of his subterfuge. But the bigger question was whether he had planted another bomb and where it might be ticking. Her old feeling of inadequacy was rearing its ugly head. Once again, Philip had bested her. Anything might lie before her.

"I eat anything," Doug said. "You know that. If you want to order from the Lego place, I can pick it up. And I'll take clean-up duty."

"Yes, please. I love Lego pizza best." Emma licked her lips.

"I'm glad to know you're not totally deaf," Lily said.

"Ashley at school says it's her favorite too."

"Ashley?" Lily almost fell off her chair. Emma still had never mentioned anyone to her or to Ruth. "Is she your friend?"

Emma nodded. "Can we call her to make a playdate?"

"Of course we can." Lily almost needed to fan herself. She needed good news. This was about the best she could have hoped for. "I'll call tomorrow."

Vicki and Doug both wore expressions of delight, much as Lily was sure had to be on her own face. Emma seemed totally nonplussed as if she'd always had friends in Fellowes Hollow. Nothing unusual.

After Vicki, by Emma's special request, had tucked her in for the night, Lily decided to break the news.

"I have a bottle of Prosecco in the fridge. I think we should celebrate."

She received two blank stares in response. With one finger

in the air, Lily turned and left, leaving the suspense hanging until she returned with the Prosecco and glasses.

"I ran into Rez this afternoon. The council has agreed to the proposal. I'd only given it to him on Wednesday, so I think we broke a speed record. Two days. But the final vote is Monday night, so don't mention it to anyone yet." She filled the glasses and handed them out.

"I knew you'd do it, Lily." Vicki held her glass in the air.

"It wasn't only me. He said they approved it because of what we did to this house. We inspired them." Lily felt a blush of pride creep up her face. "Becca isn't the only one with a new sign. Did you see Mel's hand-painted General Store sign? It's out of the 1880s. Rez thinks we created a tidal wave."

"Exactly our vision," Vicki beamed.

"Your vision and Doug's," Lily said. "If only they knew I had no idea what to do most of the time, they wouldn't be so impressed."

"No one knows anything about anything until they learn," Doug said. "Trish enlisted me to work on your backyard. I don't know much about gardening, but she'll teach me. This place will be so charming quilters will flock here."

"I'll do the PR. And how about we comb some antique stores for a pair of rockers for the front porch? Unless you want to buy them at Cracker Barrel."

"Shh, don't mention Cracker Barrel to Emma." Visions of Emma stuffing pancakes in her mouth lightened Lily's spirits. "Remember, she's a pancake monster."

"She is that," Vicki said. "It's good to see her finally turning a corner, even if she is becoming a bit cheeky. I hope nothing sets her back." Her smile dropped from her face. "But what about you? You have the money. When are you going to order and set up shop? I thought you'd have done it this week."

"I'm procrastinating." Amazing how fast spirits can rise and sink. "Ever since Simon handed me that check, I keep thinking I'd be better off using that money to pay back a big chunk of what I owe Philip."

"Are you seriously going to let him stop you?" When his anger flared, Doug looked as if he wanted to punch something. He was flaring brightly at that idea.

"It isn't only that. It's that I feel settled. I love this house and living in town. Emma's doing better. Maybe after all this, Philip was right. I don't need to take this on. I could enjoy being retired as I had planned to do."

"As you had planned to do while you had Amanda and Matt." Vicki's eyes glistened. She had loved Amanda dearly. It was part of the reason Vicki had become so attracted to the idea of living in a small town. "I'm sorry if I hurt you by saying that, but your life is very different now."

"I know." Lily refilled their glasses while she thought about her answer. "It's that once I commit, there's no going back. I'm in a good position now. I'm not sure I want to chance failing, but mostly I want to be completely free of Philip. Who knows what other trip wires he's planted?"

"You've let that guy get in your head," Doug said, his temper not completely cooled. "You're not going to fail."

Vicki leaned forward, holding her champagne flute out in a toast. "And you're forgetting that I helped Simon with his website and advertisement last week. He may yet find a partner."

"I haven't said I'm never going to do it. I'm just making sure. There's no deadline."

The three of them sat silently for a minute. Whether Vicki and Doug were thinking about Lily's future or their own, Lily was thinking of all three. If they both lived in Fellowes Hollow, she wouldn't need the shop as much as if Vicki stayed in Pittsburgh and Doug left to go wherever. And as long as she owed Philip money, she risked his interference. She could wait a little bit to see if anything sprang up.

"What about your business, Doug?" Vicki asked. "It sounds like you have plenty of jobs."

"I do. It all happens by word of mouth."

"That's because you're reliable and talented," Lily said. After that meeting, he'd been accepted by the townsfolk. He no longer feared anyone finding out he lived with her.

"Right now, I'm sprucing up an older couple's house. They're moving to The Village too."

"Ruth told me all the ladies still talk about you and what you did for Jack," Vicki said.

Doug's face didn't go dark at the mention of Jack.

Lily pulled her elbows back to stretch. "I'm going to make a cup of chamomile and go to bed." It was time to leave the two of them alone.

In the kitchen, even with the kettle on, Lily could hear Doug and Vicki talking. She clattered a few dishes, but they didn't seem to notice or care. Their conversation wasn't about anything Lily didn't already know, so she sat and waited for the kettle to boil.

"You can't give Billy or Jack back their lives. All you can do is honor their memory by living a good life for them."

"I know."

"Do you though? Do you know it here or here?"

Lily imagined Vicki tapping Doug's head and then his heart.

Vicki continued, "People love you. Lily and Emma love you and they need you. And it's because you loved Billy so much that you feel so guilty. It's time to forgive yourself."

Doug snorted. "That's what they say at the VA too. And this lady whose house I'm working on said that the way I visited Jack and let him think I was Billy was one of the kindest things she'd ever seen. Of course, she doesn't know I did it to make myself feel better."

"You're making my point. When I first met you, it didn't make you feel better. It dragged you down, but you did it anyway. You only felt better when you realized you were making Jack happy."

Score one for Vicki, but as curious as Lily was to hear if

she could get through to Doug, she didn't want to eavesdrop. Their conversation might venture where it was distinctly none of her business. The kettle beeped. She poured her tea and didn't wait for it to steep before taking it upstairs. If Doug could forgive and open his heart, who better to give it to than Vicki?

Chapter 34
Cemetery

From the top of the hill, Lily and Emma could see the double headstone at the bottom of a grassy slope. The late August day was full of sunshine and soft breezes rustling the leaves in the trees, the air full of birdsong. Peaceful and beautiful, unlike the awful day the year before when the sky was gray and riddled with thunderstorms, the ground soggy. Lily and Emma held hands as they took the narrow path and stood at the foot of the graves. Amanda and Matthew Levin. Beloved wife, mother, daughter. Beloved husband, father, son.

"They would be so proud of you." Lily was unsure what to say and words were difficult to get out, the dragon churning the molten reservoir that filled the place where Lily's love existed. Not in her head, not in her heart, but in some elusive region that had no name.

"It makes me so mad I want to scream." Lily had promised Emma she wouldn't hide her grief anymore.

"It makes me sad." Emma crept to the headstone as if afraid to step on the earth above her parents. She ran her fingers over the inscription.

Lily held her close, wanting to protect her, steal her grief, and hold it as her own. But she also knew Emma needed to feel it, to own it. "We have our memories and we have each other. Your mommy and daddy would want you to grow up, to live a good life, to remember them, and love them always, but also to be happy."

"Gammy, they'd want that for you too."

"You're right. They would." Lily kissed the top of Emma's head. Her Auntie Vic haircut had grown into a shaggy mass, sparkling with golden highlights under the sun. Emma had changed in the past year, as all kids do, but more so because she'd been wizened by tragedy. Her blissful ignorance of how cruel life could be was gone. "And they would want us to be happy together."

That was what Lily would have wanted if she'd met an untimely death and left Amanda behind. She wouldn't have wanted her to suffer. But it wasn't easy to be the one left behind. Especially for Emma, so young to lose both parents at the same time.

Lily had poured her soul into raising Amanda, supporting her in all she did. And in the space of a few seconds, when she'd answered the knock at her door, she'd gone from being a contented mother and grandmother to a sack of dry bones without sinew or cartilage.

No wonder she had persisted in renovating that old house and holding on to the dream of opening Amanda's quilt shop. She'd avoided grieving by sinking herself into the work. Since she and Emma had allowed themselves to go through the process, feel the pain, the anger, Lily had accepted the loss. Not that she wouldn't give her life if she could make it different, but that she could go on living. As she'd told Doug and Vicki a few nights before, the shop didn't feel as important anymore.

"We've come a long way together, you and me," Lily said.

Emma didn't answer. She stood stoically, her eyes dry but unfocused.

"Are you glad we came to the cemetery?" Lily asked.

"Yes." Emma fell to her knees and lay on the ground over her mother's grave, pressing her cheek into the grass and murmuring. After a few minutes, she rolled onto her father's grave, continuing her conversation.

If she could, Lily would bear every sadness for Emma, but while the journey through grief could be shared, in the end, it was a solitary process. Lily sat at the foot of the graves, giving Emma space to roll back and forth and talk to her parents. She could only imagine the words. Emma spoke too softly to be heard. Lily would tell Amanda that she was finding her way, that she believed Emma would be okay. They would both be okay. They'd already made a good life together.

Emma sprang up and climbed into Lily's lap, nearly knocking her backward.

"We take care of each other now," Emma said.

"We do."

"And we take care of Doug and he takes care of us."

"We do, but remember, he may not stay with us forever."

"He might though." She cocked her head, finger to her lips. "If he and Auntie Vic get married, can I call him Unckie Doug?"

Lily laughed, feeling the sunshine again warming her inside and out. "Let's not assume that will happen, but if it did, you'd have to ask him that."

"I hope it happens. He likes her."

"He does. And she likes him, but that doesn't—"

"I know." Emma wound her arms around her chest.

"Are you ready to leave?" Lily stood and reached for Emma's hand. "I have an idea. Since we're already in Pittsburgh, how about if we see if Grandma and Grandpa are around?"

"That's a good idea." Emma bit at her lower lip. She had something on her mind.

"But? You have a different idea?"

Emma blew out her breath, then sucked another back in, still unable to say what she wanted.

"What is it?" Lily crouched to look her in the eyes.

"I want to help you make the quilt shop."

Visions darted through Lily's mind, Emma placing bolts of fabric on the shelves or organizing spools of thread by color on the rack. Side by side, they'd make it happen. Except school would start in only a few weeks and Emma would be gone all day.

"Are you sure this isn't because you don't want to go back to school?"

"It's not like when I didn't want to go to school." Emma did an about-face and rubbed the back of her hair. "My hair doesn't make me pull it anymore."

"And it's not because you're afraid to leave me?"

She nodded furiously. "I think it will be more fun, and I can see Ashley more."

They'd had a playdate and, in the way nine-year-olds can, had quickly become best friends. "And when I come home, I can help you. And Walter will check my homework."

Did Lily want to open the shop? Not to keep Amanda alive. Not to keep her and Emma from being devoured by despair or to heal Emma's heart, but because she, Lily, wanted it. The new Lily. Strong and capable. Unafraid of failure or of Philip getting in her way. Do it because she wanted it for herself?

If she didn't at least try, would she regret it? After setting the rest of the town in motion, was she going to stand back and be a spectator? That wasn't the woman she'd proven herself to be. That wasn't the woman she wanted to be.

"Then how about if we go visit some of the quilt shops while we're here? There's one I still haven't been to."

Chapter 35
Magazines

"Doug, are you up here?"

Lily shouted up the stairs from the basement. When she got no answer, she asked Emma to run to the barn.

They'd been to Costco and IKEA with Vicki and had returned with the truck bed stacked with boxes. When they'd left, Doug had been with Trish and her club, planting shrubs and flowers along the driveway at the side of the house. Trish wouldn't quit until the whole yard had something green on it. The back was as colorful as the front with variegated foliage spotted with gold marigolds and purple petunias. Borders made from bricks that matched the house lined the beds and everything was rich with brown mulch.

"Wow, they got a lot done. This place is ready for publicity photos," Vicki said. She'd come to stay with Lily for a trial run of living in Fellowes Hollow. It could be because of Doug. Although, it could also be her promise to the town and to Lily, to help put Fellowes Hollow on the map. "You just need a sign, Lily. Have you settled on a name?"

"Emma and I have brainstormed a few but haven't decided."

Doug emerged at the top of the basement steps, his eyes red, his hair tousled.

"Did you have a bad night again?" Vicki's forehead creased with concern. Lily had no doubt she'd make a great mother if she wanted to be one.

"It's not as bad as it used to be." He leaned over the kitchen sink, splashed water on his face, then turned to Lily. "What do you need?"

"The back of the truck has the tables from IKEA. The boxes are heavy. If you could take them into the basement, that would help a lot."

"I'm on it." Doug was halfway down the steps before Lily could say thank you. She turned to Vicki. "I hope the new Wi-Fi system gives you a better signal." They'd bought a Wi-Fi mesh at Costco.

"I'm sure it will, but are you sure you don't mind me staying here? I feel like I'm imposing." She'd been there for a week and was having trouble with the Wi-Fi in her bedroom.

"I don't mind at all. I'm happy to have you here for as long as you need to decide if you're staying and, then, until you find your own place."

"Okay, then, if you're sure." Vicki gave a mischievous grin, and like Doug, bolted down the steps.

Lily shouted after her. "If you see Emma down there, tell her to grab her own things and take them to her room."

A surge of nostalgia swept through Lily as she remembered those days when she, Amanda, and Sam would work as a team to complete chores. They were a small but tight family. With Vicki and Doug, it had a similar vibe. In the ten days since Lily announced she'd changed her mind and was going forward with the shop, they'd accomplished a lot. Of course, even if Vicki stayed in Fellowes Hollow, she'd move into her own place. Doug's future was more uncertain. He was making a life in Fellowes Hollow between the jobs he got on his own and working with Trish and her club. He'd promised to stay until Lily didn't need him anymore but not beyond that. Her best hope was they would remain nearby. And that eased her loneliness.

"I've got everything unloaded." Doug stopped in the kitchen where Lily was giving Emma lunch. "I can build the tables later. If you don't need the truck, I'm going to the Taylors to finish that job."

"Emma is going to Ruth's Saturday knitting class. Can you drop her at The Village? Ruth can put her on the shuttle home, or I might walk over there later and pop in to meet the students." Lily air quoted the word "students."

"Ruth likes it when I help her," Emma said. Since school had begun, she could only do it on weekends.

"Are you ready?" Doug took the truck keys off the peg and bowed to Emma. "Your carriage awaits."

Emma put her plate in the sink, moistened a sheet of paper towel, and wiped her fingers and mouth.

"Any idea when you'll be back?" Lily asked Doug. "I'm making a roast chicken for dinner. It doesn't matter exactly what time. It just helps if I know."

"Maybe five or six. I'll text you when I have a better idea." Doug had recently bought a new cell phone and tools for the barn with money he'd earned.

"If you have other plans, that's fine," Lily said. "You don't need to eat here just because I'm cooking." Since he was beginning to have a life outside the shop, she didn't want him to feel obligated.

"What could be better than a roast chicken dinner with my favorite women?"

Lily laughed. "I hadn't thought of that, but you are with three women."

"Lucky me. I'll text you later."

Rarely did the old somber Doug come out anymore. Lily gave all the credit to Vicki. When she told him things, he seemed to believe them, take them to heart.

While Lily finished her dinner prep, Vicki roamed the house with her laptop open. A few minutes later, she settled at the kitchen table. "Good signal everywhere. Mission Accomplished."

"Glad to hear it."

"Can I help you with dinner?"

"Nah, I know chicken dinners seem like a lot of work, but they're not too bad. Mostly it's a matter of waiting for the oven to do the cooking."

"And you love it."

"I do love cooking." Lily thought about that. "But what I love best is feeding people. Especially those I love most."

Vicki blew her a kiss. "I think I'll go to the Wine and Spirits store to get a nice bottle of something."

"I have plenty of wine." Lily pointed to the great room. When she'd given up the idea of the shop, she'd moved her china cabinet into the great room. The cupboard on the bottom had a wine rack. It would need to find a different place to live. That and a bunch of other things.

"I know, but I want something special, and since you don't let me contribute while I'm here—"

"You're a guest," Lily interrupted.

Vicki swiped her hand as if to shoo Lily's objections out the door. "It's the least I can do. Anyway, you can't stop me, but is there anything you need while I'm out?"

"Nope." Vicki had raised Lily's curiosity. "What's up that you need a special bottle of wine?"

"You need to wait until tonight. When we're all here."

"You're a cruel woman to keep me in suspense."

"If you say so, but I know you'll change your mind when you hear it."

After Vicki left, the house became oddly quiet. Since Doug had moved in, Lily had rarely been the only one home. But with Emma in school again and Doug working jobs in other places, quiet was becoming more frequent.

As she put the chicken and vegetables into the roasting pan, she thought of Philip and how he loved it when she made roast chicken dinners. She hadn't spoken to him since their big fight. Except it wasn't exactly a fight. Fights end, friends make up. Someone apologizes, or they compromise. What had happened between them was a revelation that caused a parting of the ways. Lily didn't see any way they'd ever repair their relationship. How could anyone she'd known for over forty years be so different from what she'd thought? The man that Rose had loved. The same man who had helped her after Sam died, who had made the funeral arrangements for Amanda when Lily couldn't breathe. It made no sense.

Lily entered the password for the new Wi-Fi on her iPad. The email she was hoping for had arrived. Shipping confirmation for her first order of fabric, thread, and notions due to arrive in three days. Excitement and anxiety flapped like a caged bird inside her. Focusing on the positive always helped. With bolts of fabric arrayed on the shelves, the place would look like a real, honest-to-goodness quilt shop. And it was hers and Emma's.

Vicki returned with a Cheshire Cat smile and a package.

"Where's your wine?"

"Where's Doug?" Vicki asked in answer.

"He isn't back yet, but if you don't tell me something, you won't see him when he gets back because I might have to strangle your secret out of you."

"You don't frighten me." Vicki puffed her chest out.

"We all have dark sides, you know."

"Okay, I'll tell you, but only because I can't delay gratification any longer. I'm bursting to say." She pursed her mouth and blew out her cheeks like Emma would do when she had something she really wanted to tell someone. "Sit down."

Lily sat.

"I have three PR things lined up for you. An article about you and the town revitalization in *Pennsylvania Magazine*." She held up one finger. "Another spread about the hidden gem of Fellowes Hollow in the Sunday *Post-Gazette*." Two fingers. "And best of all, an article about you and your destination quilt shop in *Quilter Magazine*. We just have to coordinate your grand opening date."

Lily's mouth dropped open. She had no words. She could

only grab Vicki's three upright fingers and pull her forward for a hug, nearly unseating her.

"One more thing." Vicki wriggled out of Lily's grip. "We have a summer intern in the office who is a quilter and is dying to design a few logos for you to look at."

"Wait, back up to the first part. Magazine spreads about the town? Does Rez know you're doing PR for the town?"

"Is that what you're worried about? No. I didn't do it for him. I did it for you and the other shop owners."

"And you said you don't earn your keep. I'm blessed to have you in my life."

"I want you to be a success. A wild success. For you and for Amanda's memory. And maybe most of all for Emma."

Lily slid into a chair, breathing in the intoxicating smell of roasting chicken like an elixir. "I'm really doing this, aren't I?"

"You are. Doug and Emma and me and the quilt ladies and the town. All because of you. You are the force that made this happen. I only helped."

"I'm in shock. I can't believe I made it. After all the times I thought—"

"You're doing it because you can. One thing Amanda always told me about you was that you were the most capable person she knew and the last one to know it."

"Sam knew it," Lily said, her voice coming out as a whisper. "He always came to me when he had a problem. He said I always found a solution. I had forgotten about that." She wiped a tear from her eye. Not from sadness but from joy. Her heart had been empty for so long, and suddenly it was overflowing.

Vicki came behind Lily, laid her head on Lily's shoulder, and kissed her cheek. "Lily Wolfe, I love you like a mother. And you know who loves you too?"

"I hope he stays in town," Lily said.

"I know you do. And I hope he never has to leave. You are good for each other. He needs you and he would do anything for you. Tell him you want him to stay."

"I've told him," Lily said. "I don't want to pressure him." Same as she didn't want to pressure Vicki by expressing the same wish about her.

"Tell him again. I think he may be ready."

Chapter 36
The Quilt Ladies' Plans

After Lily's order arrived, getting Emma to go to school required promises that there would be jobs for her to do in the shop when she came home. Lily didn't mind. Emma wasn't clingy like she'd been the year before. After two weeks of school, she hadn't pulled out her hair or punched anyone. Best of all, she proudly displayed her finished homework without being asked.

Lily would pull bolts of fabric and pre-cut fabric, leaving them for Emma, who'd meticulously fold the fat quarter yards into perfect rectangles and arrange them by color in baskets. Then she'd tightly re-wrap the bolts and, with the aid of a step stool, put them back on the shelves.

With Doug's help to move all the furniture around and bring the shelves back up from the basement, the great room had become the rainbow of cottons, batiks, and spools of thread Lily had so often imagined. She still wasn't ready to set a grand opening date, despite Vicki's insistence on needing one to advertise. One thing at a time. There were still too many unknowns and much to do, like ordering sewing machines for the classroom, stocking up on supplies from rotary cutters to quilt patterns, books, and rulers. She had settled on a name though. Doug and Ed were planning to install the sign that morning before the quilt ladies came, so Lily could show off.

Lily, Vicki, and Doug stood around the coffee pot and muffins from Becca's in their morning routine of comparing schedules for the day.

"I have the quilt ladies coming. They're begging to see the place and I think Trish is anxious to show off the back garden."

"Ed should be here any minute," Doug said. "We should have the sign hung before they get here."

"And I'm going to be stuck behind my computer all day," Vicki said. "But first I'm going to make an appointment with Greta to go house hunting."

Lily nearly choked mid-swallow. She'd begun to wonder what Vicki was waiting for. Except for a few trips to get things from her apartment, she'd stayed in Fellowes Hollow for the last three weeks.

"Hooray," Lily said. "I kind of thought so."

"That's fantastic," Doug said.

He and Vicki were getting along quite cozily.

"I can go with you if you want," Lily said.

"I was hoping you'd say that. I know nothing about houses."

"I do," Doug said. "At least about their building condition. I couldn't tell you a thing about market values or locations."

"I'm only starting to look. I need to be sure. Buying a house is a big deal."

"There's no harm in looking around to get a feel for things," Doug said.

"I'm not kicking you out. You know that." Lily worried Vicki felt rushed to leave, especially with the shop almost ready.

"I know. But I can't leave my apartment until I have a place to move my things to and it's crazy to keep paying rent for an apartment I don't use."

"You could put your stuff in storage," Lily offered. "Take your time."

"We'll see, but I have to do something. I might just rent for a while."

But she'd still be nearby. Lily's heart swelled. At least one of her kids, as she'd come to think of Vicki and Doug, would stick around.

The quilt ladies arrived in separate cars. Lily watched out the window as they each pulled into the small lot behind the shop. Lily had five spaces denoted by crisp white lines. She could squeeze in a few more cars if they blocked the barn door, but soon they'd need more parking. Although the town had approved turning the lot next to Gus's gas station into public parking, change was slow in coming.

Lily ran to the basement to greet them at the back door. They were unloading boxes from the backs of their cars. "What are you doing?"

"We're not taking no for an answer, so you need to shut up and listen." Lily had never heard Maggie speak so sternly, not even to a dog.

"Do I get a treat if I obey?"

"No." Robin slammed the trunk of her Toyota Avalon. "This may be about you, but it isn't about you."

"She's right," Trish said. "At least it isn't about you until after everyone turns around and looks at the garden."

The vegetable garden was inside a neat wooden frame covered on the top and sides with wire. Critter control. Trish had found mature vegetable plants, gently transplanting and staking them. It was already mid-September. With luck, Lily would get to enjoy at least a few tomatoes and peppers before fall set in. The rest of the bed was filled with ornamental grasses, white hydrangeas, three redbud trees, and a riot of flowering annuals poking out between the rest. Lily had trouble finding time to tend to it all, but Doug, in his amazing way, usually had everything taken care of before Lily even went outside.

"Okay, help us carry all this in." Maggie was clearly the one in charge.

"Maybe drive around the front," Lily suggested. "Then we won't have to carry it up all the steps."

"No need. The heavy stuff is for the classroom." Robin sagged a little from the weight she was carrying.

Once everything was inside, they unboxed things. Between the three of them, they'd provided enough old but good sewing machines. Maggie had one, Robin had two because she kept upgrading, and Trish had five because she used sewing machines like hair dye, always changing.

Lily put up her hands, barring them from putting the machines on the tables. "I can't accept all this." Her voice came out in a whisper, her airways clogged by what felt like a tennis ball in her throat, fuzz included.

"We're donating, but if you can't accept our love, then you can borrow them, return date unspecified." Robin had clearly planned a response to Lily's objections.

Before long, they'd unloaded enough fabric and batting to make a dozen or more quilts. They'd covered the tables in the basement with boxes full of rotary cutters and mats, fabric shears, rulers, hoops, needles, and thread. None of it was new and couldn't be sold, but they would save Lily from having to buy extras for the shop and the classroom.

Maggie cleared her throat to get everyone's attention. "Do you want to hear our plan?"

Lily nodded. She had ceased trying to speak because each time she'd opened her mouth, she'd been told to shut up.

"Then let's sit."

They pulled up folding chairs to the tables, then talked all at once, making it hard to understand, but the gist was that they had arranged appliqué and hand-quilting lessons in the retirement home. They weren't going to charge for the courses but would for the kits that included the materials, which they'd make in the shop. All proceeds would go to Lily to reimburse her for the cost. They had also brought fat quarters from their own stashes. "Because you can't have too many," Trish said.

"We have to let Emma refold them." Lily got a sentence out before Maggie shushed her.

"There's more. We're volunteering to work in the shop until you have it running well enough to hire help." Maggie crossed her arms over her ample bosom. "We want this shop as much as you do, maybe more. So, it is totally selfish on our part, and therefore, you cannot refuse."

Tingling ran up Lily's spine and the tears came in an ugly, uncontrollable shower. What had she ever done to deserve such wonderful friends?

"Get her a shot of something," Maggie said. "Port? Do you have port, Lily?"

Lily pointed to the ceiling, afraid to open her mouth in case a howl came out. Trish found a box of tissues in the bathroom, and after a few cabinet doors banging and glass clattering, Robin returned with a small measure of ruby port. "Here."

The warm, sweet liquid melted her vocal cords enough to speak. "I love you all."

"It's been a hard year for you, Lily. We're your friends. It's what we do," Trish said.

"Don't pretend you wouldn't be standing in one of our places if one of us was standing in yours." Robin put her arm around Lily. "We're here. You are not alone."

Trish stood. "It's time for the walls. We brought loaner quilts to display and I have tools to hang them. So, let's go find places for them."

"We should wait for Doug to do that. He'll be able to reach better than any of us."

"Okay, but we can figure out what goes where." Trish was already sizing up the basement walls, getting ideas.

"You're the expert on color, Trish. I'll go with whatever

you decide." Lily trusted her completely.

"I was hoping you'd say that. It's like the best Christmas toy I ever wished for, but you can change it if you want. I won't be offended."

"Have at it then." Lily laughed, her vocal cords loosened by the port.

Upstairs, they threatened to tie Lily to a kitchen chair if she didn't stay put while they unfolded quilts, checking for size, then deciding where to hang them or drape them.

"The town will be beautiful, but nothing will be more beautiful than your quilt shop," Maggie said, turning a circle to take it all in.

"Even Rez is inspired," Robin said. "I just need to light a candle under him to get some of these town projects going. I was thinking I might run for town manager."

"You want to be the manager?" Lily didn't believe her.

"No. Of course I don't. It's a dreadful job. But . . ." Robin wagged her finger. "It would stoke fear in the man, and he might move a little faster."

"Brilliant idea," Trish said. "We have the park well underway. We'll be done soon. Then all we need is for the town to provide a few benches and a monument."

Robin snorted. "One can hope."

"I'm a hopeful person." Trish smiled. Lily hadn't noticed before, but her rose-colored lipstick matched her hair.

"Did you get the lipstick to match your hair?" Lily asked.

"Of course. I'm full of good ideas."

"Speaking of ideas, any idea when you're going to open?" Robin had her schoolmarm look on, eyes narrowed, lips tight. She wasn't going to take no for an answer.

"I guess I don't have a reason to procrastinate anymore. I just need to place one more order."

"So, you'll give Vicki a date for the grand opening?" Trish bit her lower lip as if willing her racehorse to the finish.

"Will the third Saturday in October please you?" Lily felt

her stomach tighten and flutter a few times. She'd have little more than a month to get her last order delivered. "I just have to check with Vicki to make sure it works with her publicity."

"Group hug," Maggie shouted. Lily could hardly breathe as three sets of arms wrapped around her like an octopus.

"I'm so proud of you, Lily," Robin said, wiping a tear from her eye as she backed out of the hug.

Maggie walked to the window, her back to the room. Lily was pretty certain she was crying too.

But Trish beamed. "You did it, Lily. I'm thinking about following in your footsteps and opening an embroidery shop in the vacant space next to Becca's. I spoke to Ruth. She's thinking about a yarn shop, so we might do a joint venture. I just don't know if I could do what you did."

"Seriously? Do you think I believed I could do this? I still don't believe it. Every night I lie in bed scared I'm going to fail dismally. You ladies will be my only customers."

"Us and a ton of people from The Village and from all over Western PA." Maggie rejoined the group, a crumpled tissue in her hand.

"I hope so. I'm counting on it and Vicki is amazing with what she does." Lily thought about where she was when she'd first walked into this dilapidated, filthy, dry rot-infested house. "The best advice I ever got was from Becca. She said the way she did her cafe was to not think about the end but to solve each problem as it arises. And maybe the most important thing of all is one I learned by myself. Ask for help. If you do it, Trish, I'll help you all I can. Where would I be if I hadn't had Doug's and all of your help and encouragement?"

"Hopefully, not married to Philip," Maggie said, practically spitting the words.

"It doesn't make sense the way he behaved." Lily still couldn't grasp how he'd worked against her, yet she was defending him.

"It makes perfect sense," Robin said. "He wanted you to be

his wife, not an independent shop owner."

Lily couldn't deny that anymore. They'd been right all along, but there had to be more to it. She had never known Philip to be that selfish. She wished she understood how a forty-year friendship could go so wrong. And she wished she could be certain he hadn't set any more booby traps.

Chapter 37
Philip

When the doorbell rang early on a Saturday morning, Lily assumed the mailman or UPS driver was leaving a package. Deliveries of boxes, once a rare thing, had become common. Each one adding goodies to her growing inventory.

Instead of a box, she met Simon, wearing the brightest grin she'd ever seen on him.

"This is a surprise." Although she'd known and worked with Simon for years, he'd only been to her house two times. First when Sam died, and again for Matt and Amanda. He'd never been to the shop. "Come in."

Russell wagged around his legs, demanding to be petted. "Hey, guy." Simon indulged him briefly. "I didn't know you got a dog."

"More like he got us, but we love him to pieces. Especially Emma."

"I can't stay long." His eyes grew wide. "Wow. The last time I was here was when Matt showed it to me. Right after they'd bought it. I can't believe I'm standing in the same place."

"Thanks. It took over a year to get here, but next week is my grand opening." She wrestled into submission the hummingbird that had taken up a nest in her former dragon's lair. The closer the date, the more she felt the need to keep her eyes to the sky looking for anything else that might drop on her. "Can you stay for a coffee? I'll put on a pot and show you around."

"I wish, but I don't have that much time. I just couldn't wait to give you the news." Every one of his straight white teeth showed as he beamed at her. "Your friend Vicki is a genius. I had two potential partners within a few weeks and I just signed the contract with one of them." He reached into his inner jacket pocket and withdrew a piece of paper. "Here's the balance. I wish I could have given you all of it sooner, but it looks like everything worked out."

Lily heard Simon as if he were far away. If not for the support of the wall behind her, she might have dropped to the floor as she stared at the amount written in Simon's familiar hand. One word swirled in her head. Freedom. She'd pay off Philip and have a cushion until the shop gained customers. Her gratitude overwhelmed her, stealing her breath. She squeezed out two words. "Thank you."

"The accountant worked up the numbers, plus interest. You can talk to him if you don't think it's right."

On an impulse, Lily hugged Simon. She had never done it when he was her boss, but it felt like the only way to express how appreciative she was. "I'm very happy you found another partner. I know losing Matt was a huge setback for you."

"Without you, I never would have met Matt. I'd still be in the old office, partnerless. And I'd be there again if not for Vicki."

"I wish you and your partner all the success in the world."

"Thank you. He's a younger man. Lost his wife recently. Cancer. Terribly sad. Has a daughter around Emma's age. I think they're at the cafe now. Would you like to meet him?"

"You bet." Lily called Emma downstairs to come with her. Russell gave his best sad dog face as they stepped out the door.

"You aren't allowed in the cafe." Emma stooped and hugged him. "But I'll bring you back a treat."

When they entered, the bell on the door gave the familiar

tinkle. Simon led them to the counter where a rather attractive man was talking to Becca.

"John, I'd like you to meet Lily. She's my old receptionist, the one I've told you about."

John extended his hand and said, "It's nice to meet you. I think Simon still misses having you around."

Lily shook his hand and introduced Emma.

"Emma," Becca handed her a plate with two brownies on it. "Why don't you share them with the girl over there? Her name is Jessie."

The girl was reading a book. As Emma walked over, balancing the plate, John said, "That's my daughter. She's going into fourth grade at Fellowes Hollow."

"Emma's in fourth too," Lily said. "Maybe they'll be friends."

"That would be a good thing for her. I don't know if Simon told you about my wife. It's been a rough couple of years for us." John pinched the bridge of his nose.

"Unfortunately, we understand that all too well. Matt was Emma's father."

"Yes, Simon told me that. I'm sorry."

After an awkward pause, Lily said, "When are you moving in?"

"As soon as possible," Simon interjected before John could answer.

John shot a look at Lily as if they were sharing a joke. "Tomorrow, but Simon wishes I could start this minute."

"We're totally booked today. I could use the help," Simon said. "Speaking of that, I need to get to the office. Join me in a bit, John?"

"I will, but I have to bring Jessie. I haven't found a babysitter yet."

"Give me a sec." Lily stepped away and called Emma over.

"Jessie's daddy needs to go to work. Would you like to have her come over to play now?"

"Yes." She bounced on her toes.

"I'll see if her daddy says it's okay."

He wouldn't have been able to say no if he had wanted to. The two girls were ecstatically clapping and jumping. Not too long ago, Lily had wondered if she'd ever see that again.

After John left and the girls were reabsorbed by brownie consumption, Lily whispered to Becca, "John seems like a nice man. You two seemed to be enjoying your conversation when I walked in."

Becca smiled, her chin tipped up.

Lily waggled her eyebrows. "Did you know he was widowed about two years ago? Came here looking for a new start. Maybe my dear friend Becca might be ready for one too?"

"I might be."

"Your parents would be happy."

"Okay, Lily, now you're getting carried away."

"Just saying. A wise woman once told me you only need to do one thing at a time. I bet he'll be back for coffee soon enough."

Becca flicked her towel at Lily. "You're just trying to fix me up, so you have more people to feed."

When Becca smiled, Lily was reminded of how beautiful she was. "I'm sure I could find space for two more chairs at my table. Looks like Emma would like that idea." The two girls were giggling about something, already fast friends.

Becca closed her eyes in mock exasperation. "You are easy to love, Lily. I'm more prickly."

"Not really. You only try to be prickly."

Becca's face turned steely. Lily was about to say Becca didn't need to prove it when she realized Becca was staring at something over Lily's shoulder.

Philip had walked into the cafe.

He headed straight toward Lily. He must have seen her through the window. Lily closed her eyes, trying to regain her composure. This couldn't be good.

"Hello, Philip. What do you need?" Lily didn't recognize her own voice, steely as Becca's uninterrupted stare.

"Can we talk somewhere else?"

"You can go in the back." Becca addressed only Lily.

Lily swept her hand across the counter to steady herself as Philip followed her. She registered Becca's new industrial-size mixer, the bowl large enough for Emma to hide in, but nothing could crowd out the sense of impending doom pressing down on her.

"So, this is how she gets all those baked goods done." Philip flipped his chin toward the mixer and to the back of the kitchen where two six-foot-tall baker's racks were in the corner next to a humongous double oven.

"What do you want?" Lily couldn't bear to listen to small talk. "Get to the point."

"I hear you're getting close to opening." Philip picked at his cuff.

Lily had to remind herself to keep breathing. She fingered Simon's check, which she'd put in her pocket. Philip couldn't hurt her anymore, could he? "I am. I am also going to be paying you back in full."

"You don't need to hurry on that." He wasn't making eye contact.

"But I do. I want to be rid of your interference as soon as I can." Words were coming out of her mouth, but she felt like it was someone else was talking.

He cocked his head, brow furrowed as if he was perplexed by what she said.

"Simon told me you lowered the amount of money he'd said he could pay me. You made me think he had nothing more to give me unless he sold the practice. You knew I would never make him do that."

"Lily, you told me you didn't want him—"

"Stop. Just stop." Lily backed away from him. "You may think you meant well, but you have tried to make this hard for me from the beginning. You turned in Doug. You lent me money, but only because you thought it would make me get rid of him. You put a lien on the property and refused to lift it when I needed more money. And you withheld the tax bill, hoping it would mess me up." She still didn't want him to know that it had worked.

"That was an oversight."

"Don't lie." Lily sounded scary even to herself, unrecognizable. And it felt good. "You are fastidious about those things. You were the one who transferred the deed into my name, so you would have been the one to decide where the bill was sent."

He lurched as if she'd smacked him, which she would have loved to do, but that was beyond how far she could go.

"I always meant to help you. I thought I was helping you. You were so deeply in grief and so worried about Emma. I was afraid you'd ruin your retirement and not be able to care for her." He couldn't look her in the eye, his gaze firmly on the giant mixing bowl. "I underestimated you."

"That wasn't your only reason, was it?" She tried to keep the spite out of her voice and instead sounded like a courtroom prosecutor about to get a conviction. "You didn't want me to have the shop because you wanted me to be your wife and take care of you."

"Take care of each other. I thought ... I think we'd be good together. I wanted to make your life easier."

"But you didn't think about what I needed. What I wanted. And Emma too."

"Believe me, I thought I was thinking of both of you." He reached for her hand and she swung it away.

"That is my shop." She pointed at the wall, her arm straight as a spear. "I did it." She pounded her fist against her chest as if she could make him understand how proud she was. "I appreciate that you lent me money when I needed it. I appreciate our friendship for all these years, but I am so angry now.

I don't have strong enough words. When I think of all the trouble I could have avoided."

"I came to say I'm sorry." He looked it. Even his suit, normally crisp, seemed to have wilted under her wrath.

She almost felt bad for him. Almost wished she'd gone a little easier on him. Almost. "I think you should leave now. I'll have your money on Monday."

He paused for a moment as though he was going to say something but turned, head bowed, and left. Lily pressed her cheek on the ceramic tile wall, letting the cool surface calm the flare. She couldn't think of a time when she'd let her anger out like that, but then she'd never been that angry. She hated the feeling of hurting someone but, at the same time, felt powerful and proud.

She wasn't the same person anymore. Although she'd never mend from the loss of her daughter, she'd grown, she'd expanded. Despite the pain, the loneliness, the uncertainty, she'd prevailed. She'd accomplished more than she'd ever imagined she could. And she wasn't done yet.

Chapter 38
Doug's Monument

The sidewalk on Fellowes Run Road was buzzing with activity. Lily stood with a reporter and photographer. Customers had come from as far as Youngstown and Pittsburgh, shopped in all the stores, then clogged up both the diner and the cafe. Several women passed Lily, then ascended the steps to the quilt shop, disappearing through the oak doors. Trish and Robin were greeting the new customers, cutting fabric, and making sales. Real sales, cash, credit cards, whatever. So far, everyone Lily had seen exit the shop was carrying a package.

The reporter was interviewing Lily, one of the opening-day events Vicki had planned. Every time the photographer's shutter clicked or the flash blinded her, Lily felt on display, her flaws exposed. She kept the smile on her face and tried to focus on the excitement.

After a while, as Lily recounted the state of the house when she'd first seen it and the hurdles she'd had to pass, the photographer and his camera faded into the background. She spoke about Amanda without tearing up, gave shout-outs to Ed and Becca and other townsfolk for their businesses.

It wasn't hard to sell Fellowes Hollow, despite the town not having completed the new street lamps or repaired the sidewalks. The shop owners had done a fabulous job with their signage and spruced-up facades. Downtown was a slice of northern Appalachia preserved by the interstate that had separated them from Ainsleyville. Beautiful, idyllic, and ready for a postcard photo.

The reporter, a twenty-something with long, brown hair curled perfectly at the ends, turned to her photographer. "Grab some pictures of the Veteran's Park. I'll be right behind you."

"I wish you luck." The reporter shook Lily's hand. "Your shop and the town are charming. And that park is such a lovely tribute."

"Someday we'll have a monument." Rez's generosity hadn't extended that far.

"Oh?" The reporter tilted her head, a skeptical glint in her eye. "Rez told me he ordered benches and a stone with the names of all of Fellowes Hollow's fallen heroes."

Lily felt her expression mimic the reporters. "I guess that's why you're a reporter. You know more than me. That's good news." It seemed Rez had changed his mind or grown a heart.

The Village shuttle stopped at the curb, letting Emma and Jessie jump out. "Bye. Thank you, Charlie." The driver waved back to the girls and drove off. He was used to their Saturdays at Ruth's knitting class.

"Look, Gammy, Jessie knit her first square."

Jessie held up a variegated pastel square, a little misshapen but a good start.

"You'll be knitting hats and scarves in no time," Lily said.

Jessie put a hand on her hip, her nose wrinkling. "Is your name really Gammy?"

Before Lily could answer, Emma did. "No, it's from when I was little and couldn't say grandma. Now she's stuck with it."

"I like it," Jessie said.

"Thank you," Lily said. "I like it too."

"Let me get a picture of Gammy with the two of them." The reporter, clearly amused, waved to her photographer to return.

Lily sandwiched herself between the girls while the photographer took a few shots.

"Okay, go to Becca's now. She has a treat for you both." Jessie was hanging with Emma until her father finished at the dental office, but with the grand opening in progress, Becca had offered to keep them there for the afternoon. Although, with the unexpected crowd, she might have to send them back to the quilt shop. Lily thought she should check. Trish and Robin would be fine for another few minutes.

The cafe was scented with coffee and cinnamon as always. Becca had added a tiered, rotating refrigerator case where she kept pre-cut slices of cake from the bakery, neatly wrapped on glass plates.

"Can I get a piece of that?" Jessie pointed to a towering slice of strawberry shortcake.

"Jessie, that's kind of big for you and I don't think your daddy would want you to have that much. Maybe Emma would split it with you."

Emma agreed. Becca took the cake to the back to slice it. Lily followed.

"You seem to know a bit about Jessie and her dad. Have you been seeing the dentist?"

"Maybe," Becca said coyly, but a rosy glow crept up from her collar.

"I'm thrilled for you. He's a nice man. Simon couldn't be happier."

"They're an excellent addition to the town, no doubt." Becca had recovered her composure.

"Speaking of the town, that reporter told me Rez ordered benches and the monument for the park."

Becca's mouth opened without words as if she wasn't sure what to say.

"Why are you looking at me like that?" Lily feared bad news.

"I'm not. I'm just surprised you didn't know. Philip donated the money."

"Philip?"

"The very one. And he asked Doug to name the park."

"Philip donated money for the park and asked Doug to name it." Lily repeated the words back slowly.

"Are you all right?" Becca was staring at Lily as if she was daft. "That's what I said."

The words were beginning to settle into an intelligible form. "How is it that you know, and I'm clueless?"

Becca put her hands up as if she could push away blame. "I found out because I ran into Doug and Trish in the park discussing placement for the benches. I assumed you knew because Philip was the benefactor. It never occurred to me to mention it."

"It's a complete surprise to me." But not so long ago, it wouldn't have been surprising for Philip to do something like that.

Underneath, she wasn't sure what to think. She wanted to believe it was goodness on Philip's part, but what if he'd done it to get back in her good graces? More manipulation? Maybe. Since she'd told him off, she had dropped the check with his receptionist but hadn't seen him then or since.

"That was a kind thing for him to do." Lily didn't have time to think about it more. "I have to get back to my shop and you must have a line five deep by now."

The following day, at the start of business, when Lily turned over the open sign on her front door, Philip was waiting on the porch. No flowers. His hands at his sides. His face with a day's worth of beard.

Lily's spine didn't stiffen, her fists didn't clench. All she felt was pity. He had become a desperate, lonely man. Maybe he deserved it, but he wasn't all bad. No one was.

"Can I come in, please?"

She stepped aside for him to pass. "Let me call Vicki down.

Someone has to be here for customers. We're hopeful for another crowd today."

When Vicki saw Philip, surprise flashed across her face, but she cordially said hello. Lily took Philip to the back room, choosing her quilting chair, leaving Philip alone on the couch. He seemed smaller, dejected, disheveled, as if he'd lost his pride.

"I came to apologize to you. I know I was selfish. I know how badly I hurt you. I was stupid and insensitive. I should have trusted your opinion of Doug. I should have trusted your opinion about everything and been there to help you." He finally drew a breath and blinked, his eyes red and shining. "I'm a jerk. I have no defense. And I have no business asking you to forgive me, except I miss your friendship. I'm all alone. You were my only friend. What can I do?" He didn't try to hide the tears that leaked down his cheeks. "There must be something I can do?"

The only time she'd seen him cry was when Rose died. The frost in Lily's veins melted slightly. She wanted to forgive him. Not that things could return to what they had been. For one, she'd never depend on him again. She wasn't the same person anymore. But maybe neither was he. Maybe he really had learned a lesson.

"I heard you donated the money for the fixtures in the park and the monument."

"I did. For Doug. It seemed a small way to make amends to him."

"So, you didn't do it to make amends with me?"

His eyes got wide, and he shook his head quickly. "No. Not at all. After what I'd done to mistreat Doug, who deserves the praise of all of us, I thought the least I could do was honor his loss. I didn't think about whether it would make you happy, but it's a bonus if it does."

He sounded like the Philip she used to know. Brusque but caring.

"Thank you. It will make a lot of people happy. It was a generous gift."

"Lily, I came here because . . ." His chest heaved as if he sucked back in a sigh. "The truth is, I don't do well on my own. My sons hardly visit. I have work, but I go home alone every night. My dinners with you and Emma were the best part of my life. I didn't want to lose that, and in my selfishness, I drove you away. Can you please forgive me?"

Could she? Would she trust him again? Many times, over many decades, he'd been there for her in hard times. Being angry and carrying a grudge wasn't in her nature. It weighed on her like a lead apron. In her own way, beyond the anger, she missed him too. He'd been a good friend for over half her life.

"No more booby traps? Have you laid another problem in my path?"

A glimmer of hope shone in his eyes. "No. I haven't. I won't. And I'll help you any way I can. Like I used to."

"Maybe. Give me time. But I have a shop to run, so I have to get back to it."

Lily watched his back as he left.

"What was that about?" Vicki asked.

"One of the saddest apologies I've ever gotten."

"He needs you." Even Vicki had sympathy in her eyes.

"I always thought I needed him and it turns out he's the one who needs me." Lily had to admit, though, he'd shifted something inside her. "I guess we're bound together. He's a square in my quilt."

"So, you forgive him?"

"I don't know. Not fully. Maybe a little. Probably." She didn't have the heart not to.

Chapter 39
Amanda

"Don't you worry about a thing." Trish shooed Lily away, flapping like a flounder. "I've got this. Go get your dinner ready." After five months, the shop was making money and although Lily could hire an employee, the quilt ladies loved working there and continued to help out.

Trish turned Lily by her shoulders and pushed her toward the kitchen. "It's no biggie. We close in half an hour, anyway."

Lily was having ten people that night, including John and Jessie. Becca had stopped pretending there wasn't anything serious going on between them. Lily was all too happy to encourage it. Becca and John were good for each other.

Doug had installed pocket doors to close off the kitchen and back room from customers. Lily slid it shut and put the expansion boards in her table. Even her kitchen had worked out well. She could fit ten people.

Shortly after the grand opening, Vicki had found a house. A few weeks later, Doug moved in with her, but since Lily had given him the barn and all the tools for his business, she saw him every day. He was too old to be legally adopted, but he was as close to a son as someone could be.

Russell had been a little miffed when the house filled with customers six days a week. And there were a lot of them. Especially after the article spotlighting Amanda's Quilt Shop and Lily's story came out in *Quilter* magazine.

They were getting guests from as far as Maryland and central Ohio, passersby on the interstate deciding to make the shop a stop on their journey. At first, Russell stayed in the barn, or Doug took him on jobs when he could, but within a couple of months, the gregarious dog had become the shop mascot.

For Lily, as long as she had a place where she could feed people, she could handle having most of the house taken over by the shop. At six, closing time, Lily took a go box to Trish. "Dinner for you and Carson."

"Thanks. You didn't need to do that."

"I know your husband loves my food, so it's a pleasure. Don't worry about tidying the place. I'll take care of everything later. I really appreciate you filling in."

A few minutes after Trish left, Vicki and Doug arrived. Emma and Russell hurtled down the stairs. "Unckie Doug, I made you something." She handed him a long scarf knitted from chunky gold-and-brown yarn. "I know it gets cold when you have to work outside."

"That's so thoughtful, Emma." He scooped her up for a hug.

"It's beautiful," Vicki said. "Show Ruth. She'll be proud of you."

"They'll be here soon. And Becca." Lily gave a knowing smile. "And John and Jessie."

"So, he and Becca are a thing?" Vicki asked.

"Seems so."

"And Jessie's my best friend."

"I know that," Vicki said, then turned to Lily. "Can I help in the kitchen?"

"Sure. We need to finish setting the table, but I think I have everything else under control."

Doug and Emma went to shoot monsters on the PlayStation in the back room. Once the robot sounds and explosions began, Lily whispered to Vicki. "How is Doug? When I ask, he only tells me he's fine."

"He still has his dark moments, but they're less frequent and don't last as long. He's keeping up with therapy. I think he'll be okay, or at least okay enough. He takes pleasure in life again."

"And he loves you," Lily said. "That might be the thing that serves him best."

"He does." Vicki rubbed her sternum with her fist. "I've never known a man like him and I've never loved anyone like I love him."

"There will always be chairs in my house for both of you." They made the absence of Amanda and Matt easier to bear. Lily had a family again and Becca, Ruth, and Walter completed it. "The others will be here soon. Would you open some wine and fill a water pitcher?"

A few minutes later, Vicki handed her a glass of wine. "Rosso Toscana. I thought it would pair perfectly with your lasagna."

Lily clinked the rim of her glass with Vicki's and then with the side of her lasagna pan, resting on the stovetop.

The last person to arrive was Philip. He came bearing a bottle of one of Lily's favorite Montepulciano wines. He had changed. Beyond his donation for the park, he'd apologized to Becca, seeking nothing in return. His edges had softened. No one cringed when he walked into the room anymore. When Lily decided to let him back into her life, everyone accepted him.

At the end of the meal, while Lily and Doug were clearing the table and getting ready for dessert, Vicki tapped on her glass, the clink of crystal echoing as all went silent. "I have an announcement."

Doug froze in place with a soapy dinner plate in his hand.

"Doug and I are getting married."

Everyone talked at once and Emma, loudest of all. "Oh, my gosh. If you have a baby, can I call it Cuzzie whatever-her-name-is?"

"I'd be disappointed if you didn't," Vicki said, blowing a kiss to Emma.

"And can I babysit?"

"Of course, but if you're not yet old enough, you can certainly be my number one helper."

Lily suspected it wouldn't be long. And a baby would be a blessing. Yes, lives are lost, but new ones are created. Love grows to accommodate them all. And Lily's heart had grown in just the last minute.

She stood on tiptoes to whisper in Doug's ear. "I'm very happy for you."

Doug wrapped his arms around Lily and kissed the top of her head. "It's all because of you, Lily."

After everyone had left, and Emma was tucked into bed, Lily went back downstairs to straighten the shop, readying it for the morning's business. While she tucked loose edges of fabric back into their bolts and put away scissors, Amanda's spirit lurked in the corners and in the shelves. "We did it, my darling daughter. I'm okay and so is Emma." Lily spoke softly. She still had moments of extreme sadness, when she'd feel the dragon's fire, or forget to breathe, but those moments were slowly becoming a comfort to her. They kept Amanda alive inside her.

"I hope we made this place as beautiful as you would have." Lily took one last look at the shop. Amanda's shop. Emma's shop. Lily's shop. She inhaled the scent of fabric and wood, then went to the kitchen to make a cup of chamomile.

 THE END

acknowledgments

A little more than a decade ago, I had a story forming in my head. I decided to write a novel. About all I had going for me was that I knew I had a lot to learn. It's been a long journey. While this is the first novel I have published, it's the fourth one I have written, leaving me with an extensive list of exceptional people I need to thank. I will start at the beginning, with a collective thanks to the many authors I have read, both fiction and non-fiction, all of whom I have learned from.

Pennwriters is the first writer's organization I joined. I was a novice, and through their patience and counsel, I became a novelist. Many Pennwriters members helped and inspired me. Most notably, my dear friend Janet McClintock, who brainstormed with me to grow the tiny seed of an idea that became this story.

My darling daughter Rachel, who from the time she was still in high school, read for me and fixed my commas. More than anyone, she kept me sane when I thought I was crazy. And she still does.

I wouldn't be writing this acknowledgment without the Women's Fiction Writers Association. Some of the most talented and amazing women I have ever known, they graciously and generously share their wisdom and encouragement. I hope I give back to others as much as I gain through their friendship and guidance.

I must pour a trough of love and appreciation on my Early Bird Writers. Virginia McCullough, Pamela Toler, Joan Fernandez, and Della Leavitt spurred me to find a publishing home for this book. Without them and Catherine Matthews and Heather Carter, I'd still be procrastinating.

I have a special thank you to the TGIF Rogue Writers for

laughing at me when I needed it. You pushed me out of my comfort zone and helped to keep me going. I love you all.

Then there are my first readers. Gabi Coatsworth, Lorraine Norwood, Sue Martin, and Tara Baisden who gave me enough positive feedback not to quit. I can't thank them enough.

Here's an honorable mention to a few dear writer friends who helped me get where I am. Kelly Hartog, editor extraordinaire, had the patience to turn the mess I wrote into a proper synopsis. Kathryn Dodson, my mentor, taught me not to hide behind my computer. Kristi Leonard, my writing partner, rides the rails of the writing life with me. You all mean more to me than you know.

I wouldn't be here without the magnificent team at Atmosphere Press. Thank you for believing I had something worth publishing. A special shout out to Megan Turner, whose editorial insight made this a better book.

A huge thank you to my husband Andrew, my father Sol, my son David, and my daughter Rachel (worth a second mention) and son-in-law Nick. No one is more important than you.

Finally, dear reader, there would be no point in any of this if not for you. I hope you enjoy the book, and I hope you find inspiration and comfort in its pages.

About Atmosphere Press

Founded in 2015, Atmosphere Press was built on the principles of Honesty, Transparency, Professionalism, Kindness, and Making Your Book Awesome. As an ethical and author-friendly hybrid press, we stay true to that founding mission today.

If you're a reader, enter our giveaway for a free book here:

SCAN TO ENTER
BOOK GIVEAWAY

If you're a writer, submit your manuscript for consideration here:

SCAN TO SUBMIT
MANUSCRIPT

And always feel free to visit Atmosphere Press and our authors online at atmospherepress.com. See you there soon!

About the Author

STEPHANIE CLAYPOOL, a native of metro New York, weaves her diverse life experiences into heartfelt and captivating novels. From London to San Diego and Annapolis, her journey eventually led her to call Pittsburgh home, where she lives with her retired Navy husband, her father, and a menagerie of beloved pets.

Beyond her writing desk, Stephanie is an enthusiast of cooking and wine, fountain pens and notebooks, and fabrics and threads. Her greatest joys are the simple things in life.

She hopes the pages of her novels will bring hope, strength, and gratitude into the lives of her readers.

9 798891 324183